# Lewis Crofts

Lewis Crofts was born in 1977 and grew up in Somerset. He has lived and worked successively in Germany, France, the Czech Republic and Belgium. His fascination with Egon Schiele was sparked while living in Prague. He is currently at work on a second novel.

www.lewiscrofts.com

# THE PORNOGRAPHER OF VIENNA

## LEWIS CROFTS

Old St PUBLISHING

First published in Great Britain in 2007 by Old Street Publishing Ltd

This edition published 2008 by Old Street Publishing Ltd
28-32 Bowling Green Lane, London  EC1R 0BJ
www.oldstreetpublishing.co.uk

ISBN 978-1-905-847-48-8

Many thanks to Michael Hernandez for permission to use his font 'Ever After'.

10 9 8 7 6 5 4 3 2 1

A CIP catalogue record for this title is available from the British Library.

Printed and bound in Great Britain

To Lynda, Gordon and Russell

*To restrict the artist is a crime; it is murdering life in the bud.*

**Egon Schiele**

*And, if baits laid by nature or art*
*Ever trapped the eyes to possess the mind*
*With human flesh or its portrayal,*

*All of these together would seem nothing*
*Compared to the divine pleasure that shone before me*
*When I turned to see her smiling face.*

*Divina Commedia, Paradiso* XXVII, **Dante Alighieri**

# THE
# PORNOGRAPHER
# OF
# VIENNA

# ONE

# BEGINNINGS AND ENDS

While on honeymoon in Trieste, Adolf infected his wife with syphilis. On their first night, side by side between the chafing sheets of a hotel-bed, Adolf reached over and turned off the gas lamp, black-blinding Marie. His wheezing drew closer, a finger and thumb clawing at the embroidered chest of her nightgown, her spine arching away from her railway inspector husband. Marie threw back the blankets, scurrying out of the room and up the corridor to the communal bathroom where she sat on the edge of a copper bathtub, her legs crossed and her nightshirt buttoned up to the throat. That first evening, Adolf followed his bride and tapped at the bathroom door, whispering pleas through the gap in the frame. On the second evening, he was begging Marie to come to her senses and rest her head in their marital bed. By the third evening, he was bellowing at the door, ordering Marie to fulfil her wifely duties, shouting over her whimpers and the protests of hotel-guests. Adolf never joined his weary-eyed wife in bed on the fourth evening. After dinner, he left her sitting in silence at the table and walked down to the promenade on the seafront. Within half an hour he had procured a prostitute and a reasonably priced room three doors down from the hotel where his new wife pretended to sleep.

The following morning, Marie was still sitting at the breakfast table when Adolf's lean frame came in through the main entrance.

He saluted her ironically, placing an index finger on the peak of his hat, and continued through the hall and up the stairs. Their paths did not cross again until dinner when Adolf re-emerged from the bedroom, refreshed from his daytime sleep, and strode through a bustling restaurant to her table. Marie had been waiting in the hotel bar the entire day, making only occasional trips to the bathroom on the fourth floor, climbing the staircases to tread carefully past their nuptial room, pressing her ear against the lock to hear her husband's somnolent breaths. Over dinner they talked. For the first time in four days, they smiled at each other, discussing the charms of the sun-baked houses along the promenade, the lilting accent of the waiter and the countless embellishments they would make to the bourgeois life awaiting them back on the banks of the Danube. After dinner, Marie got up from the table and placed her hand in Adolf's. He smiled, leading her through the foyer and back up the four flights of stairs to consummate their marriage, planting the seed of infection in their sweat-soaked union.

For two weeks prior to Egon's birth doctors shuttled back and forth along the thirty-kilometre stretch of track separating Vienna and Tulln. They rushed into Marie's room, confronted with her knotted and swollen body, sometimes naked, sometimes mummified in warm towels. After the requisite checks they packed up their instruments and were sent away.

'I tell you: it could be any day now,' said Adolf to one of the doctors as he closed his leather bag and climbed back on the train. 'I'd be grateful if you could remain on call. I'll be sure to contact you as soon as...'

'She seems to be progressing just fine, Herr Schiele. I doubt it'll be necessary to return for at least another week.'

'But what if...'

'As I said, she is progressing fine.'

Adolf pressed a booklet of rail-tickets into his palm.

'Just to be on the safe side, why not come by tomorrow.'

The doctor flicked through the booklet. Adolf pulled a second one from his pocket and handed it over.

'For the lovely Frau Neumann. I'm sure she'd like...'

'The day after tomorrow you say?'

'Tomorrow would be better.'

'I'll be here.'

Adolf knew how to flatter the handful of birth specialists already acquainted with the complications of Marie's womb, that fickle chamber which had given life to two daughters and stolen it from three of their stillborn siblings. Such incentives ensured the doctors kept coming until Egon's fragile body finally appeared one sunny morning in June 1890.

As Marie's womb contracted around what was to be her third surviving child, Egon's elder sisters, Melanie and Elvira, waited in the neighbouring room on the top floor of the station building. They barely heard the intermittent wails of their mother over the whistles of passing trains. They sat at their bedroom window, their elbows on the sill, looking out at the rolling countryside, watching it disappear momentarily behind swirls of coal smoke. Egon's two sisters had sat through this same experience three times before, each operatic week ending in the hushed sobs of their mother. Each time, a doctor (rolled-up sleeves and blood-streaked forearms; thick, matted adult hair) would exit the room with yet another of their lifeless brothers nestling in a bucket under a spattered towel.

Egon was the exception: the only surviving male before his mother's womb reverted to type and produced one final daughter. Unlike his brothers before him, Egon did not leave the upper room with his back cold against the insides of the dented bucket; rather, as he took his first breaths, he was wrapped in a woollen bed-cloth and lowered into his mother's limp arms. She grimaced, revealing a row of irregular teeth, their calcium sucked out by those who came before him. She looked Egon in the face and then between his legs, passing his pink, puffy body back to the doctor. Her arms fell by her sides and the muscles in her face relaxed into well-worn ridges.

'For Christ's sake!' The gaggle of midwives and maids leant in around her bed. 'One of you go down to the signal box and tell him he's finally got a son.'

As Egon grew, his mother dressed him in tailored suits in the winter, in a sailor's costume in spring, and in summer in the striped garb of South Bohemia where she had been brought up. On the porch of the station building, Adolf sat the boy on his knee, bobbing him up and down as trains pulled in and out. Egon slept through the screeches and the avalanche of descending boots thumping the platform. The night cargos trundling towards Danube ports failed to rouse him from sleep, snuggled in a cot in the corner of his sisters' room. Soon, thick dark tufts of hair began to spread across his scalp, hanging over his ears, a moor of unruly divots which he was first unable to tame and with time willingly cultivated.

The tale he would recount as his first memory was entirely manufactured: the burial of one of his elder sisters. Over time he groomed the falsified anecdote, describing how the half-size coffin of ten-year-old Elvira was lowered into a hole in the town cemetery; he mentioned the burnt umber soil sweating in the heat and the staccato scratch and thud of the wood sliding and resting in its pebble-strewn grave. But beyond the artificial constructs of memory, at the precise moment that Elvira's coffin was being drummed with lumps of clay dropped from trembling hands, Egon sat on the floor of his bedroom in the station building, scribbling coloured twirls on old newspapers. While Adolf led his wife away from the graveside, their shoes clogged with fresh mud, the boy surrounded himself with crayons and cascades of colour. The maid watching over him turned away, hiding her reddened eyes from the child.

Egon's earliest genuine memory was far less lyrical than Elvira's funeral. Buried deep in the shadows of his mind was a summer afternoon when one of the many traders who passed through the station approached his mother on the porch, addressing her in the same vernacular Slavic she used when out of Adolf's earshot. The peddler stepped off the train from Znojmo on market day and raised his hand to Marie.

'*Dobrej, paní Schielová.*'

'*Dobrý den, pane.*'

Every market day Egon would witness the role-play of his mother rising from the bench at the front of the station and greeting the peddler in her native packets of vowelless clicks and rolls. He rarely heard the rest of their conversation, their hushed voices drowned out by the clamour of the platform; instead, he sat captivated by the bag swinging around the trader's neck. He sucked his thumb and waited for his mother to return with a sugar-coated treat – dug out from the worn leather bag – which she placed in his mouth, smiling as he squirmed with the dancing sensation on his tongue. Through citrus tears he watched his mother saying goodbye to the trader; Marie opened her purse to pay him, resting her hand on his for an instant as she placed several coins in his palm. In turn, he twisted his shoulder back and fished out a folded square of paper from his satchel, pressed it into her hand and then stepped back up onto the train.

His mother's blunt yet musical greeting quickly became associated with the fizzing numbness in his mouth, the gravel-like texture of rough-cut sweets which sparkled behind his eyes. As she picked him up and repositioned him on her lap, Egon said proudly:

'*Dobrý den, paní Schielová.*'

The smile melted from Marie's face as Adolf appeared in the doorway. He picked Egon off his wife's lap and pinched the boy's chin with a calloused hand before slapping him across the cheek.

'*Guten Tag.* Round here it's *Guten Tag.* We're not peasants like your mother's lot.'

'*Guten Tag,*' Egon repeated.

'Again.'

'*Guten Tag.*'

'Enough of that Slavic filth.' He turned to Marie. 'Watch your bloody mouth, woman.'

Adolf stood up, ruffling the spiky crop of hair which hung over Egon's forehead and strode back into the station building.

That was Egon's first memory.

He came to admire the Austrian State Railways, marvelling at everything from their imperial reach, mapped out on the faded charts above his father's desk, to the unbearable beam of their headlights. Tulln was a transit station, a passing point for most cargoes entering and exiting the capital. Egon's father was a respected man; although of middling rank, he ran Tulln impeccably, forging its reputation as a place where trains stopped on schedule and made up time lost at more slovenly stations out in the provinces.

He grew up against the backdrop of wagons linking and unlinking, hobnail boots embarking and disembarking, containers loading and unloading, and the babel of passengers' tales. The fabric of his clothes carried the industrial odour of oil and coal despite his mother's scrubbing. The boy would sit on the platform for hours, watching the machines as though they were beasts emerging from the folds of the countryside and then disappearing into the hills and valleys behind a veil of smoke. To Egon the steel dragons were more vivid than the beasts that populated the picture books on his shelves; they were more alive, more physical, ingesting black food and billowing darkness from their lungs. As a nine-year-old, he would walk alone to the end of the platform and wait for one of the few trains to pass which did not stop at the station. The driver's whistle would warn him off, but he remained rooted to the spot. His toes stuck out over the edge of the platform and the swirling waves of air, pushed away from the front engine, wrapped around his small body, spinning it, caressing it, until the last carriage passed and he exhaled, stumbling backwards engulfed in smoke.

As Egon grew, Adolf granted him free local tickets, enough to transport his introverted son away for an afternoon, dropping him a mile or two up the track next to the Danube in a nether land of limitless escape. Occasionally, Egon would take an early morning train and disembark just as the sun was rising. On a roll of waste paper picked up from his father's office, he would spend the sunlight hours outlining engines and rolling stock. Initially, everything was in pencil, scribbled on the backs of old maps and timetables; then briefly, he used lumps of charcoal that tumbled from passing wagons, but the rocks drew uneasily on the page, his penknife unable to hone their irregular edges. Finally, he settled on stolen ink.

One afternoon, Adolf came looking for his son. He found him in a clearing of trodden meadow, lounging among papers, pencils and pots of colour. Egon looked up at the figure silhouetted against the sun and cowered; a raised hand threw shadows over his sketches. Instinctively, the young boy stuck out his ink-stained hands for inspection. Adolf bent down so close that a small black speck on Egon's thumb smeared across his father's cheek.

'Where did you get all these things from? Have you been snooping around my study again?'

He removed a handkerchief from his top pocket and dabbed his face until the spot appeared on the white cloth. Egon bowed his head.

'Answer me! Where did you get this?' Egon shrugged. 'If I find out you've taken this from the office you'll get the belt. In fact...'

Adolf reached for the boy's arm, raising it and twisting his body to expose the backs of Egon's naked legs. As he did so a bundle of papers spilled out onto the ground, the wind filling their sails and sweeping them into the cords of grass. In an instant, Adolf glimpsed the elaborate patterns of steam engines, complete with windows, cabins, chimneys and pumps. Father and son stood still and watched as the pictures bounced, rolled and danced over and through the grass.

'Gather this rubbish up, boy, and get home. Your mother's got the dinner on.'

'Yes, Father.'

'You will study to become an engineer,' said Adolf, leaning forward on his desk, his sleeves rolled up. Egon looked at the map behind his father, tracking the lines north to Prague, west to Munich, east to Budapest, all converging on Vienna, *regina urbis*, the star of Mitteleuropa. 'Following this, it is my intention that you join the Bohemian railways.' Egon's eyes wandered to Trieste. 'Look at me when I'm talking to you.'

'Sorry, Father.'

'Like others before you, you will become an inspector. If – and I stress *if* – you show promise and work hard, I'll see to it that you take over the running of Tulln.'

'That would be an honour, Father.'

'Indeed, it would. Now get out of my sight and don't let me catch you stealing again.'

Egon never recorded the exact order of the schools he attended nor the circumstances of his expulsions; the terms just slipped into each other with the seamless progression of the seasons. The colour of his cap or the hoops on his socks would change according to the school, but each time it ended in the same way: disgrace, punishment, and imprisonment in the coal shed.

It started when he was ten. Adolf fetched his son from a dusty classroom in Tulln early one afternoon, yanking him down the corridor and into the yard, shouting obscenities while small round faces appeared at the windows. After a night in the coal shed, Adolf put the boy on a train to nearby Krems, with a letter for the head-teacher and a scribbled map in his pocket indicating the location of his new school.

When he was expelled eighteen months later, Egon arrived home with an envelope from his teacher, which he left propped between the ashtray and the gas lamp on his father's desk. The envelope stood there, covered in swirls and jagged pencil lines scratched by his bored hand on the train home, until Adolf returned from the night shift and tore it apart. He only read the first two lines before storming upstairs to drag Egon from underneath his feeble defence of blankets and pillows. After two nights in the coal shed, Adolf sent him to Klosterneuburg, the only local school left which might make an engineer out of the softly-spoken youngster.

One year on, and Egon was wandering slowly home, unwilling to hasten the confrontation with his father. Scrunched in his fist was the offending sketch the teacher had torn from an exercise book and launched across the room. There had been just enough time to stuff it into a pocket before the teacher grabbed him by the neck and bundled him out the door.

With the sun already low in the sky, Egon appeared on the station platform, a bag slung over his shoulder, his jacket hanging over the strap of the bag. He unfurled the sketch and looked again at the comic penis protruding from between the figure's legs.

His father's office door was open and he was sitting at his desk with a file of papers in front of him. Egon stood in the doorway for a moment, expecting his father to look up, pull from his pocket a telegram or some other incriminating evidence and point in the direction of the coal shed. Instead, he just sat there, sorting through the embossed share certificates which he usually kept locked away in a safe-box under his desk. Egon had only seen them once before, several years earlier when Adolf had waved them drunkenly in his wife's face, threatening to leave and take the family's fortune with him. But now, Egon watched as his father held each of them up to the low flame of the desk-lamp to reveal the blue ink against the pale watermark of the Austrian State Railways. Adolf read the number aloud before closing his eyes, bobbing his

9

head and repeating the number first forwards and then backwards under his breath. He then laid the certificate back into a maroon-leather file, adorned with a bronze and gold buckle, and removed the next one.

'Two-two-six-one-nine-eight-zero. Zero-eight-nine-one-six-two-two.'

Adolf opened his eyes, checked the numbering was correct and moved on to the next, holding it up to the lamp.

'Two-two-six-one-nine-eight-one. One-eight-nine-one-six-two-two.'

Egon took two steps back and walked up the stairs and along the landing to the room he shared with his younger sister, Gertrude.

'He's been at it all afternoon.' Her voice was muffled in the bedcovers. 'Yesterday, too.'

'On his own?'

'His neck was bleeding again.'

'Did you fetch Mother?' Egon watched the back of her head shake, her face pressed into the pillow. 'Always go find her. Remember what she said?' He took off his shirt and trousers and climbed into bed alongside her.

She rolled over and into his arms, murmurs barely audible through her cupped hands. The two siblings lay there, listening to their father's voice at the bottom of the stairs, counting back and forth every single share of his life's investment.

'Story please.'

'I'm too tired.'

'The one about the magician and his helper.'

'You had that last night.'

'I want it again.'

'It's too late. And besides I don't want to light a candle.'

'You know enough of it by heart anyway.'

'Can we just get some sleep? I've had a long day.'

She rolled over, turning her face in towards the wall.

'How was school?' she mumbled.

'Fine.'

Egon was too young to recognise the symptoms eating away at his father, but alongside Gertrude, he witnessed Adolf's mood-swings, the wild unpredictability of his palm. Their mother's crowing echoed around the house as she shouted back at her husband, devoid of sympathy for his crumbling body and the disease he so deserved. As Adolf retreated into the darkness of his study, she stepped out of his shadow; she hurried the children to school in the mornings and had them washing and cleaning the house in the evenings; when once she would have remained silent, she now spoke out openly, addressing the peddlers in her mother tongue, bossing the station-workers on the platform and chastising her children as her husband had done. Melanie, Egon and Gertrude observed the switch, watching the gradual withdrawal of their father, hearing his words from their mother's mouth instead. Meanwhile, paralysis crept through Adolf's body: he stopped trains at a whim, ordering the passengers and the entire crew to dismount; he demanded to see their tickets, folding them and then biting each one between his back teeth as if checking a coin; he insisted on laying an extra place at the dinner table, ordering Marie to make enough food 'for our guest'; unprompted, he asked Egon what his three favourite boys' names were; he demanded Melanie sleep in her shoes.

Eventually he retired from work, encouraged by a colleague to take a break. As his children's bodies filled out, his own creased flesh began to hang from his neck, the skin peppered with weeping sores. For the last months of his life, he sat at the upstairs window above the porch and looked out at the trains pulling in, waving as they pulled away.

One afternoon, he was discovered lying motionless on the roof of the porch, several feet below his window.

'What are you looking at!' screamed Marie at her children. 'Go to your room and don't come out until I say so.'

Egon and Gertrude dropped below the windowsill.

'Did you see it happen?'

'No. You?'

'He just collapsed over the window ledge,' he started. 'His arms tucked into his sides.'

'Stop it!'

'And the dent in the porch roof. The tin cushioned his fall.'

'That's Father you're talking about.'

'Do you think he was trying to kill himself?'

Gertrude pulled a blanket around her head and rolled up against the wall.

'I don't want to hear you mention any of this,' Marie shouted up at the landing. 'It was an accident. That's all. The Hallings. They waved to him from the midday train. He lost his balance.'

'But...' said Egon, leaning over the balustrade, looking down at his mother.

'Neither of you are to disturb him. He'll be in bed for a few days. Do you understand?'

'Yes, Mother,' they answered in unison.

From then on Adolf was confined to his room, initially by force and later by necessity. First, leather straps, which had once held down cargo on transit hauls, bound his sinuous limbs to the bed frame. They were later removed when he resigned himself to the steady atrophy of his mind and body. Doctors carved slits over his paralysed back, applying warm jars of morphine; mercury was rubbed into his neck. Some days the pain would vanish and he would make it over to his barred window and look out; other days, as if cured, he would make sudden, worrying appearances at meal times, longing for the company of his family, his daughters squirming at his lesion-ridden face. On some days he was an immovable hunk of opium-scratched flesh; on others, he would come into the children's room at night and sit at the end of Gertrude's bed, her shoes in his hands, picking her fine ginger hairs off the blanket. They began to lock the bedroom door.

'There's someone outside,' whispered Gertrude.

'Don't be stupid.'

'They're on the platform.'

Gertrude rolled closer to Egon, putting an arm across his chest.

'It's just the mechanics. Now go back to sleep.'

'And that noise?'

'Go back to sleep!'

An hour later, Egon opened his eyes. He saw the familiar flickering glow of open flames, different from the headlights he had learnt to recognise. He slipped out of his sister's arms and walked to the window. Down on the platform, he saw Adolf standing in front of a roaring bonfire on the tracks, watching as it tossed flakes of ash into the air. He took his coat and shoes, unlocked the door and joined his father on the platform, placing an arm around his waist.

'Come on now. You'll catch a cold. Back to bed.' Adolf stared at his son vacantly, gave a near imperceptible nod, turned and walked back inside, his face red with the glow of the flames.

Egon waited for the door to close behind his father and then picked up a bucket of water from the coalhouse, taking it over to the fire. He raised the bucket and looked down at the ashes which were already scattering across the platform. He could just make out the singed remnants of his sketches: the smouldering corner of a train carriage, the charred branch of a lime tree, a church, a barn, a river. He put the bucket down on the floor, resigned to the loss of his sketches, and looked behind him to see Adolf walking slowly up the stairs, his white nightshirt floating like smoke past the windows as they glinted with the reflection of flames. Egon stood there until the fire subsided, opening his coat and letting the heat wash up over his legs and chest. He saw old train tickets, the occasional corner of one of his pictures, the wicker weaves of an office chair, the spines of novels, and, at the bottom, where the embers still flushed with swirls and gusts, he saw a bronze and gold buckle and the delicate pastry of four hundred leaves of charred paper, packed tightly together, their blue ink occasionally burning with the orange flame of a water mark before passing into ash.

# TWO

# CRIMSON FLUSH

Nine days later, when the family's most valuable possessions had long dissolved in rains and dispersed on winds, Adolf died. New Year's Day put an end to a torturous period of humiliation for the insane man. He suffered a stroke in his sleep and the children no longer had to fear pulling back the curtains one morning to see their father's body broken on the platform, a bloody delta cast out from his skull into the snow. Instead, his coffin was covered over one wet winter morning and the family returned relieved to the station building.

'What did he say?' asked Egon as he and his two sisters sat around the kitchen table, listening to their mother.

'They won't make us leave, will they?' pleaded Gertrude. 'It's not fair. They can't just…'

'Rheingold said we can stay on for a bit. He'll be round to take back some more of the furniture though.'

'Like what?' asked Egon.

'The desk. Maybe the bed.'

'Ours?' said Gertrude.

'No. Mine.' She ran her hand across the sideboard and turned to her children. 'There's nothing we can do it about it so I don't want to hear any whining. I'll only say this once so listen up. You must stop your stupid antics from now on. There's no place for them here. I don't have the time to go chasing after you, Gerti. You'll go to school and stay there. And you, Meli – you'll have to find a job otherwise we'll all be out on the streets by winter.' The eldest sister nodded and Marie slowly turned to Egon sitting at the end of the table next to his father's empty chair. 'And the same goes for you, lad. You're the head of the family now.'

The January rain fell in torrents, washing away the wild flowers Melanie had laid on her father's grave. His armchair was empty but the cushions sagged where his folded body once rested; the air in the drawing room was thin, unpolluted by his thick German tobacco; his razor rusted in its pouch next to the mirror before Egon had a chance to use it; cracks appeared in the uppers of his shoes, abandoned in the coal-house, gasping for polish. Marie tried to break her children's lingering attachment to the man who, in death, no longer instilled trepidation or pity but rather admiration. She banned his name in the house and commandeered his once sacred armchair, embroidering a floral cover over the marks which, like a shroud, seemed to bear the photographic negative of his limbs. Melanie left the house before sunrise, trudging through empty streets to the local warehouse, where she stitched workers' shirts, pricking her thumbs with misguided pins. Gertrude and Egon were banished from their father's old study, spending their afternoons in the attic instead where Adolf's possessions had since been stored. They sifted through the obscure artefacts he had horded throughout his life, inventing crude new versions of chess with his collection of butterflies and minerals. They created the spectre of a caring guardian out of the boxes of clothes, papers and contraptions that lay about them. Memories of his swiping hand or grating voice dissolved into the past and the children were left with the embellished smiles and embraces of an absent father figure. The more Marie moved to stifle any remnant of his existence, the more the children clung to their dead father.

'I've seen him, Mother, I swear.'

'Don't talk such nonsense.'

'He comes to me in my dreams.'

'Stop that right now!'

'And sometimes during the day, too.'

'Once more and you'll get no supper.'

'But I wrote down everything he said.'

Egon pushed a script of oneiric discussions across the kitchen table.

'Get those things out of my sight!'

'But, Mother, I have some sketches as well…'

'I'll burn them.'

'Why don't you…?'

'Egon!'

Marie spent her days alone on the platform, watching the passengers come and go, smiling at the commuters and chatting to the traders. She only saw her children at meal times when she would lay the table, moving Egon's chair to where his father used to sit. Egon moved it back, sitting in his customary place next to Gertrude.

He barely spoke to his mother. She would send him on errands, rebuke him for not repairing a hinge, and mock him for his incompetence at replacing a windowpane. But through all her chastising never once did she compare him to his father, never once did she mention her husband's name. Finally, as Egon's muscles started to fill out the twisting frame of his fifteen-year-old body, she moved Adolf's clothes out of the attic and into her son's wardrobe; and with that gesture her husband was officially forgotten. Meanwhile, Egon's sketching progressed from crude representations of the rolling stock to watercolours of the Gothic churchyards and sloping vineyards of the Danube valley. When Marie began to confiscate his materials, locking them in the empty pantry and sending him into the yard to repair fictitious breakages, Egon took refuge in the lime tree next to the stationhouse, his legs dangling down from a gnarly branch out of her reach. He balanced a sketching pad on his knee and glanced up at the top window. While he drew the station-workers shovelling fresh coal into an engine below, he looked intermittently to the barred opening, imagining his father's face had ducked away an instant before his own eyes could fully focus. Meanwhile Marie dozed all day in a chair on the platform, watching her son's legs grow thick and hairy, his face darkening with the advent of summer until he had taken on the features of her despised husband. She never told him that it was in fact her own mother – a Slavic-speaking farmer's wife from Bohemia who had made portraits of local aristocrats – from whom he inherited his talent. After all, it had been decided long ago: Egon was set for a career on the railways.

A squat lady opened the front door, took Egon's coat and pointed him towards the end of the hallway. She hobbled on ahead of him, stopping to rearrange a vase of fresh azaleas. She tapped two knuckles against the tall white double doors and waited for Egon to catch up. His shoes sunk into the carpet as he approached, hands clasped behind his back.

'*Komm' rein!*'

Egon placed a sweaty palm on the cut-glass handle and pushed the doors open. The sun shone in through the high window at the far end of a large room, catching the parquet and glinting against its chessboard patterning. Around the room were palms in porcelain pots, vases, clay models and statuettes. In front of the window was a grand piano, bordered with gold leaf filigree. At the keyboard sat a grey-haired man with a cropped beard and moustache. He did not look up, fixated by the black dots of music propped on a brass rim above the keys. He raised his hands a few inches and then, to Egon's surprise, hammered them down onto the keys, his body thrown forward. When the last resonance had dissipated, he stood up.

'What, may I ask, can justify this disturbance?'

'Forgive me, Sir. I'm here on your invitation.'

'And you are…?' He leant forward and looked over the top of his glasses. 'Yes, yes. Of course. I'm glad you came. Good to see you after all this time.'

'It is a pleasure to see you, too, Herr Czihaczek,' replied Egon, leaning forward to shake the old man's hand.

'Please. Please. You can call me Uncle, can't you?'

'Of course, Uncle Leopold.'

Czihaczek stood up, looked over his half-moon glasses and examined Egon's wispy face and neck-tie. The edges of his mouth turned downwards for an instant and then he sat back down on the piano stool.

'I was sorry to hear about your father. Your aunt has been quite beside herself for months.' Egon watched Czihaczek as he fingered the sheets of music. 'Well, I presume your mother has explained matters to you.'

Egon nodded, fingering the hem of his jacket.

'And what do you have to say for yourself?'

'I'm very grateful, Uncle.'

Czihaczek waved away the response with an open hand.

'You're a man now, Egon. You'll learn sooner or later that it's not a matter of gratitude, but of duty. Do you understand?' Egon nodded. 'You must start taking responsibility for yourself and those around you. A guardian cannot do that for you and Marie cannot be expected to put up with your youthful whims anymore. Do you understand?'

'Yes, Uncle.'

'You're the paterfamilias now.'

'Yes, Uncle.'

'How old are you, lad?'

'I'll be sixteen next month.'

Czihaczek grimaced, tapping a nail against clenched teeth.

'Old enough. Anyway, it's not just a question of maturity, Egon. It's a question of money.'

Egon nodded, avoiding eye contact. Czihaczek gestured for his nephew to sit down on the other end of the piano stool as he got up.

'And this place?'

He moved his arm in an arc around the room.

'Very impressive, Uncle. Very decorative. Very attractive,' he stammered.

'Enough, enough. Do you know why I live like this?' Egon shook his head. 'More than just hard work, I can tell you! Plenty of fools work hard but earn nothing. Plenty of fools. What do you think that scum do out in the fields?' Czihaczek pushed past the curtains and opened the window, the rattle of carriage wheels washing into the room. 'Scum! Scum! You hear me!' He closed the window and turned back to Egon. 'The railways, boy! Our glorious railways!' Czihaczek opened his arms as if on stage, dropping them to his side, pacing back to his piano. 'The same went for your father, for your grandfather and for me. Ludwig was like me, you know: an inspector general. Your father almost but not quite, content with stationmaster, plenty good enough for most; and you yourself have been the selfsame benefactor of that profession. It is one of the finest professions an Austrian can have.'

'Yes, Uncle.'

'But there's better still: chief inspector of the Emperor Ferdinand Northern Railways. How does that sound?' Egon watched Czihaczek's fingers walk back and forth over the ebony keys without pressing any of them down. 'Do you know what that means?'

'That you are very well respected, Uncle?'

'And also well paid. I am wealthy, educated, admired. And I have the Emperor's Railways to thank for that. This is what awaits you. But you must apply yourself.' Egon nodded. 'Is this what you would like? All this?' He pointed again around the room, running a finger down the porcelain bust of a Greek philosopher, perched on the edge of the piano.

'I would be honoured, Uncle.'

'Good. Well then, you shall visit me every Thursday for lunch. Agreed?'

'Yes, Uncle.'

'The 11.20 train from Tulln should always get you here in time.'

'Yes, Uncle.'
'I will do what I can to get things started.'
'I'm very grateful, Uncle.'
'Don't be grateful, boy. Be responsible.'

Egon spent his mornings at a college studying engineering theory. In the afternoons he took the train to a local village station to help the technicians repair the tracks. Working in the yard among the steel carcasses of old engines, he would roll his sleeves up, grease and oil smeared over his developing forearms, and strain to lift cogs, barrels, runners, shafts. The fine hairs on his arms first clogged and then curled into wiry ringlets as the heat from the smith's furnace singed his skin. At dinnertime, he would return to a silent house. His mother would be sitting alone on the porch or inside next to the fireplace; Melanie would still be in the warehouse sewing shirts, earning the coins which were to sustain the family until Egon entered full employment. He would walk straight up the stairs to his room, where Gertrude would be waiting, either playing with the jewellery her mother had refused to pawn or lying on the bed flicking through her brother's sketches.

'This one?'

Egon turned around from the washbasin, wiping the soap out of his eyes.

'Krems out the back door of the tool-shed.'

She looked at it again, turning the picture in her thin fingers, analysing it from all angles, rubbing a thumb over the pencil lines, pointing at a village landscape where three lone chimneystacks punctuated a bruised skyline.

'You should do more.'

'Don't be ridiculous,' said Egon flatly, taking off his shirt, careful not to let the grease touch the bed-sheets.

'But Egon...'

'Why are you going on like this?'

'But you could be really good,' pleaded Gertrude.

'And what would you know?'

'Don't speak like that to me.' Gertrude flashed her eyes indignantly at Egon.

Her brother relented. 'You're not old enough to understand. It's impossible to make a living with that.'

'You don't *have* to be like him, you know.'

Egon paused before responding, breathing in and letting his sister's words dissolve between them.

'And how else are we going to take care of Mother?'

'If you were an artist, we wouldn't have to. You could sell portraits and send money home. We could go to Venice. Paris. Milan. You could buy me frocks. You would wear a tall hat. We could eat chocolate cake in cafés. Wouldn't it be wonderful?' She rolled over onto her back. 'Just think.'

'We'll never get away from this place.'

'Why do you say that?'

'You know why.'

'But Meli's here. She can take care of Mother.'

'On her own?'

'If Father was still alive, we wouldn't be…' started Gertrude.

'Don't you dare say that,' snapped Egon.

'Well, it's true, isn't it? If he was still alive…'

'Forget it!'

She climbed up from the bed and hugged her brother. 'It's horrible sitting around with just Mother in the house.' She rested her head on his shoulder. 'I hate being alone when you're at the yard.'

'I come back as early as I can.'

'But I'm here all day.'

'And what about school?' Gertrude thumbed the buttons on her nightdress. 'Gerti?' She pulled herself closer to Egon. 'Have you been missing class?'

'It's just so boring. It's not the same without you around.'

'And does Mother know?'

'She doesn't notice anything anymore.'

'But you should go. You need to go.'

'I want to be with you.' Gertrude rested her chin on her brother's collar bone. 'You'll never leave me, will you? Will you?'

Egon released her and continued to undress. He moved over to the basin in the corner and rubbed a wet flannel over his neck and arms.

'Of course not.'

Egon never returned to the mechanics' hut in the station yard. He never handled another track, greased another joint, nor burnt his skin on the furnace door. Instead, he came home at midday just as Gertrude finished school. They would meet a mile outside of Tulln and walk home together. Sometimes he carried his thirteen-year-old sister on his back; sometimes they raced each other home and sometimes they played in the fields; but they always came home together to a silent meal with their mother. Afterwards they would go upstairs and spend the rest of the evening in their room, dreaming of the sun setting on an unknown sea, the water lapping against the wall of an Italian port, the pair of them eating chocolate cake. They were inseparable: Egon played father, friend and brother to the girl who wanted nothing more than to escape the repressive station building.

One day a gloved fist thumped against their bedroom door.

The pair did not move. Gertrude was sitting on the floor, half-naked, strips of an unmade dress laid out in front of her and scissors in hand. Egon rose slowly from the desk where he had been sitting and walked to the door.

'I demand you come out now!' came Czihaczek's voice. 'What the hell are you up to in there?'

Egon took a sharp step back as a gloved fist thumped against the door three more times.

'I demand to know!'

Egon held a finger to his lips.

'Out, you brats!'

He took the scissors out of Gertrude's hand and stood a few feet from the door.

'Come out!' screamed Czihaczek.

He thumped the door several times before Egon heard the diminuendo of footsteps along the landing and down the stairs. He placed the scissors back on the table and put a robe around his sister's shoulders.

'Now cover yourself up.'

'What've we done?'

'Nothing. He's not angry at you. Now, please, cover yourself up.'

Egon sat down on the corner of the bed, his head in his hands. Gertrude stood up, moved over next to her brother and took him in her arms.

'We'll leave now. We can go anywhere. You can paint. I'll make dresses.'

'Gerti, please. There's no need for that. Sit back down.'

There was a crack and Czihaczek came bursting through the door, ripping away part of the frame as he rammed his shoulder against the wood. Gertrude scurried under the bed and Egon stood up to confront the old man, who was brandishing his walking stick.

'Where have you been, you little imp?' roared Czihaczek, throwing Egon onto the bed. His nephew got up only to be slapped down again with a blow across the cheek. 'Sacrilege!' hissed Czihaczek under his breath. 'Spitting on your father's grave.'

Czihaczek straightened his tie and pulled at his cufflinks until a segment of white shirt protruded from his sleeves.

'It hit her harder than the rest of…' Egon faltered.

'Don't patronise me.'

'I swear. She's not been going to school.'

'Not another word! You're as bad as each other.' He turned angrily on his nephew. 'What would he say now, if he knew? If he knew what you've turned down? If he knew what you're inflicting on your poor mother?' He paused, looked back, incredulously, at the dress. 'You're worthless, the pair of you. Worthless. You've sullied my name...'

Czihaczek grabbed his nephew, hurling him against the bed, so that, stooping, Egon was bent over the blankets. He lodged the tip of his walking stick in the back of Egon's neck. 'Don't you dare move, boy. You hear me? Don't you dare move.' Czihaczek wrenched the back of Egon's trousers, pushing them down into a black puddle around his ankles. He tapped his walking stick between Egon's knees to spread his legs and then thrashed it across his buttocks. Every sinew shortened in Egon's body as he lurched forward. 'You feel that, boy? You feel that? That's what you've been missing.' Egon turned his head to retaliate, but Czihaczek buried the tip of his walking stick in his nephew's neck. 'I'm only doing what your father would want.' The blows came shorter, whippier, the buttocks shaking with recoil as the sixth, seven, eighth and ninth blows came in quick succession. Through a sickening alignment of two mirrors – one above the bed, the other propped up on a chest of drawers on the other side of the room – Egon could see the chafed contours of the backs of his thighs and buttocks. His uncle's cane struck leaving corrugated ridges which seeped out into a crimson flush. He could hear Czihaczek's teeth grind and his breathing accelerate.

Just as Egon lost count, Czihaczek's arm dropped to his side. He removed a glove, took a silk handkerchief out of the top pocket of his waistcoat and wiped it across his face, down his beard and then along the shaft of his blood-spattered cane.

'Where's that other brat?'

As he pulled his trousers up, Gertrude shuffled under the bed, crawling further into a corner.

'Please, Uncle. She hasn't done anything.'

Czihaczek caught his breath. 'I just want the best for you all,' he said. 'The best for your poor mother. You should show her more respect.'

'We know that, Uncle,' said Egon, refastening his braces.

Czihaczek exhaled, too tired to raise his cane again. He flicked a pile of papers into the air with the metal tip of his walking stick. 'I wouldn't wipe a donkey's arse with them! There's Melanie toiling in that place and you waste your time on this. Cravats and coffeehouse nattering.'

He walked to the door. On the floor there lay an engineering handbook for the Northern Railways, its cover scrawled with doodles. He picked it up and placed it on the side table.

'It's for your own good, you know. These scribbles will never pay your way.' He shook his head and walked out.

Marie soon tired of the arguments, the reproaches, and, most of all, the bloated silences. She wrote to one of her sisters to ask if she could find Egon a post in a firm of graphic artists run by a distant relative. It was meant to be a compromise between art and engineering, a middle ground where Egon could nurture his talent but still bring food home to the table.

A week later, Marie opened her sister's response and read only as far as *unfortunately* before tossing it in the fire under the stove.

'You know well enough what's best for him,' Czihaczek had said to her. 'I shouldn't have to tell you what to do.'

'But you've seen how he reacts. He won't have anything to do with the railways.'

'It's what Adolf wanted.'

'I know.'

'I'm not going to let him get away with it.'

'Threats won't work.'

'I warn you that if this adolescent antagonism continues, you'll all feel the pinch soon enough. I've heard what they get up to, you know. I know what you let them do.'

'What am I supposed to do?'

'They're *your* children. People are talking.'

'I can't stop that.'

'Just remember: if these improprieties don't cease, there'll be nothing. I'll send through whatever I can for you, but if you can't rein them in, don't expect me to foot the bill. It's you I care about.'

Czihaczek continued to provide subsistence support to the family, but he severed all links with the rebellious boy and his younger sister. And, as news of their behaviour filtered back along the iron arteries which fed the city, he reduced the family's allowance even further until there was barely enough to support Marie. While she sat blank-faced on the platform, too proud to beg from the disembarking passengers, the whole family relied on Melanie whose face had begun to wear the expression of a woman twice her age; the months of steam-filled warehouses ate away at her complexion until she was almost indistinguishable from her mother.

One afternoon, from the barred window upstairs, Marie watched Egon and his sister returning from an afternoon in the countryside, chasing each other and then walking and then chasing again, their laughs and shrieks out of time with the movements of their lips. Gertrude wore a coronet of daisies and Egon's shirt was strung around his waist, fluttering behind him like a skirt, their dancing feet scuffing up dust on the station's path. They stopped as they caught sight of their mother at the window. Gertrude removed her garland and Egon slipped his arms back into the shirt. Marie confronted them at the front door as they entered the station building.

'Where are they?'

'What?'

'I won't ask again, Gertrude.'

'Sorry, Mother. We forgot.'

'I give you one simple task and you can't even do that.'

'We said we're sorry.'

'So, what are we going to have for dinner tonight? Bread and water?'

'There's some cabbage in the…' started Gertrude.

'Eggs and milk! That's all I asked for. Go up to your room, I want a word with your brother.'

Gertrude trudged up the stairs, looking back over her shoulder, and Egon followed his mother into the kitchen.

'Now, there's an easy answer to all this,' she leant in towards her son, 'and a difficult one.' Egon looked up, his lips pulled tight. 'If you want to stay here then you must at least pretend to play by Leopold's rules. He pays; we obey. Do you understand?'

'Yes.'

'This is your last warning.'

'But you know I can't...'

'Silence!' Marie slammed her hand down on the table, a cup falling on its side and rolling until it hit its handle. 'There's too much of that diseased old bastard in you.' She walked away and stood looking out of the kitchen window onto the meadows beyond the tracks. 'If you carry on like you are round here we'll have nothing left. So I'm sending you away.' Egon took a step back, supporting himself against the sideboard. 'I've arranged for you to become an apprentice in Klosterneuburg.'

'To whom?' said Egon, scratching his thumbnail along the knife scars in the wooden surface.

'Joschka from the works knows these three painters. They're a bit wily but he's spoken to them and they've agreed to see you. If they still like you after a month then you can stay.' She paused and laid a hand on her son's shoulder. 'This is what you wanted, isn't it?'

Egon looked up at his mother, the usual resentment fallen like scales from his eyes.

'You'll spend weekdays in the town. Joschka says they'll provide lodging and you'll pay for your tuition by doing chores around the house and running errands. You are to do everything they ask. Understand?'

'Yes, of course.'

'You start next month.'

Egon walked towards her and laid a hand on her shoulder. She turned back from the window. He kissed the mother on both cheeks and then the backs of her hands.

'I will not disappoint you. I swear.'

'You already have,' she whispered, her voice tailing off.

He kissed her again on the forehead before running upstairs and slamming his bedroom door behind him.

# THREE

# SLAUGHTERED ANATOMIES

Every Sunday evening, the sixteen-year-old Egon took the train to Klosterneuburg on the northern outskirts of Vienna and walked from the station through the rancid streets to the artists' house. By the time he arrived, the men were draped across a table like soiled napkins, asleep and snoring. Egon would creep upstairs and curl into a ball on the mattress in the corner of their studio, making space among the piles of Caravaggio reproductions and Rembrandt copies. He rose early to scrub sheets, chop vegetables and sweep steps, the hours of tedium diminishing with the rising sun. The cycle of chores went uninterrupted for weeks; the painters avoided his company; they sent him on drawn-out errands to other villages, forcing him to come home after nightfall; they requested he fetch logs in the middle of the night to keep the fires going; they made him eat alone in the kitchen. In all that time, Egon never once touched a paintbrush other than to put it back in a jar.

One day after lunch he was summoned to the table in the front room by the greying voluptuaries: Max Kahrer, Karl Strauch and Wolfgang Pauker.

'You're not quite Paris, but you'll do, I suppose,' said Kahrer. 'Don't look so glum. You won't have to choose between us, lad. We're bloody almighty but we're far from being goddesses.'

'Speak for yourself,' blurted Strauch, wiping a trickle of wine from his jowls. 'I've always thought I'd make a rather fetching Aphrodite. And frankly, with your Latin-this and your Greek-that you could probably pass for Athena.'

'That would logically make me Hera,' added Pauker, sitting up proudly. 'I can see why people would think that.'

'What's the matter, lad?' asked Kahrer, laying a hand on Egon's shoulder.

'I don't understand what you're talking about.'

'The Apple of Discord?' said Strauch.

'Paris?' continued Pauker.

Egon shook his head.

'The conundrum of beauty?'

Egon shook his head again.

'We're going to have some trouble with this one,' added Strauch, taking Egon's chin in the palm of his hand. 'Bit of a heathen. Not like Jens. Now, *he* was quite something. Ah, my cup-bearer, my Ganymede. Are you sure you want to go through with this, boy?'

Egon nodded.

'Then your tuition will start tomorrow. As promised, we'll supply you with paints, paper, brushes and from time to time a strip of canvas, if you work hard enough. We'll also ensure you have the peace and quiet you don't have back home. Where is home by the way?'

'Tulln.'

Pauker looked at Strauch and laughed.

'In return,' continued Kahrer, 'you will rise at five. Do your duties by midday… cleaning the rooms, airing the bedclothes et cetera, et cetera… and you'll prepare us goulash – or some such dish – for lunch. After that you will paint. You will not complain. You will not answer back. You will not question our methods. Agreed?'

'Yes, Sir.'

'Good. You may return to the armpit of Austria on Friday afternoons to visit your family, if you so wish. If you don't, we quite understand. If your work – both domestic and artistic – has been satisfactory, you will receive offal and fruit to take home. Is that clear?'

'Yes.'

'Yes, what?'

'Yes, thank you, Dr Kahrer.'

Like their self-styled goddesses, the three painters divided themselves neatly into the wise, the powerful and the sensuous. After lunch every day, Strauch undressed and stood for Egon, striking flamboyant poses, while the young man learnt to paint the landscape of the aged male abdomen, the rugged channels and grooves that sagged between Strauch's muscle and bone, the mottled sexagenarian skin, speckled with black and red. In the afternoon, while the other painters slept, Egon took a sketching class with Pauker. The artist would return from the market at three o'clock with a butchered animal slung over his shoulder in a dappled rag. Before it was skinned, gutted and dropped in the pot for dinner, Egon would sit in the kitchen and commit the slaughtered anatomies to paper. Pauker would sever the paw of a rabbit and thrust it in front of his young student, tugging at the tendons, easing back the fur, talking Egon through the varying properties of flesh. Pauker worked methodically from one end of the butcher's stall to the other, each day making Egon sketch a different cadaverous fragment: the open-eyed head of a chicken, a curled cow's tongue or the creaseless surface of a pig's liver. In the evenings after dinner, they would drink cheap schnapps and argue around the kitchen table. Egon would sit quietly, the day's labour tugging at his eyelids, and slowly register the artists' affectations and mimicry.

'Your uncle's stopped writing,' said Kahrer, wiping a sleeve across his bearded chin.

'Fat-headed shit!' Crumbs spurted from Pauker's toothless mouth. 'He can't stop you.'

Egon took a cloth from the front of his apron and gathered up the debris on the table.

'Doing what, Sir?'

'Leaving.'

'But I don't want to leave.'

Pauker and Kahrer looked at each other for an instant and returned to their food.

'But you can't stay here forever,' said Kahrer, pausing to swallow. 'Much as we've all learnt to deal with your erratic little quirks…'

'Listen, boy,' interrupted Pauker. 'We won't keep you here for months on end. That's not how it works. Once you've learned what there is to learn, then you'll be on your way.'

'And not before.'

'But it's barely been…'

'School!'

'But *this* is my school. You agreed that with…'

Kahrer put his fork down, cleared his throat with a sip of wine.

'We agreed nothing! You will play by our rules or not at all. Is that clear?'

'Yes.'

'Now, the old bastard's given up blocking your application. You should make the most of it.'

'But I haven't applied for anything.'

Kahrer stretched across the table and took the tankard from Egon's hands.

'Go and press your best clothes and get a good night's sleep.'

'But I don't want to leave!'

'You're on the first train tomorrow.'

'What about the cooking? I need to get to the market tomorrow, otherwise…'

'We'll take care of that.'

'This is not the time for dithering,' bellowed Kahrer as Egon stepped back down from the carriage. 'Get on that bloody train before I throw you on!'

Kahrer removed his broad-brimmed hat and flapped it at Egon. Egon placed his portfolio on the ground, leaning it against his leg.

'Listen to me, boy. This thing's leaving any moment now and if you're not on board you might as well run back to Tulln on your own because the other two won't let you back in the house if they find out you lost your nerve.'

'I haven't lost my nerve, Sir.'

Kahrer looked up and down the platform at the last passengers boarding the train.

'You do want to be a painter, don't you?' Egon nodded. 'So, I'm right in thinking that you're not planning to swill out our piss and shit for the rest of your days?'

'Of course not.'

'So, get on that damn train then!'

'Leopold will desert us. There'll be nothing left.'

'He's already deserted you, my boy. We've never received a thing from him.'

Egon leant to pick up his portfolio and then retracted his hand.

'But she's suffering enough as it is.'

'What do you care? If you're trying to tell me you won't get on that train because you want to go home one day and wipe your mother's arse and comb her hair, then you're a liar.'

'But she can't afford to live without Leopold's support.'

'And you're just going to forget the past six months?'

'No.'

'Well, get on that train. Don't try and tell me you want to go back to the coal face for the rest of your days just for the sake of that syphilitic old crone?' Egon's protest was drowned out by the platform attendant's whistle and a drum-roll of carriage doors. 'Do you think you would ever have come here in the first place if she didn't want you to take that bloody examination? Listen to me, you stubborn little sod: you have waited your short, grotesquely talented life for a chance like this. Now stop being an imbecile and get on board.'

On the journey home, Egon already knew he had failed. The examiner had been briefly drawn in by his portfolio – flicking past the still-life sketches, pausing on the landscapes and anatomies – but Egon was wooden in the interviews. He answered vaguely, ineloquently, incorrectly. He knew little of art history and nothing of chromatography. He sweated, he stuttered; his throat dried, his mind stuck; his voice box betrayed him, switching octaves arbitrarily; he failed to explain how to prepare a canvas or mix balsam, turpentine and mastic varnish; he shook his head at a print of *The Procession of the Magi*. When the ordeal was over, he stood up from his chair and grasped prematurely for the examiner's hand, shaking his limp, clammy fingertips. He walked out of the room only to turn back from the door to retrieve his portfolio. He glided along the wooden-panelled corridors in a daze and across the atrium under the scrutiny of the other students and applicants. Reaching the front door, a gust of cold air from the street brought him back to his senses just in time for him to stretch out towards one of the pillars and launch the contents of his stomach down the School's front steps. A stately professor took a stride away from the impact, placed his hat under his arm and walked around Egon and in through the front door.

Back in Klosterneuburg, Egon walked resolutely to the post office to pick up the telegram with the predicted rejection. He stuffed the note into his pocket and returned home, leaving the message on the kitchen table for his tutors to read. He avoided their states over the following days, setting about the chores in the mornings and his lessons in the afternoons, diligent and silent.

A few days later Egon received a letter from his uncle, offering him, for the last time, a post with the Imperial railways. Czihaczek had negotiated a second apprenticeship with a stationmaster in Eisenstadt: *an exceptional opportunity – too good to pass up*, he wrote. *For your mother's sake. Word has reached me of your talents but, as I have said, there is only one career for you, and only one career your father wanted for you. This is your final chance.* Egon jammed the letter into the frame of the mirror next to a pencil sketch of Gertrude, refusing to paint or sketch for a week. The delicately scripted word *chance* poked out from underneath the fold, demanding to be read once in the morning while washing and then once again before going to bed. Egon would take the letter down, open it in his wet hands and refresh the terms in his mind, a self-imposed temptation meant to harden his resolve.

Egon lay awake on the mattress in the painters' studio, his toes gripping at the sheet, his back sticky against the mattress and a hand feeling out for the spot where his sister would have lain. His eyes, long accustomed to the room's penumbra, flicked towards the door as footsteps echoed in the hallway. The door swung open and the room was bathed in the amber glow of a shielded lamp. There was more shuffling and then the drag and scrape of books coming off shelves and fingers scrabbling through papers.

'Dr Kahrer?'

'Go back to sleep, lad.'

An oversized nightgown hung off the mentor's plump body.

'I'm already awake.'

'Do what I say!'

Egon rolled over, pulling the pillow around his ears, blocking out the shuffling and stertor. Objects thudded around his mattress and he raised his head again from the pillow.

'Did you not hear me, boy?'

When Egon awoke at dawn the next day, streaks of sunshine coming through the roof-lights, it seemed his bed had been moved in the night. A makeshift wall had sprung up, imprisoning him on his mattress in the corner of the room. As he rubbed the residue of sleep from his eyes, he saw that around him were piles of books, canvases, *objets d'art*, tables, still-life artefacts, fabrics, easels, chairs, jars, palettes, all assembled in a jumbled blockade. At the foot of his mattress were two buckets: one containing water, the other bread and fruit. Next to them were a pile of blank paper, a jar of pencils, three brushes and some paints. A sheet of rough-cut paper hung over the lip of one of the buckets: *Only move or remove one of these objects once you have either read it or drawn it. We refuse to see you until the studio is returned to its antediluvian state. Do not disappoint us. Kahrer, Pauker & Strauch.*

Egon tested his weight on a pile of books and then climbed over the blockade. He pulled his trousers on, easing the braces over his stiff shoulders, and walked to the door in the opposite corner. It was locked. He took one of the models' chairs from the middle of the room and positioned it under a roof-light but could not reach the catch. He looked towards the fireplace where a steel rod usually stood to open the large panes of glass but it had disappeared. He climbed down from the chair and went back over to his mattress. He emptied the bucket of food – apples, bread rolls and a dried sausage dropping onto his bed linen – and prepared to do his morning ablutions.

Egon endured the anodyne repetition of pencil strokes, the parrot-learning of *The Glory of the Old Masters*, the immersion of artificial colour and natural light, and the ascetic starvation. Every third day, the door swung open and two fresh buckets of water and food were exchanged for his bodily wastes. Egon hurried forward to glimpse the corridor over Kahrer's shoulder before seeing it vanish behind the thick studio door. He then returned to his work, picking each artefact up off the pile and placing it in front of the easel. When the light dimmed, he laid his brushes and pencils down and read books by candlelight until his eyelids dropped only to be woken an hour later by the drunken laughter of the tutors downstairs.

When Kahrer reappeared twelve days later, he nodded approvingly at the bookshelves and easels returned to their natural state; he smiled at the piles of Egon's papers, picking sketches at random, perusing images through a monocle. He looked up at Egon, his fingers lingering on a sketch.

'Progress of sorts, lad.'

'Thank you, Sir.'

Egon held his chin high, regaining some of the dignity lost during the solitude of the preceding days.

'It's not just because you're anxious to leave this place, is it?'

He picked a large, leather-bound book off the shelf and thumbed through its pages. He licked his forefinger intermittently, turning each leaf until he arrived at a picture of a woman brandishing a sword and clasping a severed head out in front of her. He held it up to Egon.

'*Judith with the Head of Holofernes*, Sir.' Kahrer's eyes narrowed on his student. 'Lucas Cranach the Elder.'

He nodded to himself, flicked further through the book and held up a second plate.

'*The Fall of the Angels*: Giordano.'

'Year?'

'1666.'

'Just a few months short of Milton's offering,' he muttered to himself.

'Sorry, Sir?'

'Not important.'

Kahrer moved from the shadow of the bookshelf to the middle of the room and looked up at the roof-light, bathing him in a circle of sunshine.

'You must be missing it.'

'Yes, Sir.'

'Washing and sweeping?'

'No, Sir. I miss the air. The light.'

'A true painter will paint in any conditions.'

Kahrer moved his hands in the shafts of sun, casting shadowed shapes on the floor, moving in and out of the pools of darkness around him, spinning and squatting.

'Truly marvellous. Something you must never take for granted.' Kahrer spun again in the light, his gown catching and reflecting the folds of brightness. 'Leonardo's ten attributes of sight: number one, light.' The painter stepped sideways into a shadow. 'Number two, darkness. Next?'

'Solidity and colour.'

'Good. Next.'

'Form and position.'

'Continue.'

'Distance and propinquity.'

'And the last two?'

Egon wiped his forehead with a sleeve, looking round the room for inspiration. He saw the shadows of statuettes; he saw the sharp structures of easels; he saw the graded transparencies of cloths.

'Tell me, boy.'

'On the tip of my tongue, Sir.'

'Come on! These are the basics!' Kahrer rushed from the centre of the room with arms spinning like windmills at his sides, stopping dead an inch from Egon's face. 'Look at me for Christ's sake!' A drop of spittle hung on his beard, perched on the brittle hairs beneath his bottom lip.

Egon's eyes dropped to the floor.

'Think!'

Kahrer waved a hand past Egon's face and then froze, his arm stationary in mid-air.

'Motion and rest, boy. Motion and rest.'

Kahrer stood up straight, repositioned the smock on his shoulders and strode to the door.

'You're not ready yet, boy. I won't let you fail a second time,' he said, turning the lock behind him.

When Egon heard the rusted grind of the lock a week later, he stood to attention in the middle of the room, the midday sun casting pure light down on his grubby shirt. The room was immaculate: the artefacts had all been placed once again on their shelves and in their corners; his works were propped up against the walls of the studio, lined next to each other along the skirting board. All three painters entered the room, walking in circles around Egon and his sketches, thumbing papers, checking the likenesses of still-lives, holding canvases up to the light.

'Not as good as that young lad from Brünn we had last year.'

'The anatomy is distorted in this one,' said Pauker, brandishing a sketch of two entwined bodies. 'Makes El Greco look like a graphic artist.'

Strauch took the picture, removed a lens from his inside pocket and scrutinised the forms. He took a handful of other sketches off a table, flipping through each one before letting them drop, cradle-rocking in the air before skidding across the floorboards. A minute later he looked up at Egon.

'Atrocious abuses of dimension. Tell me: lying down, what fraction of his original height is man?'

'A ninth, Sir.'

'And kneeling: what fraction of his height does he lose?'

'A quarter.'

Strauch passed the sketch back to Pauker and walked to the corner of the room.

'A few more weeks and the boy'll be just about ready, I should think.'

Egon's face dropped.

'With respect, Sir, I don't think I can survive another...' Egon stopped mid-sentence. He cleared his throat and threw his head back. 'I am a painter, Herr Doktor Kahrer. Not a boy.' His voice faltered, his eyes fixed on a point on the wall just over the painters' heads. 'If I am to realise my potential I need a more suitable environment.'

'We'll decide on that, not you,' said Pauker.

'I've painted everything in this room,' continued Egon stoically. 'Three times at least and far better than any of those books can replicate. Now, please let me out. I need fresh inspiration.'

'Fresh inspiration or just fresh air?' challenged Pauker.

'Both.'

Pauker walked over to the mirror and plucked Czihaczek's telegram from under the frame. He tore it several times, sprinkling twenty-four equally sized segments across the studio floor. He then pulled a book off the shelf, leafed nonchalantly through its pages and ripped out a picture. He stuck the paper in the letter's place under the mirror frame.

'Dürer, boy. Dürer. The kind of painter who would voluntarily lock himself up to master his art.'

'That's quite enough, Wolfgang,' interjected Kahrer. 'Egon, you may leave. The rest of the tuition we can complete as usual.' Egon walked towards the door. 'I hope you understand that this will serve you well in the long run. You'll thank us after we've finally got you into that Academy.'

'If it ever happens.'

'Now go and get yourself washed. It stinks in here.'

A month later the three painters were slumped over the kitchen table passing a telegram and a bottle of wine amongst themselves. Kahrer had picked up the note from the post office earlier in the day while Egon had been sweeping the backyard. When their protégé came through the back door into the pantry, they fell silent, gesturing for him to take up the fourth chair. He propped his broom up against the table and undid the top button of his shirt. Strauch poured him a mug of wine.

'Go and pack your things, lad.'

Egon's head dropped as failure loomed over him again, his fingers interlinking behind his neck. He pulled his hands forward over the crown of his head and onto his face, hiding his eyes behind palms. Under the table, he pushed his heel into the ground to stop his leg twitching.

'There's nothing more we can do for you here.'

The broom slid along the table's edge and cracked onto the tiled floor. He looked up and met the smiles of the three painters. Egon twisted to pick it up.

'Leave it, lad. There are more important things.'

On the table in front of him was a folded paper. He opened the telegram. It read: *PASSED STOP COMFORTABLY STOP ACADEMY OF FINE ARTS VIENNA.*

The three painters stood up to embrace Egon before toasting his health and opening another bottle. They drank and drank, each artist recounting his own Viennese youth: the days when they had attended the capital's colleges, sipped Moravian wine and writhed between the thighs of the city's urchins. Egon said nothing, grinned at their painless nostalgia and meticulously noted the names and places they mentioned.

'The most important thing now, lad, is to forget everything we've ever told you,' said Strauch, his lips full with a red wine smile. 'Forget the formalities, the structures, the postulating, Cranach and all that lot. Forget it all!' he shouted, dismissing bookish knowledge with a cork launched across the room and into the sink, chiming off the empty pans. 'Get out there and see what you love; see what you hate. Find out which inspires you more… and then paint it. Paint it all. And paint it however you bloody want.'

'Promise me you'll never degrade yourself, boy,' continued Pauker. 'No more churches and trains now. Forget all our nonsense as well. Particularly whatever Karl told you! Live a little. Soak it up. Eat it. Drink it. Fuck it. Revel in it. And then paint it.'

'Paint what?'

'Your subject chooses you, not the other way around,' added Kahrer, his voice less passionate than his two colleagues, his glass still full. 'You'll know when that choice has been made. You'll reach for your brush.'

'The mares on the puzsta,' said Pauker.

'For me: the cabaret dancers,' continued Strauch. 'Delightful tarts.'

'Whatever *it* will be, Egon, it will be good. I know.' Kahrer ran a hand down his beard. 'It will be great.'

'Maybe,' added Strauch.

Egon re-read the telegram, blinking hard through drunken eyes.

'Maybe,' repeated Pauker.

'Maybe?' said Egon, standing up. 'There is no maybe.' He raised his mug above the candles in the middle of the table. He breathed in, his chest swelling to its adult size. 'I will be better than all of you. I will be great. I will be the best in all of the Empire!'

'We don't doubt that. Now go and prepare our bedpans, pack your things and make sure you're out of here by the time we get up tomorrow.'

The familiar platform was stubbled with green shoots pushing up through the cracks in the paving. Coal discoloured the once white façade of the house, its dented porch sagging under the weight of passing seasons. Marie stood up from her chair to greet Egon as his train pulled in. She hobbled towards him, paving slabs rocking under her feet. They both stopped short of each other; Egon was the first to spread his arms and step forward. Then his mother followed. They held each other for a brief moment and walked inside.

'They're both very proud of you,' she said, sitting around the kitchen table. 'Gerti won't stop going on about it. She's so happy for you. And Meli asks after you whenever she's around.'

Marie straightened the front of her apron as they heard feet galloping down the stairs. Gertrude burst through the door with tears in her eyes and threw herself at Egon.

'You're going to be famous!' He pressed her body to his. 'So, when do you start? What'll you be doing?' Egon released her and gestured for her to sit down. She shook her head.

'First things first: find accommodation, register, buy some new materials and do all the paperwork. There's a lot of reading as well. Five weeks are barely long enough.'

'We'll manage together, won't we?' said Gertrude, reaching out for her brother's hand.

Marie cleared out her ear with a little finger. She brushed a crumb from the table and looked at her son.

'We?' asked Egon.

'You said we would be together. You said we would, you said we would.'

'But, Gerti, I'm moving to the city.'

'I've already packed my things.'

'You can't just…'

'There are plenty of schools in Vienna. It'll be fine.' Gertrude looked across at her mother's leathery face. 'She can take care of herself. Look at her: she just sits around all day, doing nothing.'

Egon grabbed his sister's wrist and pulled her to the table.

'Don't you dare say that in here.'

'So, you're just going to leave me with her?'

Egon nodded.

'But you said…'

He placed both hands on Getrude's shoulders, looking her in the eyes. 'I'll be back to visit. Often. I promise.'

'I can't believe you're just going to abandon me…'

Marie slammed her palm against the table. 'Listen to me, girl! You're staying here, and that is the last of it. I've had enough of all this. Tomorrow you'll join Melanie in the warehouse.' Marie raised a finger to silence Gertrude. 'Not a word, girl. Not a single word.' She leant back against her chair. 'Now, forget about your brother. He'll go off and do what he wants, just like all men. The sooner you become like your sister the better. You will be disappointed, Gertrude. Now get used to it.'

Gertrude ran out of the room, slamming the door behind her. Egon stood up, his chair scraping against the tiled floor.

'No matter how she tries to twist your arm, you're not…'

'But you know she'll just run off anyway.'

'She'll try every trick she knows. Manipulative little madam.' Her fingers crawled out across the table and up towards Egon's sleeve and then she pulled her hand back. 'She loves you, Egon. You know that, don't you?'

'Yes, of course.'

'Are you sure?'

'Yes.'

Marie shook her head and left the room.

# FOUR

# RED CRESCENTS

Egon and Gertrude packed two bags, tip-toed downstairs and were already waiting on the platform as the headlights stroked the sides of the valley. Egon had taken the keys from the stationmaster's quarters and gained entry to the ticket sales booth, pocketing the little cash there was in the till. No one disembarked as the first train south pulled into the station. Egon reached up for the door handle, helped Gertrude inside and passed her the two cases. They had left a note for their mother telling her not to worry, that they would be back in a fortnight. By the time she had opened it, her children were already taking lunch in a café in front of Graz station, the May sun beating down on the parasol above them.

Gertrude had spent countless nights pleading for a final adventure before her brother started at the Academy. She kept Egon from sleep, listing potential destinations, tugging at his elbow and hair until he finally agreed to elope to the Adriatic port of Trieste, a flourishing outpost where blue-blooded men walked arm-in-arm with the Empire's most elegant ladies.

In the carriage, Gertrude dozed, tiredness overcoming her initial excitement. Egon sat bolt upright, looking out from underneath thick eyebrows as the landscape blurred past. Within just a few months he had made the transition from adolescent to adult. His limbs had ceased straining against his body's rapid growth, his complexion no longer betrayed him and his voice had settled at a middling pitch. He held his chin up with an almost affected air, his neck straightened by a high collar and his father's black silk tie. His suitcase was above him, sitting on the meshed racks, bobbing in time with the carriage; he had packed it with care, wary not to crease the fashionable clothes which would allow him to melt into the aristocratic elite who trod Trieste's plazas and Vienna's boulevards. Underneath the heavy fabrics were his painting materials, and inside his small wooden box of oils was a packet of cigarettes: a concession to the pretensions of city-life. Egon removed a handkerchief from his top pocket, unfolded it over his lap and laid out some slices of pickled fish. He looked out of the window at the Adriatic's topaz skies and then across to his sleeping sister before sinking his teeth into a hunk of black bread.

The Hotel Immanuel was the best they could find for their means, and the only establishment that allowed the youngsters to sign the registry book without questioning them too closely.

'Herr und Fräulein Schiele?'

'That's correct.'

'We are brother and sister,' added Gertrude.

'You could be priest and bride for all I care. Just sign there. Payment upfront please.'

Egon placed the money on the counter.

'Can I smoke in the room?'

'You can do whatever you want in the room.' The receptionist pushed a key over the counter. 'Up the stairs. Third floor. Second on the left.'

The room was dominated by a double bed and a large mirror which hung on one wall. On their first night, Egon rolled over and looked back at himself, watching Gertrude's back rise and fall behind him as she slept. He got up and walked to the window. Opening the blinds, he looked out at the neighbouring house, the wind blowing at its open windows, flirting with curtains, before he turned around and watched Gertrude again, her shock of light ginger hair spread across the pillow. Every few minutes she would move one of her limbs and he would see the shadow of a joint as her body pulled against the sheets, and then stopped. He ran a hand through his unkempt hair, scratching a fingernail into the hollow at the base of his skull. He got back into bed, rolled onto his side and continued to watch her in the mirror.

Egon and Gertrude strolled the streets arm-in-arm like a stately couple, visiting the Roman ruins, singing childish rhymes in the dilapidated amphitheatre and making empty prayers in the cathedral which perched high above the town on a limestone plateau. After the early enthusiasm had worn off, the pair relaxed by the harbour, walking along the seafront, saving money on a light breakfast and an insubstantial lunch so that they could take tea in prominent cafés on the main boulevard. They sat there for hours – their cups long since empty – and nodded gracefully at passers-by. The Habsburgs' southern port was a jumble of those travellers, traders and locals who render harbour towns both seedy and opulent. With increasing bravado, Gertrude greeted faintly recognised faces with a flourish while Egon looked out into the harbour at the boats arriving and leaving, listening to the skiffs nod up and down in their moorings. As Egon watched, he memorised everything: the knots in the ropes, the links in the anchor chain, the wind-creases in the water, the algae colonising a plank, the graded shades of a watermark.

In the evenings after dinner, they would return to their hotel room. Gertrude would climb into bed and read for a short while before falling asleep, then Egon would open his suitcase, take out his drawing materials and sketch from memory everything he had seen during the day. Some would be fragments of ships, of people, of horses, of buildings, others would be full harbour scenes to which he would add colour through the night before presenting them to Gertrude in the morning. She would congratulate her brother with a hug and swap places with him. He would fall into bed, lying on the same patch of warm sheets Gertrude had just vacated, and she would get up, dress and walk down to the seafront.

One night, he sat layering oil onto a pencil sketch of a small promontory northwest of the city which he had earlier committed to card. As he built up the colours, scoring sea ripples into the wet paint, his tongue buried in his cheek, he watched the inanimate rocky outcrop and the Archduke's castle come to life. He had brought a bottle of wine up to his room and it stood almost empty on the dressing table littered with paints and pencils. He put the glass to his lips again, took a sip and placed it back on the table. A small red crescent had formed on the lace where the glass had been standing and as Egon replaced it, he twisted its stem so that the base eclipsed the sickle. He lay the card down next to the empty glass and leant back in his chair.

He heard the sliding sound of wind through cloth and turned to the open window. It was still. He looked back towards the bed and saw that the sheet and blanket had slid off Gertrude's limbs and dropped into a pile on the floor. His sister lay face down naked on the bed. Her arms were folded up underneath her body and her legs were slightly apart, her toes pointing inwards. He looked at the hardened skin on the soles of her feet, focussing on the line at which it became the soft veil on her ankles, which, in turn, merged into the plump flesh of her legs. His eye was drawn up and over the backs of her knees, along her thighs and into the crotch. He dwelled there for a moment until she moved again, her legs closing up and her torso twisting onto its side. She clasped arms in front of her, her fists shoved up close under her chin.

He watched her for the next three hours. She rolled onto her back, her arms falling by her side revealing her pubescent breasts; she held this position for some time before a dream took hold of her body, twisting her limbs into discomfited positions: her fingers spread unevenly over the mattress; her arms bent back on themselves; a heel pressed up into her buttock; a *trompe-l'oeil* wrist. Tracking each of her limbs as they sprawled across the large empty bed, Egon then took a pencil in hand and on the remaining sheets of paper started sketching. He had just enough time to commit the composition of her limbs to paper before she moved again. On each occasion, he would add only a few details. He had little time for her face: that convergence of adolescence and womanhood he knew all too well. He would sketch just a brief outline of her features, her face dominated by two back-to-back crescents which served as arching eyebrows and the bridge of the nose. A smudge of the side of the pencil was enough for the cheeks, while her eyes were never added. The rest of her body was a series of hurried lines: crooked scratches in the paper were the collar bones and ribs, while softer curves hinted at the femininity which Gertrude's body was announcing. As she shifted across the sheets, his eye continually sought out the point at which her thighs touched, which, if exposed, immediately became the centre-point of the sketch, a thick, firm pencil mark placing her lips in the middle of the paper: somewhere between a wound and a jewel, the point at which every picture would begin and end for Egon.

They left the following morning. Egon packed the clothes back into his case and helped Gertrude squeeze in the souvenirs she had bought during their fortnight stay. They paid the receptionist with the last of their coins and boarded the train.

Gertrude slept in the carriage. Though exhausted, Egon could not close his eyes. Grey-blue skies and potato-sack clouds slid by beyond the window, fields and forests alternating as they passed through the southern climes of the Empire. His case stood on the floor, rocking between his legs, occasionally steadied by an anxious hand. The carriage was empty: he looked out into the corridor which yawned back at him. He opened the case wide enough to remove one sketch with his fingertips. He laid it out on his lap and began studying the freshness of the curves, the depth of the body, the vividness of the genitals, slipping into a reverie. All of a sudden the carriage door flung back and the profile of a man appeared against the morning sun rising on the other side of the train: the hat, the shoulders, the bold stance, the Imperial uniform. Egon stuffed the picture into his jacket, before the new arrival could glimpse its contents; he snapped his knees together, forcing the suitcase closed, the lips of other sketches caught in the latch. Gertrude's eyes opened as the fresh air from the corridor swept into the compartment.

'It wasn't me,' said Egon.

'What?' said the man in uniform.

'I bought it. I swear, I bought it.'

Gertrude sat up, rubbing her eyes, swinging her legs down from the seat.

'What're you going on about?'

'The ink. I bought it. Honestly.'

The man twisted his neck, looking down at Egon who stuffed his blackened fingers under his thighs. He shook his head.

'Tickets, please.'

Gertrude glared at Egon on the opposite seat. He was transfixed by the figure in the doorway, his eyes rooted to the Imperial insignia on the man's lapel.

'Tickets, please,' the man repeated.

'Please give the man our tickets, Egon.'

The rattle of the compartment door.

'But I haven't done anything.'

'Just give the man our tickets.'

Egon shook his head and then reluctantly stuck out his ink-stained hands for inspection.

'What are you doing?' asked Gertrude, leaning over and reaching for the tickets. Egon pulled back sharply as her hand touched his chest. He buried his hands deep inside his jacket and pulled out two stubs of card.

'Thank you, Sir,' said the conductor, punching holes in the tickets and handing them back. 'Are you travelling unaccompanied?'

'Yes. We live at Tulln station,' said Gertrude.

'That's Adolf's place, right?'

'That's right, Sir.'

'Say hello to the old man. Tell him you met Johannes.'

'We will.'

'Safe journey home then,' he said.

The conductor slid the door closed after him and moved on to the next compartment.

Gertrude stared down at the suitcase clenched between Egon's knees. 'What's going on?'

'Go back to sleep. There's still a way to go.'

Egon leant his head against the back of the partition wall and feigned sleep. Minutes later, he opened an eye to check on his sister and then removed the crumpled sketch from inside his jacket. He straightened out its corners, ran a thumb over the figure and placed it back in the case. He squeezed it closed and fastened the latch.

A milk jug shattered against the kitchen door, porcelain shards skidding over tiles and spinning off chair legs. Gertrude scrambled under the table as her mother hurled more bowls and cups, tears running down her cheeks.

'How dare you!' Egon jumped backwards as a plate crashed on the floor at his feet. 'You thoughtless swine!'

'Mother, please.'

'Swine!'

'But everything's fine.'

'Fine? Fine?'

Her eyes flicked to a knife lying on a deck of onion slices, its speckled blade sullying the off-white bed. She stepped back and pulled out a chair. As she sat down, Gertrude crept out between the chair legs.

'How could you?'

She pulled a rag from her pocket and dried her eyes. Egon sat down next to her.

'We just wanted to spend some time together before I go,' he said, his voice cautious and soft. 'Somewhere nice.'

'Did you for one moment think?'

'I can handle myself.'

'Anything could've happened to you.'

'I'm nearly seventeen.'

'And her?' Marie leant forward onto the table, covering her face with her hands. 'How dare you?' She pushed the sweat-matted hair back from her face and looked across at Egon. 'Leopold will cancel your lodgings.'

'I'll go tomorrow. I'll speak to the landlady.'

She shook her head slowly. 'Why do you do this to me?' The words struggled past her lips, her voice barely audible. 'My son, my only son. Why?'

As the sun came up, Egon waited on the platform, two leather cases propped between his legs. From her bedroom window, Marie peeped through a gap in the curtains and watched her son beat his gloved hands together against the morning chill. Instinctively, Egon waved at the barred window, doffing his hat, then turned back. A whistle sounded in the distance as the train approached. He picked up the two cases – one containing clothes, the other materials – and lowered his head against the gust of the rattling engine. Behind him, the station doors flung open and Gertrude ran out, her bare feet skipping across the cold paving stones. The cases fell to the floor as she jumped into her brother's arms, the sleeves of her nightshirt – damp with wiped tears – wrapped around his neck. She grasped his midriff with her legs and kissed him. He kissed her back. She let go and ran inside.

# FIVE

# DAEDALUS

The city was rancid, pregnant with squalor behind its Imperial veil. From his room on Kurzbauergasse, Egon looked out onto the boulevards for hours on end, watching the carriages roll up and back, listening to the horses' hooves rattling off the cobblestones and onto the gravel paths, to the piercing clicks of ladies' heels. He looked down on the tall hats of the landed gentry and the stubby caps of workers, learning to differentiate the confident strides of the doctors from the sedate strolling of lawyers. Clerks, valets and housekeepers would rush down the street, reach for their master's elbow, pose a question and then scurry away with the answer. In the slice of Vienna below his window, Egon learnt to know mankind in all its colours and classes. He rose mid-morning and spent an hour at the window, munching on bread and salami, recording each of the stooping, strolling, shuffling, striding characters that passed his building. In the afternoon, he would walk down the stairs and out into the street. He would find a bench in front of the Rathaus and watch the women amble past in austere corsets. As the winter gave way to spring, he observed how the trees flanking the square blossomed and how the fabric of the women's dresses became thinner: embroidered bodices stitched with silver, splaying out and down to dresses with a hint of transparency. The richer ladies wore pastel blues and pinks, and twirled bamboo-handled parasols on their shoulders. He would look at each with care, following their swaying steps until they turned down a street or were stopped by another pedestrian. For each one that flashed by, he invented a character, a name, a complete plot, sketching out her life into a portrait he would never paint. As she moved on, he would exhale, breathing out the non-existent chance of meeting her.

Behind the gloss of the promenading gentry, Vienna's underbelly stank. It was swarming with peasants, migrants and a burgeoning middle class. Like an ailing Rome, the city overflowed with the Empire's constituent nationalities, interbreeding in mutual distaste. After a day's study at the Academy and dinner at home, Egon would venture out into the gloomy streets. He frequented bars, theatres and clubs, where he had his back slapped by Jews, drank slivovice with Moravians and rolled on straw mattresses with Silesians. He visited brothels, gambled his weekly five crowns away to Bohemians and argued with Italians. When he awoke, he crawled out of bed, stepping over the brushes and paints scattered on his floor, his head thick with cheap schnapps, and laughed at himself in the mirror. He rubbed long bony fingers over his beardless face; he tweaked and tugged his hair into artful disarray. Even after a night revelling in the city's taverns, he saw in himself a natural nobility.

His clothes hung limp across the back of a chair. The elbows of his black jacket had worn bare; his felt hat had faded and he lined it with newspaper to stop it slipping over his brow; he rarely wore underwear; he inherited shirt collars which were too old, too big and too high; on Sundays, he cut himself a fresh one out of waste sketching paper. Marie sent him parcels of her husband's old clothes, and Egon proudly slipped his arms down the same sleeves his father had so powerfully filled. He walked tall, holding his hairless chin high, his eyes flashing with disdain, dignity and charm in equal measures. His speech was laconic, his rural vowels chiselled to an urban prose; his lips bound tighter as they fought and felt their way around the city's thinner syllables. He toyed with a new brogue, a new intonation, before feeling his tongue slip carelessly towards the old rural shapes and rugged phonemes.

'The Devil must have shat you out and dropped you into my class!'

Professor Griepenkerl glowered down at the student in the dirty collar at the front of the class. He caught sight of the cracks in the uppers of his shoes beneath the wooden desk and scowled even harder.

'This is quite impossible!'

He was holding Egon's drawing with a finger and thumb as though the paper were covered in excrement. A pained expression pulled the lips back from his mouth and exposed a row of chipped yellow teeth.

'What don't you understand? You are meant to be drawing form, FORM! That means lines, contours, curves. Not genitals!'

The class fell into hysteria. Griepenkerl's eyebrows, wild and unkempt, twitched as waves of laughter broke at the front of the class.

'But Schiele's genitals *are* curved, Professor!' came a voice from the back.

'SILENCE, Peschka! That's enough from you,' he barked, looking over Egon's shoulder. 'As for you, I would expel you right this second, if I could. You know that, don't you? I'm fed up with your grotesques. I'm fed up with your filth. I'm fed up with you.' Professor Griepenkerl circled the naked model on the podium in the middle of the room. He turned to Egon and tugged his pointy beard. 'Art is about harnessing beauty, not drowning in degradation.' The class fell silent as Griepenkerl approached Egon's desk. 'Just one thing: that is all I ask of you.'

'Yes, Professor?' replied Egon, looking up, a defiant grin playing at the corners of his mouth.

'Never, ever, ever tell anyone that you study under me. Never. Do you hear me? Do that, shut up in class, keep your smutty pictures to yourself and you will graduate from this Academy. If not, you'll be on the street tomorrow.'

'Yes, Professor.'

'Do you understand?'

'Of course, Professor.'

'Good.' Griepenkerl turned his back on Egon. 'Now drag your sorry self up here, you insolent wretch.'

Egon pushed his stool back, its screech silencing the tittering of the other students. He stood in front of Griepenkerl's desk and clasped his hands behind his back.

'Now, you may presume to be the *enfant terrible* of this class, and, Lord, have we suffered often enough your depravity, but frankly that all means nothing to me; and it means nothing to anyone who knows anything about art. Do you understand?'

'Yes, Professor.'

'I'm content to go through this rigmarole every fortnight, as is your wont, if it gets it into your thick skull that we do things differently here. Read it again.'

Egon looked at the banner above the blackboard behind Griepenkerl's desk. He hesitated, turned back to the grinning faces of his classmates, and then cleared his throat. His eyes focused on the gothic script as paper pellets rebounded off the back of his neck. He looked down and recited it by heart, his voice inflated with ceremony.

'"Nor is the painter praiseworthy who does but one thing well, as the nude figure, heads, draperies, animals, landscapes or other such details, irrespective of other work; for there can be no mind so inept, that after devoting itself to one single thing and doing it consistently, it should fail to do it well."'

He raised his face to Griepenkerl who was nodding behind closed eyes.

'"There can be no mind so inept", young Schiele. So inept.'

He locked the door and spread the entire collection across the floor.

To each in turn he added strokes of reds, blacks and oranges for the hair and the genitals, leaving the rest bare. In places he embellished the shading with the side of a pencil or added volume to Gertrude's hair with fine-spun filigree, but these were exceptions. He selected a single sketch and layered it with watercolours – the surface dappling like old skin – swelling the curves of her body, until she seemed to hang in mid-air on the paper. He placed it next to his bed on a chair, looking out at him, owning the last seconds of the day, as he hitched up his nightshirt and gratified himself before blowing out the candle.

But the months apart took their toll, pushing Egon's desires deep into nostalgia, forcing him to live out his longing on paper rather than in person. He could no longer look on Gertrude's body at any time of the day, washing in the morning, running through the fields in the afternoon or reading in bed by candlelight. She had ceased to model, knowingly or unknowingly, for her brother, and instead he transferred her image to countless pictures: pictures folded under his bed, locked in musty cases, sold on street corners, propped on desks, scribbled on baker's bags, scrawled on the unseen backs of framed drawings. Initially, he wrote to her twice a week, composing accounts of Viennese life, interspersed with coded longings, knowing that the letters would inevitably pass under his mother's eyes. He included postcards, sketches, fragments of drawings, a collage from which she could reconstruct an ersatz-Vienna within the walls of the stationhouse. Gertrude's responses arrived less and less frequently: their contents superficial, their script hurried. Egon implored her to find an excuse to come to Vienna for a day, a night, a weekend; they could walk the boulevards, chat in the coffeehouses, eat chocolate cake, go to the Burgtheater, he would paint her; but Marie knew better, forbidding her daughter to board any train going south out of Tulln.

During the first few months in Vienna, Egon returned to the stationhouse only four times, stealing half-days from his study schedule to visit his mother and sisters. They sat around the kitchen table, watching him sip from a coffee cup clasped between his thumb and forefinger. While Egon selected his tales of opulent city life, his mother noticed his gestures grow more sophisticated, his sentences more intricate, his speech patterns a tangle of abstraction. During his first visit, Gertrude had been captivated, sitting next to her brother, hanging on his every word, her hand never leaving his forearm. Then, as he returned, she grew indifferent to his posturing, jaded by his metropolitan wisdom. She received his gifts with a smile but nothing more.

Within months, Egon was dragging himself reluctantly to the North Station for his Sunday trip to Tulln. He would slope through Vienna's streets with a food bundle for his mother under his arm and a sketch for Gertrude, arriving late at the station and watching the train pull away. The antics of the previous nights scouring his body, he would sit on a bench on the platform, eating the food himself and folding the sketch into his pocket before returning to the city's bars and taverns.

Egon continued to attend the Academy. He endured courses on the art of antiquity, on the study of drapes and endless composition exercises with a Bible, a skull and a sabre. Usually he finished early, painting the objects from memory, leaving the classroom and going home to sleep, waking only as the city was coming to life. He lay on his bed underneath the sloping ceiling, tearing strips off the mildewed wallpaper. He took the white paint from his satchel and painted over the bare patches, his brush stroking the wall in rhythm with the drip from the broken guttering outside, chipping away at the room's gloominess. He then put on his hat, using newspaper or abandoned sketches to set it firmly above his ears, and left the room.

He often walked the serpentine streets for an hour in the summer air, cutting left, turning right, working his way into the darker alleys, pushing past hawkers and drunks, mongrels curled up next to their owners, bottles spinning symphonic half-circles across the pavement.

He hid his eyes under the rim of his hat and pushed past the gloved hands that reached for his shoulders, the beggar children shoved into his path. When he reached the cobbled alley of Leopoldstadt, a streetlamp dribbling light past the shadows of lurching buildings, he lifted his chin and smiled at the streetwalkers. They spoke back, their faces of red and white carved open by black-toothed grins, but he moved on until he found one with ginger hair. It was never the same one: many of the women coloured their locks with crude dyes that lasted only until their next bath or the next rainstorm.

Egon leant forward and whispered into her ear. She shook her head.

'It's either round the corner or up there.'

She pointed to a window directly above her doorway.

'My place. I won't hurt you.'

''Course you bloody won't.' She laughed, pulling at Egon's arm. 'Come up stairs, lad. Do as you're told.'

Egon pulled his hand away. 'That's not what I'm after.'

'Well, that's all that's on offer!' She coughed, her head jolting forward revealing pockmarks under the powdered moonscape of her face. 'Upstairs or round the corner.'

She signalled into a cul-de-sac. Egon peered into the darkness and saw couples entwined in the shadows; he heard a concerto of grunts and groans, the ruffle of chiffon scrunched by fists and chafed against brick, the sound of belt buckles scraping along cobblestones.

'It's not far.'

He reached out to touch her hair.

'It's a crown down there or two upstairs.'

'I just want to watch.'

'Whatever, lad. Price is still the same though.'

Egon pulled a handkerchief out of his pocket, undid its knot and pushed the coins around his open palm. He looked back at the woman, counted the coins again and continued into the side-street. Walking canes crowned with top-hats were propped against the walls; white gloves stuck out the pockets of black coats; polished accents sought out knock-down prices; broken dialects listed their wares; alcohol and perfume barely masked bodily odours. A triangle of light, cast down from a broken window several stories up, struck the face of one of the girls, her features contorted, a grey beard buried in her neck as he thrust her against the wall. She opened her eyes and caught Egon's stare.

'This ain't a fuckin' theatre!'

The man pulled back from her thighs, looking over his shoulder, his trousers hanging ungainly around his ankles, his erection protruding from between shirt-tails. Their eyes met and Egon registered the twitching eyebrows and yellowed teeth. He shook his head and walked out of the cul-de-sac straight into the red-haired woman.

'Cold feet?' she said, knocked backwards.

He looked up at the lit window of the room above them, repositioned the sketching materials under his arm and followed her in through the doorway.

'As we can see from the composition, it's possible to depict man's universal struggle in a number of abstractions.' A cough came from the back of the classroom. 'To you simpletons it may look like a pell-mell heap of books, maps and instruments, but to the true artist – which so few of you are or ever will be – it tells the entire story of humankind in one composition.'

Several students raised their hands and Griepenkerl scanned the room.

'Yes, Jelenek.'

'With respect, Professor, many have claimed that the human struggle encompasses far more than just amassing knowledge.'

The other students mumbled disapproval and Griepenkerl stepped onto the podium, smoothing out a crease in the scarlet cloth on the table so that the light struck the still-life more evenly.

'Very good, Jelenek. While the sextant there on the right hand side depicts the beauty of knowledge and discovery, as do the dividers and map on the left, there is still the unavoidable transience of it all: the skull, lurking behind. Simple yet striking. It tells of the human dilemma: the quest for knowledge, its attainment and then our demise. In short: we are great but we are doomed. If that is clear to everyone then you may start. Any more questions?' The students all looked down at their desks. 'You have half an hour.'

They each took a sheet of paper and started marking down the broad dimensions of the piece. Griepenkerl circled the room, looking over the shoulders of the students, passing comment, offering advice, forcing several to reach for a new sheet of paper.

'Barely average, Schewe, barely average... Very good, Jelenek. Careful with the shading... What's that supposed to be Peschka? Start again... Steady on the sextant, Fried... Now let me see what your distorted mind has come up with this time?'

Egon leant back and let Griepenkerl peer over his shoulder at the near perfect representation of the still-life on the podium. Straightening his back, the professor studied the axes, ready to move on to the next student. As Griepenkerl began to turn away Egon removed his drawing to reveal another paper underneath. It bore an image of the professor, trousers around his ankles, a grotesque inflated penis between his legs, and behind him a woman, two jaundiced breasts hanging out of her bodice.

'We are great but we are doomed, Professor,' said Egon quietly.

Egon's classmates looked up from their desks.

'What is this, you heathen?'

'As you said, Professor,' said Egon, his voice barely a whisper. 'The human struggle.'

Griepenkerl grabbed the sheet from Egon's easel, tore it in half and half again, his fingers grappling at the stiff paper, bending and folding before he stuffed the scraps into his pocket. The professor picked a jar of paintbrushes off the nearest table and hurled it at the edge of Egon's easel. It shattered, spraying its turpentine contents across the room while the picture smeared rainbows down the front of Egon's shirt.

'This is the last time. The last time, do you hear me?'

'The last time you stick your cock in a whore?' replied Egon, wide-eyed.

The room filled with laughter. Griepenkerl spat in the student's face and turned over another easel, spilling paper and brushes across the floor.

'A street pornographer. No better than a common lecher.'

'Hypocrite.'

Griepenkerl grabbed Egon's collar and dragged him to the door to the cheers of his classmates. 'Get out of my sight! Get out!'

Egon rose half an hour before daybreak and prepared his paints and materials. As soon as the blue half-light of the morning dissipated, he started painting: first from memory and then from life as model after model arrived at his door. He stood by the window with the light shining in behind him, unconscious of the workers, the students, the valets going about their business down below. He barely raised his eyes, ordering the latest visitor to undress by the chair in the corner and prostrate herself on the rug. Minutes later, he would tear a completed sketch from his pad, toss it to the ground and bark orders at the model to lift her skirt. He paused only to refresh paints or sharpen pencils. Occasionally, he would toss his pad onto the bed and approach a model, loosening his trousers and gesturing for her to remove her dress. But, as the light began to dim, he would double his efforts, eager not to waste a second, capturing every shape and pose before dropping exhausted onto his mattress. The last model would see herself out, plucking a crown off the table, buttoning her blouse and pulling the door closed. As instructed, she would turn the lock and push the key back under the door.

Peschka was the only student to remain in contact with Egon

despite his infrequent attendance at the Academy. They spent an hour together in the afternoon, sitting on a street bench, smoking and commenting on the passing Viennese. They sketched together, played cards together, walked the streets, and boasted of their conquests. Despite a marginal age difference, Peschka looked much older than Egon. His clothes were well fitting, he carried a cane and his hat sat snugly on his head, pulled down over one eye. While Peschka was open and candid, Egon was aloof and laconic; while Peschka charmed and flirted, Egon grated.

They spent their evenings together, immersed in the stale beer stench of Vienna's suburban bars. Egon would slouch in a chair in the corner, while Peschka sat proudly at a table, an entourage of artists, performers, drunks and whores hanging off him like courtiers, the dazzle of makeup still on their faces, freshly emerged from the groping shadows of dancehalls or piss-sprayed doorways nearby. Peschka was a raconteur, an arrogant, robust man with a glint of talent concealed in the messy artistry of his appearance. While in class he toyed with the Academy's classical ideals, at night he descended into the sub-genre of stage painting, loitering in the coulisses of burlesque performances only to accompany the troupe afterwards into the smoke-filled backrooms of a brothel to spend the takings. His hair parted in the middle and rested in two cow-lick curls on his forehead. His brow was heavy, scoring hard lines above thickly-lashed eyes. His nose had the misfortune to be both long and thick, a plump plumb line splitting his eyes and disappearing into the moustache beneath.

Peschka gave his friend free tickets to vaudeville shows, initiating him into the posse of vagabonds, drunks and acolytes that met every evening in a different bar down the same street. After a night's revelry, Egon would walk home with Peschka, a lithe, dark-skinned dancer strung between the two of them, their arms interlinking behind her back. They would clamber up the carpeted stairs of Peschka's apartment, their berth too wide for the staircase, their combined weight too much for the floorboards. Arriving at the door, Peschka would invite the girl to fish the keys from his cock-filled trousers. She would drop them then scrape against the lock to a chorus of complaints from the neighbours. Finally, they would stagger inside. The dancer would remove her shawl and over-garments, draping them across lampshades, *chaises longues* and picture frames, her mystique struggling to hide behind layers of perfume and powder. Peschka would smile at his friend and follow her into the bedroom. Egon would take his coat and a pillow, settling down on the rug in front of the ash-strewn fireplace.

Peschka had reserved a prominent table between the revolving door and the gateaux counter. There were four chairs around a marble-topped table spread with newspapers and periodicals. Four dust-caked lamps hung above them, wisps of smoke swirling in their pool of light. The waiter sidled over and at Peschka's request removed one of the chairs, returning with two coffees. Egon sat with his back to a mirror, a broadsheet strung like a sail between his two hands, while Peschka was a small distance back from the table, his legs crossed, his trousers riding up to reveal a roll of pale-skinned calf.

'Just don't make a fool of yourself,' whispered Peschka.

'I'm not the one who risks doing that.'

'Oh, and I am?'

'He needs you,' said Egon. 'Not vice-versa.'

'He needs Konstantin, not me,' scoffed Peschka.

'Everyone needs your uncle: hundreds of factory workers, your Magyar maids, the Academy… even you.'

'And Klimt?'

Egon refolded his newspaper and laid it on the table. 'He has the same problems as everyone else. He needs patrons. We all need patrons.'

'But his work's everywhere: the frieze, the portraits, the posters. It doesn't look like he needs any help getting work.'

'Maybe, but the Emperor detests his every muscle.'

Peschka dismissed Egon's claim with a shake of his head.

'Uncle's shrewd enough. He'd never've set this up if that was true. Anyway, he knows full well where his money's going. He's aware of Klimt's reputation.'

'His reputation for "symbolic filth"? Apparently, whenever Franz Josef is riding in town, he tells his carriage to avoid all the secessionist buildings en route. There are stretches of the Ringstrasse he refuses to go down.'

'Oh, come on! That's just the nattering of bars and taverns.'

'Perverse and amoral. That's what they say. I'd hardly call that nattering. I doubt your uncle will want to fall out of favour with the Emperor over commissioning a couple of erotic sketches.'

'Keep your voice down,' hissed Peschka. 'Anyway, you've never met him. He's so charming you'll agree to something before he's even asked you.'

'The plain sycophancy of society artists.'

'And what makes you the judge?'

'They'll all kowtow to anything if it gets their names mentioned over stewed dumplings at the Tscherny household.'

'You don't even know him.'

The gentle hum of conversation died out leaving just the tap and slide of chess-players and backgammon chips. Peschka looked over Egon's shoulder and in the mirror behind him saw Klimt's bearded face and dark eyes. He swivelled round in surprise to face the older artist. There was an isolated clump of grey-streaked hair on the top of Klimt's balding head and his beard was pointed like a satyr. His auburn eyes sat deep in their sockets.

'Whoever wishes to know something about me should first observe my paintings carefully and try to see in them what I am. You should know that by now, young Anton,' he said extending his hand. 'If you're that curious, come to my studio sometime.' Peschka sprung up and greeted Klimt. 'Pleasure to see you again.'

'Likewise, Herr Klimt.'

'I'll forget I heard the rest.'

Both men sat down and looked around the room.

'Anyway, how is your uncle?'

'Very well, Sir. Very well indeed.'

'Good to hear.'

Peschka looked across at Egon and then rose again, snagging the tablecloth on a ringed finger.

'Excuse me, Herr Klimt, this is my friend and classmate Egon Schiele.'

'Of course.'

Egon stood up, bowed and they shook hands. He watched Klimt's over-developed thumbnail – hardened paint accreted underneath – dig into the back of his hand.

'Pleased to meet you, Herr Klimt.'

'Likewise.'

'I'm a great admirer of yours.'

'And me of you, Egon.' Klimt sat down, leant back in his chair and waved at a passing waiter. 'How fortunate I can finally add a face to a name.' Peschka looked back and forth between the two men. 'It's astonishing how much juvenilia sloshes around this city.'

Peschka turned away, holding a palm up to his burning cheeks.

'A surprise and honour, Sir,' started Egon. 'I had no idea my meagre efforts were known to you.'

'Yes, well, whenever I hear the old guard mouthing off at some profanity or other, I can't help but chase it up.'

'All Vienna speaks your name, Sir; your works are celebrated; you are considered brilliant, elegant, elaborate... decadent, if I may say so. Herr Klimt, you are simply unrivalled,' Egon stopped short, leant back and raised a cup of coffee to his mouth, hiding an expression on his lips.

Klimt pushed his chair back, crossing his legs and interlocking his fingers over his knee.

'That's quite enough. Thank you, Egon. I didn't come for the flattery.' He undid the middle button on his jacket. 'Anyway, it's a privilege to sit here with you two bright young sparks. How is life at the Academy? Up to no good as usual?'

'Things are progressing fine, thank you, Sir,' replied Peschka.

'I should hope so; your uncle is paying enough for it.'

Klimt reeled off a list of mundane questions, pumping swift and workmanlike responses from Peschka, gracing them with nods and smiles, punctuating the answers with simulated sips from an empty coffee cup. Egon watched as they courted each other, tossing compliments back and forth, participating in a decorous role-play where both ensured they obtained what they came for. They dropped names, going through the city's aristocracy as if crossing titles off a list. Egon was silent, ignorant to the counts, barons, princes, and the multiple beat of *von* sprinkled through the titles.

'Indeed, I saw Graf Kinsky last week at my uncle's house. He was in excellent form. Such an admirable and witty gentleman.'

'What a coincidence. I saw his son several seconds before coming in here. Accompanied by a sumptuous young lady, whose name, criminally, I can no longer recall. Although, I'm sure I saw her on someone else's arm a few weeks ago at the Burgtheater.'

Klimt drew breath, swivelled in his chair and turned to Egon.

'Have you met Graf Kinsky's son?'

'I have yet to have the pleasure, Sir.'

'But you know him?'

'Unfortunately not.'

'He was in the street outside but twenty minutes ago. You must have seen him.'

Egon shook his head.

'Well, whom did you see before you came in?'

'No one, Sir,' responded Egon.

'Try again,' said Klimt, his voice more forceful. 'Whom did you see?'

'A middle-aged woman shopping for vegetables, Sir.'

'Who else?'

'A group of clerics. Five or six, I think. Just before I turned into the road.'

'Anything else?'

Peschka looked anxiously at his friend.

'I don't know, Sir. I think I saw a grey mare down where the carriages are, but I'm not sure.'

'You are thinking. Not seeing. What did you see? Directly before you walked in. Out there, by the pavement.'

'A girl, Herr Klimt,' interrupted Peschka. 'There was a girl with a child on the pavement just outside the door. Her sister.'

'That's right.' Egon looked down, feeling Peschka's gaze. 'She's from Silesia and that's not her sister. She says she's thirteen, although I doubt she knows exactly. I'd say she was eleven. Her father is a drunk; her mother is a washerwoman for an acquaintance of mine. She sits there every day and we all stroll by. Myself and Kinsky's son included. If it's our job to depict life, gentlemen, to depict the universal in the specific, that's where we should start. She's hardly brilliance, elegance, elaboration, decadence, as you so formulaically put it, Egon. But then again that's not life. Is it?'

Peschka turned to his classmate, expecting a reply. Egon took a cigarette from his pocket and placed it between his lips.

'I know you saw her,' started Klimt again. 'In fact, you saw her more clearly than anyone else in this room. More clearly than Anton here. More clearly than the old man at the door who'll look at anything in a skirt. You see it all, Egon. You see it all far more clearly than I do.' He gestured for a cigarette from Egon and lit it off the candle. 'We're living in a collapsing world, an afflicted generation that art has as yet failed to depict, that *I* have failed to depict. I'm the last man of that generation. But it will pass… and the Empire will pass with it. As will I. The most I could hope to be is the last man of one era and the first man of the next. But that I am not. A new age is coming and it will be yours.' He waved to the waiter who brought over a bottle of brandy and three glasses. Klimt poured himself a drink and then pushed the bottle over to Peschka. He leant back in his chair and turned towards Egon. 'I've seen those incomplete scribbles you leave behind in the classroom. What you discard, the rest of the room could not hope to produce in their combined lifetimes. What you reveal, others can only hint at.' Peschka cleared his throat. 'I have seen your work, too, Anton. It shows much promise. Your uncle can be proud.'

'Promise but not talent.'

'You will be a fine painter if you choose to be.'

'But a talentless one?' asked Peschka sarcastically.

'I didn't say that. I simply said your friend shows talent.'

'How much?'

Klimt mopped up some cake crumbs from the table with a damp finger.

'Much too much.'

Egon exhaled, a cloud of smoke hanging around his head, hiding his glowing eyes from the others.

'Listen. Why don't you both come to my studio? Shall we say two weeks on Thursday?'

'I'm afraid I'll be out of the city, Herr Klimt,' said Peschka. 'Uncle has asked me to accompany him to Brünn that week.'

'Of course, the grind and fizz of the steelworks. And you?'

'I am available, Sir,' said Egon, with a hint of embarrassment.

'Well, why don't you come along on your own? Anton and I can fix another date. And tell your Uncle Konstantin that he is welcome as well this time. I should like to do a portrait of him: such unique features, a quite remarkable physiognomy. By the way, you can tell him your work is coming along excellently. He should be very proud. In fact, I shall write to him to say as much.'

'Thank you, Herr Klimt.'

'Be sure to pass on my regards, won't you?'

'Of course.'

The painter stood up, straightened his jacket on his shoulders, shook hands with the two young men and walked out, stopping in the doorway for a second then disappearing.

Egon stood at the front door, readjusting his hat and wiping palms on the seat of his trousers. A line of blonde moustache graced his upper lip; under his hat he wore a bandana of blue and white checks. As he heard footsteps from inside nearing the front door, he pulled it from his forehead and stuffed it in his pocket.

A girl opened the door, the rust shade of her hair accentuated by the ribbons on her twin pigtails: crimson bands hanging down, pulling her scalp taut against her skull. She said nothing but ushered Egon in and led him up the stairs. He watched her black-stockinged legs in front of him as she walked up, a translucent linen dress dancing over her thighs. She took his coat and hat, leading him into a large, brightly lit studio. Indian idols and Italian busts were tucked into corners and heaped on tables; ugly-thumbed books and brochures spilled from shelves; a sprinkling of plaster-of-Paris dust lay under a table, defiled by paw-prints. The girl smiled at Egon – her mouth a jumbled mess of tooth and gum – before disappearing behind a thick blue curtain imprinted with overlapping leaves, fruit, berries and birds. They fluttered momentarily before Klimt brushed the curtain aside once again and approached Egon, a finger to his lips. He wore a light brown smock and dark trousers, both flecked in paint; he went barefoot, single hairs sticking up from the tops of his toes. He extended a hand to Egon and then retracted it when he saw streaks of blue and yellow glistening on his own palm. They nodded at each other in silence. A tabby cat circled around Egon's feet and then sloped off through a gap in the curtains. Two easels were set up at the other end of the studio next to the window; they were positioned around a small dais covered by dark blue cloth of the same material as the curtains. A young woman lay on her side, asleep. She was curled up as if she had once been in the foetal position but had then stretched out while dreaming.

Klimt moved to stand behind one of the easels and Egon looked over his shoulder at the unfinished canvas; the painter had drawn the outline of the woman's thigh and buttock, placing it in the centre of the canvas, a plain of chaste skin dominating the picture. He had started to add meticulous layers of gold and silver leaf, building up a pattern on the blue background as if recreating the flicker of night sky. Egon watched as Klimt went about his work, fleshing out the woman's organic contours, giving depth to the unshadowed surfaces of her skin which appeared like gauze in the daylight. Gradually, he compiled a mosaic of colours and shapes, curling foreground lines rolling over her legs and breasts, merging into the leafy patterns of the material lying about her.

Klimt pointed towards the second easel and waved at Egon. He walked to a chair in the corner, took off his jacket and tie, rolling up the sleeves of his dress shirt. He pulled off his collar, rolled it into a ball and threw it onto a pile of used paper. He moved over to his easel, took a black pencil in hand and began to sketch.

After twenty minutes Klimt leant over and viewed Egon's efforts. He smiled through tight lips and passed him a new piece of paper.

'Sharper lines,' he whispered. 'Decisive.'

Egon set to work and twenty minutes later Klimt passed him another fresh sheet.

'Less Gustav; more Egon.'

This procedure was repeated twice more before Klimt finally laid his brush down and came over to stand behind Egon. He took his protégé by the hand and led him to the dais where the woman still slept.

'Close your eyes.' Egon glanced around the room. 'Close your eyes. Just let your arm go limp,' he whispered.

Klimt opened out Egon's hand and, starting at the woman's ankle, ran Egon's bony fingers up the length of her leg, over her thigh and onto her stomach. She flinched, jerking her head round and blinking incredulously at Egon through blurred eyes. He retracted his hand and began mumbling an apology.

'Frederike. It's only me.'

Egon tried to extend his hand and shake hers but Klimt still had hold of him. He took Egon's hand and ran it over the model's belly; he closed his eyes as his hand went over a mound. Klimt guided the tips of Egon's fingers up and over her full breasts, along her collarbone and onto her neck. She shivered again and sniggered.

'Take a break if you like, darling,' said Klimt.

Frederike shook the sleep out of her limbs and stood in front of Egon, presenting her hand. Egon took it, bowing to plant a kiss on her wrist.

'Pleased to meet you, Sir.'

'His name's Egon.'

'Pleased to meet you, Egon.'

She picked up her robe from a chair, wrapped it around her shoulders and walked out through the curtains.

'The goose bumps, the warmth, the shiver, the sinew, the flesh. Touch everything with the allure of the muses.'

Unexpectedly, Klimt stripped off his own smock and shirt and stepped out of his trousers. He stood naked in front of Egon, his chest covered in tightly curled hair, his arms and stomach muscular, his legs shoulder-width apart and his genitals hanging between them.

'Close your eyes.'

Klimt took Egon's hand once again and guided it over his own body.

'Now, go back and do it properly.'

Egon walked round the easel and took a new sheet of paper and a pencil.

'What colours do you want?'

Egon shrugged.

'Think, Egon. Think! What do you need?'

'I haven't really…'

'Take that tray of watercolours,' he said pointing over to the sink, 'a piece of charcoal and some gouache.'

Klimt sat down on the dais, leant back and opened his legs.

'You may start.'

'It won't make you any friends. You know that, don't you?' Klimt moved back from the easel. 'It may get you girls. In fact, I am sure it will get you girls, but only harlots.' He laughed to himself. 'But that in itself is not necessarily a bad thing.' He took two steps to the side to observe the painting from a different angle. 'It may bring you admirers, but not necessarily the people you want to admire you. It may make you infamous, but it will not make you friends.'

'I don't need any.'

Klimt raised his eyebrows, tilting his head at Egon. 'People think I'm like a fading flame, not worth tending since my candle will burn out sooner or later. But believe me: I am worth having as a friend.'

'I didn't mean to offend, Herr Klimt. I would be honoured,' said Egon putting his hand out and bowing. Klimt waved him away.

'How much do you want for it?'

Egon looked over at the portrait and then back at Klimt. 'I couldn't possibly…'

'How much?

'I really can't accept anything.'

'I won't ask again.'

'I suppose I could swap this for one of your sketches,' proposed Egon nervously.

'Don't be ridiculous. This is worth six of mine.'

'Please, just take it.' Egon took the picture from the easel and passed it to Klimt.

'Take my advice: don't make a habit of this. You won't always have affluent friends to bail you out. Wally!' shouted Klimt suddenly. 'Bring Egon his coat and hat please.'

The curtain fluttered and a hand parted the folds. The girl stepped into the room, her russet hair resting on naked shoulders. She held out Egon's coat and he bent to slip his arms into the sleeves while she strained on tiptoes to reposition it on his shoulders. She straightened his lapels and moved to Klimt's side, putting her arms around his waist and kissing him on the side of the mouth. Klimt leant over, adjusted the girl's hair so that it hung equally across her shoulders, and kissed her, gently, on the parting.

'I'll have time again a week Wednesday.'

'Anton will be back from Brünn by then.'

'Come alone.'

'But you said…'

'And bring some sketches.'

'I have plenty at the Academy.'

'No, no, no. Something new. They must be new. I'll turn you away if you besmirch my studio with Griepenkerl's faeces.' They walked to the door. 'I want to see something deviant. Something decadent. Something cocky.' He leant in towards Egon and whispered: 'Like fucking in the back of a church.' Klimt laughed and disappeared through the curtains at the back of his studio. 'So uplifting. Wally, see him out.'

The curtain rustled and then settled back behind the elder painter.

Valerie led Egon out of the studio and down the stairs, hopping from step to step until she arrived at the door. As Egon paused to adjust his hat in the hall, she kissed him on the cheek, pushed him out and slammed the door.

They took it in turns to paint each other, sometimes individually, sometimes sketching their entwined bodies together in a large mirror. They learnt each other's moods, copied each other's styles, and drank absinthe from a shared glass. Meanwhile, Klimt coaxed Egon along the spider-web of Viennese life, offering advice and contacts, an entrance into the insular world of portraiture.

'Pastiche! Worthless, facile, sanitised pastiche!' Klimt struck the canvas off the easel and kicked it across the room, fallen bottles rolling parabolas across the floorboards.

'It's all they'll take. The rest won't sell,' said Egon defensively.

'Newton's own spectrum lodged in the end of your brush and that's all you can come up with?'

'We're not all like you.'

'But create your own style! Don't ape mine.'

'I'm just making ends meet.'

'Feeding shit to hypocritical bastards! Crapulous old men buying gifts for their mistresses.'

Egon leant against the studio wall. He rubbed a palm over his face, pulling his cheeks down from his eyes. 'Old men with full pockets,' he mumbled.

'You just don't see it, do you?' said Klimt. 'You don't hear it. The mindless chitter-chatter. The brainless grinning. The perfumed stench. You don't see them, your patrons, their hands up the skirts of young girls, their beards bristling with dribbled schnapps…'

'They commission works.'

'Greek gods and muscular prophets!'

'I'm more subtle.'

'Subtle? They don't deserve subtle. They deserve to be defrocked, unpicked, their bespoke jackets torn from their mangy bodies, their polished buckles bent until they're naked, flaccid in their decay. You still have so much to learn,' said Klimt, approaching Egon with a smile on his face. 'But then again, so perhaps do I.'

# SIX

# PETALS AND SPLIT STEMS

Egon walked out through the double-doors at the front of the Klosterneuburg town hall and into the road. He looked back at the banner tossing the wind-bent letters of his name above the entrance. The Jugendstil typeface hunched the script up close, shunting the title of the exhibition to the end of the cloth: a mere after-thought in the wake of his grandiose name. He looked over towards the school on the opposite side of the street, its front yard still strewn with the gravel and sand which tore knees and clogged grazes. A familiar teacher's voice teased a memory back to life and Egon stepped back from the gate. His brief life seemed compressed into that bare stretch of road. On the one side was the town hall, an awkwardly civil site for his first public exhibition, and on the other the institution which had expelled him several years earlier. And there, fifty feet down the street, Egon could see the house of Pauker, Kahrer and Strauch: the roof-light propped open, smoke pouring out of the chimney. A young boy beat a rectangle of carpet against the top step, swarms of dust floating around him.

The exhibition lacked professionalism. One of Klimt's clique had made a generous and unconsidered offer to stage the event and he had agreed. But they hadn't thought it through. Ignoring the protests of Professor Griepenkerl and the Academy, who insisted it was too soon to exhibit without having graduated, he listened only to Klimt, and found himself hanging his unfinished sketches and paintings on the peeling walls of the town hall. Klimt had attended the vernissage, saying little but prodding and poking Egon to speak to the right people, content to see his abrasive charm light up the room. He nurtured his protégé, a languid arm over his shoulder and a finger pointing out a sharper colour, a tighter perspective, a richer businessman. For months, Klimt had arrived unannounced at Egon's cramped studio; he had sat quietly on a stool and watched as the young artist painted an even younger model. When Egon retired to his mattress with her, Klimt stared at the half-finished painting, a palette in hand, its traces left on the brutalised flax canvas. On leaving, he salvaged a crumpled sketch from the bin and closed the door behind him.

Gertrude sat at the door to the town hall, a purse on her lap in which she collected the entrance fee. After pleading with her mother, she was granted a few days leave from her duties in Tulln and she travelled each day to Klosterneuburg to help with her brother's inaugural exhibition. Her hair was pulled back, exposing a neck which had grown longer and more elegant in the fifteen months since she lay folded across a Trieste mattress; her skin was pale with grainy foundation and her eyebrows had been plucked into symmetrical arches. She tapped a knuckle against the rim of her chair while Egon stood in a corner of the empty hall speaking to Peschka, arguing over the distribution of pictures. She tapped again.

Three days after the vernissage, the flow of visitors had dried up. Only the wind came in off the street, blew through the hall's echo and out the cracked windows. The local residents had stopped coming, their deferential smiles faltering before the array of misshapen bodies. Egon had sold nothing and word of the exhibition's lewd tendencies had spread.

A tall man passed Egon and entered the town hall, tucking a top hat under his right arm. Egon turned and followed him in, his eyes on the silver-tipped cane that brushed the floorboards and scuffed the half silence. The man paused in front of Gertrude and dropped two coins into her purse.

'Thank you, Sir.'

'No, thank *you*, gracious lady.' He bent down, whispering in her ear: 'And here's another little something for you.'

He dropped an extra coin into her lap's taught dress; it slid until suspended above her groin; she palmed it and looked away. Eau de cologne wafted through the room as he bowed his head to Egon and Peschka and moved past the landscapes without breaking stride, his metal-tipped shoes emitting metronomic clicks. At the far end of the room where the portraits were hung he paused. He leant in towards a picture, ignoring Egon at his side, passing his eyes over the canvas, nose wrinkles gripping a pince-nez.

The thin wooden frame held the body of a young girl with knotted ink-black hair. Her mouth was closed, picked out by a flash of pink – the same pink which Egon had daubed around her nipples and labia. The rest of her body was shades of grey and sepia, teasing the contours of her developing curves, the shadows of her loins. Egon had applied the stretcher frame in such a way that the picture cut off the girl's legs just above the knee, leaving two thick bands of black stocking at the base of the canvas.

'A cheap publicity stunt, I suppose?' asked the man, still leaning in towards the picture. 'Doesn't seem to have worked, though,' he added, pocketing his pince-nez and looking around the room. 'I seem to be the first visitor of the day.'

'I'm sorry; we haven't been introduced.'

'Judging by your work, I don't imagine we shall be.'

The man leant backwards as Egon stepped between him and the painting.

'You may leave whenever you like.'

'I am quite aware of that.'

The man walked to the door pausing in front of Gertrude.

'I apologise young lady, it's hardly fitting or decorous to have pictures of such women gracing public walls, *n'est-ce pas*?'

'Such women?' she replied.

He stepped to the picture hanging by the door. 'A series of squelches and an eternity of ceilings. Your brushstroke is far too assured to hide anything other than first-hand experience.' He raised his hand as if holding an imaginary brush and etched a curve through the air. 'Then again, pornography will always sell – even pornography with such audacious *morbidezza*.'

'I think it's time you left,' said Egon.

'The more you are denounced, the more you will sell… in certain circles.' He smiled, toying with the ebony handle of his cane. 'Such delusions of grandeur at your age.'

'And what might that be?'

'Surely, you're not a day over seventeen.'

'I'm eighteen,' said Egon defiantly.

'Eighteen? And you already paint girls like that?'

'So, they're fine in your bed at night, but not on my canvas by day?'

'How dare you!'

'Hypocrite!'

'You'll never…'

'You're all the same! Your hand cradles your Parisian hat by day and by night it gropes cunts.'

The man burst out in laughter, holding his sides until suddenly falling silent and staring Egon in the eyes. There was a short pause and the man resumed tapping the uneven edge of a floorboard with the point of his cane. He pulled Egon to one side and took several bank notes from his inside pocket. Egon unfolded them and checked their value, whispering numbers under his breath. Only Gertrude's voice could be heard at the door as she chatted to Peschka.

'*Ça suffit?*'

'Sorry?'

'Is that enough?'

Egon shook his head and handed the money back. 'That and the same again.'

The man burst out in laughter again. 'You have much to learn.'

'There's already been an offer for this one.'

The man frowned, clasping the papers in his gloved hand. 'From whom?'

'A lawyer in Vienna.'

'Why didn't you accept it then?'

Egon looked across at Gertrude. The sun poured in through the open doors and burnt down on her face while Peschka crouched next to her, a hand across the back of her chair, a blue-striped cravat peaking out from underneath a cream waistcoat. A streak of grass stained the side of his linen trousers.

'Have you ever actually sold a painting before?' asked the man.

'I don't have to stomach such comments from you.'

'For how much?'

'Pay what it's worth or leave.'

'I'm just interested what range you put your work in. Name a price.'

'I'm not going to negotiate with you.'

'Well, accept my price then.'

Egon extended his hand, took the notes once more, and stuffed them into his waistcoat pocket.

'Could you wrap it?' asked the man, watching Egon intently.

Egon looked over towards his sister.

'Anton! Get the paper.'

'One of yours or mine?'

'Just get the paper, will you?'

Peschka stood up slowly, his hand sliding off the back of Gertrude's chair. He pulled his trousers straight and rolled the stiffness out of his neck. He ambled into a side-room and returned with a roll of brown paper and string. He dropped it at Egon's feet, the paper spilling out in a coffee-coloured carpet across the floor.

'Do it yourself.'

Egon watched Peschka return to his sister's side at the door and knelt down to wrap the portrait.

'Certainly very original,' said the man, as the paper folded across the face of the portrait. 'You seem to have come up with a technique entirely of your own.'

'So that I don't have to ape the styles of others,' he muttered to himself.

Egon pulled a hand out of his pocket, releasing the bank notes from between his sticky fingers, and bade the man farewell. He walked out of the hall with the painting under his arm, pausing only to drop another coin into Gertrude's lap.

Egon woke to the collage of white paint and wallpaper swarming above him. He ate nothing before leaving the house, a cup of burnt coffee sloshing in his stomach as he ran down the stairs. Expectation was stuffed into his mouth like a kidnapper's handkerchief on that bright April morning. He grabbed a letter off the table in the lobby and hurried off to the Academy to see if his months of study had yielded a tangible result, something he could hold out to his mother to show that her disappointment had not been in vain.

As he walked he read. His eyes scanned the letter, first recognising the scrawl and then alighting on individual words: *military, Austria, honour, respectable*. He paused and pulled his father's old watch from the inside pocket of his waistcoat. Vienna's morning crowd of traders and factory workers milled past him. He raised the peak of his hat to a smiling stranger, and looked back down at Czihaczek's letter, reading the final lines. *It is your last chance to do justice to his memory. Either you sign up or, contrary to the supplications of your poor mother, I will terminate her allowance before the paint dries on your latest rubbish. You will not hear from me again.*

That afternoon, Egon left the Academy with a certificate in his pocket bearing the ignominious yet satisfactory news that he had passed with the lowest grade possible. He strode out of the building and weaved past hawkers and traders to a back-street bar where Peschka was waiting with a jug of cold beer. He had his arm around the barmaid, one hand dangling above her open bosom and the other slammed firmly across his own certificate, the word *distinction* visible between his fingers. He paid for the jug to be refilled and they carved the date and their names into the tabletop, singing bawdy songs about Silesian girls. Two hours later, they stumbled over the doorstep and

THE PORNOGRAPHER OF VIENNA

out into the street. They found their way through the city's streets
to a grey municipal building with queues of men snaking down the
pavement, hands in pockets, threadbare caps pulled down over their
eyes, necks bent forward like sacrificial bulls. Egon stopped to listen
to their babbling dialects, a cacophony of jingoism. He removed a
paintbrush from his pocket and turned back to Peschka, clicked his
heels to attention and saluted, his paintbrush leaning against his
shoulder like a miniscule rifle.

'Fine servants of the Empire! Off to defend what's right!' he
shouted, strutting back and forth in front of the line. Jaded faces
looked up but most turned their backs, an iron fence of protruding
spines. 'My orders, please, Field Marshal Peschka!'

Peschka gave a dishevelled salute and did his best to look grave.

'Private.'

'Yessir!'

'On the orders of Corporal Czihaczek, you shall enter the ministry
building immediately by the foremost aperture and return to me
forthwith bearing your conscriptional papers.'

'Yessir!'

Egon saluted again, swivelled, lost his balance and stumbled
several paces before dashing into the ministry, barging to the front
of the protesting crowds. A quarter of an hour later he re-emerged,
his arm aloft, crumpled yellow documents brandished like a paper
thunderbolt. Peschka pushed himself up from the side of the road
where he'd been dozing and returned Egon's wayward salute.

'My papers, Field Marshal.'

Peschka straightened the pages out, his eyes swirling over Egon's
name and number at the top of every sheet. A drop of sweat nestled
in the dimple of his hairless chin.

'There seems to be something missing, Private.'

'Really, Field Marshal?'

'How dare you bring me incomplete papers!'

'Please forgive me, Field Marshal. I know not...'

'Silence!' shouted Peschka. He took several paces back and bent
down towards the gutter. With the conscription papers placed on

the palm of his hand, he picked up a straw-filled sod of horse dung, folding the paper back around it, creating a parcel. He took a piece of string from his pocket and tied it up.

'Where are Corporal Czihaczek's barracks, Private?'

Egon paused and then recited the address of his uncle's townhouse, which Peschka then wrote on the paper, the pencil tip occasionally piercing through into the soft excrement.

'That should do it. Dismissed, Private.'

Egon took the parcel from Peschka, saluted and turned back into the street, giggling. Within seconds he had collared a passing child, pushed a coin and the bundle into his palm and pointed him in the right direction.

Peschka and Egon knocked at the door in unison, an arm around each other's shoulders, splashback-specks of urine on their shoes. They leant forward again and thumped their fists in the centre of the door, rattling its hinges.

'Open up!'

They laughed at each other and thumped the door again.

They waited for another minute, propped up against each other until they heard the patter of feet on the steps inside. The door opened slowly and the streetlamp threw dirty light over the face of Klimt's young model. Her rubicund cheeks had grown fuller, flushed beneath locks of russet hair hanging across her face. Egon caught a glimpse of a naked shoulder underneath her robe.

'He's not in.'

'Don't give us that!' blurted Peschka.

She pushed the door back, leaving a streak of streetlamp to shine through the gap and illuminate the perspiration on her forehead and a strip of nightgown.

'The window's open and the curtains are drawn,' said Egon pointing up to the top floor. 'Just let us in.'

'I'm sorry.'

'Come on, girl! We've got something to celebrate,' said Peschka stepping right up to the door.

'He's not in,' she continued, the gap in the door inching closed as she recoiled from the cold.

'Please, Wally.'

Egon and Peschka surged forward and pushed at the door. She slammed it shut and their feet slipped in the worn gully on the top step. They collapsed in a heap on the pavement, the bolt sliding back into place as they descended into mirth.

'Please, just go away,' came the muffled voice from inside.

Egon got to his feet, pushing against Peschka's crumpled body.

'I have to see him. Wally. Open up!'

Egon heard the tap of her heels going back up the wooden stairs. He bent down and pulled Peschka upright. They interlocked arms and walked away. As they reached the end of the street, Egon stopped and looked back up at the window just as a naked arm emerged from a gap in the curtains; a flash of light cast out into the night and then the curtain blew back across.

'Mischievous harlot,' said Peschka, laughing. 'Almost as fiery as your sister.'

The gentry flocked to Vienna from the provinces, their bejewelled wives swinging like puppets beside them. All were desperate to see and be seen at the first exhibition of the Neukunstgruppe, a band of disaffected students whose new style railed against established tastes. Egon had founded the group a few days after his nineteenth birthday, and now he stood as its figurehead, a cocky young man straining at the leash of Viennese society.

Egon joined Peschka and their fellow-artists in flitting from one fawning huddle to the next, spouting pleasantries to dandruff-dusted magistrates. As founder of the group, he worked the hall more fervently than anyone, straining to overhear snippets of conversation, gauging reactions to their work. He walked tall as the words 'shock' and 'disgust' floated over the crackles of conversation. Only once did he stop to confront a critic. His stride halted when he heard the rasping phrase 'pleasantly repulsed'; he leant into a gathering of barber-clipped necks and shook the gentleman's hand.

'Thank you so much, Sir. Magnificent insight.'

Egon straightened his tie and excused himself from the crowds. He made his way to the back of the room where Gertrude stood in a corner, loitering between a table of discarded wineglasses and a vase of flowers. She turned sharply as a cork thudded into a towelled hand.

'Just another hour or so, Gerti. I promise.'

'Don't rush because of me.'

'But you should be off soon. I can't keep you hanging around here all night. If Mother knew…'

'Please, Egon. I'm fine to stay for a while longer. It's interesting to watch all this anyway.' She looked over his shoulder. 'Peschka seems to be enjoying himself…' Egon turned to observe Peschka, who was surrounded by a group of collectors, their heads tilted to catch his words. 'You know what he's like. He was brought up on all this. I can't stand all the handshaking and small talk.'

'Why not be grateful, for a change?'

'…that he likes flirting with the money-makers?'

'Someone has to.'

'He – of all people – doesn't need to.'

Gertrude pulled her brother's arm.

'He's been very kind to me tonight. Don't be ungrateful.'

The tapping of a metal-tipped cane on the marble floor drew their attention to a tall man with a top-hat under his arm. He was dressed in a dark brown suit with a matching waistcoat and tie. His hair was short and receding at the temples. A thick grey-streaked moustache graced his top lip. He switched his walking stick to his left hand and greeted Egon.

'Arthur Roessler.' He handed the artist an embossed card. 'Rather more auspicious surroundings than before.'

'Perhaps. But I imagine a man of your taste is equally at home in both.'

Egon fumbled in his pocket.

'No need, Herr Schiele. I prefer your other calling cards.'

Egon put out an arm and ushered Gertrude forwards. 'May I introduce my sister, Gertrude.'

'Forgive me, we have met before, I believe. *Enchanté*, Fräulein Schiele.' Roessler kissed her hand as she curtseyed.

'I must say I didn't expect to see you again,' interrupted Egon.

'Well, I made a purchase, didn't I?' He sucked his teeth and looked down at the floor. The chandelier reflected off his pitted brogues. 'Maybe something a little less risqué this time, present company considered.' He placed a hand on Gertrude's gloved forearm and smiled. Gertrude curtseyed again, dropping low enough for Roessler's hand to fall away. 'Permit me to be so bold as to ask if you have made any sales this evening?'

'Personally, no.'

Roessler raised an eyebrow. 'Not even that lawyer from Vienna?' he asked.

'They seem to be going for the more sanitised work of my colleagues.'

'Of course. They'll never purchase anything so audacious in front of their peers... or indeed their wives.'

'Lucky you are here on your own then,' said Egon rudely.

Roessler threw his head back in silent laughter. 'Frau Roessler is unfortunately not accompanying me this evening. *Ars longa, vita brevis*, as she never says. I find she has too great an effect on my taste.'

'If it would be easier, there are some other works not publicly exhibited. You might be interested in coming to the storeroom?'

Egon's sister gave a complicit nod while Roessler's eyes trampled over the front of her dress.

'Not just now, thank you. There's some excellent work here, but, I am afraid to say, it won't make you and your friends any money. Not here. Not with these people. The horde is here out of association rather than appreciation.' Roessler laid his arm across

Egon's shoulders, coaxing him back to the centre of the room. 'Will you excuse us a second please, Fräulein Schiele?' Gertrude repeated her curtsey as the pair walked off. 'They adore you, Egon. If I may call you Egon? Graf von Schwarzenberg, Doktor Tewes, Viscomte Deneuve, Konstantin Tscherny. The men admire your brilliance and envy your exhibitionism, and the ladies… well, *ça va de soi*.'

'But they do not buy my work.'

'Young man, it goes without saying that these kinds of people do not hang such pictures on their smoking-room walls.'

'Then they're all hypocrites.'

'Almost certainly,' said Roessler, smiling. 'Almost certainly.'

Egon turned in a full circle, scanning the room, looking again at the white-gloved couples talking past each other.

'Portraits. They all want portraits. Pamper them, court them, massage their *amour-propre*.'

'Supping with the devil.'

'They are your paymasters.'

'But that kind of tripe goes against everything you see on these walls.'

'Unless you have another plan, at the end of the evening your paintings will still be on these walls and your pockets will be empty.' Roessler took two flutes of sparkling wine from a passing tray and pushed one into Egon's hand. 'Take Benesch, for example,' he said, pointing at a barrel-chested man, whose face was the same shade of crimson as his waistcoat. 'Chief Inspector Benesch: exactly the kind of egocentric philistine who would happily have you immortalise him on canvas.'

Roessler caught Benesch's eye and raised his flute. The chief inspector bowed, the candelabra glinting off his polished scalp, then turned back to the pack of besuited men around him.

'Or Kosmack.'

'The publisher?'

'Never was there a man more in love with himself. A fine gent. A very particular flavour of haughtiness.'

Egon finished his glass and looked around for a waiter. He caught sight of Gertrude at Peschka's side in the group of art collectors, their faces angled in towards her, their eyes sparkling with wine. As Egon placed his flute on the tray, Roessler leant forward and took another glass, its stem clinked against his ringed fingers. He cradled the glass in a crooked hand, hugging it between breast and bicep.

'I will start with you,' said Egon abruptly.

'Me?'

'You have the money.'

Roessler threw his head back, a dirty laugh climbing out of his throat.

'Bold, Egon. I like that.'

'Well, are we agreed then?'

Roessler took the hand of a passing woman and planted a kiss on her black silk glove. 'Frau Kosmack. A pleasure as always.' The slender lady inclined her head fractionally towards Roessler and gave a counterfeit smile. The light slid over her powdered face and down into her cleavage, picking out the glow of a pearl necklace. She wore a fine grey-white dress with black frills down the sides and around the hips, and held a small gold-embroidered purse in her left hand. Turning towards Egon, she smiled once again, the first etches of middle age framing her mouth like brackets.

'Frau Kosmack, may I introduce the founder of the Neukunst-gruppe, Egon Schiele.'

Egon took her hand and kissed the back of her glove just below the wrist.

'Congratulations, Herr Schiele. An impressive array of work. Not for the faint-hearted though.'

'Thank you, Frau Kosmack. I'm flattered.'

'We are all intrigued as to what your next subject will be.'

Egon looked over the pale skin of Frau Kosmack's shoulders. She turned to follow his gaze, their eyes meeting Gertrude's across the room. Frau Kosmack blinked slowly.

'Herr Roessler.'

'Arthur?'

'He's just agreed to have his portrait done.'

'Really, Arthur? How valiant of you,' she said, bringing her silk-covered hands together in a silent clap. 'I never thought lawyers could be so audacious.'

'A man of great taste and great foresight,' blurted Egon before Roessler could open his mouth.

'Well, we will look forward to the end result. I do hope they hang it in the courtroom.'

'Perhaps Herr Kosmack might be interested in a similar undertaking?' asked Egon.

'I am not sure Eduard has the gall,' she said. 'Frankly, I would rather put myself in your hands.' Her delicate fingers lay for a moment on his forearm. Then she excused herself and walked away, her dress fluttering layers of sound behind her.

'I will do it for half the standard price,' said Egon.

'I'll pay for materials. Nothing more,' replied Roessler, a cupped hand at the side of his mouth.

'You need me, Sir,' continued the artist, raising his voice. 'A gentleman like you surely wouldn't let one of his peers upstage him over a mere portrait.'

'Don't get all brash with me, young man,' he said, pulling Egon to one side. 'Anyway, I think you'll find you need *me* more than I might ever need *you*.'

'I need money: that's all.'

'And practise.'

'I already have your address, Herr Roessler. I will need a series of two-hour sittings. Preferably at midday. At the latest early afternoon. Write to me when you are ready. In the meantime, I will purchase materials. Enjoy the rest of the evening.'

Egon offered his hand to Roessler, who, with a mischievous smile on his lips, took it in both hands, squeezing the artist's forearm. Egon approached a group of ladies with their naked backs to him as they admired one of his paintings. Having planted kisses on their gloved hands, he directed them towards the exit where carriages were waiting to return them to hotels and urban residences. Meanwhile, the gentlemen moved to the drawing room to concentrate on the graver business of acquisitions, cigars and mistresses.

'A carriage is waiting for you outside, Gerti,' said Egon, pulling her away from the huddle of men.

'But I'm having a lovely time,' said Gertrude, flushed with wine.

'Listen. All this will be wrapped up in a couple of hours. You can't get home now but you can stay at mine. I'll be back as soon as I can, but don't wait up for me. Please.'

'I'd like to stay. I don't see why...'

'Not now, Gerti. Please, go back.' Egon pulled a watch out from his waistcoat pocket. 'It's already...'

'But I want to stay,' said Gertrude, crossing her arms.

'If it's a problem I'll take her back.'

They both spun around to see Peschka standing behind them. Gertrude's shawl was folded over his arm.

'Thanks, Anton, but she'll manage on her own.'

'If you're insisting I leave now at least let him accompany me,' protested Gertrude.

'I'll take care of her,' added Peschka, wrapping the shawl around Gertrude's shoulders. 'Anyway, I've had enough of this lot for the evening.'

'Don't be ridiculous! This evening is what we've been working for.'

'There'll be other opportunities, Egon. Konstantin knows most of these people, anyway. Come on, Gerti, let's go.'

'The carriage driver knows where to take her,' said Egon. 'She'll be fine on her own.'

'If mother knew you were making me travel this late...' started Gertrude.

'If mother knew you were in Vienna... God knows! Now, this is the last of it. I'll speak to the driver and make sure he has my address. He'll see you in.'

Gertrude kissed Egon on both cheeks, turning her back to Peschka, allowing him to reposition her shawl.

'I'll go with Anton,' she said firmly, and walked to the door.

Peschka held out an open palm. Egon looked down at it and then across to his sister, before digging into his pocket. He dangled a key over Peschka's hand.

'I'll get her home safely.'

The key dropped into Peschka's palm.

'Don't even think about it.'

'About what?'

'I trust you, Anton.'

'And Gerti?' With a mischievous wink Peschka turned to join Gertrude. Egon stood still and watched them leave.

'Let's hope you live up to Arthur's occasionally erratic judgement.' Eduard Kosmack strained to keep his head still, the sunlight streaming in from the window onto the profile of his granite face. 'Roessler seems to think you could be the new Klimt.'

'I doubt that.'

'I trust his foresight will be right this time, though. I quite like the idea of being venerated in more than just print.' Kosmack gave a guttural laugh and stood up. 'That's quite enough for the first session, I think. My neck's stiff as a board. How about a glass of cognac?'

Egon put down his pencil and rolled his shoulders in tight circles.

'That would be most welcome, Sir.'

Kosmack tinkled a bell on a side table and removed his tie, pacing around the room, stretching his legs and loosening his belt. He was a tall, ungainly man with a high forehead and closely cut dark hair, greying at the temples. A narrow moustache bristled on his top lip. A girl entered the room with a tray, backing into the door and then turning to face the men. Egon rose from his stool.

'Herr Schiele, my daughter, Anna.'

She placed the tray on a table and held out a hand which Egon left untouched: his own fingers were peppered with ink and paint. She curtseyed instead and left the room, turning to look back before closing the door behind her.

'The apple of my eye, Herr Schiele. The apple of my eye.' Kosmack waited for the rattle of a passing carriage to subside and turned back towards Egon, cradling the glass in his hand. 'I have a proposition.' Egon shifted in his chair. 'I have been considering commissioning a pamphlet from you.'

'On what, may I ask?'

'Not sure yet. My artistic taste is famously fickle. Depending on the outcome of our current project, I would very much like to be the first to publish a selection of your works.'

Egon wiped his fingers on a towel and picked up his glass.

'I would be honoured, Sir. I could think of no better publishing house than yours.'

Kosmack turned away, holding up a hand.

'Alright, alright.' He sipped his cognac, waiting for the burn to rise up his throat before exhaling. 'There are a couple of pieces from the exhibition I think should be included, but I'd rather have something fresher, something the masses have yet to see.'

'I would be…'

'…I'll give you a couple of months to conjure up something special and then we'll sit down with your twenty best pieces and see what's what. Agreed?' Egon leant over and the men shook hands. 'In the meantime, let's finish the portrait. I age quicker than you draw!' Egon gestured enquiringly at his bag of paints and brushes. 'Not now. Come by the press at the end of the week and show me today's drafts, then we'll see if we can agree on a pose.' The men shook hands again and Kosmack walked to the door. 'Please accept my apologies. I have an excruciatingly busy afternoon.'

He stopped in the doorway. 'One more thing.' He pulled a black fountain pen from his inside pocket and scribbled a figure on the bottom corner of one of the sketches. 'The starting figure for the portrait,' he said, handing the paper to Egon.

The painter screwed his face up, stroking an imaginary beard. 'The figure I had in mind – including materials – was somewhat larger.'

'Go on.'

'Half as much again.' Kosmack inflated his cheeks, puffing shafts of air out through gritted teeth. 'With respect, Sir, I have so many requests and only time for a limited number of portraits. I have to make ends meet and…'

Kosmack's frown morphed into a smile and he raised a hand.

'I should've known better.'

He removed the cap from his pen once again and scribbled another number on the coarse paper.

Egon stretched his neck to decipher the figure, mimicked a mental calculation and then nodded. 'That will be fine.'

'It will have to be. Anna will see you out. Goodbye.'

Egon turned as Kosmack's daughter came into the room. She picked up her father's empty glass and placed it back on the tray. Egon finished his and handed it to her, its base slipping on the silver tray. For a second their fingers brushed around the cupola of the glass before she pulled away, knocking one against the other. As she walked to the door, Egon stepped forward quickly and grabbed the handle.

'Thank you, Sir.'

'You're welcome.'

She paused in the doorway, turning back. 'May I ask you a question, Sir?'

'Go ahead.'

'Why do you paint women like that?'

'Like what?'

'The way… they say you do.'

'Have you ever actually seen one of my paintings?'

She looked down at the tray and shook her head. 'But you are the one everyone is talking about?'

'The one?'

'The painter.'

'Well, I am a painter,' he said pointing at the pencils and unfinished sketches. 'Whether or not people are talking about me, I cannot say.'

'They always are in the backroom. They argue about you. Papa as well.'

'That comes as no surprise.'

'I never know if they love you or loathe you.'

'The one invariably goes with the other, Fräulein.'

The girl looked down at the sketches in Egon's bag.

'I can't see what the fuss is about.'

She blushed and walked back through the open door, the glasses clinking on the tray.

Egon's boots dropped flakes of mud on the carpet as he made his way down the hallway. He leant against the first door, stumbling into a darkened study, and then tried the second, opening out onto a candlelit passageway to the scullery. He put a hand out to steady himself, swiping a photograph from the wall. It fell, its frame striking a chest of drawers and dropping forward, its glass cracking across the throat of the schoolboy imprisoned inside. Light spilled through chinks in the third door. Egon grasped twice for the handle, turned it, and staggered into a smoke-filled dining room.

Three men sat on high-backed chairs, pouted lips sucking on cigars. The long table in front of them was strewn with sauce-smeared plates and glasses; the candelabra shone down onto the mother-of-pearl handle of a large spoon poking out of a terrine. Opposite the men were three empty chairs, pushed back from the table, crunched napkins discarded like tissues on the places set in front of them. The men had been passing various small sketches and drawings amongst themselves, but stopped as Egon crashed into the room.

'Whatever is going on?' said the eldest man, looking up at Egon through the thick smoke.

Egon stared back, hanging onto the doorknob. The capillaries in the old man's face and cheeks were cracked around a bulbous, pitted nose; his eyebrows hung like willow over their sockets; his hair was stuck back with pomade and his beard ran into scrub at the base of his neck.

'What are you doing here at this hour? Explain yourself or I'll have you removed from the premises immediately.'

Egon pointed through the smoke at a familiar, mocking face. 'Peschka, you two-faced shit.'

'Sir, how dare you?'

'With respect Herr Tscherny,' started Egon, swaying as his eyes sought a path through the forest of candles, 'your nephew is no gentleman.'

He lurched towards Peschka but slipped on the carpet and fell, his fingernails scragging on the thick cotton of the jacket that hung on the back of Peschka's chair. His leg struck the table and a vase of lilies fell mutely onto the carpeted floor, a cascade of white and water covering his trousers. He kicked and swore, writhing on the rucked carpet, Peschka's jacket twisting round his arms, petals and split stems littering the floor. The table shook again and a carafe of Beaujolais toppled, its blood sea running out over lace, seeping first into the fabric and then dispersing along tributaries.

Tscherny eased himself from his chair, its leather seat groaning as it released his heavy frame, and pulled Egon to his feet. The door opened again and a butler appeared, rushing towards Egon, a walking-stick raised above his head.

'That won't be necessary, Rainer.'

The butler stopped, lowered the stick behind his back and straightened his tie.

'Yes, Sir.'

'Clean up the mess will you. That will be all for the moment.'

'Yes, Sir. Of course, Sir.'

'Now if there is nothing else you wish to break, young Schiele, I suggest you go home and sleep this off. We can talk about this tomorrow.'

'Not coming back to this shit-hole tomorrow,' replied Egon, twisting a torn sleeve straight.

'I suggest you refrain from that language. Now, here's some money, take a carriage home.'

Egon swiped at Tscherny's hand, knocking the coins across the room in a shrapnel shower over porcelain and glass. He reached for an ornamental cutlass above the mantelpiece, but lost his balance and crumpled into the fireguard.

'A duel, a duel!' he bawled from the floor, the brass guard folding on top of him.

The butler reappeared instantly. 'Sir?'

'Hail this man a carriage, will you, Rainer? Get him some clean clothes and a strong cup of coffee. And get him out of here!'

Tscherny pulled the fireguard off Egon and leant it against the wall. Egon staggered to his feet, slapping away helping hands.

'Get off me!'

He lurched forward again, but this time Klimt , who was the third man at the table, stood up and stepped into his path, catching Egon's beating fists on his broad chest. Klimt placed an arm around his back and under his shoulders. 'Come on now. Let's get you home.'

'And leave my sister here with that shit!' snarled Egon.

'She's not here, Egon,' said Peschka from the refuge of his chair. 'She went back to Tulln this afternoon.'

'Liar!'

With thrashing arms he freed himself from Klimt's grasp and staggered over to the opposite side of the table. He approached the empty chair opposite Peschka and ran his hand over its seat. He picked up the napkin from the table and shook it out, holding it to his nose.

'Keep away from her, you hear?'

'Come on, Egon. Let's go,' said Klimt, leading him to the door.

'Away!'

'Shut up! I'm taking you home.'

'What have you done to her?' He caught sight of a sketch on the table opposite Peschka. 'You bastard!'

Peschka threw a napkin over the picture and Klimt pushed Egon out into the hallway, slamming the dining room door behind them.

'What in hell are you doing?' The butler arrived with a cup of coffee, which Klimt refused, taking instead the spare coat and wrapping it around Egon's shoulders. 'Let's get you out of here.'

Outside, the puff-pant of horses waiting in the street ruffled the night air. Klimt helped Egon down the steps, across the pavement and into the carriage. Egon hung his head, pulling the sodden trousers away from his shins. The elder painter moved to lay an arm around his friend's shoulder but Egon pushed him aside, climbing down from the carriage and elbowing his way past the butler in the doorway. The door slammed behind him and he looked up to see Gertrude standing in the corridor.

'It's alright, Rainer. Give us a moment, will you?'

'Yes, Fräulein Schiele.'

The butler tugged an imaginary forelock and walked off down the passageway towards the scullery.

Gertrude stood tall, her chin held high, her fingers interlaced around an embroidered handbag. Egon looked at the floor. He felt suddenly at a loss.

'Does Mother know you're here?'

Gertrude shook her head.

'Just sits on the platform. She never says anything anymore.'

'And what about you coming home late?'

'Piano lessons.'

Egon scoffed and pulled the coat around his shoulders.

'Surely Uncle Leopold knows.'

'He doesn't care. He doesn't give us a penny these days.' She turned, hearing voices coming from the dining room. 'She just wants to stay in the station. There's nowhere else for her to go.'

'I'll send her something.'

'A sketch won't get her much down the market,' said Peschka, standing in the doorway to the dining room, a fire poker dangling at his side, tapping lightly against his calf.

'Anton, leave us a moment, will you?' pleaded Gertrude.

'I'm not leaving you here alone with that drunk.'

'Anton, just one moment. That's all.'

Peschka laid a hand on Gertrude's shoulder.

'Are you sure?'

Gertrude nodded.

'If I hear one squeak, I'll be straight back out here, darling.'

'She saw your mention in the paper,' said Gertrude, oblivious to

Peschka. 'She asks after you every time I return from the city.'

'And?'

'I tell her you're doing well.'

'No more?'

'She's in bed before it gets dark. If I'm there by sunrise she's none the wiser.'

'Gerti's not a girl anymore, Egon,' said Peschka, leaning against the doorframe, picking dirt off the front of his shirt. 'She doesn't need you looking out for her at every twist and turn.'

'Anton, will you just leave us for a moment. Please!' implored Gertrude.

'Don't tell me what I can and can't do with my sister!'

'He's got nothing to worry about. Has he? Tell him he hasn't,' said Peschka. 'I always treat my models with the utmost grace.' Egon's head lolled on his shoulders as he looked back and forth between his sister and Peschka. 'She makes such an exquisite picture. You know that yourself.'

'How could you?' asked Egon, grabbing her hand.

'You're not my keeper.'

'How long has this been going on?'

'Let go of me!'

'Weeks? Months?'

'What does it matter to you? You've always had your own girls.'

'I thought we had an understanding.'

The scullery door creaked open at the end of the passageway.

'I'm not your little sister anymore,' shouted Gertrude.

'But not him. Please, not him.'

'I don't belong to you.'

'Why can't it… everything will be…'

Egon drew Gertrude towards him. Pictures crashed to the floor as he wrapped his arms around her, enclosing her legs with his, forcing her face into the hollow of his shoulder. She raised her knee sharply between his legs and he folded, falling away, his head striking a brass umbrella stand as his body crumpled on the floor. Peschka hurried to Gertrude's side and pushed her dress back down, holding her shaking body to his chest. Tscherny emerged from the dining room.

'Rainer!'

The butler shuffled out of the scullery and along the service passageway.

'Yes, Sir.'

'Get this wretch out of here.'

The butler tugged Egon by the neck of his shirt, the paper collar coming away in his hand. He tossed it to the floor and dragged Egon to the front door. A cold wind blew in. Klimt was still waiting in the carriage, the front legs of the horses bent in ballet-pose. He returned to Egon's body, took a fistful of scalp and pulled him to his feet, leading him half-crouched to the steps. He pushed him down the slippery sandstone into a heap on the path.

'Go to hell, the pair of you,' muttered Egon through bloodied teeth.

# SEVEN

# GOD'S PRIMARY COLOURS

The sketch curled and twisted as it floated down from Egon's window. It dropped until caught in the slipstream of a passing carriage, tossing it up then down into the street. The wind dropped and it came to rest in the dip of the gutter. Face down, the heavy paper soaked up moisture until it took on the colour of the street, hugging the gaps between the stones, saturated with the detritus of the Kurzbauergasse. It remained there for an hour, the watercolours seeping out into the putrid leaves of the street, until a carriage, turning sharply to miss a stray dog, dissected the paper, chewing it up among the leaves and transporting half of Gertrude's headless body down the street.

Egon lay upstairs on his bed, the commotion of street life blowing in through the window. He looked up at the collage of wallpaper and white paint above him. The candlelight cast hallucinatory images of inverted bodies and battles over the piebald surface. He noted them down on scraps of paper, furiously recording half-pictures of twisted corpses, prostrate women, shrouded monks and the pierced torsos of saints.

He sat up abruptly when he heard a knock at the door.

'Schiele?'

Knock. Knock.

'Herr Schiele? Anyone in there?'

'Who is it?' he mumbled.

'Kosmack. Now open up!'

Egon swung his legs off the bed, pushing scraps of sketches into a pile at the end of the bed, buttoning up his shirt and pulling on braces. He shuffled over to the door, unbolted it and kicked away crockery from the floor. Kosmack slipped in sideways through the half-open door, his back brushing against the frame, and stood looking open-mouthed at the chaos surrounding the young painter. Egon shuffled back to the bed, blinking furiously, licking his fingers to dampen down sprigs of hair.

'People like you try my patience, Herr Schiele. I have very little time. So little that I don't expect to be wasting it chasing you up for something I was unconvinced of in the first place.'

'Sorry, Sir.'

'What the hell are you playing at?'

'I've been unwell.'

'Unwell? For five months? Give me one good reason why I shouldn't terminate this whole charade.' His tongue flicked out and stole a globule of spittle from his top lip.

'Forgive me, Herr Kosmack,' said Egon, sitting up. 'I've been somewhat distracted these last weeks. I can come next week if that suits you.'

'You can't just turn up as your whim takes you!'

'I can come tomorrow.'

'I'm a busy man, Schiele.'

'This afternoon?'

Kosmack stood up and moved to the window, pulling the curtains back. 'Come at three tomorrow. We'll make time.'

'Thank you, Sir.'

'This isn't the way to go about making a career for yourself.' He stood up, removed a glove and shook Egon's hand. 'I'll see you tomorrow.'

He waited on the far side of the room for Egon to spring up from the bed and open the door.

'Just one thing, Sir. What about the pamphlet?'

'You should have thought about that earlier.'

'But you are still interested?'

'One thing at a time, Herr Schiele.' He stopped in the doorway. 'Make sure you have a bath before tomorrow.'

Egon removed his hat and placed it on the hall table as he stepped over the threshold.

'Please accept my apologies,' said Anna. 'He knows you're coming, of course.'

'That's quite alright.'

'He's working all the hours that God sends,' she said, showing him into the study.

An old lady in an apron at the end of the corridor put her mop down and curtseyed as they walked past.

'I'm happy to wait.' Egon moved over to look out the window at the street traffic while Anna milled around the room, repositioning ornaments and winding up a carriage clock.

'May I bring you something while you're waiting?' she asked.

'No, thank you. I'll be fine.'

'A schnapps? A glass of water?'

'Not this early in the day thank you.'

'I'll bring some cognac anyway. Papa demands it.'

Anna left the room and reappeared with the customary tray and two glasses. She passed Egon one and waited for him to take a sip.

'I hope you won't be offended it I keep you company. He may be some time, you see. I will, of course, leave if you have preparations to make.' Egon nodded as she took the second glass and perched on the edge of the long sofa, her knees pressed together, cradling the cognac in both hands. 'I know I'm not supposed to but Mama turns a blind eye. Besides, Papa says it's good for my constitution.' She swallowed hard and closed her eyes. 'I was wondering when you would return.'

'There have been a few distractions.'

'Papa's been looking everywhere for you.' Egon turned away from the window towards Anna, who was looking down into her lap. 'He sent one of the staff out to Leopoldstadt, going door to door.'

'That wasn't necessary.'

Egon caught her image in profile and glimpsed the scissors behind her on Kosmack's writing desk. For an instant she seemed perfect for a silhouette, cut out of the beige writing paper piled on the desk: her pointed chin and Roman nose; the high brow with distant hairline; the shallow curve of her neck which tilted her head forward. Anna was the visual antidote to the painted ladies who crossed Egon on Vienna's night streets, an innocent with no echoes of the streetwalkers and harlots whose muddied fingernails dug into his back. Her hair hung down in honey ringlets over the shoulders; her lips barely moved as she spoke.

'People have been talking again.'

'Again?'

'I'm afraid so.'

'Have they got nothing better to do?' Egon pinched the bridge of his nose. 'So, are you going to tell me?'

'I'd rather not say.'

'Why?'

'Please, Sir. I'd rather not say.'

Egon stood up from the stool, wandered once around the room, studying the certificates on the walls, and sat down at the other end of the sofa.

'It doesn't bother me, you know. You can be sure that most of it is not true.' Anna's cheeks were glowing as she took another sip of the cognac. 'You shouldn't drink too much of that,' he found himself saying.

Anna rotated the glass in her hands. 'Is it true what they say about your sister, Herr Schiele?'

'Have they got nothing better to talk about?'

'It's just what I hear.'

'And what do they say?'

'That she's "accompanying" Anton Peschka.' Egon took a large swig of cognac. 'They say you are hostile to their friendship.'

'Where do you hear all this?'

'Papa's drawing room.' She swivelled on the couch, her satin dress sliding against the leather.

'Does your father know you eavesdrop?'

'I can't help it. They talk so much. So many names.' Egon shrugged. 'Please forgive me, I hardly know you.'

'It's fine.'

Anna was about to say something else, but just then they heard the front door slam. She poured the remains of her cognac into Egon's glass and then hid her own in the corner of a bookshelf. The door flung open and Kosmack walked into the room, his coat folded over his arm.

'Apologies, apologies. Let's get straight on, shall we?'

He kissed his daughter on the cheek.

'I brought Herr Schiele a cognac while he was waiting, Papa.'

'That should have loosened him up. Perhaps he'll be a little more lively today. I'll have one as well.' He tossed his coat onto the sofa. 'I had a few finishing touches to make to some edition of mundane verse that's going to press next week. Waste of bloody time, if you ask me. I hate the stuff. I'm assured it will sell like proverbial hot cakes though. Right, let's get on with it. Where do you want me?'

Egon directed him to his usual position by the window. He took the stretcher frame in hand and started scraping away at some of the old paint, brushing powdered colour onto the floor. As he set his easel straight, laying out his portable rainbow on a small side table, his eyes rested on Anna as she poured two more glasses of cognac. She passed her father a glass and moved towards Egon. She leant across him, positioning the new glass on the side-table and removing his old glass. The satin of her sleeve coasted across his stubbled cheek as she stretched. He caught the fragrance of rosemary woven into her hair, closing his eyes as she withdrew and left the room. He looked down at his glass, watching the cognac wallow like caramel in the cupola. Underneath its wide base, he could see the folded corners of a square of notepaper. He drank the cognac, palmed the note, and restarted the portrait.

Klimt and Roessler took it in turns to drop by Egon's room, knocking until he trudged to the door and turned the key. He would walk away and climb back onto his mattress leaving the men in the doorway. They abandoned conversation and dropped a bundle of food by his bed before gathering up near-finished works, wrapping them in sack-cloth and feeding them to the community of Vienna's collectors. Egon's name dripped off the lips of the city's self-styled cognoscenti but his paintings sold slowly. He received letters requesting audiences, probing the motivations for his style, scoping him out for future exhibitions; but the envelopes collected on the chair next to his bed. He toiled every waking hour, spending his meagre funds on materials and neglecting the portrait requests which could have paid the bills. The little money Egon earned from the city's upper-middle classes soon evaporated, stuffed into the aprons of barmaids, the underwear of whores and the grubby hands of models. Meanwhile, every other day there would be a knock at the door and another of the city's usurers would be standing there, a thick-necked henchman treading the corridor behind him. Egon paid any paltry sum he had earned from the sale of a painting, but their visits grew in frequency and soon they were refusing his portraits and sketches as deferred payment. Egon stopped answering the door, creating a coded knock for his models of long and short taps followed by fingernails scraping anti-clockwise around the door handle. Before the girls left, he would go through the ritual with each of them, tapping away at the wood, synchronising their scrapes until there was no doubt they could repeat it blind, drunk or exhausted. If, on any occasion, Egon heard a standard thump at the door, he would remove his shoes and tiptoe around the room, extinguishing candles with a moistened thumb and forefinger until the room hissed into darkness. Afterwards he would sit down on the rug in the corner and listen to the graphic threats coming from the corridor.

She was a girl without a past and whose future was laid out before him like an untarnished canvas, ripe for the palette of his desires and neuroses. She was the perfect remedy to the spectre in red and black burnt on the inside of his eyelids. He courted her vagabond glances every time she entered the room with a tray of cognac, her gait extravagant and womanly. He allowed their hands to brush every time she placed the glass on the side-table, lingering as she turned to leave. When she returned he would press a note to the bottom of his glass as he placed it on her tray, giving her time to push it up the sleeve of her blouse before approaching her father.

Every day Kosmack sat for the portrait, Anna would pace around the room behind him while Egon took a scrap of paper, placed it on the easel on top of the canvas, and sketched her: arms crossed, elbow perched on the windowsill, enveloped in a leather armchair. He produced three or four such sketches every time he went to their house, immersing himself in her simple image until Anna's mellifluous locks had replaced the red hair, until her natural poise had superseded his sister's posing. Arriving home, he pinned the sketches to the ceiling slanted over his bed, creating a sprawling mosaic, forcing her image upon his tired eyes until the memory of Gertrude had been buried behind his retina.

'What are we going to do when you've finished it?' she whispered as Egon pulled on his hat and coat in the hallway.

'I can stretch it out another few weeks at most, but I'm running out of excuses.'

'We could find another time?'

She laid a hand on Egon's forearm.

'But he could turn up at any moment. Anyway, the maid will know I've been here. She knows everything.'

'What about somewhere else?'

'I could show you round a gallery.'

'Unaccompanied never. He knows your reputation… whether he believes it or not. Anyway, you can't risk the pamphlet.'

Egon moved to pull Anna towards him but the study door opened and Kosmack appeared.

'Is she wasting your time?'

'Not at all, Herr Kosmack. I was just enquiring as to the brand of the cognac.'

'Well, if you can finish this bloody portrait before I turn completely grey then I shall give you a bottle. See you next week.'

'It's Herr Eilers,' announced Anna, entering the room. 'He says it's something to do with the printers. A carriage is waiting outside.'

'Bloody good-for-nothings!' Kosmack stood up, grabbing his jacket and coat from the arm of the sofa. 'Third time this month. Can we continue next week, say, Thursday at three?'

'Of course, Sir.'

'Be so good as to see Herr Schiele out, will you Anna?'

'Yes, Papa.'

They shook hands and Kosmack strode out into the hallway, his raised voice still audible until the carriage had pulled away. The house fell silent. Anna's arms dropped to her sides as Egon approached.

'I don't…'

He leant forward and kissed her, swallowing a half-formed sentence on her lips. He ran his fingers down the sides of her unbent arms and onto her thighs, her body rigid as he pressed against her. She raised her hands to the back of his head, pulling his mouth closer to hers. In an instant they had slipped onto the couch in a series of grapples, limbs jarring against armrests and naïve fingers clawing at buttons.

When she came into the drawing room several weeks later, devoid of her usual welcoming smile – no note slipped under the cognac glass – the instant's joy had already etched around her eyes the first traces of a lifetime's pain.

'First it's bad light, next it's illness, then it's unavailability! How much longer are you going to draw it out?'

'It's got nothing to do with you.'

'I always like to know what my rivals are up to,' said Roessler, sitting on a simple chair in his conservatory, his arms crossed and his head pointed away from the dangling leaves of plants. 'Particularly when we are suffering the same tedium.'

'Keep still, please,' replied Egon, his voice tired and low.

'I don't know what I'll be forced to do if you finish his before mine.'

'If you keep talking, it'll take even longer,' mumbled Egon, biting a long-handled brush between his teeth. 'And for the record, I completed it last month.'

'A masterpiece, no doubt.'

'He has refused to pay up.'

'If it would help, I can take another batch of those ones of the two dark-haired sisters. That should tide you over for a couple of weeks.'

Egon removed the brush from his mouth and poked his head around the side of the canvas.

'They'll be ready for next time.'

He ducked back behind the easel, the scraping of spatula on palette audible over the buzz of flying insects. He switched his weight from left to right, the toes on his bare feet clawing at the ground. Roessler closed his eyes as the wind blew in and tickled his face.

'I haven't seen his daughter for months,' he said nonchalantly, his eyes still closed. 'Kosmack refuses to bring her to any soirées. Must be those grisly suitors who come crawling out of the cracks.' Egon continued his work in silence. 'There are only so many times a man can hear a rumour before it becomes truth. You know how they thrive off hearsay. I can imagine it hasn't been easy avoiding all the speculation.' Egon's spatula ground crescents into the canvas. 'I hope you feel you can tell me about it.' As if he hadn't heard, Egon placed a brush on the rim of the easel and selected another.

Roessler stood up from the stool, rolling his shoulders to ease the stiffness of sitting unmoved for half an hour. He approached the easel, looking over the top of the canvas at Egon whose head hung down, consulting his tray of paints.

'It's not exactly a well-kept secret, Egon.'

'Please, I'm trying to concentrate.' He looked up at Roessler's face. 'Sit back down! You've ruined the entire last session's work!'

Egon placed a brush between his teeth and muttered an obscenity.

'Is he prepared to pay?' continued Roessler, walking round the easel and confronting Egon.

'What are you talking about?' came Egon's tired voice.

'Don't take me for a fool. The whole city knows about it.'

'Please, Arthur, will you go back to your seat.'

Roessler sat back down, facing the painter.

'Raise your left hand; it was on your right arm, just above the bicep.'

'I won't move until you tell me what has been going on.'

'Silence!'

Roessler stood up from the stool. 'I can pay for it, if needs be.'

'We agreed you would anyway.'

'Not the portrait. The operation.' Egon sat down, his head in his hands. 'I would have thought after all these sessions you would have told me if something like this had happened,' continued Roessler. 'I mean, we're friends, aren't we? Admittedly, I'm a little older and far more charming, but still.' Egon looked up and tried to smile at Roessler. 'Just forget about his portrait. That's lost money. But at least let me pay for the operation. There's one thing making an enemy of a man on business terms, but poisoning a relationship with his daughter is a hundred times worse. Particularly in his case.'

'I never intended for this to happen, you know.'

'No one ever does.'

'It's not all how it looks, you know.'

Egon rubbed his hands across his face, drawing his cheeks down, pulling the skin away from his eye sockets.

'I know a good doctor. I'll send him to see her tomorrow morning. Make sure she's ready and that Kosmack's not at home. He'll need plenty of warm water and clean towels. Can you take care of that?'

'I'm barred from the house.'

'I'll send her a message then. Get out of the city. Go and visit your mother tomorrow. It would be best if you weren't around. Take a day off. Go and get some country air. Understand?' Egon nodded. 'I think we're done for today. Go home. Get some rest. You look terrible.'

As the sun rose, Egon was lingering across the street from the Kosmacks' house, having spent the night tossing handfuls of gravel at her window. At nine o'clock a carriage drew up at the front door. The metal foot rail rattled open and a bearded man stepped down. In his right hand he carried a brown leather holdall and with his left hand he held the rim of the carriage to steady his step. The front door opened just as his finger pointed at the bell. As the door thudded closed, Egon loped to the other side of the street and sat on a low wall, waiting there all morning while diabolic scenes of slaughter played out upstairs, brutal instruments piercing the woman's body, limp child-like limbs being pulled from between the splayed legs which had wrapped around him a few months earlier.

At midday, an old maid in a black dress, a white apron and a headscarf appeared in the doorway. She looked up and down the street, propping the door open with a mop before going back inside. A moment later she reappeared placing a bucket on the top step before darting back inside to the hollow ring of a service bell. Egon's eyes never left the bucket during the three minutes she was away. He scanned its dents, its smears and grime, examining its discoloured sides as if at any moment his vision would penetrate them and reveal the bucket's broken and bloody contents. When the maid returned, her apron was streaked with red down the front. She picked up the bucket, one hand on its base, the other on its handle, and drew it back behind her. Egon stood up from the wall and ran into the street. A frozen, soundless scream wracked his body as she swung the bucket back and hurled its contents down the front steps of the house.

Egon collapsed as he watched the dirty water flow from step to step, across the pavement and down into the gutter. The grey-brown liquid glossed over the stones, darkening them before the remainder spread into tributaries between the cobbles. The maid pulled a broom from inside the door and brushed each step with four brisk swipes. It was only when she finished the final step and arrived at the pavement that she looked up to see a man crying in the street.

Later that day a carriage pulled up and took away the bearded man. He handed his leather bag and a string-tied bundle inside to a travelling companion and eased his way up the metal rungs. The stones outside the house had dried and the curtains on the top floor were drawn, strips of cream fabric flapping out into the street. Egon came back the next day and the day after, sitting on the low wall and watching the windows, waiting for midday when the maid would reappear with the bucket.

On the following day, Egon obtained the gynaecologist's address from Roessler and walked to the other side of the city, his stride long, his face sebaceous and his lungs screaming for air. He waited half an hour in the lobby, pleading with the assistant to let him in to see the doctor without an appointment.

Erwin von Graf's oak-panelled office was narrow, with rows of statuettes and Latin-spined books lining its walls, their continuity broken by loose-leaf manuscripts poking out from the weightier volumes. A corridor of light emanated from a gap in the velveteen curtains, was filtered through lace, and split the room in two. Next to the door stood a pointed coat stand, rising up like a Viking's helmet. The doctor sat in an armchair behind a mahogany desk, his hands interlinked on his lap; behind him the leather bag slouched on top of a chest of drawers. On the wall hung a framed copy of the Hippocratic oath in Gothic script. A gust of air surged into the lung of the room, filling the yellowing lace and lifting it away from the window. Sheets of paper on tables around the room lifted up like outstretched wings.

'I know why you've come,' said von Graf, rising from his chair. 'I heard your name mentioned several times. You cannot imagine what you inflicted on that poor girl. Well, say what you have to say. I would appreciate it if you were brief.'

He gestured for Egon to sit but the painter remained standing, shuffling towards the doctor's desk.

'Come on, I don't have long.'

Egon worked the brim of his hat through both hands.

'I need to see him, Herr Doktor. Please.'

'Whom?'

'My son.'

The doctor pulled his glasses from his face, their curled tips springing from behind his ears. He leant forward onto the rectangle of green on his writing the desk, rubbing his eyes with a thumb and forefinger. 'Sit down, please.'

'I would rather stand.'

'Sit down!' Egon took two paces backwards and stumbled into a chair, slipping in off its worn arms. 'Now listen to me carefully, young man. I will only say this once. I induced Fräulein Kosmack to eject the foetus. She never gave birth.'

'But we had a baby.'

'She was twenty-two weeks gone. What was expelled from her body did not resemble a child as you know it.'

'But… the baby?'

'There was no child.'

'Our son!' Egon sprang to his feet, pacing in and out of the shadows, muttering under his breath.

'There was only a foetus. Ejected from the body prematurely.'

'His face. Hold him.'

Von Graf slammed an open palm onto his desk. A fountain pen sprang out of an inkpot and threw blotches of darkness over his hands.

'Look what you've…!'

He walked to a basin in the corner and dipped his fingers, flicking drops back into the cloudy water. Egon looked at the doctor and then turned away, his eyes darting across the room, alighting on medical statuettes, anatomical drawings and organs floating in jars.

'He must be…'

The doctor grasped Egon's arm and pushed him back into the chair.

'Listen here, you reprobate! It barely resembled a child. Neither was it fully developed nor did it have the features of a child or baby. You did not have any off-spring. Nothing.'

'But I must see him.'

'The abortus was disposed of by the family.'

Egon's head shook, at first slowly and then more erratically. He chewed the callous on the back of his thumb.

'Where?'

'That's none of your business.'

'Please, Herr Doktor, please.'

Von Graf plucked a handkerchief from his breast pocket and wiped the sweat off his neck.

'Now, if I tell you, will you leave?'

'Yes.'

'Alright, then legally speaking it must be in a mortuary.'

'Which mortuary?' said Egon reaching out for von Graf's forearm.

'Please leave.'

'Just tell me where.'

'I will not ask you again.'

'Is it buried?'

'For Christ's sake, man! Just forget it. It's in a box somewhere. You are relieved of your paternal obligations. You're off the hook. You're free. The bill has been paid. You owe me nothing. Now just get out!'

'I have to know, Herr Doktor, please.'

'Clear off! Don't you dare mention this to anyone. It's not my custom nor my responsibility to mop up after the likes of you.'

Egon had barely eaten or washed during the preceding seven days. His eyes were puffy with grey rings in their sockets; the pores of his nose were wide with serum; his fingers were bitten past the cuticles, and his teeth were furred with a yellow ochre that darkened at the roots. He sat on the chair in his apartment, his legs extended, resting on the bed, his eyes glazed with the images which had kept him awake since he first appeared outside the Kosmacks' house. One moment, the graceless fumbles on the couch would revisit him, Anna's stockinged legs slipping against the leather, struggling until he hitched his nails over the tops, her warm skin gaining traction; the next, under-developed humans would appear before his eyes, held upside-down by the bearded doctor, viscous, blood dripping off their skin, coagulating in misshapen circles on the off-white bed-sheets.

He looked around his room, the walls covered in sketches and spattered with white paint. He glanced over the myriad women his pencil had known: guttersnipes, models, brief lovers, prostitutes, imagined aristocrats, waitresses, relatives. He looked at the sea of limbs swirling around him, the landscape of flesh and bone, contorted and abrasive. Despite the composition of their limbs – their jagged lines – something was missing. He examined the looks on their faces, the expressions painted into their crescent eyebrows and lips. The turns at the sides of their mouths, the pressurised distance between the eyes, it all seemed to point to every possible emotion, from lust to fatigue, flirtation to consummation, joy to melancholy, but something was missing.

Egon took his feet down from the bed and stood up. He took his pencils off the table in the corner and walked out the door.

'I'm from the Medical Faculty.'

'And?'

'I was told I could gain admission for studying purposes.'

'Depends,' said the elderly lady at the front desk. 'This place is packed with your lot. D'you have the permission slip?'

'Isn't that just internal Faculty stuff?'

'D'you have it or not?' asked the woman, a crude hat pinned to her grey hair.

'I didn't know you needed to see it here.'

'Usually, yes.'

'I've been here before, though. With Doktor von Graf a few months ago.'

'Who?'

'Doktor Erwin von Graf.'

The woman shook her head, flicked through the register on her desk and shrugged. 'What department?'

'Obstetrics.'

'Don't suppose it makes any difference. Just make sure you don't upset anyone. This place is miserable enough without you lot making the girls feel any worse.'

'Of course. Thank you.'

Egon followed her directions and went through double-doors into a corridor. He put a hand to his mouth, flinching at the stench of blood, chloroform and sweat. Then came the chorus of groans, screams and sobs. The corridor was lined with girls, plundered washerwomen, gypsies, deformed prostitutes, fallen women of all provenance, some holding babies to their chests, others bent double over swollen stomachs, their children tucked behind them, their faces covered with rags or splayed fingers. He walked down the passageway, the tearful, bloodshot eyes of harridans rising briefly towards him and then returning to their own worlds of pain and disgrace. Every few yards doors led off to side-rooms where Egon glimpsed the bottom of beds or the silhouettes of white-jacketed doctors. The wails of new-borns were indistinguishable from the soprano screams of their mothers.

A hand pulled at the bottom of his trousers, bitten fingers sliding between sock and shoe.

'Just a crown, lad. Just a crown for the little one.' The woman was slumped across the floor. 'Please!' The red dye in her hair had long since washed away but her eyes were familiar as was her sing-song accent. 'When I get out you can have a couple of jumps for free. I swear.' She exposed a toothy grin. 'Wherever you want.' Egon dug into his pocket, pressing a coin into her palm. 'I'll be out soon. Come down whenever. I'll be lookin' out for you.'

Egon nodded and walked on, turning his face away from the girls clogging up the clinic's arteries. He turned at the end of the corridor into another passage similarly crammed with prostrate bodies, driven out of respectable homes or fleeing worse fates on the streets. He stepped into a doorway and heard the condescending voice of a young doctor. The medical faculty sent its outcast students to the clinic to cut their teeth, tucking in blankets around doomed babies, stitching up mothers, running their hands over burning foreheads and tear-streaked cheeks.

'Can I help you?' said the doctor as he left the room.

'I've come to see her.'

'Who?'

'This one.'

'If you say so.' Egon raised a hand to scratch his cheek. 'Go on in.'

'Thank you, Herr Doktor.'

'By the way,' said the doctor, stopping in the doorway. 'She lost it.'

Egon waited until the doctor's footsteps were drowned out by the clamour outside and then he stepped back into the corridor, walking in the opposite direction.

He moved to the next doorway. A woman was lying asleep on the bed. Her eyes opened wearily and as she moved to sit up, several stitches on her stomach wept blood through a gap in her dress.

'I'm from the Faculty. Please, get some rest.'

She nodded and her head dropped back to the pillow.

He looked down at the end of the bed where there hung a blackboard smeared with chalk dust. It bore no name, neither a street pseudonym nor a disrespectful soubriquet granted by a doctor. He pulled out a pencil and a piece of paper and began sketching the woman's features, the wretchedness which painted itself not just over her face but the body in its tangle of stained bedsheets. He packed his paper away, stroked her ankle and left the room.

Egon moved down the passageway, from room to room, always checking that no doctor was present. He spoke softly to those who were awake, calming their nerves, raising their spirits, while he carved their bodies, their knees together and their hands interlinked over swollen bellies, reliving the journey to motherhood he had never witnessed. Their eyes were full of pity for the children waiting in their wombs, infants about to be born into a cruel and prejudiced world.

On the following day, he strode past the old lady at the front desk and down a flight of moist redbrick stairs into the basement. A rusted door screeched open and at the end of a corridor sat a bald man behind a desk. He was thin with angular shoulders and pasty skin. The veins on his neck spread into a network of sapphire rivulets along his jaw line and cheeks. His eyebrows were thick, nearly meeting between his blue eyes. He looked up sluggishly as Egon approached the desk.

'I'm from the Faculty.'

'I don't care,' he said, returning to the newspaper on his desk.

'I'm here to conduct some anatomical drawings for my thesis.'

'I said, I don't care.'

'But the doctor said…'

'We don't allow your lot down here. Besides you can only get authorisation to see a particular corpse. You can't just browse like it's some bloody hat shop.'

'I'm here to see the Kosmack boy.'

'Are you bloody deaf? I said we don't let you lot down here without express authorisation.'

Egon put a hand into his pocket and placed a crown on the man's desk. He took the money and carried on reading. Egon placed a second coin in the middle of the paper. He pocketed the money and inspected the register to his left.

'There's nothing under the name of Kosmack in there, I'm afraid. Goodbye.'

'May I have a look for myself?'

'I said this wasn't a fuckin' hat shop, didn't I?'

Egon dropped a third coin onto the table. It rolled on its edge before spinning to a halt on the wooden surface.

'How long d'you need?'

'An hour.'

'For what?'

'Please, just an hour.'

'Thirty minutes.'

The warden stood up and unlocked a second steel door leading off the corridor. 'If anyone arrives in the meantime, you're out of there in a flash. Understand?'

'Yes.'

'If you get caught, you say you broke in. Right?'

'Yes.'

Egon retched as the door closed behind him. He took a handkerchief from his pocket, tying it behind his ears, and opened his sketchpad, drawing anything he could find before the stench became unbearable. He moved from table to table, pulling the covers off corpses no larger than plucked pheasants, recording their features on paper, their stiff bodies hanging in time and space, cramped in the middle of the sheet. He pushed the barriers of anatomy, expanding their heads, sprinkling them with adult hair, their eyes swallowed up in inflamed sockets, their gums blue, their skin flecked with purples, blacks and reds against the grey of their hardened flesh. Their stomachs were even more bloated than those of the pregnant ladies upstairs; their navels, disgorged of the umbilical cord, were like open wounds, while their puffy sexual organs found their way into one of the main axes of the paper. Within minutes, he was treating the still-borns from the mortuary like the new-borns from the clinic upstairs; he sculpted both as shrivelled homunculi, their eyes swollen in dented faces, their bodies stained with red and black.

'God's primary colours,' he whispered under his breath as the warden appeared at the door.

# EIGHT

# SLOW-MOVING WATERS

The wood gave way as the lock bit a chunk out of the doorframe. A thick-set man stumbled into the room holding his shoulder. He wrenched Egon out of bed, his naked feet slipping on the floor, and grabbed a palette knife, holding it to the painter's throat.

'By noon. I swear.'

'Bullshit!' he spat, pressing the blunt knife into Egon's Adam's apple.

'I swear I'll have it by noon.'

The man tossed the knife onto the chair and walked around the cluttered room, heavy with the odour of sleep. The centre of the floor was covered with paint-spattered rags and soiled clothes which he kicked up in the air. Half-finished sketches and canvases were propped against the walls and he flicked them over with the toecap of his boot, their frames cracking against the floorboards as they fell. He passed his hand over the bristles of a jar of upturned brushes and went behind a curtain to where the washbasin stood. Egon listened to the stallion thud of fluid hitting porcelain, followed by a trickle which spread out into an ever-widening puddle underneath the hem of the curtain, extending across the floor, seeking out Egon crouched in the corner. In a few seconds the rags on the floor were dark with wetness and the reek of ammonia reached his nostrils. The creditor re-emerged, straightening the front of his trousers.

'This place stinks.' Egon squatted on his haunches in the corner of the room, holding the palette knife in both hands. 'I'll be back at midday and if you don't have the money by then, guess what that might mean.'

He walked out the room laughing. He pocketed the key from the butchered lock and left the door open.

By mid-morning the room was empty.

Klimt was the first to step down from the cart when it arrived at the castle gates. He tossed the cases out and then followed, jumping onto the cobbles. Egon helped an elderly lady climb down from the tailpiece, and when the trailer was empty the driver cracked the reins and the horses pulled away. Klimt and Valerie paused, breathing in the clean country air and watching Egon cross the small bridge into the heart of the fortified residence. Then they set off after him, walking side by side, Valerie looking to the left, Klimt to the right.

As they reached the bridge Valerie stopped, staring down into the debris-filled ditch that surrounded the castle: there, in the shadows, four ceremonial bears moped over tree trunks and boulders, tugging at their rusty chains. She stood utterly still, watching, until a call from Klimt sent her skittering over the bridge to join him. They walked in under the vaulted ceiling of the tower building and were momentarily drowned in shadow before emerging in the light of the first courtyard. Egon waved them on and they followed him through a series of passages and elaborate courtyards. Each space was more enclosed, the walls higher and the passageways narrower, until they had passed through the heart of the castle and arrived at the ramparts on the south side. Egon was already standing at one of the oval openings in the wall when Valerie and Klimt emerged from the last courtyard. He beckoned his friends over, their footsteps echoing off the walls behind them. They bent down, leaning into the slits in the opposite wall – the archers' defence centuries earlier – and looked out over the town.

The castle was situated high above Krumau on an outcrop whose serrated rocks morphed seamlessly into the smooth sides of the fortifications. A grey-turreted tower on the east side, painted in strawberry and cream, held court over the smaller residential buildings alongside it. Behind their glass were the ostentatious rooms of a withering noble family. Inside, the velour curtains had faded and the furniture remained unvarnished; outside, the windows gave out onto hills soaked in June sun, modestly cloaked in pink blossom; the windows facing south peered down at the summer tapestry of walls, roofs and washing lines which made up the settlement of Krumau.

The heart of the town was squeezed into the meander of a river, whose slow-moving waters had isolated a circle of land over the millennia. It was packed with low-ceilinged houses, their roofs similar shades of terracotta and their walls a collage of ochres: yellows, beiges, oranges and browns. Each building seemed to merge into the next as if belonging to one large interconnected complex. The streets were an intricate web of grey cracks and creases, a jumble of houses, shops and churches heaped together on the parcel of land. The river charted a line of dark green-grey around the settlement, one side forming the moat to the castle's south wall, the other spreading out into rich green banks. The furthest tip of the horizon was hazy with woodland.

'Which one is it?' asked Klimt.

Egon took Valerie further along the wall to a place where they could get a clearer view of the town. He scanned the settlement, looking first at the nucleus of buildings and then beyond the banks to the larger houses. He stepped back and walked to the next slit.

'Memory failing you?'

'Give me a minute.'

'Been paddling in the waters of Lethe?'

'Shut up, please.'

Egon moved to the next gap in the wall and scoured the town, tracking the line of the river, past the women washing clothes in the foam of the weir and further up to the pebble deposits heaped in the hook of the meander.

LEWIS CROFTS

'Was it in the middle there or up out the other side?'
'I can't remember.'
'Hurry up!'
'It was next to the river. That much I recall.'
'The river's everywhere.'
Valerie placed a hand on Egon's shoulder.
'Take your time. It'll come back to you.'

The townsfolk barely raised their heads as the threesome made their way through the corkscrew lanes, over the wooden bridge, along Rybářská street and into Egon's mother's house. They dumped the cases on the porch underneath the rickety roofing and Egon dug out a spare key from a brick behind the doorstep. He blew off the rust-coloured dust and it ground into the lock. Klimt and Valerie followed Egon inside, pulling sheets off the furniture, tossing up clouds of dust whose particles hung in the beams of sunlight. They moved from room to room, feeling the house give under weight its floors had not felt for years. A family of starlings had made a nest in the bedroom, their excrement casting streaks of grey and green across the bed linen; the imprints of their claws had left hieroglyphics in the dust on the windowsills and cupboards. Fingers of ivy had spread through window joints and reached into the room before recoiling from the shadowy corners; a couch bore evidence of the fevered scuffles of young lovers; the mirror above the fireplace threw back a fragmented picture of Egon, red-black spots of rust crawling across the glass surface and into his face.

Marie had brought Egon here only twice while her parents were still alive: first, when he was three, sitting him on the lap of an old woman, whose toothless mouth repeated *babička* at him. Then, several years later, Egon had spent a month with her, swimming in the river and running around the castle's courtyards with a sword made of two pieces of driftwood nailed together. When they returned to Tulln, Egon's father banned any further visits to his wife's parents: rural Bohemia with its misfits and peasants was not the place for his son.

Marie had returned once a year but without the children. For her,

Krumau was a refuge, an asylum to recover when her capricious womb cheated her again, whenever the worldliness of her husband became too much, whenever she wanted to wallow in the simplicity of life before trains. The visits stopped once her own mother had succumbed to influenza, borne into the town on the river's cold winter waters. Nevertheless, Marie still groomed memories of Krumau, entertaining the children with tales of the mythical settlement where she grew up. She elaborated stories of princes and princesses, dragons and bears, and Bohemian kings who valiantly defended the town from the castle ramparts; she spoke of the nymphs who swam in the meander, creeping out at night to seduce the husbands; she sung lullabies in the abrasively melodic tongue of her parents; she created epic tales around the butcher, the violin teacher, the cobbler, the silversmith and the painter (all of whom Egon learnt to know by name), building up the cast of a society her son would always know but would never recognise.

On the first morning, Egon rose well before Klimt and Valerie. They lay next to the smouldering fire, folded in each other's arms, their limbs interlocked under the blanket, elbows and knees jutting out through the fabric. He sat on the front step and slipped his boots on before walking down the bank to a small footbridge, over the river and into the heart of the town. He stopped at an open door and collected some dew off a windowsill, wetting his hair and washing a face still creased by a crumpled pillow. He went down two worn steps under a quintefoil rose and into the shop, scraping his head on a beam in the process. He rocked back and forth, grains of sand crackling under the soles of his boots.

'*Abyste neuklouzl, pane!*'

Despite the warning, Egon slipped and staggered into the room. The shop-owner giggled and then continued her discussion with an elderly lady who was loading eggs into a basket. She spoke in words at once familiar and unknown to Egon, a Slavic dialect which fitted snugly in his ear but failed to conjure up the relevant images: *malý, vlak, úsměv, tatínek*. When he spoke the words tripped out in urbane German and the women stopped talking. He greeted them both and – pointing – purchased a loaf of bread, some eggs and a stub of bacon. He heard their encrypted discussion resume as he stepped up to street level.

When Egon returned to the house much later that morning, Klimt and Valerie were sitting on chairs in front of the stove, the ornately carved legs of a kitchen stool sticking out of the flames. The kitchen drawers hung open and the table was castellated with bottles and glasses, crystals of evaporated vermilion around their bases.

'Glad to see you've settled in.'

'We invited Bacchus round for the morning,' said Klimt, a glass pinched between forefinger and thumb.

Valerie got up and moved over to the couch, pulling a rug around her naked body. She raised her glass to Egon. He shook his head.

'Where did you get all that from?'

'You know those rusty old shears out on the terrace? Well, we traded them in with one of the farmhands for a few bottles of homemade.'

'And the bread and coffee? The soap?'

'Elixir, my friend! Elixir!' Klimt raised his glass and emptied its contents. 'The only path to true inspiration.' Klimt's shoulders shook as the wine worked its way through his body. 'And besides, you said you'd pick up the bare necessities.' He gestured towards the bundle under Egon's arm. 'Very good of you.'

'We should be sparing with the firewood,' said Egon firmly. He put down the supplies and ran his finger through a puddle of red wine on the table.

'For God's sake relax. You've nothing to worry about now. You're away from it all!' Klimt poured him a glass of wine. 'Take some medicine, you'll feel much better. There's time for everything.' He danced to the couch where Valerie was curled up. She opened her blanket and Klimt ducked under her arms, sliding up against her warmth. 'No one will find you here.'

'We could go swimming later, if you like,' she said, her voice quiet like a girl's. 'You could watch me dive off the bridge. I'm an excellent diver, aren't I, Gustav?'

'Indeed you are, darling.'

She ran a hand over Klimt's balding head and down his neck, her fingers innocent, their placement assured. Egon had seen her grow up on the fringes of his friendship with the elder painter to whom she was, at various stages, model, mistress and maid. While others came and went, Valerie had always been in the studio, both as a young girl and later as a growing woman, her feet falling more heavily on the steps as she ran down to open the front door. The ribbons she had worn in her hair were gone and now her natural reddish-brown colour spun out over the grey blanket was enough to catch the eye of its own accord. In some moments she was innocent and childlike, hanging around Klimt's neck like a pre-pubescent admirer unskilled in the tenderness of her touch; in other moments she was an experienced seductress, aware of the dimensions of her muscular body, striking seemingly natural poses which would have middle-aged townsfolk craning their necks in the street. Her jaw no longer bore the petite chin of childhood, now statuesque and occasionally heavy when caught from the wrong angle. Her eyes were a shallow blue, tucked into the hollows either side of an aquiline nose. She passed her hand over the rough leather of the seat and smiled at Egon. Her pupils were pinpricks in the azure of her eyes.

'It's a lovely day for it.'

Egon turned away and walked into the kitchen.

'Have it your way,' added Klimt. 'We're only here for your sake.'

He studied the town-whore, just as he had studied others before, carving out her birthmarks like knots in old wood, pulling the skin tight across her joints with bold brush-strokes. Klimt directed him from the bed at the back of the room, recommending colours, demonstrating angles. But Egon found himself choking at the sight of her lived-in womanliness. He hesitated each time he dipped the tip off his brush into the seething black to layer on bands of raucous hair. He stopped and started, hurrying through the work, flicking his brush against the paper, adumbrating the clefts of her pubis and armpits.

With gritted teeth Egon added an untainted cream wall behind the woman's body, editing out the cracked plaster, the stains and the mouse hole. He accentuated her breasts, pulling out their tips and raising them an inch above their middle-aged sag. But he did not paint her eyes, hiding them instead below a wide-brimmed hat, which he asked her to pull down over her face. As the whore sat, she gradually eased her legs open, only to shut them again when Egon snapped at her. She laughed it off, cackling at Klimt and Valerie who languished in an opiate daze on the bed behind the painter.

Egon laid his brush on the edge of the easel, wiped his hands down the front of his smock and sat on a chair in the corner of the room. Klimt looked up, blinked and then slumped back onto the bed.

'Is that all?' asked the prostitute. Egon took a dress off the back of the chair and threw it at her. 'So, we're done?'

'You can go.' He took some coins out of Klimt's jacket and held them out to her. She raised her arms, dropped the dress over her body and took the money. 'There's no need to come back again, thank you.'

'But he's asked me to come back tomorrow.'

'Well, this is my house and you shouldn't listen to him.'

'I'm not here for the fun of it, you know.'

'Look, I'm sorry to have troubled you. But there won't be any more of this from now on. Now please finish getting dressed and leave.'

'What is it with you lot?'

'Just get out!' shouted Egon.

She spat on the floor between Egon's feet and stormed out. Klimt stood up, pulled a rug off the bed and walked over to the easel. He stood in front of the picture casting his eyes over its length and breadth.

'It will come back.'

Egon struck the brushes from the easel.

'No more… not here…'

'You just need time.'

'No more.'

'I'll find you a younger one. I saw a girl up by the church this morning. She would be exquisite.'

'No more! If you want all that, then you can get out as well! Go on, get out!'

Klimt pulled the blanket tighter around his shoulders and shuffled back to the bed.

'Don't you dare turn your back on me, Gustav!'

The elder painter looked back at Egon, smiled and collapsed face down next to Valerie.

'Patience, my boy,' he muttered into the pillow. 'It'll come.'

Egon picked the canvas off the easel and went onto the terrace. With both hands he hurled it out into the long grass.

'I suppose you think you're helping,' he shouted through the window at the couple. 'Waste your days however you want but leave me alone. Just go! Leave me in peace!'

Egon sat down on an upturned bucket and put his head in his hands. A strand of spittle fell slowly from his mouth into a molten pile between his feet. He spat, and a stripe of blood from his bitten lip flecked the floorboards.

Klimt and Valerie spent less time in the house as the summer gathered pace and the days drew longer. They frequented inns around the town, joining the burlesque plays of travelling troupes. Klimt's notoriety attracted revellers and admirers, a curious clan of townsfolk, pseudo-artists and social climbers who gravitated from bar to tavern until the night drew to a close and they returned with their leader to the house by the river. There they loaded up the stove with boot-cracked furniture and mixed dance with song with sleep with intoxication with flesh. Egon kept himself apart. He would rise just before first light and walk down Rybářská street along the riverside, listening to the birds and insects darting over its surface as the sun rose. Then he would make his way through the narrow streets as shutters began to clap open, and stop at the shop before heading up to the castle.

'*Dobrý den, paní Gottová*,' said Egon, greeting the shopkeeper, who appeared from the backroom before the door chimes had subsided.

'*Dobrý den, mladý pane. Ráda vás vidím. Jak se daří?*' She pulled a wrapped cloth from underneath the counter and handed it to Egon. 'Your usual, Herr Schiele.'

He felt the hard grains of the fresh loaf through the material and smiled as she slid an open bottle of Budějovické across the counter.

'*Moc vám děkuji.*'

'*Nemáte zač.*'

The rattle of freshly soled shoes on floor-tiles heralded the arrival of the shopkeeper's daughter. At the sight of Egon the little girl slipped past her mother, ducking under the counter, and ran towards him. Smiling with pleasure he picked her up in his arms, spinning so that her legs forked out like a swallow's tail. She kissed him on the cheek.

'Can I come again today, Herr Schiele? Please. Can I?'

Her voice dealt adroitly with the inflections of German. Egon flattened down her fringe, straightening it across the level of her eyebrows.

'You'd better ask your mother first.'

Egon turned so that the girl could face the shopkeeper while still remaining in his arms. She spoke quickly, breathing in the wrong places, abandoning the rest of her sentence to end with just *prosím, prosím, němčinu, prosím, prosím, mamčo*.

'You go up to castle like always?' asked the shopkeeper, biting at the German words as she spoke.

'Near the rose garden. I'll be there most of the day.'

'You must say when you want that she stays here.'

'Honestly, she's no distraction. She's always good as gold.'

She switched back into Czech, issuing stern instructions to her daughter, who lifted her chin with exaggerated nods, blew a kiss, climbed down out of Egon's arms and ran out the door.

'I'll drop her back here when I'm finished, Frau Gott.'

'Not later than four.'

Egon walked out the door, the wetness of spilt beer spreading down the front of his trousers. Jana skipped as she followed him down the lane, her legs taking two strides to his one.

Egon spent most of the daylight hours up on the castle walls, searching out new perspectives of the town's stooped buildings. From his viewpoint, he could follow the tight curve of the meander, jerking left and swooping across the tapestry of rooftops. The settlement was like a human body: its joints angular, its arcs gentle. In the early morning as the sun crept over the castle and fell on the houses, their wood and walls would creak and expand, like limbs stretching underneath a mantle of light. Windows would open and the clink of cutlery on crockery would chime out into the streets while housewives readied their breakfast tables. Next would come the thump of boots on cobbles as the men trudged off to work. Mid-morning, young girls would pour down to the riverside by the wooden footbridge, baskets of laundry in their hands. As the wind swirled in the valley a fragment of song or chatter would sometimes be swept up to the castle top, where Egon would pause to listen, his brush poised above the paper.

Although the songs tempted him, Egon would not climb down to the town. The stigmata of exile still throbbed in his palms. He stared out from the walls, brush in hand, a blank paper on his lap. The settlement was like a dying body, a jumbled heap of rachitic limbs trapped in the autumn of life. For him, the walls were weatherworn and crumbling, stooped like drunks supporting each other; the roofs sagged like worn hats; the streets were lonely. Every day he would watch the town unfold in front of him through the sunshine hours before folding back up again as night fell, a circuit of life and death which followed his moods. To Egon, Krumau crouched next to the dark waters of the Moldau, as if it might submerge at any moment.

Jana accompanied him all day. In the mornings, bright with excitement, she would embark on breathless monologues about school, her cats, life beyond the town's perimeter, the ponies in farmer Schneemann's top-field, how strong her father was, how Jarda pinched her during class. At lunch time, she would dig her milk teeth into the hard-grained bread, exhausting her jaw on her mother's crusts. Egon would allow her two gulps of beer to help it down and then she would doze on the rug next to him, her head resting against his thigh or arm, her fine brown hair flecked with dust from his clothes, her chest rising and falling with shallow breaths.

In the afternoons, when Jana awoke, Egon would turn his back on the town to pace around the grounds of the castle, stumbling and striding as ivy wrapped around their ankles. He gathered wild flowers to sketch while Jana plucked fully grown blossoms out of amphorae. Egon would lean his back against a tree, the wind ruffling its leaves to reveal their lighter undersides. He watched Jana as she ran her fingers over the speckled centre of a sunflower, smearing her hands with pollen which Egon wiped away with his sleeve before she spoilt her dress. While she played among the beheaded flowers, her own pencil long since abandoned among the leaves, Egon would commit his own sunflowers to paper: their heads drooped, their petals dimmed, their dark cores spread to the edge of the flower, and their leaves browned with the advance of summer. Equally, saplings, pushing upwards for their first summer sun, ended up as frail lines, stretching like bony arms out of the ground. Meanwhile, Jana continued with her stories, applying new German words and expressions which she had heard from his own mouth only minutes earlier. Sometimes she would fall silent and watch her handsome, gaunt friend as his hands crept over the listless drawings.

'It's always the same things: houses and flowers.'

'Not always.'

'Why do you never paint people?'

'I don't do that anymore.'

'But why?' she said, drawing shapes in the gravel with her finger.

'Not even the bears. The bears are lovely.'

'I know.'

'We can stay down in town next time. You can paint some people. By the river. It's boring up here. You've done it all. Houses and flowers. Houses and flowers.'

Egon closed his portfolio and turned to Jana.

'Alright. Just once. Next time we'll go down by the footbridge. But you know your mother doesn't let you down there. So, don't be surprised if she says no and we come back up here.'

'I'll go anywhere with you.'

'We'll see.'

Egon lined up his brushes and pencils in their wooden case and slipped it into his trouser pocket. He emptied the water jar and screwed its lid on, stuffing it into his other pocket.

'When will you paint me, Herr Schiele?'

'I just told you: I don't paint people anymore.'

'But I'm not like that woman who lives in your house.'

'I'm sorry, Jana. I've stopped doing that.'

'Why?'

'It makes me sad.'

'But I want you to paint me. I want a nice big painting of me in my Sunday dress. With the blue bows in my hair.'

'Someday,' answered Egon.

'Today?'

'No.'

'Please!'

'Someday I will.'

She hugged Egon, gravel dust smearing over his white shirt.

Egon and Valerie watched as Klimt slit open the letters with the point of a carving knife. He pulled the fragile papers from various envelopes while Valerie sat opposite him at the kitchen table, her hands cupped together. Egon loitered next to the window. Klimt opened out two sheets, passing his eyes over the inked scrawl.

'Don't jump ahead! Read them out like you usually do.'

'I'll do what I want, young girl.' Valerie leant across the table and Klimt slapped her across the knuckles. 'You can't read anyway.'

Egon recognised Roessler's handwriting on one of the envelopes and grabbed the letter from the table before retreating to the corner of the room. Klimt was unmoved. He bent the crease out of the first letter and cleared his throat.

'"Dear Gustav,"' he started. '"I trust this missive finds you well. You are doubtless still revelling in the bounteous excesses of Bohemia. Oh, how we all envy you here! Lord knows we all fear staleness. And what better than the bucolic breast of Bohemia to suckle you back to full magnificence?"'

'What's bucolic?'

'Be quiet, girl. "Nevertheless, the Viennese summer is simply wonderful. You are missing a real treat: the sun pounds down on the parasol-toting ladies on the Opernring; the scent of honeysuckle hangs in the air and the city is alive with the furtive glances and bare ankles of summer. You missed a terrific soirée at Uncle Konstantin's last week. Everyone was there. Even Deneuve. Rumour has it that he was spotted in flagrante delicto with one of Zarncke's daughters…"' Klimt read on to the solitary gasps of Valerie, sighing with each revelation. She held the handle of a kitchen knife and spun its point on the wooden table, gouging a cone of wood out of its surface. '"…I hope your time away from the Empire's cradle of culture is feeding your artistic flame. Suffice to say – even in your absence – your latest works have incited the usual bifurcation of praise and aversion. Goltz always does such a good job at that. It is as though a certain kind of Viennese will never manage to stomach your flirtation with our darker sentiments; for me, you are still a Titan among shadows…"' Klimt's voice faltered as Egon stepped out onto the terrace, slamming the door behind him.

When Valerie came to find him a few minutes later he was sitting on an upturned bucket picking dirt out from underneath his nails. The Bible-thin pages of Roessler's letter were crumpled in his fist.

Klimt's voice was still pouring out of the kitchen window.

'Oh my God!' Valerie hopped in the doorway. 'You'll never believe it, Egon.'

'Come back inside,' shouted Klimt through the window. 'Anton's got news – praise be to Hymen!'

'I don't care what that bastard has to say.'

Egon kicked over the bucket and walked to the other end of the terrace, looking down towards the riverbank.

Valerie shrugged and spun back into the kitchen, to find Klimt scouring the cupboards for a bottle of wine. She fetched three empty glasses from the main room, rubbing lip marks off the rims with a thumb while Klimt scuttled around the house looking for the corkscrew, pushing aside piles of streaked plates, eventually giving up and forcing the cork in with the handle of a knife.

'He's cut the announcement out of the paper,' Valerie shouted through the window to Egon, looking back into the envelope. She held it aloft and then gave it to Klimt. 'What's it say? What's it say?'

'"On August 14 in the Christuskirche…"'

'Where's that?'

'It's in Hietzing, darling. Now can I please go on?'

'Yes. Yes.'

'"…Herr Anton Gottlieb Peschka of Hietzing…"'

'Gottlieb? I never knew.'

'Will you please…?'

'Sorry.'

'"…of Hietzing, Vienna, graphic artist and portrait painter, will marry Gertrude Schiele, daughter of Adolf Eugen Schiele of Tulln (stationmaster Imperial Austrian Railways; deceased) and his wife Marie. Pater Rudolf Schering will preside over the ceremony."'

She ran to the terrace waving the clipping in the air.

'If it hadn't been for you…'

Klimt followed her out through the back door, bearing three glasses of wine, crimson streaks down their sides, trickling over his hands and onto the floorboards.

'That was last week,' said Klimt to an empty terrace.

Egon awoke two days later and crawled up on the planks of the footbridge. His pockets were laden with stones and his head distended with cheap schnapps. He rolled over and eased himself up, wiping the dew off his face and hair, straightening his twisted trouser legs, pulling splinters out of his jacket sleeves. He sat with his back against the side of the bridge, looking up at the sky, blinking through blood-shot eyes. A stone dropped out of his jacket pocket onto the bridge, rolling off the boards and into the water. Slowly, he removed more stones one by one from each of his pockets, lobbing them over the side into the slow-moving waters. At his feet was a piece of rope wrapped clumsily around a metal bar – once a section of locomotive drive shaft – its knot abandoned. When he picked the final stone out of his jacket pocket he found Roessler's crumpled letter at the bottom. He unfolded the sheets of sodden paper, the ink having run, and rubbed his eyes. He laid each of the sheets out on the bridge, weighing them down with small pebbles. He closed his eyes and waited for the morning breeze to dry the letter.

As Egon finished the first page his stomach contracted, bilious vomit dribbling down the front of his shirt. He wiped his mouth with the back of his sleeve and read on, Roessler's measured prose recounting the wedding guest list, the opulent décor and the gifts. He paused, stood up and hung over the bridge's railings, looking at his murky reflection in the water below. He waited, half-expecting a tear to drop into his mirror image, but his eyes were too bloated to cry. He scrunched the first sheet in his hand and let it go: it floated, bobbing on the ripples, before growing heavy and sinking into the shadowy waters.

He picked up the second sheet, flicking the stone into the water with the tip of his shoe, and read on. *Your minor indiscretions are forgotten: merely the recklessness of youth. Collectors have moved on, courting the Academy's latest batch of talentless, production-line epigones. None of them have your gift, none of them see the world as you do, but they are here, right at the heart of it all, milling around with the kinds of people you so despise but on whom you are ultimately dependent. Collectors are buying their simulacra for lack of choice. Just one of your most paltry sketches would wipe away this mediocrity. Just one! But where is it? Where is that simple scribbling from your hand? Where is it? All the hard work you have done to establish yourself, to create a new art – it's all going to waste. Vienna misses you. We all miss you. I miss you. Gustav tells us nothing of your progress. He writes only of countryside idylls and simple folk. Please write. We are so worried.*

Egon rolled up the letter into a ball and held his hand over the side of the bridge. He left it there for a second before shoving the ball into his pocket and walking home.

When he opened the front door Klimt and Valerie were lying in each other's arms on the couch. Two young farmhands were asleep at the kitchen table. A third man spun misshapen pirouettes around the room, a bottle held in the crook of his arm.

'And finally Homer reappears…!' declared Klimt, looking up from his embrace. 'Gracious Calliope has returned him to us!' The dancing man stopped and shook his two companions at the table. 'We were wondering how long it would take for you to climb down from your mountain,' continued Klimt.

'I went down to the river.'

'To swim with the sirens?'

Egon walked through to the kitchen and drank a ladle of brackish water out of one of the buckets. It trickled out of his mouth and dribbled onto his shirt.

'I've never seen you like that before.' Klimt stood up from the couch, buttoning the flies on his trousers and slipping the braces over his shoulders. 'I didn't know you could… I mean it stands to reason… But anyway, even the tears at the end. Marvellous. The glory of the epic tradition. The power of slivovice.'

'Just forget it.'

'They were dumbstruck, of course. I mean no one had a clue… they'd give this summer's harvest to see it again. They've been asking me to persuade you to join the troupe… but I won't let them have you, my dear Apollo! You serve a greater god.'

'I serve no one.'

'You serve your art.'

'Bullshit,' spurted one of the men at the table. He thrust his arm around his companion's shoulder and they both launched into song.

Valerie threw back the blanket and danced around the room, darting from foot to foot in time with the fists banged on the kitchen table. Klimt joined Egon out on the terrace.

'Wherever did you learn that?' he asked.

Egon's head dropped, his face burying itself in cupped hands.

'School,' he mumbled.

'Even with all the different voices?'

'Can we just please forget it?'

'It was exceptional.'

'You're the one always spouting the classics.'

'But to perform like you? Not a slither of a divine chance. That's not the species of wisdom I learnt at school.'

'I'm not in the mood, Gustav.'

The two men sat on the terrace listening to the vulgar chants inside, hearing Valerie's cracked contralto whistle above the men's bass. They watched as the sun crept over the tops of the houses.

'Your little fairy woke us up yesterday.' Klimt moved to the side of the terrace and began urinating into a bush.

'What did she want?'

'Same as the rest of us. To know where in heavens you'd been. No one had so much as glimpsed you since you stormed off the other afternoon.'

'I don't have to tell you where I spend my nights and days.'

'Indeed, you don't,' said Klimt, fastening the buttons at the front of his trousers and turning back to face Egon. 'But you ought to tell the little girl. At least out of courtesy. She was distraught. Then again, I'm sure a performance of *The Magician's Apprentice* would win her over. That is, if it hasn't already.' Klimt blew the contents of his nose into a shirtsleeve. 'So, where did you disappear to? Some lucky farm lass enjoy the delights of your brush?'

'I went down to the river.'

'Hippocrene?'

'I'm back now.'

Jana ran her hand through the grass on the riverbank, tapping the pollen-charged heads of wild flowers, coughing colour into the wind. Egon worked at the sketch on his lap. He heard the soft plop of rounded pebbles dropping into the water. The wind swirled along the surface of the river, spilling up its banks, rippling grass and flapping the laundry which hung outside the houses on the other side. The individual slates on their roofs were lined up like the cracked spines of books in a giant library, each segment of terracotta a different colour. The town now seemed vibrant, the glorious insignia of stockings, jackets, sheets and dresses strung in front of the sullen walls, blowing forth from darkened windows, moving in the wind like spirits. From the riverbank, the town was no longer a jumble of roofs and crumbling walls but a tapestry of moving colours, interlinked and living.

Jana threw her arms around Egon's shoulders, looking down at the paper nestling in his lap.

'You see, it's nicer down here, isn't it?'

Egon nodded, stroking his rough palm over her thin forearm.

'Where is everybody?'

'Mass.'

'Won't your mother be worried?'

'She never notices anyway.'

'You should really be there.'

She let go of his shoulders and lay back in the grass, rolling onto her side and resting her head on folded arms.

Egon looked back up at the vacated houses on the far bank, watching the wind blow ghostly limbs into the empty clothes. He opened his box of watercolours, its sticky reds and blues – so well licked that the enamel gleamed in their cavities – and started to embellish the laundry which flapped in front of him. There was a tin clatter every time he mixed colours on the inside of the lid; his jar of water clouded with murky hues. He paused, looking along the bank at the laundry waving its arms and legs outside his mother's house.

A flash on the terrace caught his eye. Through the swirling fabrics, he saw a flicker of naked flesh. He watched as Valerie stood up in a bathtub, and Klimt rubbed a cloth over her shoulders and down her spine. He raised a porcelain jug and poured water over her hair, her body jerking against the cold, sending a drift of soap bubbles down her back. He took up the rag again, passing it over her face, digging it into her ears with a pointed finger. Egon was transfixed, watching Klimt work the curves of her body, following his hand as he pushed his palm against her spine until she leant forward and he could pass the cloth through the cleft between her legs. Valerie kissed him and climbed out of the bath – her toe dripping back into the tub – and the pair disappeared into the shadows in the back of the room.

Egon added detail to the pencil sketch of the couple which he had scribbled in the corner of his picture. He quickly finished the rough dimensions, put his pencil and brushes away and blew on the paper. He pulled back the sun-soaked straps of his satchel and laid the paper inside and looked up, feeling Jana's eyes on him.

'Did you have a nice sleep?'

'I wasn't asleep,' she smiled.

'But I saw you close your eyes.'

'Maybe.'

'I'm taking you back.'

'Show me your picture first.'

'I've put it away for now.'

'I want to see it.'

'Not now.'

Jana got to her feet, tugging her skirt straight and smoothing it over narrow thighs. She leant forward and looked at her hand, watching a swelling rise up under the skin, first white, then pink, then white again until a fleck of blood appeared in the bite marks. Egon stood up and watched it weep in the sun before scraping an indiscriminate nail over its peak. Blades of grass slowly rose from their depression underneath Jana and they looked down at the offending beast disappearing into a crack in the dried soil.

'Does it hurt?'

She shook her head. Egon took her hand, examining her palm criss-crossed with the pink and white pattern of the riverbank, a crushed seedpod lodged in her lifeline. He stroked her hair, baking at the back and moist at the temples, and lowered his mouth onto her palm. He blinked as salt drops were released over his brow. Jana pulled her hand away and went on ahead, her legs striding against the tall grass. He watched as she paused on the bridge and looked back at him, her eyes searching the houses on the riverbank, her shoes tapping on the planks. She walked several yards in front of him, hopping, stopping, pausing, skipping, running her hand down the flaky plaster of façades, stroking the mobile meander of a cat's tail. She waved back at Egon and skipped down into her mother's shop.

Egon passed Frau Gott the empty napkin and placed the Budějovické bottle on the table.

'Děkuji vám ještě jednou.'

'Bitte schön.'

She took the bottle and placed it behind her on a shelf. Jana ran towards her mother, pushing past her apron and the layers of self-tailored cloth until she felt the softness of her petticoats. She let go, the layers of skirt falling back like a curtain.

'Where were you this morning?'

'At the front, in the first pew,' said Jana, feigning sudden interest in a speck of dirt on her mother's skirt.

'Don't lie to me.'

'We were the first out. I was with Katka on the left.'

'If I find out you were…'

'She was there, I assure you,' said Egon soothingly. 'She hasn't stopped singing all day.'

Frau Gott knelt down and straightened her daughter's hair, brushing dust off the front of her dress. 'She behaved good?'

'I didn't go in the water once.'

'Hodná holčička. She was no trouble, I hope,' said Frau Gott, turning to Egon and smiling.

'Not at all. She's really come along this summer. She'll be able to pass for an Austrian most of her life.'

'That's not what husband wants.'

Egon smiled, waiting a polite second before moving to leave.

'*Auf Wiedersehen.*'

'*Auf Wiedersehen.*'

As his heavy boot passed over the sand and struck the worn step, Jana spoke. 'You'll never guess what we saw today, *mamčo.*'

She spoke in German, forcing Egon to pause on the steps.

'What, my darling?'

'We saw a girl bathing.'

'Now listen to me,' said Frau Gott, switching back to Czech. 'I've told you a thousand times you can't swim in the river. I don't care what paní Rendtová lets her daughter do.'

'No, *mamčo*, bathing,' she interrupted her mother's Czech with German. 'In a bath.'

'What?'

'Look at his painting.'

'Herr Schiele! Show me your picture.'

Egon turned slowly, the sand grinding under his boots, and approached the counter. 'It's not finished.'

'I don't care. Show me.'

Egon turned the brass buckle and pulled out the sketch, pushing it across the counter with his index finger. She took it in her bony hands, flipping it over, holding it up to the light. Jana stood up on tip-toes and looked at the picture.

'I see no bath.'

'But, *mamčo*, we saw this man,' Jana paused, sniggering. 'They kissed.'

Frau Gott turned to Egon.

'Is this true?'

'Well, there was this… she was…'

'Where?'

'It was one of the windows. I thought Jana was asleep.'

'*Rybářská, mamčo.*'

Frau Gott threw the paper to the floor. 'Where you take her?'

'To the river, as you said.'

'And how she saw this?'

'She was asleep, I didn't know...'

'It was the people in your house, yes?'

'No.'

'The man and the girl? Everyone knows. You...' she searched her vocabulary, grappling for a word which was not there. She hurled a beer bottle across the shop floor at Egon. '*Drecksau!*'

She came out from behind the counter, striding towards Egon.

'Frau Gott, please. It's not what...'

'*RAUS!*'

Egon slipped up the worn steps and fell into the street. A beer bottle smashed on the ground next to him.

The late summer sun shone in through the terrace door onto Klimt's grotesque buttocks. He turned to smile at Egon, a brush between his teeth, a palette in his hand and pubic hair running up the curve of his overhanging stomach. He gestured for Egon to join him, pointing forward to Valerie's body on the couch, her limbs woven in and out of towels and cloths, foot-shaped patches of wetness on the rug in front of her. Klimt picked up a piece of charcoal and held it out to Egon.

'A true nereid,' whispered Klimt.

Egon walked past Klimt, knocking the charcoal out of his open hand, striking a black line down the elder painter's leg. He picked a shirt off the back of a chair and laid it over Valerie. She jerked awake, mumbling through dried lips.

'We're going to paint you together, darling,' said Klimt.

'Get dressed, Wally.'

'Don't you do anything of the kind. Don't move a muscle.'

'I would appreciate it if you would both get dressed.'

Valerie began feeding her arms into the shirtsleeves. Egon pulled the rugs straight on the couch.

'What is it?' asked Klimt, standing naked in the doorway to the terrace.

'Cover yourselves up.'

'It will come back. I promise you.'

'You look ridiculous.'

'I know what you need.'

'Get dressed, Wally.'

'Wally, stay where you are. Egon's going to paint you.' Klimt held out a brush. 'Come on.'

'I need peace and quiet, not a house full of lechers and drunks. Now if you don't mind...'

'Your paintings will sell; I know they will.'

'Put some trousers on, for God's sake!'

'People will know your name, Egon. I promise you. But you don't need that. You need something entirely different, something far greater.'

'I need you out of here. Now, will you...'

'You need something stirring; something to make you scared and infatuated, desperate and proud...' He ran a golden finger down Valerie's cheek and into the opening of her shirt, leaving a glitter trail on her skin. 'Come, Egon. Let's paint this delightful nymph.'

'Leave now!'

'It won't change anything.'

Egon looked up and down Klimt's naked body.

'Just leave, will you.'

'We're not going to abandon you like this. You're not ready to go back. Four months isn't enough.'

'I'm staying.'

'And you'll start painting again. We'll paint together.'

Klimt held out the brush again, pointing towards an easel.

'You don't belong here, Gustav.'

'What?'

'You have one week.'

# NINE

# HONEY AND BLOOD

Egon stepped over the gutter, across the pavement and up to the house. A swarthy man speaking in broken German opened the door – its grain gaping with the waxing and waning of the seasons – and directed him down some stairs. Uncertainly, Egon opened a door to a small, dark room, and stepped into a haze of steam and stale clothes. She was hunched in a chair, the shape of her body indiscernible under the layers of blanket. The light shining in through the door picked out a ring-clad finger. A candle was lit in the corner of the room, casting light onto curling postcards and yellowing photographs on the wall. She looked up, glimpsed Egon and lowered her eyes again.

'Hello, Mother,' he said, advancing. 'You're looking well.' He bent down and kissed her on the cheek. Her skin was wrinkled against his lips.

'Days, months, years. Makes little difference now.'

'It's been too long.'

'Don't make excuses.'

'I only got back to Vienna yesterday...'

She pulled a blanket around her shoulders. 'House still standing?'

'Of course.'

'Rendt wrote to say he'd seen some people staying there.'

'I was going to ask you but then...'

'It's as much yours as anybody's.'

'I should've written though.'

'When are you going back?'

'Tomorrow.'

'But I'm worth the trip?' She coughed and Egon held a handkerchief to her face. She dismissed it with a shake of the head. 'Get me something to drink, will you?'

Egon walked to the corner of the room where a jug of water stood, a curtain of bubbles hugging the sides of the glass. He poured some into a tin cup and brought it over to her. She took a sip and lowered it onto the dunes of blanket in her lap.

'The room's not much, I know, but Anton's uncle is paying for it. And frankly, I don't have the choice. The Serbs upstairs don't stop fighting.' She took another sip. 'Can't understand a word anyway.'

'I'm sorry I wasn't around to help.'

She shook her head.

'They organised everything. Anton and that nice man Roessler. I don't know what I'd have done otherwise.'

'I shouldn't have left you like that.'

'You've done it before.'

'That's no excuse.'

'I was hardly expecting you to come running through the top field and whisk me away in a horse-drawn carriage.' She paused, wiping the side of her mouth. 'There's no one left now anyway. Even Melanie's gone. She always hated that town.'

'She never writes.'

'Neither do you.' She took another sip of water and coughed. 'Married a tailor from Klosterneuburg. Poor girl.'

Egon pulled up a chair next to his mother and pulled the blankets tighter round her shoulders.

'I bet you no longer have the gall to ask for what it is you came for,' said Marie, watching him. Egon looked away. 'All that I have is in the drawer over there.' A crooked finger appeared out of the folds of her shawl. 'Take it. Just leave enough for this week's supplies.' Egon did not move. 'Go on. Take it.' Egon opened the drawer, looked at the small pile of bank notes folded in perfect squares next to verdigris coins, and closed it again.

Marie's eyes were still fixed on her son. She gestured over towards the tall mirror leaning against the wall in the corner. 'Look at yourself. You used to have such beautiful hair.'

Egon ran a hand across his scalp. He walked closer to the mirror: his hair was patchy, cut by his own hand; it had soaked up the odours of the river air, the locks dry and frayed like sailor's rope. His morning swim by the bridge had left traces of algae, and his face was pallid, the uneven sprigs of a beard darkening his complexion.

'His honeymoon present. God knows why I keep it.'

She was quiet for a while. Egon ran a hand down the side of the mirror's frame, thinking she had drifted off.

'He's not worth it you know,' she said suddenly. Egon turned and walked behind his mother, avoiding her gaze. 'I bet you thought back then that you would make him proud. Just look at yourself,' she said, craning her neck to see Egon behind her. 'You're from his stock. But that was nothing to him. Nothing at all. His legacy isn't worth mentioning?'

'Please stop talking like that.'

'I don't need to linger in his memories like you do. There's nowhere on this earth that he lives on.' Marie pushed a leg out of the shroud of blankets, exposing a ladder of scars up her shin and a patchwork of twisted skin across her thighs. Egon extended his hand, moving his finger towards the ridges of hardened skin. She retracted her leg sharply.

'Every time you and your sister got up to something. If there's one thing he couldn't stand, it was disobedience. It was *my* fault for not bringing you up properly. Every complaint from a teacher, every time you were expelled, every mouthy piece of disrespect from you was meted out on me long after you'd all gone to bed.'

She looked across at Egon. He went down on his knees, wrapping his arms around her legs, squeezing against her through the blankets and coats. She laid a hand on his back as he shuddered with tears. His mutterings were inaudible through the coarse fabric. She continued stroking his back, running her long, thin fingers over his jacket and down the sides of his torso, feeling the ridges of his heaving ribs.

'Up you get now.'

'I'm so sorry.'

'Your sister will be along in a minute. You don't want her seeing you like this.'

She squeezed his arm and Egon pushed himself up from the floor, wiping his face with a sleeve.

'She's coming?'

'Every Friday afternoon. I'm sure she'd like to see you. She always goes on about how she hasn't heard from you for ages.'

'It's only been a couple of months.'

'Since the wedding.'

'I never received the invitation.'

'She'll be here alone. Anton's away on business.'

'Please, Mother. Another time.'

'There won't be another time.' Marie held his gaze until he looked away.

'I'll be back. More often. I promise.'

'When you do, take the mirror with you. I can't stand to look at it anymore: not at my reflection, nor at the frame. Please get rid of it.'

'I will do. If I come back. When I come back.'

She looked up sombrely from her chair. 'You can always come here, you know.'

Egon looked around the small room: the stove crouched in a corner, the basin and jug of water next to the strip of window. He walked back across the room to his mother, leant forward, took her in his arms and kissed her once again on the cheek before leaving. After the door had slammed behind him, he stood on the steps outside the house for a minute, adjusting his jacket. He tucked his shirt collar in, rearranged the buttons, which he had done up incorrectly, and rubbed the tips of his shoes against the backs of his legs. He threw his head back and took a deep breath. Winter was flirting with Vienna and the wind carried the hint of the frosty night to come. He pulled the collar up on his jacket and dug his hands into his pockets. Inside were four folded bank notes. He smiled at his mother's legerdemain, half-turned to go back inside and then hurried off.

As he reached the end of the street, pausing at the market stalls, he saw her: she was walking slowly towards him, wearing a full-length black coat with six large, silver buttons down the front; he saw flashes of a red and green dress underneath, the lines of her hips fitting snugly to the coat's tailoring. He stood, feigning interest in a chestnut seller, and gazed at her hungrily. In the hollow at the bottom of her throat hung a water-drop necklace: a pearl held precariously in a wire frame, flanked by two yellow-red opal stones, echoed in her earrings. His gaze was drawn upwards, past a white shawl to her face. Her cheeks were full and healthy with rouge; tears hung in her eyes, filling against the breeze. A moment later and she had passed him on the street. He turned, and caught the flash of her russet hair before she disappeared around the corner.

Egon scraped the soles of his boots on the balustrade, clods of mud thudding onto the hollow terrace. As he opened the front door a mouse scurried under his legs, scampering over the lip of a plank into the grass of the riverbank where it was swallowed by the wash of breeze and swaying meadow. The wind blew off the river and up to the back of his house, bringing with it the hint of blossom sharpened by the chill of impending dusk. Inside, unopened letters stood to attention on the kitchen table propped between chipped mugs and corkless bottles.

A fist banged at the door.

'Is anyone there?'

A young woman's voice.

'Hello?'

He stood up and placed his ear next to the door jamb.

'Please open up if you are there.'

A fist. Egon moved back from the door.

'Please open up.'

'Who is it?' he asked.

'Me.'

'Who?'

'Wally.'

'What do you want?' he asked through the gap between the door and the frame.

'Please let me in.'

He unlocked the door, peering out into the street.

'Thank you.'

She stood alone, a suitcase in each hand. She wore a long, thick coat and a threadbare hat hung down behind her neck on a ribbon. Her eyes widened at the sight of Egon, his hair straggly, his face pinched and gaunt.

'I've disturbed you.'

'Not at all. Come in.' Egon leant forward and took her bags, beckoning her inside. She walked in and removed her coat, laying it over the back of a chair.

'It's not quite as welcoming as you remember, I suspect. Still, make yourself at home.'

She looked at the piles of sketches tossed on the floor and cluttering the surfaces. Layers of dust blunted the colours of trees and flowers, the papers curled and torn, strewn like leaves, the detritus of a past season. She looked over at the crude bed in the corner, its blankets still in the shape of the body that had vacated them several hours earlier. The couch was laden with clothes and smeared crockery.

'There's nowhere to sit.'

'You'll have to sit on the floor, I'm afraid. Firewood over comfort.'

Valerie knelt down then extended her legs in front of her. 'I've disturbed you, haven't I?'

Egon closed the door to the terrace and turned back to Valerie. He sat down opposite her on the carpet, putting a hand to her chin and raising her damp eyes to his.

'Don't be afraid.'

She smiled, the expression releasing two tears down her cheeks.

'Why have you come, Wally?'

'Gustav sent me.'

'What's happened?'

'Nothing.'

'Is he ill?'

'Not particularly.'

'So, he's gone some place?'

'No.'

'An argument?' asked Egon, puzzled.

'No.'

'Has the old bastard thrown you out?'

'Not really.'

Egon walked out on to the terrace and pulled a rotten balustrade out from under the banister. Its soft wood broke easily over his knee. He returned and knelt down next to the fireplace, pushing aside the ashes with the back of his hand.

'So, he's still in Vienna?'

'He told me that you needed something.'

'He knows I can barely support myself, let alone someone else.'

'I should never've come.' Valerie moved to stand up but Egon laid a hand on her shoulder and held her back.

'No, please. You're welcome to stay. I'm sorry, I just don't understand what he's up to.'

She pulled her legs up to her body and held her knees.

'I am to model for you.'

'He knows I've stopped all that.'

'He said you could sell the paintings. He wants to help.'

'You belong in his studio.'

'I don't belong anywhere.'

Egon scraped a match against the fireplace and held it to the corner of a crumpled sketch. The paper caught fire and he laid the balustrade on top, prodding it with a chair-leg. She raised a finger to her eye and picked a tear out from next to her nose.

'I'm a gift. From Gustav.'

Egon straightened the bedsheets. 'I'll take the couch. Now let's get some warm food inside you.'

He went into the kitchen and started opening cupboards and drawers while Valerie wandered over to the pantry. She recoiled as she opened the door, her fingernails grating on the varnished surface. Egon sprang to her side, laughed and then picked up a dead rat by its tail, flinging it out over the terrace into the grass.

'He won't bite.'

Outside on the terrace Valerie pulled a loose piece of wood away from the corner of the flooring and returned with a rusted paintbox. Egon opened it and she placed a finger inside, pushing the coins around and counting under her breath.

'How much?'

'About three crowns.'

'Let's go and get some dinner,' said Egon.

'But we'll need this to buy supplies tomorrow.'

'I won't be alive tomorrow unless we eat now.'

They put on their coats and walked over the footbridge into town. As the tavern door opened they were hit by the crescendo of violins and the cymbal crash of tankards. They were engulfed in the hubbub of a room packed with revellers, dancers and drinkers. Next to the door a large fire sizzled and spat with roasting boar. As they picked their way through the crowds, a gypsy grabbed Valerie's wrist and tugged her into the middle of the room. The crowds closed around Egon as the young gypsy, white shirt open to the navel, sweat trickling in rivulets down his chest, took Valerie around the waist, twisting and turning with her in time with the violins' erratic tune. He released her and she spun off into the crowds, bouncing off men and women, beer spilling onto the stone floor. Egon caught her and they made their way laughingly through to the back of the room where there were empty tables under low-arched stone-ceilings. A waitress slammed down two tankards of beer and a jug of wine on the table.

'Good to see you back, miss. Them out front have missed you.'

'Certainly felt like it.' Valerie gulped hard at one of the tankards.

'Don't mind me asking but is Gustav not with you this time, miss?'

'Not this time, Radka.'

'We'd love to see the old chap, if he ever makes it back.'

'I'll tell him that.'

'Well, I'll leave you two to it. Usual for you, miss?'

'Yes, please.'

The waitress waddled back to the kitchen, her ample rump draped in a stained apron. Valerie and Egon glanced nervously at each other and then looked away.

'You don't have to stay,' said Egon eventually.

'I promised Gustav I would.'

'I won't play his little games.'

'This isn't a game. I'm here so you can paint me.' She drank again. 'He said I'm not to leave you until you paint me better than he does.'

'You don't have to do what he tells you, you know.'

'You're already a better painter than him.'

'So, leave now.'

'No.'

Egon looked up as the waitress slid a board of roast meats and mustard onto their table. Valerie tore off a chunk of beef, stroked it across the tip of the mustard and dropped it into her mouth.

'Why are you doing this?'

'For you.'

'Not for Gustav?'

'I've known him as long as I can remember,' she said, chewing. 'I've very few memories of what things were like before I met him. Anything in my life that is worth remembering has something to do with him. He's like a father to me.'

'A father?'

'And more.' She swallowed another piece of meat and followed it with a gulp of wine. 'Like you and your sister.' Egon looked up sharply. 'That's what Gustav used to say. '"We're like Egon and his sister."'

'What's that supposed to mean?'

'I'm just telling you what Gustav said. Ask him yourself.'

Valerie tore off another slice of meat, cocked back her neck and lowered it into her mouth.

'She used to model for me from time to time.'

'Then there's your answer.'

As Egon ate he watched Valerie chewing on strips of roast beef, drips of warm juices running over her fingers. She tore the meat away with the side of her mouth, gripping hard with her molars and then ripping with the strength of her neck. They sat silently opposite each other, their hands and faces glistening in the candlelight with the trails of wine and meat juices. Valerie lowered her head into the crook of her elbow and pushed a lock of hair away from her face. She smiled at him with an uneven grin.

'So, when are you going to start painting me?' she asked, a morsel bolting down her throat.

'Nothing's changed.'

'Still just pictures of trees and crumbling houses?'

'I don't paint people.'

'Am I going to have to write to him to spur you on?' she grinned.

Egon looked back at her, his face taught and emotionless.

'I will not be forced.'

'We start tomorrow.'

As she lay out in front of him on the terrace the following morning, sunlight bathing her body, Egon adapted her imperfections. He widened the eyes which looked back at him, stretching them out into the elongated face of an icon. He softened the bridge of her nose, allowing it to disappear into the canvas, leaving two lakes of sky-blue dominating the top half of her face.

'I can see why Gustav kept you so long.'

'He never *kept* me. I wanted to stay.'

'How could he send you here then?'

'I wouldn't have come if I didn't want to.' Valerie looked away across the river towards the town.

'Keep talking.'

Egon watched as her lips moved back and forth, revealing crooked teeth like gravestones sunken in subsiding ground. He straightened each one on the canvas, producing a face more vivid, more striking than her real one, which he watched switch between three simple expressions: a smile, an indifferent frown, a toothy piano laugh.

In the following days, Egon continued to work, adding freshness to her sometimes hollow cheeks, painting her as both virgin and femme fatale, goddess and whore. Each time her face seemed more noble, firmer than the unformed softness of her teenage complexion. Her skin tone warmed and cooled with the hours of the day: in the morning she had full rosy cheeks, and in the gloaming she appeared pale and translucent like unblemished marble. She never became strikingly beautiful: rather her face was always – in the words of Klimt – "interesting".

They brought the house back to life over the following weeks. Valerie threw open the doors and windows; she went down to the river to wash the sheets with the other women from town; she cut down the grass in the yard with a rusty hand-scythe; she filled the larder with dried meats and eggs which she charmed off the neighbours; she rearranged the furniture, letting sunlight fall afresh on previously hidden surfaces. She took one of Egon's shirts and dyed it bright red, the ink remaining on the backs of her hands and in the crescents of her nails for weeks. She wore it religiously, rolling up the sleeves and tying it above her hips when the weather was hot; when the wind blew cold she would fasten all the buttons up to the neck and roll down the cuffs, retracting her hands inside.

One evening, as the sun set against a sky of water and ink, Egon returned home with a dead rabbit earned from the butcher in exchange for repainting a shop sign. In his other arm, he carried his portfolio and a box of paints. He arrived at the front door but chose to walk around the side and into the house via the terrace, leaving the rabbit hanging out the back. As he turned the corner he saw Valerie lying on a blanket on the terrace. He hurried towards her, thinking she lay injured, but then stopped as he heard the cavernous wheeze of her lungs. Her red shirt had fallen open and her face was pressed into a rolled-up coat which served as a pillow. She raised an instinctive hand to her face, scratching away vagrant strands of hair, and rolled to the side.

Egon sat down on the upturned bucket. He watched as she twitched at gnats buzzing above her and shivered at the wind blowing off the river, up the bank and into the kite-wings of her shirt. She moved her legs under the blanket, a strip of flesh visible between the loose shirt and the top of the rug. A suspicion of contentment played at the sides of her mouth as she slept, while her left hand cradled a breast inside the open shirt. He watched as the air entered and exited her lungs, first convex and then concave ripples arching over her rib-cage. She bent her leg until her heel pressed up into her buttock and then raised a hand to her reddish hair. It fell across her face and momentarily concealed her identity.

Egon undid his shirt, and stepped out of his trousers. He folded them and hung them over the balustrade next to the dead rabbit. He pulled back the blanket and slipped in next to her.

'I said I'd never leave you,' he whispered.

She stirred, nestling the crescent of her back into his chest. He kissed down her neck and over her shoulder, passing his arms around her waist and up under her breasts. She responded by reaching back for his thigh, pulling him closer to her. Slowly, he rolled her over – the blanket twisting underneath her – and manoeuvred himself behind her parted legs. He rocked slowly at first and then faster; her groans were buried in the rolled-up coat.

When Egon chose not to paint, they spent their afternoons together, dining on a frugal picnic by the river, walking in the hills around Krumau or weaving through the town's serpentine streets. On the days when he busied himself with paints and brushes, the taverns welcomed Valerie's return, beckoning her inside for wine, asking after Klimt and then posing questions about the shy painter who spent his days up in the rose garden. Several regulars from the inn at the end of Rybářská street stopped by one evening to invite their reclusive acquaintance up to the tavern for a drink. They looked over Egon's shoulder at Valerie wrapped in a sheet on the couch, smiled knowingly and staggered back to the tavern, their jokes continuing long after Egon had closed the door.

Steadily, word spread around the small community that Valerie had returned and was staying alone with the painter. Within a month the townsfolk began to recognise him in the street. The washerwomen greeted him as he walked over the bridge at midday; barkeepers and traders remembered his name; the bears looked up as he crossed the bridge into the castle courtyard. His notoriety was enhanced by Valerie; everywhere he went, she would be close by. As he walked down the street from his house, faces would appear at windows and oriels, glimpsing the dazzling girl in the red shirt. She smiled at everyone. She smiled at the old and infirm; she smiled at the youthful and innocent; she smiled at the adult and flirtatious. Most of all, she smiled at the innkeepers and shop-owners who would extend them credit before Egon had even reached the counter. People would frown, too, when the couple did not attend mass on Sundays. Rumours of indiscretions, of flashes of naked flesh on the terrace, would filter down through the men in bars to their chattering wives and their imaginative children. Everyone had an opinion on the exact nature of the couple's relationship: friends, lovers, siblings, heathens, urbanites, perverts – or a combination of all.

When Egon and Valerie entered the chapel one stifling Sunday morning, the priest stopped mid-sentence and the entire congregation craned their necks towards the door. The church air chilled their blushes as the pews creaked and the townsfolk exhaled disapproval at Valerie's flamboyant shirt. She smothered a laugh while Egon gave a deferential bow.

'God be with you all,' stammered Egon.

'And also with you,' replied the priest.

The pair shuffled out, bursting into laughter before the doors scraped closed behind them.

As they sat on the steps outside the chapel, holding each other, their bodies shaking with laughter, the door opened again. A girl touched Egon on the shoulder. He looked round, his eyes full of tears.

'Yes?'

'Herr Schiele?'

Egon rubbed his eyes with a sleeve and looked at the girl again.

'My Lord, where've you been?'

He stood up, opened his arms and pulled the girl's unbending body to his. He pushed his cheek towards her but she refused to kiss it. He let her go and her arms relaxed as she stepped away.

'You never come by the shop anymore.'

'I've been busy.'

'Is it because of *mamča*?'

'Of course not.'

The girl frowned, looking down at the ground and then across to Valerie.

'Wally, this is Jana. Jana, this is Wally,' he said pulling the girl by the wrist towards his companion. Valerie bent down on one knee to greet the girl. She turned her cheek away.

'Aren't you happy to see me?' asked Egon.

'You never go to the castle anymore.'

'I needed a break.'

'But you could still come and see me. You haven't been since she arrived.'

'I've been at home.'

'You're always there now.' She looked across at Valerie, pointing. 'With her.'

She kneaded the folds of her dress with twisting thumbs and fingers.

'Come on now. Don't be like this. We'll all have fun together. We can go up to the castle later. All three of us.'

'But I want to go just with you.'

'We can do that, too,' Egon said, looking at Valerie out of the corner of his eye. 'Please don't be grumpy.'

He spread his arms wide, gesturing for another embrace. Jana did not move.

'You can come round to our house if you like and we can sit out on the terrace, drink barley water, go down to the river…'

'*Mamča* won't let me.'

'You don't have to tell her. Just come over on your own.'

'She knows she's here. She told me not to see you. You're a "bad influence" or something, she says. Everyone's talking about her.' Egon turned away from the child and smiled at Valerie. '*Mamča*'s inside at the moment, you know? I said I was going to be sick so I could come outside.'

'You shouldn't lie.'

'But you lied to *Mamča* before.'

'Jana!'

'I can't come with you to the castle. She knows we went there. And people will see us as well. *Mamča* has told Frau Herold, who told the Mittelstädts and the Tichý. They all know about you.'

'Well, you'll have to come round to the house then when things are quiet. We'll sit inside. No one will see us. We can play together. You can tell me everything I've missed.'

She nodded.

'But I don't want her to be there,' she added.

'Wally's just a friend. You can bring a friend, too, if you want.'

'I don't like your friends.'

'Don't be rude. You'll get on really well. But just remember, it's our secret, alright?'

'I don't know,' she said, running back up the church steps, pulling hard against the heavy door. 'It's not right.'

Egon looked down from the castle garden onto the clutter of roofs and spires. He watched the townsfolk coming and going from house to house, shop to shop, stopping each other in the street, talking, arguing, joking. He rubbed his eyes and took a sheet from his portfolio, preparing to commit the lively townscape to paper. He flexed his fingers and the pencil hovered above the blank page as he listened to the hum of conversation, the rattle of cartwheels and the chorus of farm animals carried up from the streets on the wind. He placed the tip of his pencil in the middle of the paper, calculating where he would set the town square.

He closed his eyes and dropped back onto the grass. The colourful figures of daily life, which had captured his attention for an instant, vanished, as did the concerto of insects and rose-tainted fragrances wafting through the garden. He lolled on the grass, his senses overcome with the memory of the body he had left slumbering that morning. The point of his pencil started scratching at the paper still resting on his chest, as if blindly transferring the image engraved in his memory. Almost without looking, he proceeded to fix the picture of her body on the paper. He painted her from the marks she left on his skin; she had pressed herself hard against his body throughout the night before withdrawing her limbs as he clambered out of bed that morning; she had left white patches on his skin – a near perfect imprint of her body – until the blood flooded back. It was as though her limbs had left a series of indentations all over his flesh, a network of impressions and dimples, which, when taken together, were the sum of her body, a moving, living mass of joints, bones and muscle.

He started with her shoulder, the last place he had kissed before leaving for the castle. He sketched the line of her collar bone, adding the tendons, linking the shoulder to the elbow; then the elbow to the wrist; then the wrist to the hand and eventually stretching the sinews – which had flexed around his body the night before – all the way down to the finger tips which had clawed at his back. He captured her in a dimension beyond time and space; a zone where her gaze seemed both eternal and fleeting, where her skin was both pure and etiolated, where their affection was both corporeal and ethereal: an ever-changing muse.

He came down from the castle with a portfolio of sketches under his arm. A wheelwright looked up from his work as Egon passed, the hammering resuming when his back was turned; groups of school girls cackled to each other in small posses; a man carrying a bag of potatoes on his shoulder raised his cap to him; and several lace curtains rippled on the ground floors of houses as he passed. He paused at the door to Frau Gott's shop, thirsty for a cold Budějovické, but moved on, deciding on the tavern instead on the way back to the house. He sat on his own at a table in the corner, placing his portfolio on the seat next to him. The innkeeper brought him a jug of beer, drops already condensing on its porcelain surface. Egon poured it out into a tankard which he then drained in several gulps before pouring himself another. He looked around at the other drinkers, mostly men guzzling beer between the fields and home, the soil streaked across their clothes and patches of grain dust on their faces. They chatted, interspersing their conversation with belly laughs and fists banging on tables. Egon drank another tankard of beer and smiled to himself. He paid the innkeeper and ordered him to take the remainder of his jug over to a table of farmhands. They raised their tankards to him as he stepped out the door. He waved back and walked out into the street, listening to the muffled chants of his name.

Valerie provided for the daily groceries, bartering ornaments and broaches which she had fashioned from scrap and embellished with gimcracks Egon's mother had hidden at the bottom of drawers. Meanwhile, Egon's reputation trickled into the provinces and reached a local aristocrat, who commissioned a landscape and several portraits of his children. Egon duly obliged, waiting every morning for the carriage to pick him up at the castle gates and take him through the woods to the count's country residence. Egon sat in the reading room, the sun shining in through tall windows framed by thick magenta drapes, sketching spoilt children who refused to pose. After lunch, he would walk out onto the terrace and down to the French garden. He would wait a moment by the man-made lake, watching the bees fly from petal to petal, before taking up his position on the edge of the haha to paint the vast acreage of the count's estate. Most days he returned promptly in time for dinner and Valerie would be waiting for him, a bowl of thick soup and a doorstep of bread sitting in the middle of the table. Despite his hunger, he would first take Valerie out onto the terrace where they would embrace and tell each other of their day. Egon would remain silent, listening to Valerie as she recounted the mundane occurrences of her afternoon. Eventually, he would sit down at the table, his soup now cold, and she would take up a chair next to him, smiling with wifely pride.

Arriving back in Krumau one afternoon, Egon found his house alive with female voices and the tinkle of children's laughter. Entering the main room he saw Valerie, dressed in her red shirt, stretched out on a rug with Jana and another girl. They were surrounded by hundreds of small patches of material which they had sorted into colours like tesserae in a mosaic. Valerie, needle in hand, was sewing them into a larger cloth.

They all looked up when they heard Egon cough in the doorway. He bent down onto one knee and opened his arms. Jana already had an arm around Valerie's shoulder but with her encouragement, she let go and walked slowly over to the painter. He grabbed her around the waist.

'What's going on here then, *Janičko*?'

'We're making a dress.'

'Who for?'

'Probably for me. Maybe for Katka.'

Egon looked across at the second girl who had both of her arms around Valerie's neck. He released Jana and she went back over to the rug in the middle of the room.

'How long has it taken you to do all this?'

'Ages. She helped. So did Katka.'

'I see.' Egon stared at Valerie. 'You must have been working very hard together.'

'Katka and me pick the colours and Wally sews them together.'

Egon took the dress in his hands, admiring the patchwork of colour. 'Well done, girls. I'm sure it will be beautiful when it's finished.' He turned to Valerie. 'Would you get me something to drink, darling?'

She stood up without objection and walked into the kitchen. Egon followed her to the open window, the sound of the breeze drowning out their whispers. On the riverbank, elderflower blossoms swayed in the wind.

'Does her mother know anything about this?' demanded Egon. Valerie shook her head. 'Have you any idea of what might happen?'

'But they've come to see me.'

'And what if she finds out?'

'She won't.'

'You can't trust them.'

'Yes, I can.'

'And the other girl? If she blurts?'

'It's got nothing to do with you. Anyway, I'm teaching them to sew… and they're helping me make stuff for the market. They're saving us time and money.'

'You just don't see it, do you?'

'They like it here. They like being around me.'

Egon grabbed Valerie's wrist and pulled her towards him. 'How long has this been going on?'

'A couple of weeks.'

'Why didn't you tell me?'

'You're always at the count's.'

'Come on, Wally!'

'I thought it was best if you didn't know.'

'I need to know about these things.'

Egon looked around the house, scanning his paintings and sketches which had all been turned around to face the wall.

'It's wrong for them to see your work.'

'Why? They don't understand it,' said Egon in an angry whisper.

'They're cleverer than you think. I'm sure you were just the same.'

'Well, you are the same.'

'I'm not a child.'

'Seventeen is still a child.'

She raised a hand and then dropped it to her side again. Egon looked away, their breathing stopping for an instant, and then they embraced.

'I'm sorry,' said Egon, whispering into her ear through matted hair.

'I'm just keeping them company,' she replied.

Valerie led him outside and they looked down towards the river where mothers were washing while daughters took care of their younger sisters on the bank. Egon stood behind Valerie, wrapping her in his arms; she stroked the hair on his forearms, picking flecks of paint off his skin. For several minutes, they rocked against each other and then tip-toed back into the main room. Jana and Katka were asleep on the rug, their bodies lying on a bed of multicoloured cloths, their arms raised and interlinked, lying side by side; the dress billowed out behind them like a heraldic flag; their bodies were encased in a cocoon of colour, the white of their arms, faces and legs, pushing out from underneath their skirts.

'They ought to be getting back.'

'No, Wally. Not just yet.'

The faces of the count's children were smudged and bloated with Egon's hurried paint. He sat in front of the troublesome youngsters, committing the broad lines of their faces to memory so he could fill in the detail later. Similarly, he sat at the end of the garden, twiddling his brush between thumb and forefinger before walking back into the house, explaining to the count that the light was "just not right" and then demanding the carriage take him back early to Krumau.

He always took his boots off outside before taking up a chair just to the right of the window, the light shining in and onto the girls' bodies as they wallowed in half-sleep. He started by just sketching their outlines, hurrying their figures onto paper before Valerie – always around the same time – came and tapped him on the shoulder. He would protest briefly but then give in and leave the room. Valerie would rearrange their dresses, straightening their clothes, before she cast shadows over their faces by passing her hand through the shaft of light from the window. The dancing shapes would wake the girls from their slumber; they would walk into the kitchen where they greeted Egon eating soup at the table and then leave by the back door, promising to come back the next day.

Sometimes, Egon would arrive too late and the girls would already have left; on other occasions, he would arrive too early and they would still be piecing together fabric or trinkets on the tasselled rug with Valerie. Asleep, they would shudder as he loosened their clothes, a chill nearly prising open their eyelids. Egon would then straighten their dresses again, painting the creases in their skirts rather than the light reflecting off their flesh. When close enough, his breath would ripple their hair. Valerie would watch as Egon traced their outline onto paper, his arms more alive than ever, the colours richer, his breathing faster. She crossed her hands in front of her chest, a finger slipping through the layers of cloth, past the buttons, describing small circles around her midriff.

When they awoke, Valerie hugged Jana and Katka close, their warm, limp bodies moulding to her own curves. She kissed them on the cheeks, smoothing down their hair and rubbing marks off their faces with a moist rag. Holding the children in her arms, their heads on her shoulders, she stood up.

'Just another two minutes.'

'But they're already awake.'

'Just let me get Katka's face again.'

'No.'

'Please.'

'No!'

She looked down at his grubby hands and the patches of watercolour that had seeped into his trousers. She shook her head.

'They're so angelic,' he said.

'I know.'

'Absolutely irresistible.'

'Sometimes it's not right the way you paint them, you know.' Egon frowned. 'You know what I mean.'

'They're just innocent little girls, Wally: no signs of passion, no signs of suffering. So pure.'

'Well, some day we'll have our own, won't we, darling?' She followed Egon as he walked through the kitchen and out onto the terrace. 'Some day soon?'

Egon leant against the balustrade and looked out at the sunset of honey and blood. She looked down at the two girls in her arms and then shepherded them out the garden gate.

Egon kissed Valerie on the back of the neck as she prepared dinner.

'They went home early.'

'Again?'

'Afraid so.'

'Are they unwell?'

'No. They just needed to go early.'

He placed his portfolio on the table and collapsed onto the couch.

'You're not trying to keep them from me, are you?'

'Don't be ridiculous.'

'I just want to paint them, Wally. Nothing else.'

'I know.'

'Then why won't you let them stay longer?'

'They're not your models.'

'And they're not your playthings.'

Egon was late coming from the count's residence – a mid-summer's evening having produced perfect conditions – and he walked leisurely down from the castle gates into the sticky back lanes of Krumau, his shirt clinging to his back. He had missed the girls by several hours and ambled through the streets until he arrived at the inn, pushing the door open, unsettling swirls of smoke and song inside. He dug a hand into his pocket and fished out the five coins he had received from the count that afternoon. He was greeted by the locals, some of whom knew his name, others of whom just called him *malíř*. He waved away their welcome and ordered a jug of beer before retreating to a corner where he chilled his back up against the stonewall. He laid his packed portfolio down on the chair next to him, removed his jacket and stretched out his arms all the way up the wall behind him; a quiver ran down his body.

The beer moistened his cracked lips, hurtling over his tongue and into the pit of his stomach, a pleasant shudder easing its way around his ribcage. He ordered another jug and a bowl of goulash.

'Evening, painter.'

'Good evening, Jiří.'

The wheelwright moved Egon's portfolio onto the ground and sat down next to him. 'Long day?'

'You could say that.'

'Painting again?'

'How did you guess?' said Egon, picking paint from under his fingernails.

The wheelwright ran a finger down the condensation on the side of the beer jug, rotating his tankard like a chess piece on an imaginary square. 'What you painting this time then?'

'Children.'

'What? Like proper portraits?'

'Just a few ink sketches today. For Count Rosenberg.'

'Mind if I…?'

'Be my guest.' The wheelwright filled his tankard from Egon's jug and drained its contents. 'You don't have to feign interest in my work just to fill your mug. Just go ahead and help yourself.'

'Alright.' He refilled his tankard and stood up. 'Well, I guess I'll leave you be, then.'

He moved back over to the main table, leaving Egon in the corner listening to the raucous humour of the locals, their misogyny a front for devoted family lives. The farmhands were gathered around their usual table in the opposite corner, their songs soaring over the rhythm of tankards on table. They waved, chanted a lewd song about a painter and then cheered his name. Egon nodded to the innkeeper who took a jug of beer over to their table. He eased himself up from his seat and went over to the counter, fishing another coin out of his pocket and flicking it onto the bar. He bade the owner good evening and walked out into the street, digging his hands into his pockets, bracing himself as the air blew into the back of his shirt.

'Did they come today?' asked Egon, slipping into bed next to Valerie.

'No.'

Valerie rolled over to face Egon, laying an arm over his chest. He looked down at her reddened eyes.

'What is it?'

'I want to have my own.'

'You're too young, darling.'

'Says who?'

'We should get settled before we take that step.'

'But we've been here for months.'

'I mean financially.'

'And when does the count pay up? I can't wait forever.'

'Depends when I finish.'

'When will that be?'

'Sometime next month, I reckon.'

'So, can we plan for then?' she asked, sitting up.

'Why the hurry?'

'I want us to have a real family.'

'I'll start exhibiting again soon, we'll have some extra money and then we can think about it.'

'Not now?'

'All in good time, darling. All in good time.'

Egon and Valerie had been asleep for a little less then a quarter of an hour when a brick shattered the window, striking the jug from the bedside table in a shower of glass, clay and water. Their bodies were still warm and moist, the sheet scrunched around their feet at the bottom of the bed. They jumped up as another brick came in through the window, covering them in serrated hail. Egon pushed Valerie from the bed and hustled her out of the room, snatching a handful of clothes from a chair. As they crawled into the main room, boots thumped on the terrace and faces appeared at the windows, elbows breaking the panes. Valerie was pulling on her skirt as the front door split in two and a group of farmhands came trampling in. One of them kicked over the table, a leg snapping as it fell, while another swept the crockery off the chest. Grabbing Valerie around the shoulders, Egon pushed her behind him and turned to face the intruders. A row of knuckles struck across his jaw, folding his bottom lip over his teeth, and he fell to the floor with a mouthful of red and white. Valerie collapsed onto his body, her hands passing over his face. A boot struck Egon's ribcage, searching out the fault-line of a kidney, and he brought his legs up into his chest.

'Fuckin' pervert!'

A hand pulled Valerie away and more boots drove into his body. With each blow he swallowed a scream behind clenched teeth. Eventually they stopped: Egon was left wheezing, his mouth full of blood and shards of tooth.

'Get up, you pathetic shit!'

Egon clambered to his feet, cowering from the fists raised before him. He blinked hard, seeing familiar faces among the group of men.

The innkeeper towards the back had locked Valerie in his thick, dark arms.

'Rosenberg gets this stuff, too, hey?' said the wheelwright, throwing Egon's portfolio onto the floor in front of him. The leather file opened and pictures skidded across the floorboards, fanning out like playing cards around his feet. The room grew lighter as one of the men lit the candles on the tables and cupboard. He walked closer and held a flame over the pictures. Molten wax dropped steadily onto the reds and blacks.

'There's more over here!'

As the group of men turned around, they saw rows of canvases propped against the walls, some of Valerie, some of Egon, many of both. Their eyes flicked from picture to picture, scanning the dimensions of the bodies, tilting their heads to adjust the perspective, tracing errant limbs.

'You brought my little one in here?' asked one man.

'In this filth?' asked another.

A man ran towards Egon but was held back, several farmhands pulling him away to a corner. When they relaxed their grip he made a run again, this time towards Valerie. The innkeeper shielded her from his fists until the man was bundled to the ground.

'Whore!'

A knee was pressed onto his chest, squeezing the air out of his lungs.

'Petr, leave it,' said the wheelwright. He turned back to Egon, whose crumpled body swayed in a ring of angry men. 'This place has seen enough of you, painter,' he said. 'We're going out the back for a minute. When we come back inside, you better be gone. Take whatever you need, but leave the pictures.' He struck Egon again across the face, a drop of bloodspit spurting out onto the sketches on the floor. Egon fell to his knees. 'Filth.'

He walked over towards Valerie, the group of men parting to let him through. He slapped her across the face with an open palm and then ripped her red shirt open down the front. Egon looked up but lost sight of Valerie as the group of men tightened around her. Her shrieks were consumed by their tribal chants.

'Stop!' shouted the wheelwright. The room fell silent but for Valerie's faint whimpers. 'Get outside, the lot of you. If she's still here in five minutes, have your fun then.'

The men dispersed, laughing to each other as they made their way to the terrace. Valerie was crouched in the corner, her face to the wall, oil and grime deep in the grazes on her back. Egon pushed himself up, slipping on the bed of sketches beneath him, and crawled over to her on hands and knees. She recoiled as he touched her back. He whispered her name and she turned, sliding into his arms. He held her trembling body while the concerto of men's laughter came in through broken windows; smoke from oil-soaked rags began to waft into the house. He picked her up, pulling a cloth from the table to place over her shoulders, and walked her into the bedroom.

Valerie sat in the chair, still shaking, and Egon grabbed clothes out of the drawers and stuffed them into a suitcase. He threw Valerie a fresh dress which she held against her chest. He helped her pull it over her shoulders and slip her feet into shoes. Her face, white and wide-eyed, seemed to float above the dress. He took her face in his hands: her pupils were small, her gaze distant, and Egon held her head to his shoulder, whispering in her ear. Blood began to seep through the fabric on her back. Following his orders, she went to the kitchen, took a knife and the jar of money, put them in a bag and slung it over her shoulders. They put on their coats and hurried to the front door, the raucous voices still audible on the back terrace.

'Is there anything else you want?' whispered Egon.

She looked over to the corner at the red shirt which lay in tatters on the floor, its buttons sprinkled across the floorboards like tacks. She shook her head. They opened the door and walked out. Just before it closed behind them, Egon turned back, ran across to the chest of drawers and grabbed his box of brushes and paints. He scuttled out of the house, reopened the suitcase on the porch, flinging two skirts into the grass, and squeezed the box inside. He closed the case, leaning down on the fasteners, and took Valerie's hand. A light film of rain was falling as they huddled under the small roof which jutted out over the porch. As they reached the end of Rybářská street, their lungs gasping for air, they turned back just in time to see the first tongue of fire lick the roof of their house.

# TEN

# NOT PUNISHED, JUST PURIFIED

Valerie ran a hand down the inside of her blouse to scratch at a cluster of fleabites. Egon wrapped his coat tighter and laid back, pulling hay over his legs. He tugged at Valerie's arm and she rolled alongside him, flinching at the rustle of a scampering rodent. They huddled together in the barn, listening to the screeches of hens and the braying of a donkey.

'He has a house on the main square we could use,' suggested Valerie.

'Don't even think of it.'

'There's no harm in asking.'

'I'm not talking to him,' protested Egon.

'Don't be so unreasonable.'

'I'm not.'

'But he's hardly ever there.'

'Who told you that?'

'Someone at the market. I was asking around and they said that Leopold rents out the rooms.'

'Forget it.'

'We'll be found sooner or later.'

'Why don't we just move on to the next village? We'll be complete unknowns there.'

'We are here.'

'But Leopold…'

'They said he only owns the house on the square. He doesn't actually live in there.'

'Still, I don't want…'

'We can't afford to be any further away from the city. Think about your paintings.'

'It would be the same from the next village.'

'Egon, this place is as good as any.'

The next day Valerie went into nearby Neulengbach. Egon, his body stiff and bruised, slept fitfully until she returned. She had found work, and a single room at the back of a family house nestled in behind the village's main street. They packed their case, brushed the hay off their clothes, picked the lice out of each other's hair, and returned the hayloft to its previous state. They slipped into town and collapsed on the room's cold bed, exposing their skin to a different genus of flea.

They tried to make a new start. Valerie would leave each day before the sun rose to weigh vegetables at the grocery market on the main square. Meanwhile, Egon would stay in bed, getting up only to pace the room, running his fingers over the surfaces of the furniture, or sit motionless on a velvet-covered chair. They had just the one room, with corners tucked away in semi-privacy behind hastily erected blinds and curtains. A makeshift easel dominated the space, its splayed legs crumpling an uneven rug. In the early afternoon, Egon would walk down to the market stall, pick up Valerie and sort through the leftovers to take home. She had usually put aside several potatoes, two apples and some carrots, wrapping them in a rag which she would tie with bailing string. She always hid something else on her person, revealing it only when they arrived home. Playfully, Egon would go through the routine of removing her clothes, peeling away a blouse, unbuttoning a dress, until he found the fruit – normally grapes, often plums and once an orange – which they would eat together after making love.

Later, Egon would wander the streets of Neulengbach, recording every person he saw: the powdered cheeks of the conservative ladies, the grimy fingers of labourers, the rosy faces of children playing, the knitted brows of grandfathers sitting on street-corners. When he returned, he and Valerie would talk, joking together, arguing with smiles on their faces. After a modest dinner of vegetables and any scraps of meat which Valerie had managed to barter at the market, Egon would count the coins that trickled in irregularly. Valerie would drop her day's pay onto the bed while Egon consulted his notebook and letters to see when he could expect payment for paintings long since delivered. He would then lie back on the bed and teach her to read, closing his eyes as she went back through the day's letters. He laughed as she mispronounced the simplest of words, rewarding her with kisses when she completed entire pages correctly. Soon she moved on to the newspaper, sitting with legs crossed and the paper slung between her arms, wearing Egon's hat as if she were a Swiss banker, reading the day's happenings in her scrappy regional accent. Egon lay on the bed, his shoes kicked off and an arm bent back behind his head.

'Who's written today?'

'The usual: Osen, Arthur, Goltz...' she said, sorting through the envelopes. 'And Gustav, of course.'

'Goltz first.'

'Alright.' She picked out the relevant letter.

'Has he sold any?'

'Don't think so. I can't see any numbers.'

She passed the letter to Egon, he cast his eyes down the page and tossed it on the floor.

'Promises. Promises. Money not promises.' He looked up at Valerie. 'And Arthur?'

Valerie ran a finger down the next letter.

'*Dear Egon, I hope that you are...*' Valerie sucked her bottom lip as she processed the contents. '*... he says... that he is ... ang-shus to know if you are end-you-ring village life.*'

'Enduring. Go on.'

'*… the city is still your inspiration, my friend. If not a somewhat in-sal-you-bree-us one.* What's that mean?'

Egon pointed to an unfinished painting, propped against the end of the bed. It depicted the couple, naked, fondling each other's genitals. Egon winked.

'He wants to know when he can come and visit.'

'I'll reply later.'

Egon always wrote back in neat but uninspiring letters, thanking his friends for all their interest and concern, reassuring them that he had rarely felt better. Their letters left hanging questions and open queries which Egon refused to indulge. He simply wrote that all was well and they could expect more paintings soon; he would visit them maybe this month, maybe next.

'He's offering us money,' said Egon, tossing a letter onto a pile of torn envelopes.

'But we're coping, aren't we?'

'Anything extra would help.'

'We're always borrowing off someone or other. We don't need to keep scrounging off Gustav.'

'We're not scrounging.'

'You know what I mean. We're happy just the two of us, aren't we?'

'Of course,' reassured Egon, stroking Valerie's hair. 'Things are just fine. They will always be fine.'

'Let me help you with that,' said Valerie as the grocer's daughter lugged a crate of potatoes to the front of the stall.

The girl looked up at Valerie, her spine bent under the weight of the vegetables. 'I've got it,' she replied, her voice deep for a child her age. Her forearms were like a chessboard of bruises, her flesh tarnished by sharp-cornered boxes and the traces of an adult's grip.

'Not while Vati is here,' she hissed, and continued lugging the crate to the front of the stall.

Valerie worked alongside a foul-mouthed grocer and his ten-year-old daughter. In front of the girl, the grocer would spit schnapps-flavoured insults at Valerie, chastising her for tardiness or inefficiency; then, when his daughter was away, he would squeeze and press himself against her, forcing her into the edge of the wooden table, rubbing her with his loins. She would feel his humid breath on the back of her neck and recoil at his dirt-coated fingers as they ran up the front of her blouse. Nevertheless, she endured his behaviour, more concerned by his daughter's suffering than her own, and content to fend off his brutish advances so long as she could escape later to Egon with a few coins.

When the grocer took his midday break, Valerie would watch over the stall and speak with the girl. She was quiet at first, retracted and cold. Words struggled over her lips, starting in her throat before drying out on her tongue, ending up as puffs and swallows before she turned away.

'I'm his little helper.'

'But he takes care of you?'

'We take care of each other. Sometimes he's so tired he can't walk.'

'You're on your own?'

'Sometimes there are others. They don't stay long.'

For those rare moments while her father was away from the stall, Tatjana was bolder, almost cheerful. She would copy Valerie's poses and speech patterns, adorning her dress with broaches of dandelions and her hair with sprigs of parsley. It lasted barely half an hour before the church bells struck one and she once again turned sombre, watching her father meander back from the inn on the other side of the marketplace.

'What you got for me?'

Tatjana held up the leather purse she kept on a cord around her neck. Her father emptied it out into his palm, counted the coins and transferred them to his own pocket. He grabbed the girl by the hair.

'Have you been stealing from me?'

'No, Vati. Honest.'

'If I find out you have, then…'

'She hasn't, Herr Mossig. I've been watching her all the time.'

'And why should I believe a tart like you?' he said, turning to Valerie. 'You're as bad as each other. Get back to work, the pair of you.'

After the market had closed and the grocer had returned to the tavern with the day's takings, Tatjana carried the empty boxes home. It was only a matter of weeks before she learnt to slip out of the house, eloping for the afternoon and returning in the early evening to help her father up the stairs and into bed. She would take the back streets to Valerie's apartment, where she played while Egon was out sketching in the fields or in Vienna touting his produce. Valerie would brush Tatjana's hair while the younger girl tried on outsized dresses, loose-fitting blouses and a scarf that went three times around her neck. They would make trinkets: a wire bracelet, a string band or floral necklaces made from the petals strewn around the florist's stall on the marketplace. When the time came for Tatjana to leave, she would throw her arms around Valerie, who, in turn, would kiss her and wave goodbye, watching from the window until her diminutive frame had turned the corner at the end of the street.

Back at the market, Tatjana would flash Valerie a smile in between her duties, and her eyes would sparkle even as her small feet stumbled over the cobblestones.

'Stop nattering you two and get on with the bloody work!'

'Yes, Vati.'

'Yes, Herr Mossig.'

'If you spent more time working instead of fooling about maybe we'd have some decent meat for a change.'

'Sorry, Vati.'

'Back to work… and I want you home this afternoon, not out

making a nuisance of yourself. There're chores to be done.'

'I'm not making a nuisance of myself, Vati.'

'Are you answering back to me?'

'Sorry, Vati.'

Mossig slapped her across the cheek, pulling her by the wrist until his unshaven face was an inch from hers.

'Frankly, I don't care what you get up to in the afternoons out in the fields catching butterflies or pressing flowers or whatever else you idiots do, just make sure you do your chores. Do I have to do everything for you?'

'Sorry, Vati.'

Later that evening, Tatjana was waiting by the door to help her father's filleted body into the house, up the stairs and into bed.

Within weeks Egon's room had transformed into a gathering place for the village's forgotten children. Before long Egon was used to returning home to a room of boys and girls who bounced on the mattress, played with the paints and stroked each other's cheeks with his ox-hair brushes. Egon watched Valerie from the bed: invigorated by the company, maternal in the way she brushed the knots out of the girls' hair, straightened the boys' caps or cradled the younger, sleepier children. This time, Egon did not paint them. He let the children play with his materials, paint clown faces on each other and explore the dimensions of his cramped quarters. He looked on as Valerie played with them, watching her womanly beauty unfold, content to wait until evening when the room was empty and he had her to himself.

'You up there, you little brat?'

Valerie sat up on the bed, grasping Egon's arm. He groaned, rolled away, and went on writing a letter.

'If I find out you're up there.'

She stood up, moved to the window and looked out into the street.

'Open up!'

Valerie grabbed the paper from Egon's hands. 'He's outside! He's outside!' she gasped.

'Get yourself down here right now!' came the voice again.

The sound of a scuffle could be heard, and a wheelbarrow toppled in the street, dumping its load of bricks. Egon sprung up from the bed. He went to the window, pulling a shirt over his naked chest.

'There's no one there, darling.'

'But you heard him, didn't you?' She walked across the room and pressed her ear against the door. Then she turned to Tatjana, who stood trembling behind Egon's easel.

'Your Father's come to take you home. Everything'll be alright.' She licked her thumb and wiped marks off the girl's face. 'We'll take care of everything.'

Egon opened the door and the grocer strode into the room, his head lolling on his shoulders.

'You! Get home before I beat you in front of this tart!' Mossig's twisted mouth was cruel. Valerie laid a cape around the girl's shoulders and she walked into the corridor, receiving a slap across the buttocks as she passed her father. 'What do you take me for, you ungrateful brat? You'll get the belt and more later.' At the top of the steps Tatjana paused, looking back into the room. 'Thought you'd kidnap her, did you?'

'Don't be ridiculous,' started Egon. 'She just came round to get some help from Wally.'

'From that tart?'

Egon looked down at a small bundle of wool and needles lying on the floor.

'Your daughter was knitting you something, Sir.'

The grocer looked down. He lifted his foot and planted a soiled boot in the middle of the pile, grinding streaks of horse manure into the woollen fabric. His gloating face looked back at them; then he froze, transfixed by a painting propped up on the velvet-coated chair. Valerie stretched for the picture but Mossig pushed her onto the bed and grabbed it first. He turned round and looked at his daughter on the landing.

'You seen this?'

Valerie looked at Egon. Over the preceding months he had grown sloppy, unable and unwilling to conceal all his paintings in the small room. The grocer's eyes wandered artlessly over the canvas, the breasts, the crimson sex, and then back to Valerie and his daughter.

'Answer me!' he shouted at Tatjana.

She shook her head, moving behind the banisters.

'Nonsense!'

He stormed out with the picture, pulling his daughter by her hair down the stairs. Valerie ran to the window and watched the grocer drag her down the street by the arm, her raised feet barely touching the cobbles.

The walls in Sankt Pölten prison were cracked, the plaster peeling away to reveal moist red brick underneath. Cockroaches appeared in the gaps, their antennae flicking into the cloacal air before they crawled across the tiled floor and through a crack in the opposite wall. In places, prior occupants had scraped at the plaster with gnarled thumbnails, leaving messages for future occupants or current wardens, counting days, chiselling out indecent images. The door was made of dark wood, supported by two thick horizontal metal bars. There was also a metal panel at chest height, fastened by five bolts, which would open and close at mealtimes and whenever the guard shouted abuse into the cell. The letters M.S. had been carved deep into the wood at the top of the door. The floor was tiled but the individual squares were cracked and chipped, forming a mosaic of shattered triangles. A century of inmates had looked down at lethal shards fixed to the floor by cement and dreamt of the damage they could do to a guard or themselves if only they could be removed.

Egon's bed comprised a straw mattress laid across a horizontal slab of wood, bolted to the wall and supported underneath by two vertical struts. He had two rugs. In one corner there was a simple wooden chair on which stood a tin jug of water. In the other corner was a bucket with a cloth laid over the top. The cell was almost entirely below ground level, the single window barred and flush to the ceiling, leaving only a six-inch gap at the top where light could come in. The light was dirty and grey, refracted off the yard's cobbles and filtered through the filthy glass onto the cell floor. Egon took to laying his blue handkerchief out on the chair in the corner, a source of colour which he would stare at for hours.

For the first few days he lay on his bed, the covers pulled up to his neck, a hand pushed slyly out the side, his thumb nail scratching graffito into the malleable plaster. Later, he would push the chair over to the window and look out at the feet traipsing across the courtyard. He could only see the shoes of passers-by, but from time to time they walked close enough to his window for him to catch sight of an inch of ankle or the hem of a trouser-leg. Within days he began to record the different types of boots and gaits, recognising certain figures whose feet would pass by at regular intervals, feet for which he would invent names and characters, an entire *dramatis personae* taking shape in his imagination. Most of them were guards wearing the standard issue black leather boots with thick upper, but he learnt to differentiate the rolling steps of the portly senior officers (with their clean and straight laces) from the swift strides of the indefatigable youngsters (their laces twisted and frayed). Once he saw a hand reach down and tap a pipe against the sole of a shoe, leaving a sprinkling of tobacco debris in front of his window. He never saw the slender ankle of a woman pass by his window. When he stepped down from the window he would imagine seeing Valerie from his new vantage point, how her steps would roll with the weight of her hips. He played back images of her walking up the stairs leading to Klimt's studio. She had been little more than twelve years old then, her stockinged feet sliding lightly up the steps like two black feathers blown in from the street. And always he remembered those legs as a vice which wrapped around him every night with scorpion strength, relentless and unforgiving. As the light faded, he moved away from the window and climbed back into bed, pulling the blanket over himself and turning to the wall.

At night when the prison was quiet, Egon could hear the faint rumbling of far off trains passing through the valley, the rattle and whine of carriages on tracks keeping him from sleep. The rumbles mingled with voices and with dreams and with the scraping of insects until he would jerk awake in the night, his blanket saturated and the ring of Czihaczek's reproaches still in his ears.

As the sun set on his fourth day in the cell, the hatch opened.

'I've been told to inform you that Herr Mossig has dropped the charges.'

Egon jumped up, rushing towards the door. He bent down to look through the hatch. 'Let me out, then.'

'The authorities are going to prosecute…' the guard paused. Egon could hear a piece of paper being tugged from a pocket and unfolded with awkward fingers. '… on the basis of… *moral degradation and propagating indecent pictures*. There you go, you sick bastard!'

The hatch slid closed, cutting short a burst of laughter from the corridor.

He was standing on the chair at the window, looking out at the shoes in the courtyard, when the latch slid back. He had grown to recognise the slide and snap of the hatch closing and he sprung down and ran towards the door. The lethargic hinges creaked and Valerie walked into the cell and Egon's arms. They raised their hands to each other's faces and Egon wiped tears from Valerie's cheeks, kissing her fingers. They sat on the mattress, their arms interlocked and their bodies twisted towards each other.

'They wouldn't let me bring anything in.'

Valerie looked towards the hatch and then placed a hand inside her coat, pulling out an orange which had been nestling just below her breast. Egon let the fruit roll from palm to palm and moved over to the window. Briefly, he held it up to the daylight, admiring its colouring, and then deposited it on the chair. He kissed her on the forehead.

'Have they been pestering you?'

'More came once they'd taken you away.'

'But they haven't touched you?'

'There was nothing I could do. I'm so sorry.'

'Just keep away from them. Keep out of all this. Promise me.'

He kissed her again pulling her close.

'They've taken all your work.'

'But they didn't touch you?'

'They shout at me on the streets. And down the market…'

She broke off, holding a hand to her mouth.

'All this will blow over, I promise.'

'They've thrown us out, too,' she added, burying her face in Egon's neck.

'Wally, listen to me: I'll be out soon. I promise. Soon.'

'And if you aren't?'

'I haven't done anything wrong.'

'But the guard said they're going ahead with your case.'

'It'll be over in a few days. Then we'll move on. Milan, Berlin, Paris. Wherever you want?'

'We can't afford a lawyer.' Valerie's voice faltered and she looked away. 'It's all my fault.'

Egon pulled her head against his shoulder.

'Wally, please.' He stroked her hair, pushing the dampened strands away from her cheek. 'Have you written to Gustav?'

He felt her head shake against his shoulder. 'I couldn't. You know how I feel about that.'

'Goltz?'

She shook her head. 'Something arrived from Anton though.'

'Have you opened it?'

'No.'

'Swear to me you will tear it up. Swear to me.'

She took Egon's hand. 'I wrote to Arthur instead.'

'When?'

'As soon as you were arrested.'

'Clever girl.'

'Something arrived yesterday.'

'And?'

'He'll be here as soon as possible.'

Egon kissed the crown of her head and they fell back onto the mattress. He pulled a rug over their legs.

'Everything's going to be fine. I promise.' He ran his hands through Valerie's hair, gripping the muscles at the base of her neck. 'Last night I dreamt of Trieste. Of the sea. Of expanses. I was painting it all in my mind. A plump-hulled ship, bobbing on the pulse of the Adriatic. And you on board. Your legs crossing and uncrossing as you slept. We'll leave. I promise. To distant islands.'

The keys jangled at the door and they both sat up. The door swung open.

'Haven't disturbed you two, have I?' asked the guard, not expecting an answer. 'Right, young lady. Time's up. Out you get. Unless you want to buy yourself an extra ten minutes,' he added, cackling to himself.

Egon and Valerie stood up and embraced.

'I'll come back as soon as I can.'

Egon smiled, his lips tight and down-turned, his eyes moist. Valerie left the cell, the guard watching her as she passed, his gaze remaining on her as she walked away from him up the corridor.

'Nice one you got there, hey?' he said before slamming the door closed. 'Pity you can't enjoy it.'

The walking stick tick-tocked down the corridor and tapped at the cell door. The latch was pulled back and the guard gestured for Roessler to enter. He walked in and undid the central button on his jacket, releasing a mound of stomach from its tailored constraints.

Egon stood up to greet him and they shook hands.

'A sorry business. A sorry business indeed.'

'I'm grateful you've come.'

'That fillette of yours implied you were in dire straits. Poor thing.' Roessler walked over to the window, avoiding the bucket. 'I've got my watchful eye on her though. Don't you worry. Hidden her away in a boarding house on the edge of town.' He looked out at the feet passing by. 'She's very fond of you, you know.'

'I'm grateful to her.'

Roessler turned back from the window and faced Egon.

'I passed by the magistrate's office earlier. Despicable fellow. A country philistine and an old soak. He said you are to be prosecuted for propagating indecent pictures.'

'So I hear.'

'Heathens! Oh, I shan't let it happen. I guarantee you. They wouldn't know a Titian if it bit them on the nose.' Roessler dabbed his forehead with a silk handkerchief.

Egon turned away, moving to the chair in the corner. 'I'm afraid I can't pay you, Arthur.'

'It has been taken care of, my friend. Almost.' Egon looked up at him, shuffling on the chair as Roessler paced back and forth. 'I can cover my own expenses, and I will waive the fee… in return for… for some samples.'

'Take anything you want.'

'Oh, I don't think we need to go that far.'

'I should warn you though: everything's been confiscated.'

'A minor setback perhaps, but not insurmountable. I'm sure you'll be able to knock up some new works when we get you out of here. Shall we say… three canvases and six aquarelles over the next twelve months? How does that suit you?'

'Fine.'

'If that's too much we can either extend the time or lower the number.'

'You'll have your paintings in good time.'

They shook hands again. Roessler picked up a small leather

document case which he had left on the floor. 'Well, we better get started then.'

'Where shall I begin? With the arrest or earlier?'

'No, no, no. Just legal formalities and judicial obloquy. I'll do all that. I meant the paintings.' Roessler took a wad of paper, two pencils, two brushes and three blocks of watercolour paint out of his bag and handed them to Egon. 'Just remember: don't throw anything away. I want to see it all. I don't care if you think it is only worthy of the bin.'

'Thank you.'

'Now, there's no need to get vexed by the case. I'll handle all that. You just concentrate on getting some work done. Your hearing is late next week. It may be delayed by a day or two, but they won't have reason to keep you any longer.' Roessler bowed gracefully, closed his bag and walked to the door. 'I will come back again in the next few days once I have gone through the papers and we can discuss any outstanding points. Stay well, Egon.'

When the door closed behind Roessler and the guard had shuffled out, Egon sat back down on his bed. He closed his eyes briefly and then looked across the room towards the chair. It was late afternoon and the light had long ceased to come in through the thin slit of window. Valerie's orange sat on his blue handkerchief: the room's only source of light.

'This has been the first arrest of an artist in the Habsburg Empire for over a thousand years,' announced the magistrate, his voice coarse with decades of pipe smoking. 'I hope the defendant feels suitably ashamed.'

Egon bowed his head, mopping his brow with a handkerchief passed to him by Roessler. The courtroom was muggy, the air saturated with the sweat of gathered crowds: a handful of guards, court staff and villagers. At the front sat the magistrate, his head sinking down into his neck, his eyes obscured by spectacles, his mouth hidden behind a bush of beard, a fountain pen rotating between his fingers. At the desk opposite him sat Egon and Roessler: the lawyer in a pin-stripe suit, the painter straining against a chafing collar. Egon turned around to look at the three rows of chairs behind him. Valerie sat nearby, dressed in a floral summer robe with her hair tied back. She smiled, kneading a cloth in her right fist. Behind her, Egon recognised the grocer. Next to him was an older woman and then the parents of other children who had played with Valerie on the floor of their room. Two guards stood at the back of the room by the door.

'As you know the charges of abduction and serious sexual misconduct have been dropped. Nevertheless, you still stand accused of moral degradation and…' The judge consulted his notes. '…freely displaying erotic nudes in such a fashion that… they might be seen by children. What do you have to say for yourself?'

Roessler stood up. 'As you can see from the testimonies submitted *inter alia*, your honour, the children were on the premises in entirely innocent circumstances. Tatjana Mossig and Magda Husmann have both testified that they went to the defendant's lodgings of their own free will.'

'Ten-year-olds have free will, do they?'

'Your honour, there is no proof whatsoever that the children were mishandled by the defendant.'

'That is not the charge. And that does not answer my question!'

'I can only repeat, your honour, that the children were in no way maltreated. Physically or otherwise.'

'The physician's report I have in front of me seems to suggest otherwise.'

Egon looked around at Valerie and then over her shoulder at Herr Mossig, who held his gaze before mouthing an obscenity back at the painter.

'With respect, your honour, whatever evidence of abuse there might be cannot be traced back to the defendant.'

'Are you suggesting, Herr Roessler, that another party may have been responsible for the markings on Fräulein Mossig?'

'As you are no doubt aware, your honour, none of the other children implicated exhibit any markings on their person.'

'Therefore, you are suggesting that Fräulein Mossig has somehow been subject to maltreatment?'

'Yes, your honour.'

'By the parent perhaps?'

'That is certainly a possibility.'

'Herr Roessler, that is a very serious allegation. May I remind you that this young girl has been eloping to spend the afternoons in the defendant's quarters where she has been exposed to pornographic works of the most pitiful degradation. That is the charge. Furthermore, if she was my own flesh and blood, I imagine I would consider her worthy of chastisement, too.' The magistrate sucked in air through clenched teeth. He removed his glasses and leant forward over the table, looking first at Egon and then at Valerie. 'I am fully aware that this wheedling was by no means a one-man show, so-to-speak.' He extended his pen, jabbing at Valerie. 'How would you define your relationship with that woman, Herr Schiele?'

Egon looked to Roessler who gave him a nod of encouragement. The painter cleared his throat.

'We live together, your honour.'

'I gathered that. Your cohabitation is infamous. But what is your relationship?'

Egon looked towards Roessler, his face blank.

'She is my model.'

'And how old is your model?'

'Twenty, your honour.'

The magistrate shook his head and looked over towards Valerie, raising his pen.

'Does she have proof of this?' Valerie looked towards Roessler and then down into her lap. 'I thought as much. Twenty is a little ambitious, don't you think?' He consulted his papers again, flicking back and forth past the same three sheets. 'Judging by the paintings we have confiscated, it seems to me... to my inartistic eye,' he mocked, 'that your relationship may have transgressed the usual boundaries of artist-model. Frankly, I find it deplorable that young children have been exposed to this despicable brand of muck you profess to be art.' The sombre resignation washed out of Egon's cheeks. He raised his chin, his eyes narrowing as the magistrate continued his tirade.

'You call that art?' continued the old man, pointing across at one of Egon's paintings propped up against the wall on a table. A paper ticket was attached to its frame covering the face of the model everyone knew to be Valerie. She was lying on her back, vertical down the length of the picture. Beneath the ticket, her face looked off to the side. Her shoulders were bare, the top of her dress pulled down. She had raised an elbow to the side, a gesture which had pulled a breast out from the lip of the dress. With her other hand, she covered the remaining half of her chest. Her skirt was gathered around her waist, exposing the sanguine flesh between her parted legs. The top half of the watercolour was predominantly white apart from the red-brown of her hair, the blue of her eyes and the red of her nipple and sex. The bottom half of the picture, however, was dominated by the thick black stockings which covered her legs. Above the knee the same red of her sex and nipples was repeated, stroked boldly in two bowed garters.

'What kind of hellish world do we live in, if the defendant can claim that is art? Art? It is debauched filth: a gangrenous wound on portraiture. What happened to beauty?' A globule of spit hurtled from his mouth as his lips struggled with the plosives. 'What happened to nature, the charm of life, humanity? Do you know what you're doing? Do you realise what you're doing to humanity?'

Egon moved to stand up but Roessler grabbed his forearm, restraining him.

'Your honour, I am turning humanity inside out,' cried Egon defiantly.

'Nonsense. There's nothing humane about that!'

'I reveal what humanity really is: festering, rotten. I reveal the truth.'

'The truth?'

'Each age gets the art it deserves.'

'And that's the truth?'

'I paint eyes like rocks in people's faces, like rocks because that's how they really are… lifeless, cold, death beneath the skin… poked at by the likes of you.'

The judge held up a hand as two guards stepped forward.

'Let the fool continue.'

'I show exploitation, suppression and rape. The same filth which hypocrites like you trample on in the street or fuck up against barn doors. That life which is far more elemental and tragic than any of your Godforsaken ART!'

The guards lurched forward and pulled him away from the table, throwing him to the floor. A knee ground into the small of his back. Egon's face was pressed against the tiles, his mouth filling with dust, a truncheon buried in his occiput. Valerie stood up and Roessler turned to soothe her. Herr Mossig, his mother and the other couples all got up from their seats and a babble of indignant voices filled the air.

A single strike of the gavel silenced the room.

'Sit down, all of you!'

The guards lifted Egon to his feet and held him before the magistrate.

'As stated, there is, unfortunately, insufficient proof for the mishandling of either of the children. I therefore sentence you, Egon Leo Adolf Schiele, twenty-one, bachelor, resident in Buchberggasse 29, property of the Gierlinger family, for the crime of distributing amoral works for the maximum period allowed by Imperial law: four weeks. Regrettably, since you have already served twenty-three days, you shall duly be committed to confinement for a further five days. I don't see that leaving you there any longer will do anything to pacify your diseased soul. In addition, I pronounce a public censor against your work. Furthermore, the one hundred and twenty-four works of vice confiscated from your quarters will be destroyed. And we shall start with that one,' he added, pointing to the portrait of Valerie which had slipped onto the floor in the struggle. 'Guard, take that outside, will you please, and wait for me at the marketplace. Make the relevant preparations.'

One of the guards walked over to the portrait, picking it up off the floor, and turned it over to conceal its painted surface.

'Does the defendant have anything to say for himself?'

Egon continued to struggle against the guard.

'Anything?' repeated the magistrate.

Egon looked up at him.

'It's you! You're the criminal. Art should be free. To restrict the artist is a crime; it is murdering life in the bud.'

A crowd had already assembled on the marketplace and a bonfire was roaring on the cobbles. Children tossed empty boxes and crates onto the fire, while stall-owners stoked the flames with long sticks. The guards pushed Egon through the crowds to the edge of the bonfire. He looked up and saw Valerie and Roessler on the other side of the flames, his pin-striped arm laid across her shoulders. Their faces were distorted through the heat haze.

The crowd parted as the magistrate approached, the offending painting tucked under his cassocked arm. He held it above his head, rotating so the entire crowd could glimpse its lurid image.

'May this be a lesson to you all,' he shouted over the crackling of burning wood. 'May the Lord punish all those with unclean thoughts! May the Emperor protect our land, our people and our art!'

He laid the picture face-up on the fire. The crowd moved inwards, watching the flames rise around the portrait, licking at Valerie's flesh. The surface darkened and then suddenly it was ablaze, the picture disintegrating into air and ash. The crowd cheered and Egon looked away, gazing up at the smoke swirling into the darkening sky. Roessler continued to watch as the cheap varnish on the frame bubbled and it sank away among the other logs and fruit boxes. The guards held Egon in front of his cremated work while the crowd jeered and stall-owners spat into the fire. Through the floating cinders, he saw a grey-bearded man in a high white collar and black cravat standing at the first-floor window of a townhouse on the other side of the marketplace. His hands clapped furiously in time with the crowds.

When there was nothing left of the picture, the guards wrenched him back, pulling him through the masses towards the jail. As they turned into a side street they stopped to let a cart pass by. It grated over the cobbles and the guards turned with Egon to look back at its cargo. The horses pulled a large semicircle around the square, paintings slipping in the cart as it pulled up next to the fire. The driver climbed into the back and starting hurling the portraits onto the ground. There was a roar as the villagers surged forward and grabbed canvases, frames and papers, tossing them into the flames.

'That'll teach you, hey?' said one of the guards.

Egon watched as a young villager on the fringes of the crowd picked up a sketch, flipped it over and quickly scanned the image. Looking over his shoulder, he folded it up and stuffed it into a pocket.

'Not punished, just purified,' replied Egon.

# ELEVEN

# SILK GLOVES

When Egon walked out of Sankt Pölten five days later, Valerie was waiting at the gates, the suitcase and an empty portfolio at her feet. Egon kissed her on the lips and straightened her hat. His back strained against the weight of the suitcase as they set off in the direction of the station, stopping at every street while Valerie juggled the portfolio under her arm.

'What about Paris?' said Valerie, standing on the platform, looking up at the list of destinations.

'Don't be ridiculous.'

'But you said…' Valerie leant in towards Egon. 'It would be easy. We could go into Vienna, take the first train to Munich, and go north from there. We'll make it in a couple of days.'

'Not in this state.'

'Montmartre, the Pastille, cabarets.'

'It's too far.'

'Come on. It'll be fine.'

Egon walked away from the tracks, steam fizzing above his head.

'Anyway, this place is full of…' Valerie turned around and grabbed Egon's arm. 'What's that word you use?'

'Philistines.'

'…full of philistines.'

'Gustav would be happy to hear you say that.'

'You know what I mean.'

Valerie pulled a postcard from her pocket. 'Just look at this: the Louvre, the *Eiffelturm*, the Seine,' she said, prodding the crumpled picture with a dirty finger. 'It's the perfect place for us. It's the perfect place for you.'

Valerie's conviction kept their spirits high for the hours of train rides as they zigzagged their way across the Empire. She would pull out her postcard and talk of Paris' Promised Land, a world beyond the cold floors of carriages and the broth of dosshouses. They climbed aboard the first trains they saw, dodging platform officers and ticket-collectors, sleeping in empty carriages, bartering their possessions and collecting food from the backdoors of bakers' shops. By the time they reached Munich for their connecting train Valerie's blue-eyed optimism had waned. Their meagre savings were gone and when the train pulled into the main station they stepped onto the platform exhausted.

'Watch the bags, will you?' asked Egon.

'Don't be long.'

'I'll just check the connection. I don't think the cargo trains go till nightfall.'

When Egon returned, Valerie was asleep across the suitcase, her blouse slate-grey with dust and oil, her face sallow with nights of uneasy sleep. Her dress fluttered as another train pulled into the station's dome.

'It doesn't go for another three and a half hours but we should check the loading bay now to see if we can get in before they notice us.'

Valerie shook her head. Egon picked up the suitcase and portfolio and helped her over to a bench. She looked at him, resignation painted on her face.

A cauliflower head bobbed in the sludge of urine and straw outside Egon's mother's house. Night was falling and dots of rain spattered the dark stone of the building. Unlike Vienna's coffeehouses, Marie had heard nothing of her son's imprisonment, his censorship or the magistrate's condemnation; she had become just another termite crawling in the walls of the city and such news only circulated among the theatre-going classes. She rarely left her room, rooted to her chair in the corner, reading letters, straining water through old tea leaves and mending the clothes of the students who lived in the rooms above.

'I thought you'd come,' she said, receiving her son and Valerie with little more than a pained smile.

Egon kissed her on the forehead.

'Mother, this is Valerie.'

Marie took one look at the bedraggled girl with red hair and turned to her son.

'I could have guessed.'

Marie was indifferent to her son's young companion, friend, lover, model or wife, but the likeness to her own daughter was undeniable.

'Pleased to meet you, Frau Schiele,' said Valerie, squatting into a curtsey.

'No need for that, girl. Just bring the case inside.'

Valerie dragged the suitcase and portfolio across the threshold while Egon collapsed in the corner. Marie unwrapped half a loaf of bread and a triangle of cheese on the table.

'Coffee?'

Valerie nodded, biting into the bread, failing to conceal the ugliness of her hunger.

'Let's forget the half-hearted questioning, shall we? I'm sure you'll tell me everything in good time.'

'Thank you, Mother.'

'Now, get out of those clothes and get into bed.'

'We couldn't possibly.'

'Don't be absurd.'

'I'm not letting you sleep on the floor.' Egon looked across at Valerie. 'I don't think it makes any difference anyway.'

She had fallen asleep at the table, her head resting on folded arms, a hunk of half-chewed bread still in her hand.

'Just give us a rug and we'll be fine.'

They slept next to the stove, its door permanently open, smoke tainting the icons hanging on the walls above them.

The three of them lay awake at night, regulating their breathing to feign sleep. Egon would wait until his mother's shallow breaths evened out against the percussion of the stove and then manoeuvre himself onto Valerie. Her arms would wrap around his head, pulling him tight into her. Egon's hair merged into Valerie's, spreading behind them like a trellis. A film of sweat covered their bodies like dew, and the candlelight picked out their sinewy lines as Egon's back rose and fell in slow, graceful movements. His skin was darker than Valerie's, flecked with greys and greens in the half-light. A heated minute of thrusts and it was over. The flush faded from Valerie's skin and with the slightest of shivers she opened her eyes. Meanwhile, Marie lay awake, enduring the chorus of grunts and the damp friction of their nightly acrobatics. Finally, when it was over and the two parted, the stove's flames reflecting off Egon's chest, Marie would fall asleep. In the morning, the fetid air would be suffused with odours Marie had long forgotten but still recognised.

Egon left the room every afternoon just before dusk settled on the city. He walked out through the house, planting his feet softly in the hallway, avoiding the lines of the floorboards which scored ridges in the thinner patches of the rugs. First, he would tour the tailors and barbers just as they were closing. He would nod to the owner and stride to the back of the shop through a partition curtain, where he would remove a wad of postcard size drawings. The owner would sort them through, pausing at some, skimming over others.

Depending on the establishment, some owners would take three or four pictures, others would take an entire set. When the shops closed he would move on to the taverns with what was left, notifying the bar staff and then sitting alone at a table in the corner, waiting to be approached. It only took a subtle wave and Egon would follow a potential customer out into an alleyway where he would hurry through the remaining pictures under the glow of a streetlight. If business was slow, he would end the evening going back and forth down Vienna's narrowest streets, angling for the same punters as the painted ladies around him. At the end of the night, he would return to his mother's squalid quarters, treading carefully through the hallway and down the steps, closing the door behind him before making small piles of coins on the table. He would set aside two stacks for food and three for materials; what was left – if anything – would be placed in a handkerchief under the blankets on the floor.

Day after day, Marie huddled in the corner of her bed, cocooned in blankets. Valerie would offer to rub mercury into her lesions or comb her hair, but Marie waved her way, crawling up in a ball facing the wall. Her fingers gripped weakly around Valerie's wrist as she brought soup and coffee, only for it to go cold on the bedside table.

One morning in late July, two months after their arrival, Egon dragged the case and portfolio to the threshold and went to kiss his mother on her thinning crown.

'And where will you go this time?'

'Wally's found us a room.'

'I don't believe you,' she said, coughing.

'We won't be far away. I'll come more often.'

'I know you hate living off Anton's generosity but it's not a reason to go.'

'We're making you unwell. You need your space back.'

'I'll outlive the pair of you. I guarantee you that.'

Valerie kissed Marie and walked out into the street, leaving Egon and his mother alone.

'Is this how it'll always be?' she asked.

'Things will get better.'

'Will they really?'

'I promise. I'll take care of you. I'll find you somewhere nice to live.' He shrugged his shoulders. 'I'll get you a cat.'

'I don't need a bloody cat and I don't need new lodgings.' She coughed again, wiping her mouth with the corner of a sheet. 'You just don't understand, do you? I'm not worried about me. I'm worried about you.'

'There's no need. Really.'

'Things could've been so different.'

'They will be. I promise. I'll take care of you. I'll be back to visit in a day or two.'

Egon kissed his mother again and joined Valerie outside.

They spent the day wandering the streets, knocking on doors and windows, enquiring about spare rooms, outhouses and dosshouses. By late afternoon they were sitting atop their suitcase in the park, arguing over the next steps. As night was drawing in, they walked across the city, their worn shoes moving from the cobbles of the workers' quarter to the well-swept streets of the bourgeois district. They paused outside Klimt's studio looking up at the lit window.

'I'm not going in,' said Valerie defiantly.

'Where else then?'

'What about Arthur's?'

'Arthur won't have us. Or rather, he won't have me. Not after the censor.'

'Well, we've got no choice, Egon. Anywhere, but not here.'

Valerie picked up the suitcase and stumbled away down the street. Egon stayed outside Klimt's door, looking up at the window, shadows flickering against the lit curtain. He took a deep breath and cupped his hands around his mouth. He paused and then exhaled. He bent over, picked up the portfolio and hurried after Valerie. After an hour's walking they found the correct house number and rang the bell.

'Good evening,' said Roessler, opening the door with a glass of red wine in his hand.

'Arthur, it's me.'

'Of course! Of course! Vienna's exiled son!' They embraced briefly and Roessler retreated inside the house, leaving Egon on the doorstep. 'Lovely to see you. Just a courtesy call or can I help you with anything?' he asked, looking at the suitcase at their feet. 'I'd invite you in but I'm having a bit of a soirée and things are rather hectic inside.'

'We need somewhere to stay.'

Roessler supported himself against the door handle, barring entrance.

'Egon, it's really good to see you, of course, and I'd love to catch up, but I really can't…'

'We're desperate.'

'Things are so busy. As I said, I've got guests here and I don't know if…'

'Just a couch.'

'Egon, please. Don't put me in this position. I have my reputation to think of.'

'Or the floor? Just somewhere in a quiet corner. We won't disturb you.'

'You're making things very…'

'Please, no one need know we're here.'

Roessler's eyes dropped. He looked up again and was met with Valerie's pleading gaze.

'I've already been taken to task over representing you. I can't risk that again. And please don't look at me like that, Valerie.'

'Call me Wally. Everyone else does.' She stepped up to him and placed a hand on his shoulder, her fingers brushing his neck. 'Please can we stay with you? Just for a few days, then we'll be gone. We promise. You would be helping us so much.'

'Only for a day or two,' echoed Egon.

Roessler dropped his hand from the door.

'You can take the corner of my old studio, just please do not cross the landing to my living quarters. General von Auffenberg-Komarow is next-door as we speak. He doesn't fraternise with the *plebs sordida*.'

Valerie embraced Roessler and they moved down the main hallway and through the kitchen into a backroom. The door was tight, the dust on its handle recording Roessler's palm print as it turned.

'I'm sorry,' he said, leaning his shoulder against the door. 'It's all I have.'

Egon looked around the room at the dust-covered sculptures and decadent friezes. The air was tainted with rabbit-skin glue and linseed oil.

'This is ideal.'

'How is it with a man of your talent that within just a couple of years your name can ring so hollow in the ears of the city's collectors and curators?' Roessler stood next to the window in his studio, blond-wisped calves poking out from underneath a navy-blue robe. 'It seems faintly absurd that the only work which brings you financial recompense is what men buy for small change and hide from their wives inside cigarette cases.'

'It's work.'

'...work whose scant reward is an imperceptible bulge under the mattress, insufficient even to keep dear Wally from sleep.'

'Not all of us can sup with marshals and ministers. The rest have to make their way the best they can.'

'The best you can?' Roessler picked a postcard off the table, tearing it in half. 'This brainless drivel?' Roessler walked to the easel, propped up a piece of paper, took a pencil and started sketching a copulating couple. 'Totally brainless.' He picked up a brush and started filling in colours.

Initially, Egon just watched. He sat on the mock sedan-chair in the corner, tracking his friend's hand as it flitted in and out of the colours tray, stroking over the canvas in the homely aura of a gas lamp.

'You should use less sable in the eyes,' said Egon.

'How do you mean?'

'You've made them too strong.'

'How?'

'Doesn't matter.'

'Tell me.'

'I can't be bothered.'

'So long as you are in my house, my friend, you'll answer me if I ask you something. So, what have I done wrong?'

'You're spoiling the mysticism. Look at her. She's staring out as if she's drunk.'

'If you can do it better yourself, come and show me.'

Egon picked up a fine brush, passed its tip across a blob of white oil paint, and worked on the portrait's eyes. A minute later he stood back.

'Now she looks as though she longs to be freed from the picture. She wants to be out here with us, not in the confines of the frame. You'll have to change the lips slightly if you want to alter that, but do you see?' Egon took up his chair next to the window. 'Now continue.'

Over the next days and weeks Roessler worked patiently on Egon, demanding examples, forcing his friend – often out of frustration – to take up a pencil himself and demonstrate the angle or a shadow that was missing. Once Egon had the materials in his hands, Roessler would step back and watch him sketching out shapes and mixing colours before throwing the paper down in disgust.

Sometimes Roessler took Valerie out to the city's ballrooms and restaurants, leaving the painter to curse and create to his heart's content. But Egon did not paint his own pictures. He examined his friend's work, made amendments and then stood on the balcony for the rest of the day until Valerie and Roessler came home. It was only when they began to stay out later that Egon finally took up the brush. Unwilling to venture out into the spotlight of Viennese society life, he worked for hours on old scraps of canvas. Afterwards, he left the apartment, studying the nightlife to colour in the gaps of pictures already forming in his head. Vaguely familiar men would approach him in alleyways, asking if he had any "special" sketches. He looked at them bewildered and hurried away.

In this way, with Roessler's help, Egon crawled back to the easel. Still reluctant to present himself before crowds or enter rooms of chinking glasses, he remained in the studio, producing work upon work, piling the canvases high. He worked at night in the studio, stepping over and round Valerie's sleeping body, layering colours onto the canvas, their shades emphasised by the candlelight silhouettes of his fingers. Every morning, when Roessler awoke, he crossed the landing to the studio to wake Egon, who had fallen asleep in his clothes minutes earlier. The night had given way to the first flirtations of morning and an ever-lightening blue swirled around the room, casting no shadows. Egon was spread across the couch while Valerie sat by the window, tying her hair back, her recently opened eyes puffy with sleep.

'Same as usual?'

'Let's get him to bed.'

She helped Roessler lead Egon back across the hallway into the living quarters. There, Valerie removed his trousers and Roessler helped his friend into his own bed.

'He's going to make himself ill.'

'He's doing just fine,' replied Roessler. 'A couple more weeks of this and you'll have the old Egon back.'

They walked back through to the studio to survey Egon's achievements from the previous night. Roessler gathered up the sketches and any canvases which looked suitably advanced, wrapped them in cloth and tucked them under his arm.

'They'll love this round the private galleries.'

'Does he know anything about this?'

'He turns a blind eye.'

'And the money?'

'It's all yours, Wally. Not much these days but there's still enough of it. His work needs to be seen and that will never happen from this wallpapered prison. Listen, I'll be back in about three hours. Make sure you're washed and perfumed by then. There's a robe and some jasmine soap in the cupboard. It's time you modelled for me.'

By the beginning of summer, Egon's name was on the lips of most of the city's art-lovers, yet he still refused to leave Roessler's studio during daylight hours. By day he would drift in and out of sleep on the couch and at night he would clamber over and around Valerie, shifting her slumbering limbs to paint a pose, tripping over her ankles as he reached for a canvas. Eventually, she was forced to move into Roessler's living quarters across the hallway. Now, repossessed by his art, Egon didn't even look up as she dragged the suitcase across the worn floorboards of the landing; he simply ploughed on, producing picture upon picture upon picture: self-portraits, allegories, still-life sketches, bulimic trees with arthritic branches, and again and again, differentiated scenes of a man and a woman clasping a small child.

'It's time we found our own rooms, Wally.'

'But what's wrong with it here?'

'We've exploited Arthur's goodwill far too long. I never thought he could be so generous.'

'But you like it here. I've never seen you work so hard.'

'I think we should live together somewhere. Just the two of us.'

'You know I'd like that, but…'

'I want you to have your own place to stay while I'll be away.'

'I'd be happier staying here. Arthur could keep me company.'

'I'm not leaving you behind with him. If you're concerned about company you can come along with me. You've always wanted to go to Zurich and Cologne. Paris, too.'

'But Arthur says it's fine for us to stay here.'

Egon grabbed her by the arm.

'You're not staying here with him. Is that clear?'

Egon stood at Klimt's door the following morning, squinting up at the sunlight, his neck stiff from the night's work. The dregs of the previous evening's drink were smeared across his teeth. An unknown girl answered the bell and led him up to the painter's studio. She took his coat, tossed it over a chair and shouted Klimt's name towards the back of the studio. The painter appeared from behind the blue curtain, a glass of red wine in hand.

'You're obviously busy.'

Klimt waved off Egon's bashfulness, sweeping his wine glass in an arc in front of him. The fingers in his other hand were glittering with speckles of gold leaf.

'Please, please, Egon.' Klimt embraced his friend. 'We've missed you.' The men released each other, Klimt looking up and down Egon's clothes. 'Let me guess.'

'I need your help.'

'How much?'

'About three hundred.'

'What for?'

'I have to find somewhere I can work in peace.'

Klimt tugged at his beard and walked behind a canvas on the easel, tilting his head as he queried its dimensions.

'There's a spare property in Hietzing I'm overlooking. The deposit is paid. In my name. You'll have to pay the rent though.'

'How much?'

'I don't know. I can't foot the bill for that though. I'm sure, despite your withered appearance, you're coping.' Egon looked away, unable to meet Klimt's eyes. 'I've seen your "smaller-scale" work doing the rounds. I'm sure you're managing.'

'It's not enough.'

'It's certainly getting your name out there though.'

'It's shameful.'

'There's no reason to be ashamed,' continued Klimt, putting his wine glass to one side and laying an arm around the young artist's shoulder. 'Those pictures are the talk of the city. Artistic filth has a tendency to end up in the most unexpected of hands.' The pair laughed. 'Personally, I find them tremendously uplifting. Plans may be afoot for a limited edition folio?'

'Wishful thinking,' smiled Egon. 'I'm not exactly popular among publishers.'

'Someone told me about a print-run of one hundred,' added Klimt, circling a finger over his bald patch.

'Not with my name on it.'

'Anyway, I am sure they keep the coins rolling in.' Klimt signalled to the girl and she brought a second glass of red wine, handing it to Egon. 'And the trader?'

'Nothing until next year.'

'But you're coming to Prague next month?'

'It will cost me more than I'll earn.'

'Be patient, young man. The exhibition circuit is a necessary evil.'

'Easier said than done when I can't even afford materials.'

'Where are you staying at the moment?'

'At Roessler's. Sort of.'

'With Wally?'

'Yes.'

Klimt walked over to the girl who had lain out on a *chaise longue* in the corner. He stroked her black hair and her eyes opened. Egon saw a sprinkling of gold leaf along her thigh.

'Dear Arthur's kept that a secret.'

'He's wary of it being known that I'm sponging off him.'

'We need to get you out of there, Egon. That's no place for you. Or Wally.'

'That's why I came.'

'I know. And you did right to come.'

Over the next few months Egon took Valerie with him everywhere.

Throughout the summer they lived out of suitcases and modest hotels, criss-crossing the German-speaking world to exhibitions in Hagen, Cologne and Berlin. They travelled south to Bregenz and Zurich: each time Egon's work met with critical acclaim, first in the chitter-chatter of the exhibition hall and then in journals and newspapers. During the day they visited the towns, walking proudly down the boulevards, Egon planting the copper tip of his new walking stick with precision onto the cobbles. In each city, Egon treated Valerie to the latest fashion: an embroidered purse in Berlin, French stockings in Cologne, a shawl in Bregenz, perfume in Hagen and a mauve hat with a rose corsage in Zurich. Emerging from the shops, she would tear her latest present from its box, launching tissue paper into the air. Egon watched it flutter to the ground. In Zurich, she pulled her hat on with both hands, the corsage protruding at the back. She looked at herself in the reflection of the shop window, spinning to the left and right, raising a foot with each flourish. The shop assistants looked out, sniggering at the young woman twisting in front of the window's two-way mirror.

At breakfast, Valerie would read the papers to Egon while he ate, their vitriolic ink diluted by her comic delivery.

'What does the Abendblatt have to say?'

'"Schiele's perverted mind and mary-trish-us…"'

'Meretricious.'

'"…meretricious incarnations have achieved nothing short of sullying the city's..."'

'Enough!'

'Who wrote that?'

'Biberkopf.'

'Idiot. And the Morgenpost?'

'"The exhibition reveals a pri-mor-di-al genius which at once succeeds in an arresting pictorial beauty and a ghastly exposure of human hypocrisy…"'

'That's more like it. You can always trust the Morgenpost: prolix, self-inflated and utterly correct.'

'"He depicts the vibrant seascape of the fallen body like no other…"'

What does that mean?'

'He's talking about you, darling.'

In Zurich, copies of a local magazine – carrying one of Egon's nudes on the front cover – were torn from the shelves by insulted church-goers and liberal art-lovers alike. In other cities, his scandalous reputation preceded him, forcing galleries into extraordinary session to debate whether ladies should be turned away at the door. Critics and journalists were as fascinated by the charismatic woman at the artist's side as with the artist himself. Never having laid eyes on Valerie in the flesh, the critics knew her more intimately than their own wives thanks to Egon's portraits. Some pointed out the differences between her in person and on canvas – the crooked teeth, the smaller eyes – but their natural tendency was to see through the garments to the body hidden beneath, seeking out the curves of her thighs. Journalists, critics and fellow-painters walked away with nights of Valerie-inspired dreams, leaving them no choice but to rave about the artist and his muse.

Egon put down his fork and took the paper from Valerie.

'I'll read this one otherwise you won't understand.'

'I'm not stupid, you know.'

'I know you're not. But just listen for a moment.' Egon lay the paper over his empty plate and read: '"…the artist, simultaneously haggard and slick, stands by his model, who is like a statue of Athena which has been standing too long in the rain."'

'Is that a compliment?'

'Of sorts. "…they joke with each other and with the group of onlookers who cannot help but compare the pair with the torturous portrait hanging to their left. Their eyes scan the portrait for similarities and differences, visual truths and artistic lies. They are the most precise synthesis of intimacy and community."'

'So, do they like us or not?'

Their new apartment in Vienna consisted of several large rooms, which Egon steadily monopolised, spreading his possessions across their surfaces, marking out areas next to the windows where he would place his easels. One room with north-facing windows was set aside as the studio and he filled the other rooms with long cabinets housing memorabilia, gifts, *objets d'art*, novels and almanacs. Egon laid each item out, creating a gallery of images, textures, poses and colours which he could hunt through for inspiration: the stance of a doll or statuette, the grain of a scarf or pennant, the fragrance of a tin of incense. His mother's mirror leant against the wall in the corner. Streaks of paint were smeared across most surfaces, flashes of cadmium and yellow picking out bumps on the walls or the corners of furniture.

'I've told you before: don't leave your clothes lying around. Put them back in the drawers where they belong.'

'I'll do it later.'

'This is the studio, not your dressing room.'

'If you want me to model for you, then you'll have to put up with this. I have to leave my clothes somewhere.'

Egon kicked a skirt up off the floor. It hung in the air before falling in a pile on the ground.

'So, it's my fault?'

'It's just a skirt.'

'Just a skirt?' Egon picked it up, rolled it into a bundle and hurled it at Valerie. She struck out with her hands, snagging a fingernail on the material. 'If you can't grow up and afford me some space, then…'

'Then what?'

'Just leave me to my work, will you?'

Egon spent more and more time in his studio, the door closed on Valerie's gramophone-filled afternoons. Tired, he would sit by the window, pull back the curtains and look out into the broad residential street of the middle-class suburb of Hietzing. The bedroom directly opposite Egon's studio belonged to the teenage boy of a Jewish family who spent his days next to the window grasping a mirror, examining the laborious growth of his beard, willing it on with a straining neck. Egon rested his feet on the windowsill and looked across the road.

Flakes of snow covered the town of Györ, halfway between Vienna and Budapest. Blown in from the east, they nestled in ridges and folds, tucked into the rims of barrels and boxes, spread up the base of walls like spider webs. August Lederer, a prominent brewery owner, clad in a long coat with a fur neck, was there to meet them off the train and accompany them to his country residence. As the carriage travelled out into the countryside the snow thickened, no longer just sprinkled on the lips of ruts at the side of the road, but layered up banks and hedges, weighing down branches.

'We are very grateful for the invitation, Herr Lederer.'

'I'm glad you could both come. After all the good things we've been hearing, I'm very much looking forward to seeing the portrait. I assure you my son will only be a minor distraction to the festivities.'

'I'll do my best.'

'I hope you'll find everything to your liking. You may have the choice of rooms to find one with suitable light; and a tradesman will be arriving tomorrow to offer you a selection of materials.'

'That's kind.'

'As for you, Fräulein Neuzil, my wife Elisabeth has prepared some excursions and assorted pastimes so that you will be kept entertained while Herr Schiele is painting.'

'Thank you, Sir.'

'I trust you enjoy Klopstock?'

'What?'

Egon's fingers tightened around Valerie's wrist.

'Indeed, Herr Lederer. She very much enjoys his work. Particularly the later poems.'

Lederer's house was decorated with all the trappings of Christmas, carefully arranged to display the family's opulence: candles, gilded pinecones, nuts, slices of dried fruit, glittering ornaments. When they arrived, porters took their bags up to their room and Egon and Valerie were summoned to the lounge to receive gifts. They walked through the main hall, past French cabinets and over Persian rugs, portraits hanging on the dark green walls.

'Schiller: a remarkable man and a fine dramatist,' said Egon as he peeled the paper off a volume of the German's early plays. He opened it on the first page, read the anodyne dedication and smiled. 'Very kind of you, Herr Lederer.'

'I always find a true man can never have enough Schiller, do you not agree?'

'Indeed. A fine companion for any occasion.'

'And for you, Fräulein Neuzil.'

Lederer held out another gift and Valerie tore at the tissue paper, pulling the strings and bows off. Her eyes sparkled as she removed a pair of cream, elbow-length silk gloves from the remnants of packaging. She pulled them on, flexing her fingers down the length of the material until they found their way into the slots at the end. She ran her gloved hands over her arms and shoulders, feeling the silk against her skin, grinning at Egon and her hosts, looking around the room for approval. Everyone smiled back politely, Lederer's wife adding three claps of considered applause.

'They suit you very well, Fräulein Neuzil.'

'I'll never take them off. Ever.'

'They're actually meant for eveningwear only.'

'But they're so beautiful I'll wear them all day!'

'If you must,' said Lederer's wife curtly.

Egon sat most of the day with Lederer's son, Erich, a pale-faced man of seventeen with a retroussé nose. His lips were a bold red, his ears pointed and distanced from his black hair, combed into an elaborate quiff at the front. He wore the latest fashion: a tailored dark brown jacket which hugged his figure just above the waist; a high-collared white shirt with an emerald-green tie. His trousers had the flared pomp of the *nouveaux-riches* spilling out over the top of his knee-length hunting boots.

Valerie spent the first day walking around the estate with Lederer's wife, Elisabeth, an imposing matriarch clad in a dazzling fur coat and shawl, her black hair and gun-barrel grey eyes lending her face a bewitching intensity. They only survived a day in each other's company. Elisabeth was tactful but honest, thinly veiling her surprise that Valerie had read neither Lessing nor Klopstock and was unskilled in basic casuistry. Valerie spent the remaining days rambling through the snow on her own wearing her silk gloves or sitting in the parlour chatting to the maids and cooks.

Lederer made his only other appearance on New Year's Eve. The entire ground floor of the house was swarming with local dignitaries and guests shipped in from the Empire's major cities. Elisabeth floated from conversation to conversation, her legs moving smoothly underneath a floor-length dress. As a butler sounded the gong, the guests flooded to the main hallway where Lederer appeared at the top of the staircase. He addressed the guests, welcoming in the New Year, before descending the stairs and heading straight for Egon.

'Found you at last, Herr Schiele. I'm so sorry for my absence. Always business to see to, you know… no rest for the wicked.'

'I understand entirely.'

They shook hands and Egon looked up at his host's receding hairline and the geometric precision with which Lederer had combed the remaining strands of hair across his scalp.

'So, how are things going with my son?'

'He's very patient for a man of his age. I was expecting someone far more impulsive.'

'Oh, believe me, he is. He's pulling the wool over your eyes, Herr Schiele. I thought painters were supposed to capture the soul of their models,' said Lederer, laying a hand on Egon's shoulder. 'You'll have to look a little closer.'

'I'll take your word for it,' he replied. 'But, as I said, he seems totally dedicated to the portrait. At the end of every session he analyses the canvas, asks me questions about the composition, how and why I made decisions about different sections, different effects.'

'I do hope he hasn't been disturbing you.'

'Not at all, it's rare for a model to take such interest. He has popped round to my room several times in the evening with questions.'

'You will tell me if he is being a pest, won't you?'

'He's a very engaging young man, Herr Lederer, and he gets on well with Fräulein Neuzil, too.'

'That's also encouraging to hear.'

'You certainly seem to have groomed an artistic interest in him.'

Lederer applied pressure to Egon's elbow, directing him towards the door. They walked through the crowds and into a silent room with a large billiard table.

'That's what I wanted to talk to you about, Herr Schiele. I've had the Academy in mind for Erich for some time, but I'm not sure he'll get in. The examinations are apparently quite taxing. He embarked on a course in the viola last year but that fell foul of some alternative teaching methods. The teacher took a bit of a shine to my Erich. Anyway, I've been thinking about pushing him towards the visual arts: painting, sculpture, something like that.'

'A fine idea. And rare for a father to want such a thing for his son.'

'I wanted to ask if you would be prepared to teach him the fundamentals. I would, of course, pay for your services.'

'I am honoured and flattered but shouldn't you be asking someone more accomplished? Herr Klimt, for example?'

'That's not what *he* says. Anyway, you were at the Academy yourself not so long ago. I assume you have a far better sensitivity to proceedings than he does.'

Egon turned, looking straight at Lederer, his neck green with the reflection off the baize.

'Then I would be honoured. Particularly to be associated with such an illustrious family as yours.'

'How does two hundred crowns a month sound?'

'A little more would ensure all costs are covered.'

'Three hundred.'

'That will be fine.'

'You are worth every crown!'

'That is for you to judge, Sir.'

They each took a sip of wine and surveyed the distribution of the red and white balls across the table, abandoned mid-game. Lederer moved to leave the room, glimpsing a small gathering of men milling around the door. Egon put a hand out and held his host's elbow.

'Forgive me, Herr Lederer, but one more thing. Erich would have to come to Vienna for the tuition.'

'That's right.'

'But I am leaving tomorrow.'

'Of course, of course. I thought you could take him with you. I have a brother who will accommodate him while he studies. I would be grateful though if you could ensure he gets there safely.'

'Certainly.'

'The Empire is growing fat, Herr Schiele. Vienna is the safest place for him.'

'Are you actually enjoying that?' asked Valerie, her head resting on Egon's naked shoulder.

'Of course.'

'You never used to read in bed.'

'Doesn't mean I can't now.'

'You just want to be able to speak like that lot downstairs.'

Egon closed the book and laid it on his chest, pushing Valerie's head from his shoulder. 'Stop talking rubbish and go to sleep.'

'They won't like you any more or less for it.'

'I'm reading it because I enjoy it. It's edifying. Now, go to sleep.'

'Edi-what?'

'Forget it.'

Valerie embraced Egon, her skin autographed with jasmine. He picked up his book and continued reading.

'D'you not think you can take those off?'

'But they feel so nice against my skin.'

'Not in bed for Christ's sake!'

Valerie pulled at each finger, loosening the material before sliding the glove off and dropping it to the floor. She rolled back over to Egon and ran her hands down the front of his chest and between his legs. The book quivered in his hands and then he snapped it closed.

'What are you doing?'

'It's been a while,' she retorted, rummaging under the sheets.

'They'll hear us.'

'Since when did that bother you?'

'Stop being so difficult. We're guests in someone's house.'

'You're so desperate to please them, aren't you?'

'Nonsense!'

'These were the kind of people you used to hate… these aristocrats. You used to hate their hyp… their hyp…'

'Hypocrisy.'

'Their hypocrisy.'

'I still do.'

'Then why all this?' Valerie picked up the book and held it in front of Egon's face.

'This makes me an aristocrat, does it?'

'You just don't see it, do you?' said Valerie rolling away. 'They'll all be knocked off their perch sooner or later. And you'll be knocked off with them.'

She climbed out of bed, placed a gown over her shoulders, grabbed her gloves and left the room. Egon picked up the book and continued to read.

Egon stood next to Valerie in the hallway and looked up at the drape-covered picture hanging from the wall. Lederer pulled the sheet off, studied its features and equipoise, moving in a semi-circle, feeling the portrait's eyes follow him.

'Truly magnificent.' He leant in, his nose nearly touching the canvas. 'Have you made the eyes darker?'

'You have a fine eye for detail, Sir. Just like Valerie. She corrected me to their true shade last night. They're much closer to your wife's eyes now.' Frau Lederer gave a nod of appreciation in Egon's direction. 'I hope the last minute change is to your liking.'

'You've rendered them perfectly. He does indeed have his mother's eyes. Congratulations, Fräulein Neuzil.'

Erich stood next to the painting as Lederer and the other members of the household compared him to his portrait.

'It will keep you in our thoughts when you are in Vienna.'

'Thank you, Father. You, too, shall be in mine.'

They shook hands; Erich gave his mother a kiss on each cheek and climbed into the carriage. Egon made his farewells while Valerie embraced one of the maids. She moved towards Frau Lederer holding out her gloved hands. She took Valerie's fingers and allowed her to kiss the back of her hand. Valerie curtseyed and made for the carriage.

On the train back to Vienna, Erich asked countless questions about the Empire's capital city, about its architecture, its soirées, its decadence. Egon had been awake the entire previous night putting the finishing touches to the portrait and now sleep caught up with him. As his eyelids dropped, he listened to the other two continue the discussion, their voices becoming softer and more cautious, melting into the rattle of the carriage. Valerie laid a blanket over Egon's lap and chest as he fell further and further into sleep. It was only when the cabin jolted several hours later as they approached the outskirts of Vienna that his eyes opened and he saw an exploratory finger on

Erich's left hand stroking the frayed silk of Valerie's glove.

When they arrived in the main station, Egon escorted Erich directly to his uncle's townhouse.

'All portraiture lessons will take place on these premises, do you understand?'

'Yes.'

'You are never to visit my studio, do you understand?'

'Yes.'

'And if I ever see you with Wally – or even discover you have been communicating – I will tell your father immediately. Is that clear?'

'Yes.'

'Now get inside, you little shit!'

Egon chose to overlook Valerie's minor flirtations since she, too, knew of his scuffles with models visiting the studio late at night. As had always been his custom, he picked up girls from the streets and had them sit for him through the small hours: "rough diamonds" who would simulate masturbation on a stool in the centre of his studio while he worked feverishly at the canvas, capturing their lustful desperation. As the sun came up and Egon climbed into bed, Valerie would wake, feeling the springs sag under his weight. He clambered over her and between the sheets, the scent of sex still on his skin.

Yet, these infidelities evaporated when they were alone in the apartment. Egon would still demand Valerie modelled for him, painting her as if he were setting eyes on her body for the first time, every new picture a new beginning. The following day, however, she would wake up and her half-finished portrait would still be standing on the easel while Egon stuffed clothes and materials into a leather bag. He would kiss her on the forehead and then hurry out the door, leaving her alone in the empty studio. Days later, he would return to Vienna from yet another exhibition in a far-flung corner of Europe and slip into the warm bed where Valerie lay slumbering, her limbs sprawled across the blankets and her clothes scattered on the floor. She would roll over, a tender greeting poised on her lips, but he simply pressed himself against her and fell asleep.

'It will happen. I assure you,' said Roessler, opening an extra button on his shirt.

'Maybe a regional conflict, I could see that happening. But not across the entire continent. Never.'

'Just look at it logically, though. Look at the way the continent is divided up. It's the only natural course of any conflict: war on a massive scale.'

Egon and Roessler walked out of the chill of the woods and into the unrelenting sunshine. They turned onto a path, their boots tossing up puffs of smoke on the dry gravel. The countryside around them was silent but for the wind in the treetops.

'Corrupt, arcane, hated everywhere,' continued Roessler. 'The Empire won't last much longer. Mark my words.'

'You're exaggerating.' Egon broke off a branch and cuffed at the ground.

'Just look outside of your little world for a second. Read the front page for a change and not just your reviews. Listen to some of the well-to-do bigwigs who sit for you. They'll all agree. I guarantee you.'

'Why should that bother me?'

'Why? Why?' Roessler stopped, turning to Egon. 'Sometimes I really can't believe you.' He breathed out through his nose, shaking his head. 'The only canvas you'll have will be the one keeping the rain off your head.'

'That will never happen.'

'And what if they make it to the gates of Vienna?'

'It's not the Turks, for God's sake!' Egon paused, looking away into the woods which flanked the path. 'Anyway, we can always come up here to get away from it all. No matter how war-mongering the

Russians are, I doubt they'll ever get as far as Altmünster.'

'You are short-sighted, Egon. Dangerously so.'

They continued down the country path, birds flitting between the treetops, flashes of winged-black breaking the blue canopy above them. They turned off down a narrow walkway through the woods, bees humming from the chalices of wild flowers as their legs whisked past.

'Whether you like it or not, politics is very much *de rigeur* these days,' started Roessler again. 'I know what you think but you're wrong. It's what they're all buying, believe me. I went to an atelier in Brünn a couple of weeks back and I tell you, I've rarely seen such original work being produced over the past eighteen months.'

'Just a flash in the pan. There is no conflict. There is no war. There's only good and bad art.' Egon put his hands in his pockets and went on ahead.

'You're not immortal,' shouted Roessler, decapitating a thistle with the tip of his walking stick.

'Well, what's that supposed to mean?'

'Young, talented, the grand self-styled saviour of painting, but not immortal.'

Egon turned back to Roessler and laughed. 'As intuitive as ever, Arthur! What would I do without you?'

'Be poor and unsuccessful.'

'And immortal?'

'Oh, shut up!' he joked. 'From what I hear anyway, you're doing rather well for yourself.'

'Thanks to you.'

Roessler walked up the path towards Egon and laid an arm across his shoulders. 'How was the exhibition anyway?'

'They gave me space for three pieces. Dear old Gustav took care of it all.'

'What did the locusts say?'

'One called me "Satan with a paintbrush", which I was actually quite fond of, but the rest were unerringly complimentary.'

'And did anyone deign to open their sequin-covered purses?'

'All three went.'

'It appears they've finally forgiven your rather caustic edge.'

'I think I've forgiven that, too.'

They arrived at the end of the path. There they paused, and Roessler tapped his walking stick on the gate-frame. Looking through the paddock, half-garden, half-meadow, their eyes passed over the blanket of lilac, azure and gold flowers which led up to Roessler's small holiday house at the top of a ridge in a clearing. They watched Valerie sunbathing near the back door, catching flashes of her bronzed skin and rose bathing costume as she turned on the chair.

'Ah,' said Roessler. 'Another little part of your caustic edge.'

Egon was silent for a moment. Then, with a shrug, he walked thoughtfully on.

# TWELVE

# THROUGH AN OPEN WINDOW

Outside, doors clattered closed and a man shouted insults as he tossed bags and suitcases onto the pavement. Valerie slept soundly; Egon pulled the pillow over his head, drifting back to sleep. When he rose several hours later, the ground-floor shutters of the house opposite had been boarded up. Boxes were scattered along the pavement; through the upstairs windows he saw desks and chests abandoned, their drawers hanging out like tongues.

'Herr Andert from number ninety-two said they went north,' said Valerie, appearing at his side. 'Frau Koerber thinks they're on their way to England.'

'To avoid the obvious, I expect.'

'But it'll never spread this far, will it?'

'I don't know.'

'Frau Koerber said they've got relatives in the east. Andert says that's a lie, though.'

'They'll be heading north.'

'Why?'

'Sarajevo, darling.'

'Where's that?'

'Doesn't matter,' said Egon, looking away. 'You wouldn't want to be there. Listen: why don't you get yourself dressed and go down the market. I'd like fresh fish for lunch.'

While Egon was taking a break at his window, exhaling cigarette smoke into the street, a carriage drew up outside the empty townhouse. A man and his wife disembarked and waited in the street while a labourer tore the boards from the door. They filed in, followed by their two daughters, pulling up their heavy dresses as they walked in over the front step. Throughout the day, the delivery men brought in the family's possessions: wicker baskets of china, a grandfather clock, an upright piano, a Renaissance copy hung in an incongruous frame, leather armchairs, a mahogany chest, a coat rack, a rocking chair. Egon watched each of the items being carried into the house, listening to the mother as she ordered the delivery men into different rooms, distributing the boxes and furniture about the house. The two sisters climbed the stairs and rushed to their room, which had once belonged to the young Jewish boy. Egon watched as they flung open the windows and their two faces appeared, leaning out into the street. They scanned the buildings on the opposite side of the street, caught sight of Egon and waved. He waved back, a cigarette between his fingers, and returned to his work.

He adapted his daily routine so that he appeared at his window after breakfast and could wave to the young women before starting work. Sometimes, he donned a chequered hat, other times a bow tie, walking on tip-toes in front of the window, entertaining them with jumps and pirouettes. Other times he just leant forward with both hands on the windowsill and swayed from side to side as if listening to music. The sisters sat together and laughed, aping the tragicomic gestures of the mime artist over the road.

After their father left for work in the morning, the daughters were called downstairs to help their mother, spending an hour reading correspondence and finalising letters to be dispatched that day. They would then go into town, the sisters wearing different pastel shades of the same dress while their mother wore a flamboyant hat. Climbing into the carriage outside their house, she would look out the corner of her eye up at the windows of neighbouring houses and down the length of the street to see who had noticed the grand *sortie* with her daughters. Egon would crouch behind the curtain, stealing glimpses of the three women as they lifted their pudding dresses, planting slippered toes on the carriage rungs.

On Tuesdays and Fridays, an old man would come to the house, ring the bell and stand on the porch, mopping his brow. He would be made to wait until the mother opened the door and ushered him in, picking the hat off his head and placing it on a coat rack as she passed. Several minutes later, a cacophony would erupt from the upstairs windows; there would be short periods of sparse piano music interrupted by a racket of keys and chords in butchered syncope. After an hour, the man would reappear at the door, mop his brow again before replacing his hat, and walk slowly away.

Egon began to record the comings and goings of the Harms family on a piece of scrap paper. As autumn passed into winter, and winter into spring, he constructed an elaborate calendar of the family's movements, detailing festivities, visits, appointments and customs, until his scrap of paper had matured into a colour-coded chart which he hid between old canvases. At any moment in the day he could track where each family member was and what he or she was doing, their lives seemingly oblivious to the scarcities and restrictions that preparations for war had brought for others. Johann Harms was the most predictable, his working day more accurate than Egon's pocket watch; his wife, too, ran the household with relentless rigidity: tutors, traders and guests were designated specific slots throughout the day, their paths never to cross. The daughters were less organised and more leisurely. Adele would fiddle with her hair in her bedroom mirror; Edith was often engrossed in a book or journal.

Egon winced as the doctor dug fingers into his lower back, searching out the form of his kidneys. He wiped his hands on a cloth passed to him by Valerie and picked up Egon's bedpan. He removed a pair of spectacles from his breast pocket, cleaned them on a stray shirt-tail and pinched them over the bridge of his nose, removing the cloth and reading the runes of Egon's ablutions.

'To be frank, I don't see anything untoward. Your kidneys seem in order and your discharges are by no means irregular. You say you have jabbing pains?'

'That's correct, Herr Doktor. Just here.'

Egon placed a finger on the side of his torso.

'Well, such minor discomforts are not uncommon. You should take the usual precautions to ensure it doesn't develop into anything more unpleasant. Therefore, I suggest you remain in bed for the next five days, drink nothing but water or tea and avoid draughts. The window should be closed at all times.' The doctor turned to Valerie. 'Is that clear?'

'Yes, Herr Doktor. I'll make sure he does what you say.'

'And no medication?' asked Egon, feebly.

'Considering the mildness of your ailment, Herr Schiele, and also the scarcity of resources at this time, I suggest you put your faith in rest and recuperation. I'll return in three days. Contact me if your situation deteriorates.'

'We will do. Thank you.' Valerie accompanied the doctor to the door, down the stairs and out into the street. When she returned, Egon was standing up in his bedclothes.

'You heard what the doctor said.'

'I'm not going to lie in this dreary room all day. Bring the bed through to the studio.'

'But it's too heavy.'

'You'll manage.'

Valerie slid the bed into the studio and positioned it next to the window. She filled jugs of water and pots of tea and ferried them from the stove to the side of his bed, pulling up a chair to keep him company.

'That will not be necessary.'

'Egon?'

'I need some peace and quiet, please.'

She looked out of the window and saw flashes of the women passing through rooms and down staircases next door.

'Shall I close the curtains?'

'No. It's alright. The warmth of the sunlight will do me good.'

She looked down at Egon, deciphering the lines of his frown. She ran her fingers through his hair and went to sit in the corner with a book.

'One more thing,' said Egon. 'Could you bring me a fresh pan?'

Valerie picked up the porcelain bowl from under the sink, laid a cloth over the top and pushed it under Egon's bed.

'I could do with it now, actually.'

She picked it up again and handed it to Egon. He held the corner of the pan and manoeuvered it under himself.

'Can I help?'

'You know I can't go when you're here.'

'But the doctor said I...'

'Wally, please.'

'I'll just be next door.'

Egon placed the empty bedpan on the floor as soon as the door had closed. He got up, threw the window open and laid back on his bed, pushing down the covers. His torso was naked and he allowed the bedcovers to slip further down until the tight, curly hairs at the top of his groin were visible. He rubbed his eyes and turned to the side, his smile part-concealed by the pillow. With half-closed eyes, he massaged himself under the lip of the sheet and waited for the animated faces of the daughters to appear over the street.

One hot day, later that summer, Egon walked out into the street just as Frau Harms and her two daughters were easing their way down the front steps, the hems of their dresses raised above the dust. Egon waved cordially to Adele and Edith, a pair of bashful smiles on their lips. Frau Harms watched as Egon removed his hat and bowed in the street. She nodded towards her daughters and both women sunk into deferential curtseys.

'Good morning, Madam,' he said, walking across the road.

'Good morning, Sir.'

'Forgive me for not introducing myself earlier: I live at number 101. Egon Schiele.'

'Pleased to meet you.'

Egon removed a glove and took Frau Harms' hand. 'A delightful day, do you not think?'

'Indeed, Sir,' she replied, and motioned her daughters forward.

'Are you heading into town to enjoy the weather?' asked Egon hastily before they had a chance to lay a foot on the carriage rungs.

Adele, the younger daughter, looked towards her mother for permission to answer.

'We have a reception to attend to,' continued Frau Harms. 'With Countess von Krasnik. Now, if you'll excuse us.'

She put a hand on the carriage door, ushering her daughters inside.

'I imagine you'll be well received,' said Egon. 'I have read good reports of the Count's preparations in the Balkans.'

'I wouldn't know about that,' said Frau Harms. 'We must really be going. Girls, get inside, will you, please.'

'Of course, sorry for holding you up. Do send the Countess my regards.'

Frau Harms dropped her arms to her sides, the satin gloves whisking past the dress material, and turned back from the carriage.

'You know the Countess?'

'I once did a portrait of her husband. And one of Victor Ritter von Bauer.'

'Ambassador Ritter von Bauer?'

'That's correct.'

'We have yet to make his acquaintance.'

'I am not sure if he knows of your arrival.'

'Well, we have yet to publish it in the journal.'

'I may mention it to him if you wish. Strictly *en passant*, of course.'

'I'm sure my husband would appreciate that. Enjoy your day, Herr

Schiele.' She gave him a gracious hand and ushered her daughters into the carriage. Egon watched it sag under the weight of the driver and the three women. The reins snapped and the carriage pulled away. Egon tossed his gloves into his upturned hat and went back inside, smiling to himself.

Egon became a master of chance encounters. He accosted the daughters the following day as they returned from the market, producing a bag of truffles from his inside pocket. A week later, he winked up at Adele's window as he departed for a vernissage in a top hat and evening dress. One morning in July, he bade farewell to Klimt on his doorstep, introducing him to the sisters as they climbed down from a carriage. During summer evenings, he entertained them with mime acts from his studio window. Every day, he sought out one of the sisters, either rubbing shoulders in the theatre lobby or sharing a carriage back to Hietzing. His life divided itself along the lines of their daily routine, lurking around corners or crouched behind curtains for when the girls left the house or appeared at windows. Their father would accompany them to church on Sunday mornings or the theatre once a month, but otherwise they remained in the upstairs room, venturing out only under the watchful accompaniment of their mother.

'It would give you something to do,' said Egon.

Valerie spat her wine back into its glass. She looked at Egon in amazement, shuddering at the moan of a piano streaming in the open windows.

'Just listen to that!'

'What?'

'That racket!'

'They'll get better.'

'Spend my time with those two prancers?' She moved her knife and fork into one hand and placed her elbows on the table, leaning towards Egon, pointing. 'You of all people should be able to see through them and their Hochdeutsch.'

'They speak properly.'

Valerie snorted. 'It's like cracked crystal.'

Egon placed his knife and fork either side of the plate and sat back, allowing Valerie to rant, attacking their fashions, their coiffeurs, their dainty noses and polite laughs.

'You've always hated that kind of thing,' she insisted, stopping to draw breath. Across the road the piano was replaced with the warble of vocal scales.

'I just hate to think of you here on your own when I'm off travelling. I know that Frau Harms is a bit unyielding but you shouldn't judge her daughters by that measure.'

Valerie stood up and removed the empty plates. A minute later the crockery clattered in the sink.

Egon walked through to the studio and returned with a sheet of paper, a fountain pen and several pots of ink. Valerie sat at the table, her chin on folded arms.

'I'll write to them for you. You go next door and have a lie-down.'

'But I want to see what you write.'

'I'll show you afterwards. I'll need to spend some time getting it right. You know how Frau Harms can be.'

Valerie stood up and shrugged. 'If that's what you want, I'll be in the bedroom.'

Egon took the pen, placed the tip on the thick brown paper and watched as its nib splay-seeped black ink. He wrote ornately, adding strips of reds, blues and russet to the borders and lines, layering the text until it was a work of art itself. When he had finished he went into the next room and read the text out to Valerie as she lay on the couch. He spoke in a steady, emotionless voice, omitting parts and sealing it before she reached for the envelope.

'To the cinema?'

'Why not?'

'Frau Harms won't allow it.'

'They'll pick something appropriate.' Egon held the letter out to Valerie. 'Can you pop it through their door?'

'Me?'

'Please.'

'You wrote it.'

'I have work to do.'

'And I'm exhausted.'

'Wally, please. Just do this for me.'

"We shall be delighted to accompany you to the cinema on Monday, to the Park Cinema, to see *A Woman of the World* by Ewer. Along with Valerie, of course. Who do you suggest picks up the tickets?"

Egon re-read the letter, paraphrasing its contents for Valerie. As he folded it up and placed it in his desk drawer, he cast his eyes once again over the pencil-note added at the bottom in rounded, feminine letters: "P.S. Please make sure my mummy doesn't hear a word of this. A&E."

Egon and Valerie were already waiting outside the cinema when the Harms daughters arrived. They had spent days grooming an alibi with their mother, claiming they had tickets to attend a Beethoven recital in one of Vienna's many concert halls. Edith, older by ten months, wore a patterned dress, a yellow blouse and an overcoat. Her sister, Adele, was dressed in a white blouse with black needlework down the front and a dark blue skirt. She had a blue shawl across her shoulders and her arms were folded across her chest. Valerie caught sight of them in the distance.

'Dolled-up strumpets.'

'Young ladies in the prime of life, Wally,' said Egon, unable to suppress a delighted smile.

'Strumpets.'

'I don't want another word like that out of you this evening. Give them a chance, please.'

Inside the auditorium, they sat on four adjacent wooden chairs: Adele and Egon were in the middle, while Edith and Valerie sat either side of the pair, looking up at the screen. Valerie's thigh rubbed against Egon as she tapped her foot in time with the organist. Her toe struck the floorboards on the downbeats of every bar, her fingers playing imaginary melodies on her knee. There was a whirr behind them and then a shaft of light struck the screen; it picked out the circles of smoke and particles of dust in the air, beaming its flaky, grained image onto the curtain before them.

Egon shifted forward onto the front of his chair and watched the reflection of the film's images dance across the faces of the two sisters. Out of the corner of his eye, he saw the light flick across the canvas of their complexions, skipping over the surface of their cheeks, flashing shadows down their necks and onto their chests, rising and falling to the same circus beat which he felt tapped out on the knee next to him. The projector jammed and for an instant the film stalled, a black line running down the middle of the screen. As Adele and Edith turned to look back towards the projectionist, their eyes met Egon's. Adele raised a hand to her neck, feeling it flush even in the darkness. Edith smiled gently, the reflected light picking out a mouth half-full of teeth, before her lips covered them up. The projectionist mumbled an apology and all eyes turned back to the screen for the final few minutes during which an inappropriately dressed heroine saved her unfortunate mother to the applause of the audience. They filed out of the auditorium, Egon fetching the ladies' coats from the cloakroom on the way out.

'Didn't you just love the part where the sailor took the rope and wrapped it around the big man and they all fell over and then the soldier came and the organ was playing quickly so quickly...'

Adele hopped down the front steps, turning back to look at the others.

'Amazing!' added Valerie, walking beside her.

'It is such a talent to be able to play the organ like that,' said Egon, placing a coat around Edith's shoulders. 'I simply adore that instrument.'

Edith looked at her sister and then spoke up. 'We are both taking piano tuition at the moment. Mother pays for lessons twice a week.'

'We've alr…'

'Really?' said Egon, interrupting Valerie.

'Adele's *Moonlight Sonata* is exquisite.'

'I'd very much like to hear you play sometime.'

'You should come round for tea one afternoon,' started Adele. 'We'll have Mother invite you. Edith and I will play a duet, if you like.'

'That would be lovely. Wouldn't it, Valerie?' She nodded indifferently. 'We would very much like that. Thank you.'

They wrapped their capes and jackets around their shoulders and turned down the street, walking back towards Hietzing.

'Now tell me, ladies, did you enjoy the film?' asked Egon.

'It was magnificent,' replied Adele. 'I loved the part when they went for the picnic on the sand dunes and then they went into the sea but then the man came and they had to run away and then find that other man who was in that dark hat with the woman and the boy…'

Edith laid a hand on her sister's arm.

'We miss the sea so much down here.'

'Father used to take us to the coast every weekend in Bremen. But since we moved here he never takes us anywhere,' said Adele.

'Well, we might have to remedy that. I know a lovely place on the Dalmatian coast.'

The girls smiled and walked on.

'To be honest, Herr Schiele,' started Edith, 'and do not think me ungrateful… I found the showing rather tedious. I mean what was the point of that fellow with the ridiculous hat. And the leading lady… well, I just found her nauseous.'

'Do you not think at least that the plot was mildly gripping?'

'Fair entertainment, perhaps, but… and please do not think me a killjoy… in essence, I prefer the theatre.'

Adele turned to her sister.

'You suggested we go to the cinema.'

'It was your suggestion.'

'You know full well…'

Edith pulled her younger sister again by the arm and they moved on ahead.

'Excuse us.'

Egon and Valerie followed behind, leaving the heart of Vienna and entering the wide residential streets of Hietzing. Valerie walked silently next to Egon as he looked ahead at the two young ladies. Adele, on the left, was marginally slimmer than her elder sister. She walked with a bounce in her stride, a mischievous spring that sent flutters through her dress with each step. Edith had a more conservative gait, her spine straighter, her chin higher, hinting at the poise her mother expected of her. Adele was closer to Valerie in age, she had a precocious charm that at times could either conceal or reveal a sexual charisma she was only just discovering. Edith, on the other hand, although only slightly older, had the mature bearing of an adult. Her eyes carried a neutrality that knew to promise nothing; she read the truth concealed behind the gestures of her sister, of her parents, and of the men who would approach her at soirées or cross her in the street.

As they reached the end of the Hietzinger Hauptstrasse, the sisters stopped. 'It's probably best if you do not accompany us for this stretch,' said Edith.

'Of course,' answered Egon. 'We'll wait here for a few minutes.'

'Thank you for a lovely evening, Herr Schiele,' said Adele.

'It was most pleasant,' added Edith.

'You're welcome.'

They walked away towards their house, Adele turning once to wave back at them. Egon and Valerie waited until they heard a bell and then a door slamming behind the sisters.

'Well?'

'They're both spoilt.'

'Don't be unfair.'

'I suppose Adele is passable, but she tries too hard. She's trying to impress you.'

'Don't be ridiculous,' scoffed Egon.

'The other one's a bit dull, but fairly harmless. She sniffs too much. I could barely hear the organist.'

Later that evening, while Valerie slept, her legs spread out over Egon's side of the bed, the crunch of grinding teeth audible over her breathing, he sat at the desk in the corner of the bedroom, a half-written letter in front of him. He looked up and watched as she rolled across the sheets, her legs kicking out against the worn linen. He turned back to the letter, recounting the evening's events to Roessler, describing the "brittle yet charming conversation" with the Harms sisters, the "trite" film and the *son et lumière* show across the young ladies' faces. He signed off, writing: "My friend, I am proud to be the first to tell you that I intend to get married." He rocked back on his chair and looked out the window into the dimly lit street and the lifeless house across the road. "Though not to Wally."

# THIRTEEN

# SCARLET FEVER

'I better stop in case we don't hear her come in.' Edith closed the lid of the piano and swivelled on the stool. 'If mother knew you were here, Herr Schiele…'

'She'll be another hour at least.'

'How do you know that?'

'She's never back before four on a Thursday,' replied Egon. 'Trust me.'

Adele jumped up, pulling Edith away from the piano. 'Herr Schiele's right.'

They moved over to the divan by the window and sat down. Egon looked over their heads out into the street.

'You can see the entire world go by from up here. In fact, you can see all the way into my studio.' He turned his attention back to the girls. 'I hope it hasn't been too distracting for you both.'

'Not at all, Sir,' answered Adele. 'In fact, it's one of our favourite…'

Edith tugged at her sister's arm.

'One of your favourite…?' repeated Egon.

'Adele was just saying how…'

'…how what?'

'Please excuse us.'

Egon bowed his head and walked to the back of the room, craning his neck to catch the girls' whispers.

'You two look very similar, you know?' he said, turning around. 'You'd make a lovely picture.'

'You flatter us, Herr Schiele,' said Edith.

'No more than you deserve. I don't suppose you have a piece of paper, do you? I'd love to catch the pair of you like you are just now, with the sun behind you, coming in at that angle through the window.'

'Mother says we must wait until we are twenty-one for our portraits,' continued Edith.

'This won't be a portrait. Just a quick sketch.'

Adele flicked her hair back off her shoulders and raised her chin.

'Like this, Herr Schiele?'

'Very good, Adele. Very good. Edith could you lean in towards your sister a little.'

Edith scowled but Adele pulled her closer. 'Come on, Edi.'

Egon picked a sheet of music off the piano, turned it over and rested it on the back of a book. He pulled a pencil out of his top pocket.

'That's exquisite, girls. Now it would be lovely to get some of that sun on your necks... yes, that's excellent, Adele. Edith, could you do the same? Just pull the material down a little.'

'Herr Schiele, who exactly will see this picture?'

'Edi, just do as he says!'

'It's just a sketch. A little memento for you both.' The pencil skimmed over the paper. 'A little more, Edith, just a little more.'

A horse's hooves clicked in the street and a carriage rattled up to the front door. Edith leant away from Adele and looked out the window. 'She's back.'

The door slammed downstairs and their mother's shrill voice echoed around the house. Edith got to her feet and ripped the sketch from Egon's hands.

'You must go.'

'Why?'

'Immediately.'

Adele languished on the divan, laughing to herself and slowly buttoning up her blouse.

'Use the back stairs. You know where they are?' asked Edith.

'Of course.' Egon smiled and hurried out the room.

'Marriage! We're the people who destroy such institutions, not those who willingly subject themselves to them.'

'You make it sound like it's the end of the world.'

'It's the end of something.'

Klimt emptied the glass of absinthe, grains of sugar washing back as he placed it on the table. He poured another glass and with a teaspoon of sugar broke the surface until the crystals turned green. He took a candle and passed its flame around the spoon, its molten contents plopping pyrotechnics into the glass. Egon waited until the cobalt flame burnt out and Klimt had twirled the spoon in the glass before he sipped his own coffee and uncrossed his legs. The two men sat at a table in the corner of Klimt's studio, the cat circling in and out of the chair legs.

'Besides, you barely know her.'

'A year is more than enough.'

'For whom exactly?'

'For us.'

'And for her father?'

'I haven't asked him yet.'

'We painters make poor husbands and even worse sons. He'll know that.'

'Nothing will change, Gustav. I am Schiele today and in three months time I shall still be Schiele.'

'Your name remains – what of your inspiration?'

'You sound like that doctor that's always in the papers.'

'But it's so bourgeois, Egon. You've spent your life dissecting those rotten values, exposing their artifice. And now you're ready to adopt them...'

'Why do you have to vilify everything? Particularly anything that brings love, affection, trust, a family.'

'And a higher social ranking.'

'How dare you! You've built an entire career on sycophancy.'

'There's a difference between being sycophantic out of financial necessity and wilfully adopting the mask of the bourgeoisie.' Klimt leant forward and poured another glass of absinthe. 'And what about Wally?' asked the elder painter before emptying the glass and exhaling an inflammatory breath across the table.

'She'll survive.'

'She's barely known any other life than with you.'

'I'm sure your door will always be open.'

'I can't believe I'm hearing you talk like this.'

Egon sipped his coffee and looked down into his lap.

'I don't love Wally, if that's what you're pushing for.'

'Not after all these years?'

'What are you trying to say?'

'She might not have the right accent or a cottage in Schleswig-Holstein but…'

Egon stormed to the other side of the studio. 'For God's sake! I love Wally like a sister. That's all.'

'Your brush will dry in its jar and you'll wonder how it came to this.'

'I have other models. And besides, she'll still stand for me.'

'After all this?' Klimt shook his head. 'You're lovers. Lovers! Do you think you can halt that with a wave farewell and a letter of thanks?'

'It won't end like that.'

'This place is rotting around us and all you can think of is securing your little piece of bourgeoisie.'

'Don't lecture me.'

'The most intolerable era the world has ever known and you're just going to pack up and disappear into marital obscurity.'

'Are you finished?'

'Thousands of men are dying out there…'

'In an apocalyptic mood today?'

'Go down to the hospital for an hour. Spend an afternoon in Leopoldstadt. You'll see some of the poor bastards returning from the front. They've seen more than any of our paintings can ever depict. This is no longer the age of decadence, Egon. This is the age Ares, the age of decay... and you've become cauterised.'

Klimt poured himself another absinthe and Egon came back to the table.

'Feel better now you've got that off your chest?'

Klimt smiled and reached for the sugar. Egon pushed his hand away.

'Go steady with that, my friend.'

'My teeth are already rotten.'

'I meant the green stuff.'

Klimt stood up and they embraced.

'So, do I have your blessing?'

'You're asking the second most sacrilegious painter in the Empire for his blessing?' Klimt ran a finger around his bald patch. 'If you're asking for it figuratively then...' he plucked a paintbrush off a windowsill and stroked the sign of the cross on Egon's forehead. '...figuratively, yes.'

Johann Harms had long foreseen the reason for the painter's visit. He had watched his youngest daughter toy with the artist from across the road. He had always thought her brash, striking, volatile: the kind of woman who turned heads, the kind of woman meant for a painter. She lingered at the bedroom window before drawing the curtains; she wore her hair down when her elder sister donned a bonnet; she adjusted her bodice in public and laughed off her father's reproaches.

'Well, you do surprise me,' he said, turning from the window to face Egon. 'I wasn't expecting that at all.'

'I have tremendous admiration for her, Herr Harms.'

'I will, of course, have to speak with her first.' He paused, then continued. 'Provisionally, you have the answer you came here for.'

Harms asked three routine questions about the state of Egon's finances and, satisfied, shook his hand. He gestured for Egon to rise and accompanied him to the front door. Before Egon stepped out into the street, Harms pulled him back by the elbow.

'And that young girl who lives with you?'

'A model and a lodger, Sir.'

He pulled Egon closer, breathing into his face.

'I don't care what she is. Make sure she is gone by the end of the month. If she is indeed just a lodger then that shouldn't be a problem.'

'Fräulein Neuzil will be leaving tomorrow, Sir.'

'Be sure that she does. You are aware of the consequences. These may be lawless times but certain things remain totally unacceptable.'

Later that evening Egon climbed the stairs to his apartment. He opened the studio door and saw Valerie laid out on the couch, a book in hand. She looked up at him and smiled, her hair falling rakishly over her eyes.

'There's something we need to discuss.'

Egon stood impassive as Valerie spun like a firework around the room, expecting her to drop to the ground, charred and empty. But she continued to flame. She threw knives and brushes at Egon, tore sketches in half, kicked over pedestals and chairs, until finally she ran to the window and pulled the curtains down, the fabric tearing from its fastenings. She grabbed an easel and threw it through the glass, the shattering an overture to the clatter of wood in the street. The street came to life as neighbours brought candles and lamps to their windows.

'Bitch! Bitch!' she shouted through the broken window, shards sinking into her palm as she grabbed the frame. 'Have him then, you stuck-up bitch!'

A jar shattered on the pavement outside the Harms' house. She stormed into the bedroom and threw everything she could find into a leather case. Egon approached her, calmly laying a hand on her shoulder. Feeling his fingers, she spun and slapped him in the face.

'Get your hands off me!'

'Please, calm down a moment. You can't just leave.'

'Watch me.'

'You have nowhere to go.'

'That's what you think.'

The following day, he played back over the sobs and reproaches, her questions and his evasive answers, all of which had preceded the flurry of destruction. The studio was silent. There was no gramophone song coming from the next-door room; hours passed without interruption and all around him he saw shattered crockery scattered at the bottom of walls and framed canvases with gaping foot-stamped double tears. And, over and over again, he heard her recurring threats to return and burn the house down.

Egon had cut himself shaving that morning and a trickle of red tainted his stiff new collar. He placed a finger between his throat and the rigid board, allowing a shaft of air inside his damp shirt. The sun pounded down on his dark blue jacket and sugar-watered hair as he waited outside the church, bowing to the guests as they walked in. Klimt stood next to him, drops of sweat glistening on his balding head. He breathed hard against the cummerbund squeezing his midriff.

'You'll be fine once we get inside.'

'Is it full?'

'It's filling up, but I'm sorry to have to inform you that it contains possibly the most appalling altarpiece in all Christendom. I can only recommend that you keep your eyes shut when you're facing forwards.'

'I doubt the priest will allow that,' said Egon, patting down his hair with licked fingers.

'Well, then you had better look at your wife-to-be instead.' Klimt slapped his friend on the back. 'Rather more aesthetically pleasing.

It's about time you got this over and done with. In we go.'

Klimt followed Egon into the church and they walked briskly up the aisle to the front. The room was quiet but for shuffling shoes and ivy wreaths crackling on the fringes of candle flames. As they passed, the guests on each side turned to greet the bridegroom. Egon smiled, but when he reached the altar, his stomach was tight. He looked over his shoulder and exchanged a subtle nod with Gertrude, who sat in the front row, a lace shawl around her shoulders, her tired eyes looking out from underneath a faded beige hat. She was alone: Peschka had opted for conscription, casting off his aristocratic yoke in order to "experience the real Empire beyond Vienna's sealed walls". Like many others, she received infrequent letters from the front, carrying traces of struggles in the Macedonian mud: smears across rough paper, blunt smells, the scrawl of a shaking hand. Next to Gertrude lay a bouquet of flowers, sent by their mother who had stayed home, lying in bed, a mucus-soaked handkerchief clenched in her fist and a vial of mercury by her head.

The ceremony was little more than a flurry of hymns, recantations and formulaic speeches. At one moment, Klimt reached for Egon's arm while he swayed, at another moment the priest paused over a bible reading to engage Egon's errant eyes. Finally, Klimt passed him the ring and Egon struggled as it slipped only as far as the knuckle on the bride's finger. They both leant forward and Egon, licking his dry lips, bowed his head to hers. He raised his right hand to her cheek where her skin was stretched over the fine line of her jawbone. Terror seemed to overcome him, as though caught in the eyes of an ageless portrait.

Edith took a single, shallow breath as Egon pulled her towards him. His gaze alighted one final time on her undulating features, slipping effortlessly over the lines of her face. He fixed on her high cheekbones, on the small hairs at her temples and hair-line, on the defined lines of her nose, on a thin, previously unseen scar above her right eyebrow, and finally on her lips. Looking at this face for the last time, it was the face of a woman not yet possessed. Like a traveller leaving a country to which he would never return, he breathed in the image, breathed in the memory, tilted his head to the side and laid his lips with gentle precision onto Edith's. With the lightest of pressure, she kissed back.

Rows of smiling faces stared back at them, as they pulled away from each other and turned to the congregation. Egon blushed. It was only when he looked up, beyond the hats and the tearful faces, down the aisle and into the shadows at the back of the church that he saw a flash of sienna hair framed against a grey stone pillar, but then it was gone.

After hours of fawning conversation, Egon took Edith by the hand and led her out of the reception. Roessler was sprawled on a chair in the hallway, a glass of wine threatening to slip from his fingers. He looked up as he heard the front door open.

'*Prima nocte*, young lady.'

'Good night, Arthur.'

Egon stopped in the doorway, walked back to Roessler and removed the glass from his fingers, placing it on the hall table.

'Glad you could make it, my friend. Now get on home.'

'Be warned, you toothsome little thing. He has very particular tastes.'

'Look, I'll call you a carriage. Now go and clean yourself up.'

'You're about fifteen years too old for him though.'

'My wife would rather not hear such comments. Good night.'

The door closed behind them and they crossed the street to Egon's apartment. Edith wiped her feet on the doormat and followed Egon up the stairs and into his living quarters. He took a bottle of cognac and two glasses from a cupboard, replacing one when Edith declined. She looked around his apartment, laying her eyes for the first time on the accessories and accoutrements that filled her new husband's life. He walked towards Edith and kissed her on the lips. She remained passive, her arms by her side, her feet rooted to the carpet. Egon ran his hands over her shoulders and down her arms, catching his thumbs on the lip of her long gloves and slipping them off. He dropped them to the floor.

'They're a present from my aunt,' she said bending down. 'She would be most unhappy if...'

Egon took them from her and placed them on a chair. He pulled her close again and ran his hands down her forearms, feeling the tingle of skin rising under the soft hairs. He circled her, pushing the hair away from her shoulders and kissing her on the back of the neck. She gasped as he undid the laces at the back of her dress. Her dress eased and she exhaled, the tension flowing out of her shoulders. Egon moved round to face her and raised her face to his and kissed her once again on the lips. Her chin dropped; she pushed his arm away. She took two steps back, her eyes locked on his. They stared at each other for a second before she turned and went into the studio.

Egon went back to the cupboard and poured another glass of cognac before following her through to the studio. When he pushed open the door, Edith was wrapped in a rug, pacing wildly around the room, looking from one painting to the next, flicking through piles of sketches, turning over canvasses piled on the floor.

'Edith, darling. Please.'

'I don't believe it.'

'It's all old material. I don't do that stuff anymore.'

'I never thought...'

'Please, Edith. Just leave them, come on through to the next room.'

'I thought you did portraits.'

'I do.'

'But not these kind of pictures.'

'They're old sketches, studies, worthless scribbles. Now, please, come on through next door.'

'And her! Valerie!'

'It was for her lover.'

'Her lover?'

'She's moved out to live with him.'

'So, none of these are...'

'Listen to me. These are worthless old sketches. Forget them. Now please come next door. It's our wedding night.'

'But I never thought…'

'Edith, don't make an ordeal out of this. Come next door. Please don't ruin our first night together.'

Her body hung limp as he removed her garments. She held her arms up resignedly as he slipped the remaining parts of her wedding dress up and over her shoulders. Egon rolled over onto her, the weight of his thighs prizing her legs apart. He manoeuvred himself into her, her face falling to the side, looking at the cracks in the wall. Her gasps were inaudible through gritted teeth and against Egon's groans. His hands had twisted and turned her awkward limbs, grappling against her inexperience. Then they rested, their bodies intertwined like the knotted roots of trees. Her head lay on his chest until his heart rate slowed, the pace of his breathing a gentle ebb and flow of air. Then, carefully, she slipped her head underneath his arm and got up. To one side of the bed were Egon's high-legged black boots, one lying on its side, the other still standing, its shin bent down, its tongue protruding over knotted laces. She stepped around them, gathered her things and walked across the road to her parents' house.

Egon met her around the corner from his house in a cramped backroom of Café Eichberger. Valerie had come from the other side of the city, the bottom of her dress curled and grubby with trampling heels and summer streets. Her hair was tied back, moist and matted at the temples, with a faded ribbon hanging down over one shoulder. Egon stood up from the table and kissed her on the cheek, his rough fingers fastening around her arms as he drew her body towards him. She leant away and pulled up a chair, her eyes looking over and round him. She did up the top button on her lime-green blouse and pulled the collars straight.

'I've missed you, Wally.'

'Liar.'

'I often think about you.'

'Why have you called me here?'

'I wanted to see you.'

'What for?'

'I just wanted to know how you've been.'

'That's none of your business.'

'Where have you been…?'

'Didn't you hear me? It's none of your business!'

'I just want to know you're alright.'

'You'd never approve.'

'Please, darling, just listen to me for one moment.'

'Well, get on with it,' interrupted Valerie. 'No pleading, no excuses, no nothing. Just say what you have to say and let me go.'

Egon pushed his chair back and leant to the side, feeling around in the side pocket of his jacket. He withdrew several pieces of paper and laid them on the table, ironing out their creases with his palm.

'I have a proposition.'

'Does Edith know I'm here?'

Egon leant forward onto his elbows, resting his chin on interlocked fingers.

'No.'

'She wouldn't step foot in a place like this.'

'Wally, can you just read the…?'

'You used to scowl, you know, when I stood by you in public, holding your arm while you went on about form and composition and everything. You blathered on while I sat speechless in front of whoever it was you were trying to impress. Do you know how that felt?'

'Please.'

'Of course, I don't have a wealthy father.'

'Wally…'

'I don't have a father!'

'Stop it! Please!'

'All that for the prim convent girl.' She brought her hand down onto the table. 'Four years count for nothing? Nothing?'

'You know that's not true.'

Egon closed his eyes against the smoke rolling in circles across their table.

'We could have had a family. Children, Egon. Children!'

'I wasn't ready.'

'And now?'

'I don't know.'

Valerie leant across the table, looking Egon in the eyes. 'Why have you called me here, if not to answer my questions?'

Egon gestured to the waiter to bring another candle, which shed extra light on the bent papers as he folded them back on themselves along the creases. He pushed them over the table to Valerie. She took a minute to read them, her fingers walking back and forth over the sheets, reading and re-reading passages.

'If you would. Just there at the bottom of the last page.'

Egon pulled a black fountain pen out of his jacket, removing its lid. He passed it to Valerie, pointing out the relevant area with its nib. She took the pen from him and laid it on the table next to the document.

'Is that what it seems to be?'

'It's just an agreement.'

'A contract.'

'An engagement.'

'Call it what you will.'

'Please, just hear me out. It may seem quite formal but all it does in reality is ensure that we can both, every summer for three weeks – although you may want to change that period – spend a recreational holiday together.'

'A holiday?'

'You know, a couple of weeks by the sea; a trip to Lake Ballaton; take in some shows in Paris. Whatever you like. It's your choice. Perhaps we could start in Trieste.'

'So, for a few weeks every year, I would go with you to the coast… and do what?'

'Whatever we want.'

'Whatever *you* want.'

'We'll be together. Just like before.'

'And what does *she* say to this?' Egon shrugged. Valerie drew herself up. Her face was white, her jaw clenched and tense. 'Are you out of your mind?'

'Wally, please.'

'I will not be your damned whore!'

The chatter stopped in the café and all faces turned to Egon's table. A waiter walked to their table, hands behind his back.

'The other guests would appreciate it if you could lower your voice a little, Madam.'

Egon nodded and little by little conversations restarted.

'What were you thinking?' she hissed. 'Do you honestly think that she'll agree – or indeed I will?' She pushed the papers away from her, sliding them back across the table to Egon.

Egon took the papers, folded them up along their creases and placed them back in his pocket. 'I give up all my claims, all my desires, all my memories. Now trot off with a lighter heart and a clear conscience. Go and make your prim little wife happy. And never, ever humiliate me like this again.'

Egon looked up at her, leaning back in his chair. 'It's not so outrageous, you know. Believe me. We could…'

'Stop there. You've insulted me enough already.'

She stood up from the table as Egon pulled a cigarette from his jacket pocket. She moved around to stand beside him, waiting for him to look up. When he didn't, she ran her hand down the back of his head, stroking his hair and walked out of the café. Her high-heeled shoes clicked across the floor tiles while the rest of the café fell silent. Egon watched the door close behind her and his head dropped to the table. The clang of cutlery and voices washed over him like a tide.

∽∽

Two days later, when Egon was back in his studio, a cup of camomile tea on his lap, Valerie moved out of the apartment of her new lover, Erich Lederer. She carried all her possessions in the same worn suitcase, its leather strap digging into her palm like cheese-wire. She walked through the city, asking directions until she arrived at the headquarters of the Red Cross. She registered her name in their files, her head slung back, tears welling in their ducts, and walked against the wind towards the station. She loaded her bag onto the train, finding a small, hard seat in an overcrowded carriage and pulled her hat down over her eyes until she fell asleep. A day later she disembarked in Trieste, a friendly soldier carrying her bag, and boarded a ship in the docks. It wove its way through the idyllic islands, making several stops down the Dalmatian coast, picking up the injured and exiled, until three days later it reached port in Split.

Valerie's life was never to be the same. She learnt to recognise the white lumps in the mouths of corpses as cholera; she wrapped and bound the severed limbs of soldiers returning from the front; she prised blood-stained photographs from the fists of dying servicemen, their thumb-prints leaving ridges of red across the faces of their loved ones. With a kind smile she held sodden towels to the foreheads of dying men, and gathered up boots that would never be worn again. She wrote question marks in name registers and hid her fear behind a calm face. Each night she cried to herself. Meanwhile, Egon slipped between crisp linen sheets next to Edith, a stick of incense burning in the corner of their bedroom.

# FOURTEEN

# THE GODS OF THIS GENERATION

Pressgangs trawled the streets for bodies to feed new fronts, flesh to catch the hail of Russian bullets. For most of the previous year Egon had avoided conscription, visiting complicit doctors who marked him down as having a "weak physical condition" or "poor circulation". He had stood naked in their clinics, allowing their professional hands to press against his organs. He winced at opportune moments, flinching at jabbing fingers, his voice faltering, his step uneasy. The doctors had seen it all before, but they knew his name and let it pass. Klimt, too, had slipped through the net, his fame and age ensuring that he would spend most of the war looking out of his studio window at mothers walking their children to and from school.

But four days after the wedding, Egon was served his call-up papers.

The new doctor surveyed his body, this time frowning at Egon's winces, shaking his head at the coughs dragged up from healthy lungs. He scribbled down notes in Egon's file, reporting on the state of each of his faculties, a hypotactic ink review of the body which Egon had depicted so often in paint.

'These are difficult times. You must understand I am under a lot of pressure.'

'But what if I…'

'I'm sorry, Herr Schiele,' he said, shaking his head.

Within three weeks of their wedding day, Egon and Edith arrived at the Franz-Josef I station in Prague, the tickets for their honeymoon in Livorno left behind in the studio. The platform thronged with drafted troops, fresh-faced, flag-waving crowds, kissing and crying their farewells. Egon and Edith left the smoke and leather of the station-hall and stepped out onto the main street where soldiers had collected in small groups, crushing cigarette butts under boots and laughing away their anxieties. Egon took the suitcase from Edith, grabbed her by the hand and led her to the planning quarters.

He worked long hours, sleeping on a camp bed in the backroom of the offices, rolls of orders and invoices piled next to his bed. Edith spent her days and nights alone in a cold, rented room in the district of Smíchov, a sprawl of brick, flaking plaster and immovable blocks of greyness. It was a panorama of monotony, broken only by blocks of lime or yellow shoehorned into the industrial setting. During the day, she would go out to pick up eggs and bread; she would stop at the post office to hand over her daily letter, which was taken to Egon's military station on the other side of the city; she would cover her head in a scarf, walking briskly past the soldiers whistling at her from behind, and avoid the streets where rickety vans loaded up with boxes of military supplies. Every afternoon she would hurry back to her room and wait for news of Egon, falling asleep in her clothes, a blanket pulled over her, the same old novel spilt open on the sheets. At night she would be woken by troops marching past or the clang of armaments being transported. A couple of times a week, Egon would rouse her, closing the book and placing it on the bedside table, slipping his jacket off and rolling in behind her, pulling the blanket over them both, his legs uncovered, resting his unshaven chin on her shoulder blade. Her eyes half-opened and then closed again. In the morning, Edith would wake alone, no trace of Egon's nocturnal visit other than a dent in the pillow and crumbs of mud by the door.

Once, Egon slipped out of the planning bureau at midday to meet Edith for lunch. She had come with bread and cheese wrapped in a cloth and they passed the time on a bench on an island in the middle of the Moldau, sheltered by evergreens while the dark waters rumbled by, carrying barges stacked with martial cargo.

'They're needed east. A report came in last week that things have been going badly in…'

'Egon!' snapped Edith. 'I barely see you. Can we please talk of other things?'

Egon pulled her towards him, allowing her hand to trace his ribs through a thick-weave shirt. She coughed hard.

'I'm sorry, Edi, I'm so sorry.' He pulled a strand of hair away from her damp cheek. 'Did you manage to stop by the post office?' She nodded against his chest. 'And?'

'It's a mess, you know. It takes weeks to get anything through to the provinces.'

'And nothing from Adele?'

She shook her head again.

'Just one page would be enough. Why can't she write?'

'I'm sure they're better off than we are. You shouldn't worry.'

'This isn't a game, Egon. It's not about suffering more or less than your neighbour.'

'I didn't mean that. Just that they're probably bearing up better there than here. We should just count ourselves lucky that we landed where we did.' Her head sunk into her neck, her shoulders jerking with sobs. Egon pulled her closer. 'Come on now. Things could be worse.'

'How?'

'At least we're together.'

'Together?'

'It's more than most.'

'I see you for a few minutes every couple of days!'

'This is wartime.'

'As you keep saying.' She sat up and looked her husband in the eyes. 'We need to get out of here.'

'It's not easy.'

'You haven't painted in months.' She coughed again, raising a handkerchief to her mouth. 'This place is killing us both.'

As Egon extracted himself from Edith's arms several mornings later, he caught sight of black-flecked mucus on her pillow. He leant over and examined the fluid which had seeped into the linen of the pillows. He unfolded the handkerchief lying next to her side of the bed and recoiled at its dark, viscous contents. That afternoon, he went to his commanding officer.

'I should just send you straight to the front, Private!' he said, peering over half-moon glasses. Hans Rosé looked at Egon's chin as if examining a crumb.

Mostly bald, Rosé groomed his beard to a point, teasing his moustache out at the sides. His dark green uniform was embellished at the neck with the silver stars and the gold and red piping of an officer.

'Age?'

'Twenty-five, Sir.'

'Do you realise we've got men nearly half your age at the front? Things could be very different for you, Private. They are for most of your compatriots.'

'I realise that, Sir, but...' replied Egon, raising a hand to his stubble.

'How do the Balkans sound to you? You could pop down there and sun yourself with our Empire's finest straplings.' Egon did not respond. 'You're probably not really made for that, are you? All that dirty mud and those awfully heavy guns...!'

'My skills are in alternative fields, Sir.'

'Alternative fields? What grand skills can you offer me, Private? Knitting? Crochet? I need killers, Private. Killers!'

He placed the sodden end of a cigar in his mouth and drew hard, the embers glowing.

'I am a painter, Sir.'

'Hate to disappoint but there aren't really any jobs for your sort around here. Nor in Dalmatia, you'll be pleased to know.'

'Sir, the city is affecting my wife's health.'

'Private, we are at war!' The commanding officer struck the table, a teacup tipping in its saucer. 'It affects one's health. If I listened to every soldier's worries about their loved ones we would all be living in cabins in the Alps, swimming in glacial lakes and eating grilled salmon. A lovely thought, but it doesn't contribute much to defending the Empire, does it now?'

'No, Sir.'

Rosé leant back in his chair and linked his fingers behind his neck.

'There was a lovely young lad who used to work in here a while back. The war affected his health, too: a bullet through the abdomen and subsequent septicaemia. Now, get out and I don't want to see you back in here again.'

Egon saluted, turned slowly on the spot and walked to the door.

'Hold it there, Private!'

'Yessir,' said Egon, stopping in the doorway.

'I don't care much if your type are up to their elbows in mud. Everyone is equal before God and before enemy fire, Private. But rest easy, you're not going to the front. You could come in useful later. Not for the campaign, but for something else.' He picked up the half-smoked cigar from an ashtray and waved away Egon's salute. 'They need another person in the processing camp. You start next week.'

Egon sat at a small square desk, his feet extended underneath, his elbows resting on its corners. He wore the sap green coat of the Austrian Army, the double buttons down the chest, the rough collar chafing against his neck. He held a pencil in his right hand and a thin pipe in his left, sucking in smoke with his eyes closed. At the front of the desk was his hat, which, although unsullied by battle, still bore the salty tidemarks of daily work. Opposite Egon stood a Russian soldier, his hands bound with frayed string resting between his legs; his neck was crooked forward. Behind him stood yet more, all silently waiting in the same position, trying to melt into insignificance while three young Austrian soldiers played with their rifles in the doorway. The first prisoner shuffled closer.

'Name?'

'Markov. Nikolai Mikhailovich Markov.'

'Date of birth?'

'12 June 1899.'

'Place?'

'Berezniki.'

'Regimental number?'

'14.982.169.'

With a flick of his pipe, Egon signalled for the prisoner to move on.

'Name?'

'Likhachev. Vasily Ilich Likhachev.'

'Date of birth?'

'3 December 1897.'

'Place?'

'Kursk.'

'Regimental number?'

'14.982.055.'

Egon signalled again, drew on the tobacco and the next prisoner moved on.

When he was first transferred to the sorting station on the outskirts of Prague, he struggled with the names. He transcribed them, guessing at how the Slavic sounds might be rendered in the confines of German orthography. Now he barely looked up from the register in front of him, calling out the four questions, licking his pencil and etching them into the coarse sheets of the book. He would hear the shuffle as yet another soldier drew close and sense the weight of his body leaning over the desk. He smelt the war on them: dampness, oil, muddy hair. Despair. Many were young, too young, their hairless chins smeared in grease. It was as though a whole generation of the nation's youth was hurtling west towards an unknown enemy, as if their pregnant mothers had given birth astride open graves. These were the lucky few whom war had swept off the battlefields while their brothers-in-arms lay rotting in water-logged fields.

On rare occasions, Egon would exchange a word with one of them. He would mishear their patronymic and they would stumble through the German alphabet while Egon scratched out approximations of their names: Mikhailovich, Nikolaevich, Aronovich, Yakovlevich. Whenever he looked up he saw the same resilience in their eyes. Their fine features and pasty skin would cause him to pause as he wrote down their details, sketching a character, a history and a family around the prisoner before making a sign with his pipe and watching him walk away. Days later that prisoner would be gone, processed through the camp's books and dispatched to work at another facility. Just as easily as Egon had seen a life grow up momentarily around the four entries in the register, the life would be extinguished leaving nothing but a line of numbers, a name and a place as if they were just arbitrary data collected from a scientific experiment.

However, Grigori Kladjishuili was one he would always remember. The prisoner had been unable to spell his own name, uncertain how to portray the fickle trans-Caucasian vowels in his uncouth German. Egon asked several times and then gave up, pushing him a piece of scrap paper and the pencil.

'Write it.'

One of the Austrian guards stepped forward and Egon waved him away.

Egon looked around the room while he waited for Kladjishuili to complete his long and laborious name. The young guards had returned to the doorway, joking with one hand in their pockets and the other hand holding cigarettes, rifles swinging from their shoulders. The remaining prisoners huddled together in the corner watching. As he looked back to Kladjishuili he saw him still scribbling, filling up both sides of the paper with bridges, arches, crosses and hammers interspersed with reversed Roman letters. Egon said nothing, watching the prisoner scrawl furiously, filling up every last corner of the paper.

Feeling Egon's eyes on him, the prisoner stopped and held the paper out. He blinked repeatedly.

'Please.'

'What?'

'Address. Here. Please.'

Egon looked at the paper and then shrugged.

'Here. Name. Here. Address,' he said, pointing. 'Please.'

Egon copied his name, place, birth date and regiment from the paper into the register. He held the scrap in his hand a little longer, flipping it over onto the other side.

'Please. Send. Sir. Please. God.' The words came out urgently, and the guards at the door looked up from their conversation. One of them sauntered up, raised the butt of his rifle and buried it into the small of the Russian's back.

Egon stood up from his desk, his hat falling to the floor.

'Fucking sit back down, Private!'

'But he's done nothing!'

'A piece of shit not worthy of standing on Imperial soil.'

'We have protocol…'

'We owe nobody no favours. Least of all the fuckin' Ruskies.' He kicked the body on the ground. 'Fucking animals. Bearded women and dickless men!'

The guards by the door cheered and Egon looked down at the man writhing on the floor, gulping for breath. He moved to bend down but the guard struck Kladjishuili across the jaw with his rifle again. He groaned, spitting bloody, shattered teeth from his broken mouth.

'Now sit back down and do your job.'

Egon pulled up his chair and took his place again at the table. He looked down at Kladjishuili hunched on the floor, the notches of his spine pushing through his jacket like dorsal fins. Egon crunched the scrap of paper up in his palm and as the next Russian arrived at his desk, he leant back in his chair and slipped the ball of paper into his jacket pocket.

Egon opened it in his palm when he was back in his quarters, holding it next to the candle, watching the light flicker off its pictograms. He looked for familiar shapes among the Cyrillic letters but gave up. He wrapped the note in another piece of paper, having carefully copied the name and address onto the front, and dispatched it the next morning. The likelihood of it arriving was non-existent. Postal services had all but collapsed over the previous months and even if the letter did arrive, no one would be there to receive it. Maybe, when the war was over, Kladjishuili would trudge back across corpse-filled battlefields to his family's house and find his own letter on the mat. Or maybe a fellow officer would pick up the letter at some military outpost, it would be stuffed into his pocket, passed on through myriad dirty fists until one day Kladjishuili's wife would stick her calloused thumb under the flap, tear open the binding and smile at the illusion her husband was alive.

Weeks later, Egon painted the Russian prisoner from memory, picking out the red piping on his hat and lapels with the same red as his full lips; his sunken cheeks enhancing the Russian's lifeless eyes; and embellishing a wispy moustache which had since become a full beard, fighting against the winter wind of a labour camp.

Egon saluted to the sentries as he entered the commanding officer's hut in the corner of the camp. He knocked at the door and waited for the order to enter, marching smartly into the room, saluting and fixing his gaze just above the officer's head at a picture of the Emperor on the wall: a row of medals offset against a scarlet jacket, a gold embroidered kepi, and clipped white sideburns sprouting over full cheeks.

'At ease, Private. At ease.'

Egon relaxed, looking down from the portrait to Rosé's face.

'What is it?'

'Nothing, Sir.'

'Why do you think you're here?'

'No idea, Sir.'

'Not even an inkling?'

Egon shook his head.

'Answer me!'

'No, Sir.'

'I've never been particularly fond of you. But then again you doubtless have plenty admirers tucked away in some grotty corner.'

'Perhaps, Sir.'

'Such as Grünwald. A great admirer of your scribblings. Apparently.'

'I'm honoured to hear that I am known to a senior officer, Sir.'

'There's no honour in what you do, Private. It's the likes of that old bastard that will have us lose this war. Look at me when I'm talking to you!'

Egon cast his eyes down from the portrait and back towards Rosé.

'He read the report filed over the incident with the Russian and instructed me to treat you well. He said you were quite "controversial".'

'That has been said, Sir.'

'The Empire could do with some politically volatile stuff. Quite right to stick it to them. There's nothing worse than silent obedience.'

'With respect, Sir, I'm not a political painter.'

'Not political?'

'Mainly people, Sir.'

'What kind?'

'All kinds, Sir.'

'What's controversial about that? Did you miss off some of the Emperor's medals or something?'

'I've never painted the Emperor, Sir,' said Egon. 'I paint people from all backgrounds. All shapes and sizes.'

He sat back in his chair, smoothing his lapels.

'All shapes and sizes?'

'That's correct, Sir.'

'I understand.' Rosé smiled. 'Listen, Private. Grünwald has asked me to change your duties. According to him, your place is not with the prisoners. He believes it is below a man of your calibre.'

'That's kind, Sir. Thank you.'

He rolled a blunt pencil across the desk, its serrated rattle counting out time until he silenced it with a thumb.

'I think it's bullshit. We'll never win a war with that kind of leadership. Anyway, there's little use I can make of your skills here. That is, unless you can come up with any decent ideas.' Egon glanced around the room. 'Exactly. So, I am going to transfer you.'

'Where to?'

'You have a wife?'

'Yessir.'

'Where is she?'

'In Smíchov, Sir.'

Rosé tugged at his beard, shifting in his seat, casting his eye over the papers on his desk. He pulled out a map and ran his finger in a circle around Vienna.

'How do you fancy the Imperial and Royal Commission for the Army in the Field?'

'Excuse my ignorance, Sir, but...'

'The stores, Private. Distributing supplies to our troops in the field so that they have enough tobacco to smoke away their fears as the shells are falling all about them. It's only a short trek away from Hietzing. You'll be able to cuddle up to that wife of yours at night. A drop of mercury in a sea of blood, young Private.'

'I'm truly grateful, Sir.'

Rosé ran his finger down a sheet of paper, reading out loud. 'Open every day from 9.00 until 14.00 and then again from 15.00 to 19.00. There is also a night-shift for the provision of emergency armaments.'

'I'll be available, Sir.'

'Now, I'll have to get in touch with a few colleagues in Vienna to make sure this can all go ahead, but if Grünwald is involved there won't be any complications. If you get bored of the stores – or indeed your wife – I'm sure he can organise a quick tour of the provincial headquarters to paint the offices.'

'Thank you, Sir.'

'One more thing.' Rosé looked down at the papers on his desk and cleared his throat. 'Grünwald would like something from you in return.'

'Of course, Sir. Anything.'

'He'd like a picture done before you leave.'

'A landscape of the hills at sunset perhaps, Sir?'

'Private Schiele, every soldier – including myself – will be happy if he never sets eyes on those hills again.' Rosé stopped, shuffled his papers and coughed. 'Do you remember registering a prisoner this morning by the name of Radzinsky?' he said at last.

'No, Sir. There were so many and I don't recall that particular name.'

'Quite tall. Slender chap. Thick eyebrows.'

'The lad with his side bound, Sir?'

'Dmitri Radzinsky. I think he had taken some shrapnel. Not bad enough to be admitted to the field hospital though. Grünwald examined him thoroughly earlier. It seems he has nothing to fear.'

'A lucky one, Sir.'

'Indeed. A very lucky young man.'

'And how can I be of service, Sir?'

'Grünwald wants you to paint him. He'll be out of here tomorrow and it should be done before he is relocated.'

'Him, Sir?'

'That's right.'

Rosé leant over and opened a drawer at the bottom of his desk. He pulled out a piece of paper and slid it onto the desk.

'It has come to Oberstleutnant Grünwald's attention that you already have some experience in this field.' Egon looked down at Kladjishuili's inverted face, his eyes still dripping sadness. 'The duty officer found this in your kitbag last week. Who is it?'

'One of the Russian soldiers passing through, Sir.'

'Name?'

'I can't remember, Sir.'

'Come on, Private! Name?'

'There are so many of them.'

'…but some particular ones stand out, don't they?' Egon shrugged. 'But it's hardly the work of someone as "controversial" as you.'

'I wouldn't know, Sir.'

'Grünwald does.'

'If I may ask, Sir, what is it he is looking for?'

'Private Helden is in the storeroom. He will be there to guide you.'

'I'm sorry, Sir?'

'Helden will assist you.'

'In what way?'

'He will ensure the prisoner is presented properly. This is to be a classical portrait. You know in the Greek style. I am sure they taught you that in the Academy.'

'But he's wounded, Sir.'

'You have two choices. And I suggest, if you want to return to your wife's warm bed, you do as you are told.'

'Yessir.'

'Dismissed.'

Egon put his hat back on, saluted and walked to the door.

'One more thing, Private.'

'Yessir.'

'Front on. The perspective is to be front on.'

'Of course, Sir.'

'And don't be shy. If Grünwald's not satisfied you have captured the essence of the boy, your transfer will not be processed.'

'Yessir.'

'Do you understand what I mean by capturing his essence?'

'I think so.'

He saluted again and walked out of the room past the sentries.

He stood on the path outside the cabin, wiping the sweat from his brow and looking over the camp. He saw a prisoner, lying by the side of a track, left behind as his group was marched to the fields. Egon watched him through a passing wall of Austrian soldiers, the Russian's face disappearing and reappearing as the rows of green-clad legs flashed past. He was spluttering fluid into his cupped hands. Several Austrians dropped off the back of their company and crowded around the young Russian. A rifle pressed down on the prisoner's face, grinding it against the gravel path as the rest of his body was swallowed in a sea of stomping boots. After the Austrians had walked away, a cloud of gravel dust hung over the fossilized body, his bloodied face imprinted with the tread marks of military footwear. The soldiers ran to catch up with the rest of their company, their boots crunching on gravel. The Russian twitched on the ground, his shinbone showing itself through blood-soaked leggings.

The prison camp remained a muddled constellation of such images: a collage of dark uniforms and fragmented faces, blurred snap-shots like the photograph album of a country Egon had never visited. He couldn't paint. The only works he had to show for his months of toil in the camp were a registry of Cyrillic names, the portrait of Kladjishuili folded up in his bottom drawer, and a grotesque painting hanging in the sleeping quarters of Oberstleutnant Grünwald.

Edith reached across the table, turned Egon's palm over and squeezed his fingers.

'You'll be late,' she said, wiping a flake of pastry from the side of her mouth.

'My colleague will be there already. Anyway, I'm going to stop in on Mother on my way. She never tells us when she runs out of coal.'

'They ran out down the market yesterday.'

'Then I'll take her some of ours.'

'Well, we're also…'

'…I'll bring some back from the stores.'

Egon stood up, placing the remaining bread rolls in his jacket pocket with an apple.

'When will you be back?'

'Around five or six. Maybe later.'

'Why don't you come home earlier? It's been a while since you were in the studio. What if I model for you?'

'Edith, leave it, please'

'It's something to do with me, isn't it? It is. I just know it is.'

'Don't talk such rubbish.'

'Egon!'

'I ought to be on my way.' Egon took his hat from a chair next to the door. Edith stood up from the table, walked to his side and kissed him on the cheek.

'Off you go, my soldier.'

'Please, darling. Don't joke.'

She kissed him again, standing up on tiptoes.

An hour later Egon arrived at the supply depot and took his place behind the counter, marking small numbers and crosses next to names and ranks, counting out cigarettes and bootlaces, cans and biscuits. The day passed in silence beyond the walls of the depot except for the irregular whip-crack of a bullet echoing off the courtyard walls. Egon's colleague sat behind him in the room, verifying names, striking each letter into the typewriter with a burgeoning index finger. Soldiers came blank-faced, picked up their supplies and left, exchanging vacant glances with Egon. By mid-afternoon he had returned to an empty house. Edith was still in the city's cafés mingling with officers' wives, lamenting the luxuries they had forgone that particular month. Egon changed out of his uniform and stood by his studio window, pulling back the curtains. He waited until Edith's sister appeared at her bedroom window over the road and caught her eye with a wave. In unspoken complicity, Adele pulled on her shawl, crossed the street and entered his studio.

She had been shy at first, unwilling to shed her flowery dresses and embroidered blouses. But Egon chipped away, grinding down her protests, until she no longer sat with her fingers interlaced in her lap, her back straight, looking away to the side. Now, Adele simply undressed and followed the painter's orders. She would hold the pose until Egon finished with a flourish, watching him simulate a signature and take the portrait away into the bedroom to dry. She had protested at first, eager to see how he had rendered her beauty, but she soon gave up. When he came back into the studio, wiping his hands on an old rag, she was already waiting for him, her blouse open and her skirt laid over the back of a chair.

In the next-door room the blank canvas stood propped against the side of the bed.

'One for me, one for the corporal, one for me, one for the corporal,' said Klimt as Egon changed out of his smock and into a shirt.

'At least I'm contributing something to the campaign.'

'We wage a different kind of war.'

'Here it comes.'

'A war of ideas.'

'Don't you ever get tired of yourself?'

'A war of the mind.'

Egon looked around the bare studio. 'Who's winning?'

'I'm working on it.' Klimt lolled back into an armchair, his head rolling on his shoulders. A tabby cat sprung up onto his lap and he closed his eyes as he flattened the fur on its back. 'I've produced nothing for months. Brussels was a disaster. They've all fled to the country and I can't bring myself to stare at another blank canvas for half a day.'

The blood was drawn out of Klimt's cheeks and the skin hung from his bones in folds. Sprigs of white stubble were sprinkled on his chin like grains of salt. 'So empty. No decent models. No one comes anymore.' He sat up suddenly. 'What about Wally?'

'Gone. I tried to persuade her but…'

'Shame,' said Klimt, lighting his opium pipe. He raised a hand to his face and pinched the bridge of his nose. 'Hippocrene has run dry. They may all come and go, Egon, but you'll never have another Wally. In fact, *we* will never have another Wally.'

He held out the pipe and Egon waved it away.

'Kiss Morpheus full on the lips.'

'Just put it down, Gustav.'

'Come lie with the lotus-eater,' said Klimt, easing himself out of the chair, the cat jumping down. He lay down in the corner of his studio on a bed of cushions. 'If you won't join me, help yourself to a drink over there,' he added, pointing at a tray of bottles in the corner. 'There's arsenic in the cupboard.' He opened a dark wooden box and filled the pipe, lying back on the cushions, resting it on a small stand next to his head. 'It's as though a cloud of dust has gathered... a massive, nebulous cloud and it's floating above me. Collapse, implode. Soon a gust will disperse it into miniscule particles and nothing will be left. The gods of this generation have been overthrown.'

'Give it a break, Gustav.'

'Not just in the streets and on the battlefields but even here. Death... life is passing over into death. Even my fine, graceful women, or your dirty cherubs... even they cannot escape this. It will all go.'

'Put that pipe down, for God's sake.'

'So much time looking at what is beautiful and we've forgotten what is lasting.'

'Beauty isn't lasting.'

Klimt closed his eyes and sucked on the pipe.

'You see: the nebulous cloud.'

Egon sipped at his wine while Klimt continued to draw on the pipe.

'Tell me: do you remember Peschka?'

'He's my brother-in-law.'

'Forgive me.' Klimt ran a hand over his forehead. 'Excellent with watercolours, that man. Magnificent cerulean blues.'

'What's the bastard done this time?'

'I received a letter from his aunt this morning.' Egon leant back and rested on the corner of an armchair. 'I am to make the epitaphium at the interment.'

Egon sunk into the chair.

'And Gerti?'

'I presume she knows. His aunt is paying for the body to be preserved and returned to the city, *mors mortis*. They've asked me to be present. It seems the poor young fellow used to idolise me.' Klimt sucked again on the pipe, coughing as his lungs reached capacity. 'The train comes in tomorrow afternoon. Help me with arrangements, will you? I know he valued your friendship as well.'

'I'm not sure I'd be welcome.'

'Don't be stupid.'

'I haven't – hadn't – spoken to him for years. I barely speak to her anymore.'

'Then now's the time to rectify that.'

Egon walked into the corner, drained his wine and poured a large glass of absinthe, dipping a sugar-filled spoon into the green fluid and adding a drop of arsenic. He lit the charred spoon and watched the molten drops splashing into the bottom of the glass. His hand shaking, he took the tumbler, emptied its contents and lay down next to Klimt on the cushions, severing the anchor of consciousness.

# FIFTEEN

# BRUSH STROKE

Sleet wrapped around the graveyard in sharp slices of ice and water. Two soldiers, weighed down by their saturated uniforms, slid Peschka's coffin into the family tomb, his body lined up alongside the uncle who had committed suicide months earlier, the war having left his business in tatters. The military pastor closed his bible, its pages sodden, its leather binding swollen, and turned his back to the young widow. His cassock seemed an impenetrable black, a shadow in three dimensions. He walked back to the church leaving Gertrude strung between her mother and Roessler, her body held tight as she shuddered with tears.

'Egon said he'd come.'

'I'm sure there's a reason,' consoled Roessler.

'But what could possibly excuse this?'

'He wanted to be here. I know he did.'

'And Gustav? How could they?' She broke down again and Roessler caught her in both arms, her body frail from the long months of war and her husband's absence.

Egon had not met the simple coffin off the train that morning; nor was Klimt at the cemetery to make the funeral oration he had promised. Instead, while Peschka's body lay next to his deceased relatives, the stone door grinding back over the tomb's opening, Egon was on the other side of the city crouched at Klimt's bedside.

On that same morning, Egon had left Edith at home and walked to Klimt's studio to rehearse the funeral address, passing groups of men wandering the streets barefoot, with hollow eyes and no recollection of their own address. The war was dragging to a close and the city was clogged with suffering. He knocked at Klimt's door, half-expecting to hear the painter's heavy feet walking down the steps, half-dreaming of Valerie's light footsteps. He stood back from the pavement and looked up to the top floor. The studio window was partially open and a flap of dark blue curtain flicked in and out.

'Gustav!' he called.

The disapproving faces of mothers and widows appeared at the other windows across the street.

'Open up!'

He crossed the street to the far pavement and picked up a metal tube from outside a derelict house. He wedged it in the jamb of the door and leant his weight against the lever. A window opened behind him and a voice shouted abuse across the street. He forced the door, his knuckles slamming into the wall as the jamb gave way. He swore, pulling a handkerchief from his pocket to wipe away the blood which throbbed in the grazes, marking time. He walked inside and up the steps, pushing open the unlocked studio door at the top. The room was light; Klimt had pulled back the curtains, replacing the stale air with morning chill. Egon poked his head behind the dark blue arras.

'Come on. We'll be late!'

He turned back into the studio: empty glasses and bottles were on every surface while half-finished sketches and paintings were propped against the walls. The floor was strewn with rags, clothes and cushions. He called out Klimt's name. As he approached the easel in the corner his left foot struck something. Egon bent down and saw the artist's crumpled body lying face down; his dark blue, full-length smock had made him almost invisible among the swathes of material. Horrified, Egon rolled him over and saw Klimt's vacant face, one side smeared with lunatic black and red, the other side slipped, the lips and cheeks hanging limp from his skull. He leant into the body, feeling breath on his cheek. He opened the eyes with his fingers and watched the pupils shrink like clenching fists: a mere glimmer at the bottom of a well. He pulled the body up and placed cushions underneath it, looking at the easel where infernal colours were smeared in a stripe down the length of a painting. He leant down and wiped his friend's face with a rag; a low litanic mumble came from Klimt's dry lips and Egon held him, kissing his forehead and running hands over his head. His body was flaccid, the left arm and leg flung out across the floor. Egon stood up and ran outside into the street.

Egon crouched at Klimt's bedside in a hospital packed with amputees, loud with the bronchial rasps of influenza. He held his friend's hand, whispering, raising a cloth to wipe away the spittle which ran down his grey beard. His complexion had lost is rosy glow and his once bulky frame was now a clothes-horse for a suit of skin. Egon switched back and forth between monologue and silence, talking mostly to himself but occasionally filling in Klimt's probable responses. He brought paper and pencil, and, resting the pad on the edge of Klimt's bed, he talked as they had done before, sketching out plans for an academic institute, holding the pictures in front of Klimt's empty stare, hoping for a squeeze of his hand. Day after day, Egon continued to draft and redraft the plans they had half-baked in an absinthe torpor, finally giving up when the old painter's eyes refused to open.

Egon returned every day for three weeks, pestering the nurses over Klimt's progress. He would stay overnight in the hospital, sleeping in the chair next to Klimt's bed, leaning forward and resting his head on the edge of the mattress. He would be jolted awake in the middle of the night sensing Klimt had moved; he would stand up, call the night nurse and pace the ward until finally, swallowing a yawn, he would sit back down next to the bed and fall asleep.

He started to sketch Klimt's sleeping face, his head lolling to one side of the pillow, his eyes bulging beneath their immovable lids, his face gaunt, slanting on the left, his hair uncombed. On each sketch, Egon traced the outline of a smile on Klimt's lips, turning up the corners of his mouth underneath his thin moustache.

Three weeks after the stroke, Klimt died of pneumonia. Egon returned only once more to the hospital. He followed the warden through the corridors to the back of the main building and down some stairs into the morgue. He walked to a table in the corner and pulled the top of the sheet back, folding it down over Klimt's grey chest, overgrown with tightly-coiled black hairs. Egon bent over the body and hugged the hardened flesh.

'Get off!' hissed the warden, pulling Egon away. 'Not here.'

He wiped the tears from his face and dropped the pre-arranged handful of coins into the man's hand.

'How long?'

'Until I say. No longer.'

'Alright.'

'And no touching or else you're out.'

The warden looked once over his shoulder before closing the door. Egon opened up the bag he was carrying with him and removed a piece of muslin which he placed over Klimt's bloodless face.

He walked through the blood and mud suburbs, past looted and abandoned shops, their fronts boarded up, shards of glass littering the pavement. Streetlights were bent over like half-smoked cigarettes; horse shit festered in the road; groups of men with empty sleeves and encrusted bandages roamed the streets, streaming in from all corners of the crumbling Empire, adding their horrifying war stories to the city's melancholic narrative. Egon paused outside Klimt's house.

'Good afternoon. My name is Schiele. I have come to speak about…'

The landlord slammed the broken door in Egon's face.

'At twenty-seven?'

'You're the natural candidate, *l'élu*,' pleaded Roessler.

'It's wrong to be discussing this now.'

'It needs to be done sometime.'

'It's trampling on his grave before the soil has even settled.'

'Everyone knows you're his designated heir.'

'Arthur, this is not a monarchy!' Egon rested his elbows on the desk, staring at Roessler on the studio couch.

'Lenz is backing you as well.'

'He always has.'

'And Koloman.'

'He owes me.'

'You owe him actually.' Roessler dabbed his brow with a handkerchief. 'And Orlik.'

'That makes a change.'

Klimt's death mask was propped against Egon's desk-lamp, its edges still rough, its closed eyes staring at him. Roessler removed his jacket and hung it off the corner of an easel, sitting on the corner of Egon's desk.

'Everyone knows we have witnessed the passing of a great man, Egon, but that does not mean the world stops turning. There's still the next month's exhibition.'

'So that's what this is all about?'

'Life goes on, Egon.'

'War has brought this place to its knees, hacking off provinces like diseased limbs, pumping poison through the country. And all you can think of is an exhibition!'

'And when did you start caring?'

'I've always cared.' Egon's face was colourless.

'Then you'll understand that we have to do everything we can to retain a sense of normality. Particularly here.'

'Don't be naïve, Arthur. The Federation expects us to employ all manner of pomp to prove that, despite everything else, the Empire and its subjects are mightier than its enemies.' Egon picked up a brush and pointed it at Roessler's face. 'Well, let me tell you, I'll exhibit if you want me to. I'll exhibit the best paintings I can produce, but not a single one will be for political purposes. Not a single one will glorify this despicable place, this arsehole of humanity.' He lowered the brush. 'Quite the opposite.'

Egon's life was spread across the city's galleries: whores, girls and lovers; landscapes with trains; townscapes with laundry; portraits of prisoners, soldiers and aristocrats. The sum of his life hung before the visitors like a book of a hundred characters and a hundred narratives, drafted, rewritten and rejected until all that was left were these forty-nine fragments. Valerie, long absent, still looked down from inside her prison-frame, her unblemished skin a rare sparkle among the oil-heavy canvases. Fickle Vienna, which had spurned Egon so often and so brutally in earlier years, now hoisted him onto a pedestal as a sign of the city's greatness; that same greatness which festered within the city walls and on battlefields throughout the continent. Collectors bought up his paintings; critics praised his style; aristocrats commissioned portraits; museums made their first purchases from a living artist. At long last, as the Empire's sons and daughters bewailed severed limbs and shattered bones, Egon nestled in the bosom of acceptance.

The visitors came in droves. They frowned at Valerie's nudity, admired Edith's posture and looked askance at the portrayals of entwined girls sleeping on rugs. The price of the paintings trebled; people tore the exhibition's sacrilegious posters from walls across the city, hanging them in their front rooms.

On the day after the exhibition, Egon returned to the gallery to pick up the single unsold painting. The curator had taken it down, wrapping it in cloth and leaving it on a table in the storeroom. Egon pulled the coarse material away from the frame and cast his eye over the canvas which the assembled collectors had rejected. Edith stood there, her arms long and thin, her eyes staring out of the canvas at him: a full-length portrait pose, standing unnaturally straight. Her tawny hair was up, its wavy fringe trimmed around the line of her thick eyebrows. Her eyes were wide and round, her cheeks picked out with a dash of red. She wore a long dress of vertical stripes of reds, greens, yellows, blacks and browns. Underneath she wore a white blouse which frilled out around her neck. At the bottom, her white-stockinged feet stood in white shoes. Egon rewrapped the painting, put it under his arm and walked out.

He stepped down from the carriage in Hietzing, standing for an instant at his front door, searching in his pocket for house keys. Then he changed his mind and crossed the street to Edith's parents' house. He leant the painting against his leg and rung the doorbell. Adele answered.

'What a pleasant surprise, Egon.'

'Good evening.'

'Your wife's not here, I'm afraid.'

'Actually, I was looking for your father.'

'Not for me?' She smiled coquettishly up at him.

'Not this time.'

'He's out as well, I'm afraid.'

'And your mother?'

'They've both gone to the theatre. Left an hour ago. I'm home on my own if you want to come in and wait.'

'I must be getting back actually. Could I ask you to give them this though?' He picked up the picture and leant it against the wall inside the door.

Adele untied the string and pushed down the fabric. 'Oh, I see.'

'It's a present.'

'Don't I get one?' There was a stubborn look in her eye.

'Another time.'

'Tomorrow afternoon?'

'Another time, I said.'

Egon turned away and the door closed behind him. He walked back across the street and into his apartment. Upstairs, Edith was sitting in the studio, reading the newspaper. She looked up as the door opened.

'They adore you, darling. Just adore you!' Egon kissed her on the cheek. '"Fate has decreed that he should become famous, not merely notorious, in his own lifetime. For Vienna, an unthinkable occurrence..."'

'Who wrote that bloated nonsense?'

'Arthur.'

'He really does go over the top sometimes.'

'Don't be such a bore! Why don't you just enjoy it?'

'My darling.' Egon kissed her again on the top of the head as he passed, removing his jacket and tie.

'Koller was here an hour ago.'

'Let's not get carried away now, please.'

'Dr Koller! Can you believe it? He wants you to paint his entire family. They'll buy anything if it's got your name on it.'

'You know that's not true.'

'Where do they get the money from at times like these?'

'Best not ask.'

'And another gentleman called by earlier as well. I can't remember his name. He said he already had a portrait from you, but didn't want to leave a message.'

'Did he leave his card?'

'I don't think so.'

'He can join the queue.'

She held both hands to her forehead.

'Ledermann? Something like Ledermann?' she said, looking up.

'Lederer?'

'Maybe.'

'August or Erich?'

'I can't remember.'

'Young or old.'

'Young, I think. He didn't remove his hat.'

'What did he want?'

'Why? Who is this Ledermann?'

'Lederer. Did he leave an address?'

'No. I told you he didn't leave a card. Why are you speaking to me like this?'

'He has one of my paintings.'

'Which one?'

Egon poured himself a glass of rum, drinking it down in one mouthful.

'He has one of my best pieces of work. I want to know if he still has it.'

'Why wouldn't he?'

'Sometimes people get bored, Edith, darling. They discard things they wish they'd kept.'

He rolled his tie around the palm of his hand.

'You're not making any sense.'

'Sorry, it's been a long day.'

'So, tell me: how many did you sell at the exhibition?'

Egon started counting on his fingers and then looked up smiling.

'All of them.'

'Even the one of the four trees?'

'Even that one. I know it wasn't your favourite.'

'And the one of me in that dress you bought in Leipzig?'

Egon took a gulp of rum.

'A collector from Ulm bought it.'

'For how much?'

'Several hundred crowns.'

'I don't believe you.'

'That's what you're worth, darling,' said Egon, walking into the next room. 'I sold it to him on the condition that I was able to make a copy,' he said from the corridor, taking off his shoes.

'But you never do that.'

'I did this time. To give to your parents.'

She ran into the corridor and hugged Egon, her arms high around his neck. 'It means a lot to me. I'm sure it will mean a lot to them.'

Edith chose a house in a leafy street called Wattmanngasse. It had been abandoned by a family of aristocrats fleeing north: there were tins stacked in the pantry and stained lace still hung at the windows. At the back of the building there was a large studio-sized room and a smaller nursery which faced south onto a courtyard. Johann Harms paid for carpenters and painters to renovate it, employing a handful of blank-faced men recently returned from the front.

'This room is to be for our first-born,' Edith declared.

'We agreed to wait until after the war,' said Egon.

'It should still be the best room in the house,' she continued. 'No expense spared.'

Egon leant out of the window and watched children chase each other with buckets of water and sticks, their voices echoing off the tall walls of the surrounding houses. In the background he heard the monotonous thud of an elderly lady beating the dust out of a rug. Edith grabbed Egon's arm and pulled him into the corridor.

'I'm not going to wait that long.'

'Patience, my dear. Patience.'

'The clock is ticking.'

He pulled a watch from his inside pocket and laughed. 'You're right.'

'We've discussed this before.'

'And I thought we'd agreed.'

'I married you so we could have a family together,' said Edith defiantly.

'And you will be the mother of my children.'

'When?'

'One day.'

'But I want it now. Now!'

A carpenter stepped out into the corridor. 'Where would you like the bed, Herr Schiele?'

Egon looked up and down the corridor. 'I think that's enough for today, Herr Schultz. You may leave now. My wife and I have work to do.'

'But I could do with seeing...'

'Another time. Come by another time. We have urgent business to see to. I'll be in touch tomorrow.'

'Alright, Sir.'

As the front door slammed closed, Egon pulled his wife into their new bedroom and threw her on the mattress.

Egon would sit awake at night, his wife dozing next to him after their purposeful lovemaking, and sketch small hands reaching for cups and spoons, tiny feet bathing in water and the face of a new-born baby, its mouth open around giggles which would one day pierce the nursery wall into the studio.

'What is it, darling?' she mumbled from the pillow, sensing her husband's eyes on her back.

'Nothing.'

'Shall I get you something to help you sleep?'

'No. You stay there. Now go back to sleep.'

As Egon swung his legs over the side of the bed, Edith extended her arm blindly and grabbed his hand before he stood up. She held it until she felt him squeeze back and then she let go.

'It's hardly what I was expecting,' said Roessler, walking around Egon's studio. 'I've worshipped at your altar more religiously than most, but I must confess these seem to lack your usual fervour.'

Roessler scratched nail-bitten fingers under his full beard, twisting locks of wiry hair between thumb and forefinger.

'I'm not going to explain each one to you, if that is what you're expecting.'

Roessler took a sip of schnapps and placed his glass on a small table. 'Where are the frail bodies, the strained poses, the effrontery that envigorated your old work? You did it so much better than anyone else. This is just art that looks too much like art.'

Egon shrugged. 'We all change, Arthur.'

'I get fatter and my head gets balder. *La mort d'Arthur.* That I can deal with, but I can't stomach some of these. Here you've layered the oils on too thick. And you've gone right to the edge of the canvas on these ones. It's like the poor girl can't breathe, hemmed in by that ghastly frame.' Roessler took a pair of spectacles out of his pocket and tilted a canvas towards the window so that the sun shone directly on it. 'And these dark greens and browns. Where have these come from? What's happened to the reds and blacks?'

'What do you know about colour?'

'It's simplicity that requires inspiration, Egon. Complex tricks just require technique.'

'Look, do you want to buy anything or not? There are plenty of others out there who will if you're not interested.'

'I'm sure there are.' Roessler undid the central button on his jacket and bent down to examine a canvas, wheezing as his knees bent. 'People are always in the market for sober stuff to give their salons a bit of gravitas. These days they'll buy anything with your signature on. Makes it rather difficult for an old faithful like me.'

'I don't paint like this for commercial reasons.'

'Well, why then?'

'No true art-lover would ever ask that question.'

The city's young artists began to congregate at Egon's house every week, crowding around their mentor in malfitting hats, some wearing paper collars, others striking poses to impress the master painter. He guided their brushes over the canvas, offering encouragement and making snide comments about their Griepenkerl-inspired lines. He laughed with them and told stories of Klimt, passing on the tricks he had learnt from the old master.

'Where's Jens?' He looked around the room at blank faces, eyes turned to the floor. 'Malte, have you seen him?'

'No, Herr Schiele.'

'Jan-Peter?'

'Nothing, Herr Schiele.'

'Stefan, you live near him, don't you?'

'No, Herr Schiele.'

'Well, his still-life's not finished.'

The young men looked at each other, none of them prepared to reveal the fate of their friend. Each day one more of their ranks would fail to come, sitting instead on a train, dressed in dark green, fists buried in armpits, toes frozen in boots. He would jump down from the train at a military camp and be ordered into a tent where he would curl his body against the cold, waiting for the morning which would bring the unfamiliar weight of a rifle pressed in his soft palms.

'Sorry, boys. I won't ask again.'

Egon turned a blind eye to the ever-changing attendance, forcing himself to forget particular voices which one day would fill his studio and the next day be absent. New, younger men would take their places, finish their half-completed paintings and count the days until they, too, were rotting in ditches or twitching with scarlet fever.

While Egon slept late on Sunday mornings, Edith would climb out of bed and walk into his studio, laying out a fresh shirt and placing the comb next to the washbasin. In the top drawer of his writing desk was a small red-bound book, its edges tied together with a shoelace. She would ease the drawer open and slip the lace off, leaving the knot intact. She would flick to the most recently inscribed pages and run her finger down the column of names, dates, times and occasionally prices, to see who had been to the studio the preceding week. She would trace the familiar names, seeing some appear intensively every couple of days for a month before disappearing for good. Other names would feature once next to an indecipherable note in the margin. Mostly, they were just first names or nicknames, playful monikers or the street guises of whores. She would count the numbers, calculating if Egon's week had been above or below his average of four. She measured some of the more regular names against Adele, trying the nicknames for size against her teasing character (Evchen, Bieni, Gretchen, Kati), never discovering what name her sister hid behind in her clandestine visits.

Next Edith would go to the easel to peruse the previous night's work. The faces were depersonalised masks, neither one girl nor the next, a generic façade often with a hint of her own visage. She felt nauseous seeing her own head superimposed on a foreign body, the face tilted away to the side, deprived of all identity, canvas mirrors for Egon's still unfamiliar psyche.

One morning, rising early due to sickness, she surprised Egon in his studio. He was alone, asleep in his chair, his shirt undone, his chin on his chest. She scanned the room, the usual debris of a night's painting scattered on the floor. A familiar odour was in the air and she walked quietly around, tracing the fragrance with her upturned nose, seeking out its source. Egon awoke as he felt her body leaning over him.

'She's been here, hasn't she?'

'Who?' he replied, rubbing his eyes. 'What's wrong?'

'I know my sister's smell.'

'What are you on about, dearest?'

'Don't you dare call me dearest!' She walked over to the window and threw the curtains back. 'Where is she?'

'Who?'

'How could you do this?'

'She hasn't been here. I promise.'

'Promise? You're an artist, Egon. Everything you do is lies: it's all symbol, all metaphor, all lies.'

'Sit down a moment, please.'

'With the others maybe… with Hanna, Sofie and Gretchen maybe, but not with her!' Egon stood up from his chair, undoing his shirt and dipped his fingers in the washbasin as his wife threw herself wretchedly onto the sofa. 'Don't do this to me.'

He wiped his torso with a wet rag, washing off the scent of foreign bodies. 'They're just paintings, darling. Just paintings.'

'Do you promise me that, too?'

'Of course.'

'Well, why are you so secretive then?'

'Edith, please, you have nothing to be jealous about.'

'Then why hide this from me?'

'Because I knew it would end up like this.'

She turned away from the window and the pair met in the middle of the room.

'This must stop. Do you hear me?'

'They're just models.'

'Then don't hide them from me.' Egon nodded, taking Edith in his arms. 'It can't go on like this.'

'I'm sorry.'

'I want you to be a proper father to our child.'

Egon leant back, looking Edith in the face. She raised her eyes to his.

'You heard me, Egon. I need this.'

# SIXTEEN

# RECLINING WOMEN

Egon set up a *chaise longue* next to the window in the studio, covering it in fresh canvas. The sunlight reflected off his mother's mirror on the opposite side of the room. He brought Edith the latest novels and magazines and traipsed through the city's markets, tracking down scarce fruit and vegetables to keep her strong and healthy. She complained at his molly-coddling, demanding to walk to her parents' house to take afternoon tea, but he refused, marching to the Hietzinger Hauptstrasse himself and inviting his in-laws round to the studio. They would pack food and blankets and hurry to Egon's house, spending the afternoon talking with their daughter, tossing children's names back and forth (Gustav for a boy, Michaela for a girl), discussing colours and patterns for items of clothing which Adele and Frau Harms knitted as they spoke.

Egon stayed with his wife in the studio most of the day, bringing her meals and drinks: in the mornings spring water and in the evenings a cup of warm milk. As she slept, he stroked her stomach under the blanket and mapped out his apologies and her acceptances; he pre-empted barbed conversations they would have once the child was born; he cleared up lingering questions over the troubled nights of their marriage, the inevitable reproaches; he made declarations and listened to her imaginary responses; he told stories of the past and made plans for the future. While she slept he painted her holding an imaginary child to her breast, adding his own face looking over the pair of them. Edith's body appeared shapely and feminine, devoid of the blues and reds that typified his earlier work, liberated from the shackles of contortion and claustrophobia. He watched her every day as she grew more maternal, her belly filling out before him, her breasts growing heavier, and his pencil curves thickened accordingly. He embraced the wildness of her moods and she accepted his obsession with her well-being: the intense devotion she had hardly imagined possible between a husband and a wife.

Egon left her in the afternoons to visit the gallery, where he discussed future exhibitions in Prague and Wiesbaden and made excuses to aristocrats waiting for portraits he had promised months earlier. He travelled to Zurich for a private exhibition but returned a day later, leaving an apologetic note for the event organiser and slipping on the first train out of the city.

'You would be doing us a great honour if you were to accept.'

Roessler stopped and turned to face Egon. 'I don't know what to say.'

'You don't need to say anything. Your face has already said yes.'

The two men laughed and embraced each other. An old couple on a nearby bench looked over at them disapprovingly.

'Godfather. I like the sound of that.' Roessler tapped the point of his walking stick against a paving slab, his face drawn out into a large smile. 'I really am speechless.'

'Let's enjoy the silence then.'

They walked over to a bench in the corner of the park and sat down opposite a fountain. Its basin was clogged with leaves and caked mud; the metal fixings of the fountain were corroded and green. The flowerbeds were empty and unturned, the topsoil dried to a crust. Roessler pulled a hipflask from his pocket.

'To celebrate,' he said, passing it first to Egon.

He took a swig and passed it back. Roessler drank from the silver flask and they watched a company march by, their boots crunching on the gravel.

'You'll have to travel, of course,' said Egon. 'We won't be bringing the child up here.'

'A wise decision, *mon ami*. This city's not fit for adults, let alone children.'

'I'm still owed several thousand crowns from the exhibition though.'

'Cut your losses and go. There will be plenty more to be made after the war.'

'But I need it before we can go.'

'Why?'

'Edi wants to move to the sea.'

'The sea?'

'It'll be expensive getting there.'

'Italy?'

'As far away as possible.'

'I'll lend you whatever you need. Find yourself a peaceful corner somewhere and pack your things.' Roessler passed Egon the hipflask again. 'You can't keep her here.'

'I've got commissions stacking up.'

'Forget them.'

A young man mummified in rags and cloth approached the bench. 'Please, Sirs. Can I…?' He held out a gloved hand, his muddied fingertips poking through the wool. 'It's been days.'

Egon put a hand in his pocket and pulled out a purse. He looked inside and shook his head. Roessler dropped a crown into the young man's hand. His fingers closed and he shoved his fist into a trouser pocket. Egon passed him the hipflask. He gulped hard and gave it back.

'Thank you, Sirs. Thank you so much,' he said, shuffling off towards the old couple on the other bench. Roessler wiped a handkerchief around the top of the flask and passed it to Egon.

'If business is keeping you both here for another few months, you should at least let her out more often. Being outside on a day like today would do her good.'

'She could catch something.'

'On a bright autumn's day? In the park?'

'It's reached Neulengbach and already taken Klosterneuburg.'

'That's just scare-mongering in the papers. She's as strong as an ox.'

'Have you heard anything from Kahrer?'

'No.'

'Pauker or Strauch?'

'Nothing.'

'There you go.'

'It's picking off the Jews, Egon, not us. Don't get me wrong, the influenza is not confined to a particular race; it just strikes the squalor. You'll both be fine in that palace of yours.'

'I read that it took Riegel.'

'Well, he had it coming to him then, short-sighted fool. Serves him right for locking you up.'

'Don't be so heartless.'

'You can't be feeling sorry for that bastard.'

'In times like these you have to feel sad for all victims.'

'Like him?'

'Like Anton.'

Egon stood up and moved on, pulling his hat down over his eyes. Roessler waited on the bench, sipping at the schnapps. He watched Egon walk down the path lined with chestnut trees, fallen leaves tossing up from his heels. He slipped the flask back inside his jacket and hurried after him.

They left the park by a side gate, crossed a boulevard and entered Vienna's backstreets. Mangy dogs sniffed among the rubbish, moving from house to house at the whim of their bladders. Five minutes later Egon and Roessler were sitting at a table in the corner of a deserted café.

'It all seems so sterile without Gustav.'

Roessler tugged the sleeve of a passing waiter.

'A bottle of Champagne, I think.'

'Apologies, Sir. We haven't had such wine in here for months.'

'A sparkling chardonnay perhaps?'

'I must apologise once again but…'

'Well, what do you have?'

'Beer and schnapps.'

'What else?'

The waiter looked over his shoulder to the barman.

'I think we may have some whisky left, Sir.'

'That will do.'

They waited until the half-empty bottle was deftly positioned between the candles on their table, accompanied by two glasses, and a jug of water. The waiter uncorked the bottle and filled both glasses. Roessler took a swig from his hipflask.

'To the unborn child.'

'To the unborn child.'

Their glasses clinked. Egon sipped at the surface while Roessler gulped his down and recharged his glass.

'I thought this was the only place in town where the wine cellars were oblivious to the misery everywhere else.' He drank his second glass. 'Seems not.'

'I shouldn't have come out.'

'Why not? We can celebrate in his name.'

Egon lifted his glass and emptied its contents down his throat. Roessler rotated the bottle between his palms, sucking his lower lip.

'I probably shouldn't tell you this, but you should know anyway.' Roessler swallowed a belch behind pursed lips. 'Gustav probably told you himself and if he didn't he should have.' Egon looked at Roessler from behind a raised glass and nodded for him to continue. 'He thought you had lost it. Don't misunderstand me, as far as I understood, he didn't think you had squandered your talent – far from it – he thought "technically" you were even more gifted than before. He just thought that you were no longer… what was the word he used… "inspired".'

'What kind of garbled confession is this?'

'I can't remember exactly how he put it… something along the lines that you were no longer capturing that passion which others – and he meant himself, I believe – could never hope to seize. He thought you had somehow…'

'Choose your words carefully, Arthur.'

'… become conservative.'

'I have mellowed. I accept that.'

'He said conservative.'

'War does different things to different people.'

'Goltz mentioned it to me recently as well,' continued Roessler.

'What?'

'That you no longer paint… it. You no longer paint what you're good at.'

'And what might that be?'

'The act. *La petite mort.*'

'What?'

'Sex, dear Egon. Sex.'

'Rubbish! I do it all the time.'

'You paint naked flesh, my friend… all too happily… but you don't paint sex anymore. That was what you used to do: you painted the vibrations, the rhythms, the spark of enjoined bodies. You painted the raw, pungent act. You painted Wally.' Roessler leant forward, his fingers clawing at the tabletop. 'All the others toyed with the polite forms, the lead-up, the desire, the foreplay… you know, all those lacklustre reclining women and bare backs. But you, you painted the vivid explosion. But not anymore.' Roessler gulped again from his glass. 'It used to be vivid, so vivid. It's all so dull and stately now.'

'And that's why I now hang in every gallery in the city.'

'Is that a measure of success?'

'I'm trying to build a household, Arthur.'

'And your principles?'

'To hell with my principles! I have a pregnant wife to care for, for God's sake. I need money.'

'And what about that piece for the gallery?'

'Which one?'

'The one that no one bought.'

'What's your point?'

'I heard they made you paint over the skirt. You would never have done that five years ago. You would've spat back in their faces. I mean a skirt! For Christ's sake. What's happened to the defiance?'

Egon finished his drink and stood up.

'Thank you for your company, Arthur. Your views have been most interesting.'

'Sit down!'

'I have a pregnant wife to attend to.'

'Look, sorry. I got ahead of myself. It's the whisky talking.'

'Goodbye.'

Egon walked out of the café, the door swinging closed behind him.

As Egon's work was being hung in the exhibition halls of Amsterdam, Stockholm and Copenhagen, Nurse Valerie Neuzil lay in convulsions on an army camp-bed, sweat seeping into the coarse material under her back. A simple cough had signalled the beginning and the end. Three days later she fell into a fever, a scarlet rash spreading from the armpits and groin up her body and to the neck. Her fingers clawed at her throat between bouts of vomiting. Her neck glands swelled, her tongue lolled in her mouth like a slab of butcher's meat. Within a week, her kidneys had collapsed. By the time Egon had sold his tenth portrait of the year, the frost had already prised off the corner of Valerie's tombstone. Eventually, it cracked in two, leaving just the fragment of a name which the rain quickly robbed from her.

The house had been over-run by students a few years earlier but it had since emptied, the young men exchanging their pencils for pistols. The landlord was desperate to fill whatever rooms he could, and Egon negotiated a reasonable price for two neighbouring apartments, one for his mother and one for Gertrude. They would come to Egon's studio every other afternoon and spend a couple of hours with Edith, keeping her spirits high and bringing news, sweet cakes and barley water. Marie would make her way slowly up the stairs, Gertrude moving step by step behind her to ensure she didn't fall. They would then pull up chairs around the *chaise longue* and Edith would patiently listen to her mother-in-law's advice, allowing her to pass wrinkled hands over her swelling womb.

'You've got it easy, you lucky thing.'

'Egon won't let me lift a finger.'

'Are you eating properly?' Marie fastened her bony fingers around Edith's wrist.

'He cooks well, despite the shortages.'

'My daughter won't let me down to the market anymore.'

'You're too weak for it, Mother,' said Gertrude. 'It's hellish. So many people all scrabbling after a couple of potatoes.'

'But as long as you're getting enough, that's all that matters,' added Marie.

'I am. Thank you.'

'You must stay healthy if that little Schiele in you is going to be a big strong boy.'

'Or girl.'

Gertrude endured the maternal talk, so colourful compared to her own widow's world. As Marie relived her own years of motherhood, passing on advice and anecdotes to Edith, Egon laid a hand on Gertrude's shoulder and led her into a quiet adjoining room. Various unguents, medicines and towels were laid out on the table in the middle of the room: the only evidence of impending motherhood.

'You're well prepared.'

'Sulphate of quinine. Valerian. Turpentine. Some of it has been virtually impossible to get my hands on, but it's all there in case.

Turns out, she's happy with just a glass of water in the morning and warm milk before bedtime.'

'Is she eating?'

'Mother just asked that.'

'Edith will never tell her the truth. She loves you too much for that.'

'Meat once a week; vegetables every other day. And fruit when I can get my hands on it.'

'I still can't get my head round the fact that you'll be a father in a couple of months.' A proud grin spread across Egon's face and Gertrude couldn't help but smile back. 'You'll be exceptional, I know.'

'I can't think of anyone worse prepared than me.' Egon stood up, walked to the door and looked through into the next room. Edith and his mother were still chatting. 'I always hoped that if I ever had children I would be half as good as Father. And now I find myself hoping that I'll never be half as bad as him.'

'You won't be. Anyone can see that for themselves.'

Egon sat down opposite Gertrude, lifting her chin with his hand. 'I don't know why I behaved like I did. I'm sorry.'

'Let's not talk about this now.'

'But I've never apologised.'

'It's in the past.'

'You were entitled to your happiness without me interfering.' She raised a handkerchief to her face. 'Jealousy's an ugly thing.'

She wiped her nose and eyes, stuffing the handkerchief under the sleeve of her dress. 'It wasn't jealousy.'

'I'm so sorry, Gerti.'

'It was a look you always had when Anton's name was mentioned or whenever you saw us together. I know what it was and it wasn't jealousy.' Gertrude reached out across the table and took Egon's hand. They held each other's gaze while their fingers interlocked. 'I have the same feeling when I see you together with Edith.'

Egon kissed her fingers.

'If it's a girl, I'll ask her if we can call it Gertrude.'

'She said she liked Michaela.'

'Michaela Gertrude then.'

They smiled at each other and would have embraced had there not been a row of ointments between them.

Egon stopped painting, his abandoned brushes bending on their tips in jars and mugs. Instead, he took up paper and pencil and taught Edith to sketch while she reclined on the *chaise longue*. At first, he positioned vases and crockery on the table next to her, talking her through the relative dimensions of the objects, the interplay of geometric lines and organic curves, teaching her perspective and cross-hatching until the composition was captured and he could hang it next to his own sketches on the studio walls. She protested, embarrassed at the naivety of her work, playfully angry at her husband's insistence on displaying it to all visitors; but still she practised hard, occupied through the hours of boredom and encouraged by the joy Egon took in his mission.

While Edith drew, Egon would clean the house around her, revelling in the role reversal of artist and housewife. He would lift her legs as he brushed underneath the couch; he would cover her mouth and nose as he dusted the table; and he would bring her clean blankets and sheets every second day. Meanwhile she would sketch, her pencil growing bolder, casting scimitar strokes across the paper.

One evening, Egon had finished reading the newspaper to Edith and fallen asleep in the high-backed chair, his head rocking back against the rest, a candle still burning on the table in front of him. He had endured a morning of cleaning and cooking and then travelled to the other side of the city in the afternoon to settle requests for yet more of his works. Just as his breathing sunk into the rhythms of deep sleep, he heard a scratching noise. He sat up and lurched in the direction of the noise. On all fours in front of the *chaise longue*, scrabbling around for the mouse, his startled face was met by Edith's grin. He looked across at the sketching paper she had affixed to a tray balanced against her belly. As his eyes focused in the room's half-light and Edith tilted the paper towards him, he recognised the pencil outlines of his own features. His hairline had receded and his wartime complexion was thick with stubble. At the edge of his lips was the suspicion of a smile.

# SEVENTEEN

# ICARUS

The pandemic had spread across central Asia, wrenching the heart out of the armed forces, leaving snivelling bodies shivering in mud before moving into the towns and cities, devastating vast tracts of countryside, whole networks of streets, gutting every family and farm on its way. It reached the freezing and starving lanes of Vienna, spreading from house to house, indiscriminately nipping at the lungs of rich and poor, the living and the unborn.

Egon wrapped his wife in linen cloths, lighting a fire in the studio and placing coals in a pan under her feet. He placed a bonnet on her head and wiped the sweats from her brow. He pushed aside a comma of hair stuck to her forehead and held a mug of lemon-scented grog to her lips. He visited doctors on her behalf but their practises were either closed or packed with spluttering, shivering patients. When he finally reached a Jewish doctor, huddled away in a cellar at the bottom of an abandoned street, the old man shrugged and Egon returned to his tomb-like studio.

Edith slept and woke, suffering fevers and chills as the influenza worked its way through her body. Her husband sat on the floor next to her as she lay stretched out on the canvas-covered *chaise longue*, huddled under rugs and blankets. Adele and her mother came to visit each day, handkerchiefs strung across their mouths and fastened behind their necks with ribbon; their eyes spoke of the sadness which the rest of their faces kept hidden. They brought fruits and rum, cooking up concoctions to drip past her dry lips. Edith would throw back her covers, take the drink like a live coal in her hands, and then minutes later cower beneath the blankets, eyes swollen, real tears merging with the sweats which the fever drove from her body.

'They will come for me soon.' Her voice struggled past cracked lips.

'This will all pass in the next few days, darling. Everything will be fine. You're doing well.'

'It won't survive.'

Egon watched her hands run over her belly under the blanket. 'You'll both be fine,' he said, kissing her on the forehead. 'Just fine.'

'They'll be wearing black.'

'No one is coming for you, darling. You'll be up and about next week and all this will be forgotten.'

Tears ran out the corner of her eye and onto the pillow.

'You deserve more.'

He kissed her on the lips and ran a hand over her forehead. 'You're far more than I have ever deserved.'

On the fifth night when Edith's family had left and she slept, exhausted, Egon sketched her. It took him three days to complete two simple sketches made with charcoal. Her face remained achromatic, a blank shape devoid of the crimsons and blues feeding through her lips and cheeks. As the sun came up, Egon placed the papers down by the side of the *chaise longue* and went through into the kitchen to pour himself a mug of rum. He walked back into the studio, unscrewed the bolts from the back of his easel and dismantled it into planks and slats. He pulled the blanket up around Edith's neck and then fed the wood onto the fire in the corner of the room.

Hours later, Egon was back outside, scouring the markets for medication, pawning the jewellery Edith no longer wore for a quart of rum or a wrinkled lime. He walked back through the silent streets to his house: the windows were all closed, the curtains drawn; no children played outside, no servants brushed the dust off steps. He went upstairs into his studio and glanced across at his sleeping wife. He went into the kitchen to boil some water, squeezing the last drops of juice out of a withered lemon and swigging a mouthful of rum before adding it to the mug. As he poured the hot water in, the fumes rose up under his nose.

He approached Edith, the mug clenched in his hands so as not to spill a drop. Her face was turned away into the back of the couch and her hands were clasped across her belly through the blankets. Egon gently rubbed his hand over her hair and down the back of her clammy neck. He grasped her shoulder and pulled her body back. Edith's eyes were closed. Her lips were thin, the skin around them like mother-of-pearl. A scribbled note lay by the side of the couch, made on the back of one of his sketches. He held the paper up to his face, scanning the words whose sense and order scrambled before his eyes. He kissed her on the forehead, laying his head on her chest, his fingers interlocking with the hand she had clenched over her swollen and soundless womb.

Visitors continued to come to Egon's house in those ensuing days. Edith's body had been taken to the morgue, piled up next to the hundreds of others who dropped every day under the pandemic.

Egon moved himself onto the *chaise longue* next to the window, slipping in between the same rugs, blankets and canvas which had warmed his wife's body a day earlier. The Harms family came to visit him, but he raged at them from the couch, warning them not to enter the room. They stood in the corridor, communicating with him via his mother's large mirror propped in the doorway. Over the next few days they watched his reflection grow thin, his face darkening with stubble and his eyes reddening with salt water. They brought medication which he ordered them to leave in the corridor, and when Gertrude and Marie passed by in the evening they found the untouched bottles still there, propped up against the doorframe.

'Please, you can't go in,' advised Roessler from the doorway.

He had volunteered to be the gatekeeper to Egon's tomb, sitting day and night in the corridor next to the tall mirror, pulling the handkerchief away from his mouth to turn away visitors, creeping close to Egon, placing drinks on a tray which he would slide over to Egon's bed with his cane.

'I've survived longer with something far worse,' replied Marie. She stood for a minute in the corridor, watching the reflection of her son sleeping in the mirror.

'Please, Frau Schiele.'

Marie planted her stick on the threshold of the studio and walked past Roessler. He swayed back, careful not to knock her off balance.

'I beg you, Mother, don't. Not at your age.'

'Now listen both of you,' she said turning slowly around in the doorway. 'This Spanish cough is nothing compared to what the French left us with. Now, get out of my way, I want to see my son.'

Roessler and Gertrude stood back, watching in the mirror as Marie shuffled towards the *chaise longue*.

'Keep away,' shouted Egon. 'Get out! Back into the corridor. Please, for your own sake!'

Roessler followed her in, carrying a chair which she refused. He stopped in the middle of the room as he saw Marie reach Egon, running her hand down his forearm and kissing him on the top of the head. She muttered something under her breath in a language Roessler did not understand and knelt at the side of the *chaise longue*. She kissed her son again, ran her fingers over his hair, straightening the unruly spikes. Her platinum eyes opened, crow's feet flexing in the corners of her sockets. Tears dispersed into the furrows of her cheeks.

She sat there the whole day. As night fell, she pushed herself back up on her feet, walked down the stairs and out into the street.

Three days later, the Harms family stopped by Egon's house on their way back from Edith's funeral. A wreath had been laid on her grave on his behalf. Roessler came down the stairs to meet them at the door. Adele pulled back her simple black veil and looked into Roessler's eyes. She held out a flower.

'Can you give it to him? It's from the wreath.'

Roessler looked down at his shoes and back up at Adele, giving a near imperceptible shake of the head.

Despite the frost, the soil on Edith's grave had not hardened by the time Egon's coffin was brought to the cemetery. The spades of the gravediggers slipped easily through the moist topsoil until they hit the wooden lid of her coffin. Roessler, Harms and four others lowered the box and stood back while the pastor read from a leather-bound bible. As the skies opened, Roessler accompanied Egon's mother and Gertrude back inside the church and the gravediggers quickly shovelled the soil into the hole.

Vienna was a mere shadow, its streets squalid and silent but for the occasional trudge of scavengers, moving among empty houses, rifling through piles of refuse. They were the lucky few, free to roam the streets while their companions rotted on deserted battlefields or tramped barefoot across lost territories, a weevil-ridden crust clasped in their hands.

The city had been brought to its knees: prostitutes rubbed brick dust into their hollow cheeks; fathers dozed drunkenly on benches; daughters begged on street corners; town-houses were abandoned. Egon's postcards soaked into the mud alongside family photographs and letters from home. The corridors of the academies were bare, and homeless people crouched in the covered porches of museums. Egon's paintings were left to stare down vacantly from darkened walls into empty rooms.

Elsewhere, canvases were cut from frames; oil paints cracked in dropping temperatures; portraits were removed from walls and wrapped in muslin; sketches of girls were stuffed in lofts and cellars; Krumau landscapes were looted by victors; and Valerie's delicate features were exchanged for a jug of milk or a hunk of meat.

Meanwhile, myths were being born among the chattering classes. Around dinner tables in foreign capitals, collectors and cognoscenti talked of Egon's death, of how Roessler or Adele had crouched at Egon's side while he uttered his last phlegm-soaked words. Rumours spread into the provinces, claiming Egon had reached out, his eyes heavy with tears, his voice faltering, a photograph of Valerie crunched in his hand. Newspapers began to print obituaries and eulogies, stating that he had made final sketches on his death bed, visions of heaven, hell, his mother, his father, trains, girls, bears, all flowing out of him in a final ejaculation of creativity; pictures that subsequently appeared on markets and at auction houses, the uncertain squiggle of Egon's signature forged in their bottom corners. They claimed he made plans for a mausoleum so his body could for eternity lie next to Klimt's; they said he pointed to sketches on the walls of his studio, blessing them with a gnarled finger; they maintained he composed a farewell letter to Valerie with a shaking hand, unable to sign his own name.

But no one had been there. As sleep descended on Egon one final time, he lay alone on the *chaise longue*, its canvas dark with hoops of sweat. His chest was inflated with pneumonia, his swollen gums wept blood around loose teeth. The painter pulled his legs up, rolled into a ball and wiped a sliver of red and black mucus from his lips. His eyes closed and he gripped the divan's wooden frame.

# Acknowledgements

Nowadays, for many of us, art thrives off coffee tables. For me and *The Pornographer of Vienna* it was no different, and I am indebted to the erudite and accessible work of Wolfgang Georg Fischer, Serge Sabarsky, Otto Breicha and Rudolf Leopold who have done so much to bring Schiele's work to the public eye. Furthermore, Obecní dům and Národní galerie in Prague, the Egon Schiele Art Centrum in Český Krumlov (previously Krumau), and the galleries and back-streets of Vienna have all played their part in inspiring me and others to delve deeper into the artist's life. Special thanks go to Munich's Staatliche Graphische Sammlung for allowing me access to some of Schiele's finest and least known works.

I am grateful to my agent, Kevin Conroy Scott, for looking after me and coming up with the title; and thanks must also go to my polyglot editor, Elena Lappin, and all at Old Street Publishing for their passion and creativity.

The critical input of Tom Mogford, Ryszard Szostak and Matthew Kimberley throughout composition was invaluable, as were the inspiration, distraction and correction provided by Becky Senior, Rob Heck, Thomas Greis, Rob Dinsdale, Will Gilroy, Serena Gosling, Andrew Fargus, Kate Bland, Jemma Phipps, Tom Matthews, James Dempsey, Mandy Miller, Clayton and Florrie Ponting, and Will C. Foster. The final and most profound thanks go to the project's invisible guiding hand, Míša Šilpochová, who first inspired the idea while wandering the snow-laden streets of Český Krumlov.